Thre............................eir
lives for their country, who each deserve our
respect and a special woman's love

Loving Our

HEROES

We are thrilled to bring you these award-winning writers
and proud to be working with Help for Heroes.

HELP *for*
HEROES
ENDORSED PRODUCT

One pound from the sale of each book is going
towards this important cause.

Thank you for buying this collection—
please enjoy it!

Loving Our
HEROES

JESSICA HART

AMY ANDREWS

INDIA GREY

MILLS & BOON

First published in Great Britain 2011
by Mills & Boon, an imprint of Harlequin (UK) Limited, Eton House,
18-24 Paradise Road, Richmond, Surrey TW9 1SR

LOVING OUR HEROES © Harlequin Enterprises II B.V./S.à.r.l. 2011

Last-Minute Proposal © Jessica Hart 2008
Mission: Mountain Rescue © Amy Andrews 2006
Mistress: Hired for the Billionaire's Pleasure © India Grey 2008

ISBN: 978 0 263 89045 7

009-1111

Harlequin (UK) policy is to use papers that are natural, renewable
and recyclable products and made from wood grown in sustainable
forests. The logging and manufacturing processes conform to the legal
environmental regulations of the country of origin.

Printed in the UK
by CPI Mackays, Chatham, ME5 8TD

Last-Minute Proposal

JESSICA HART

Dear Reader,

I once spent five months on expedition in West Africa, living in close quarters with four ex-Army men. That's when I learnt how to radio (Papa Bravo Tango, roger, over and out) and the importance of getting rank right (never my strong suit). I also learnt that soldiers are neat, practical, and resourceful—although not great cooks in my experience! And they are usually very, very fit.

Above all, the servicemen and women I've met have all been wonderfully, reassuringly competent. You always feel safe with a soldier, whether you're hanging off a cliff like Tilly, at the beginning of *Last-Minute Proposal*, or broken down in the middle of the rainforest, miles away from the nearest garage. That's why men with military backgrounds, like Campbell Sanderson, make such great romantic heroes.

But they don't just make fictional heroes. Every day, soldiers put their lives on the line for us all. In their courage, their dedication, their steadfastness and their ability to get the job done, *they* are the real heroes.

Jessica

Jessica Hart was born in West Africa, and has suffered from itchy feet ever since, travelling and working around the world in a wide variety of interesting but very lowly jobs, all of which have provided inspiration on which to draw when it comes to the settings and plots of her stories. Now she lives a rather more settled existence in York, where she has been able to pursue her interest in history, although she still yearns sometimes for wider horizons. If you'd like to know more about Jessica, visit her website, www.jessicahart.co.uk

"RITA® award-winning author Jessica Hart never disappoints her readers with her spellbinding and sophisticated stories, brimming with warmth, wit, drama and romance."
—*CataRomance*

"Jessica Hart is a marvel."
—*RT Book Reviews*

"Jessica Hart is 'smart, sassy and sophisticated'."
—*CataRomance*

For all those readers whose support over the last
fifty books has meant so much.
This one is for you, with thanks.

CHAPTER ONE

'DON'T let me go!'

Tilly's voice rose to a shrill whisper as she grabbed Campbell Sanderson's neck and hung on for dear life. He was rock-solid and smelt reassuringly clean and masculine. And he was the only thing standing between her and the bottom of a cliff.

Typical. The closest she had been to a bloke for ages and she was too terrified to enjoy it.

Campbell reached up to prise her hands away. 'I've no intention of letting you go,' he said irritably. 'I'm going to hold the rope while you lower yourself down. It's perfectly simple. All you have to do is lean back and trust me.'

'And how many women over the centuries have heard *that* line?' snapped Tilly, clamping her arms determinedly back in place the moment he released them. 'It's all very well for you to talk about trust, but you're not the one being asked to dangle over an abyss with only a thin rope between you and certain death!'

One thing was sure—certain death was awaiting her twin brothers, who were responsible for getting her into this mess. She was going to kill them the moment she got off this sodding hillside.

If she ever got off this hillside.

Tilly risked a glance at Campbell. It was odd to be so close to a perfect stranger at all, let alone clasping him quite so fervently, and she examined him with a strange, detached part of her mind that was prepared to do anything other than think about abseiling down the sheer cliff face.

He had glacier-green eyes that were the coldest and most implacable she had ever seen, close-cropped hair and an expression of profound impatience. Of course, that might just be inspired by her, Tilly had to acknowledge, but she had a feeling it was habitual. He seemed the impatient type. Tilly was the last person to deny that appearances could be deceptive, but there was something about the austere angles of his face and the ruthless set of his mouth that made her think that here was a prime example of 'what you see is what you get'.

And what you got in the case of Campbell Sanderson was a very tough customer indeed.

'How can I trust you?' she demanded, without releasing her limpet-like grip. 'I don't know anything about you.'

Campbell sucked in an exasperated breath. 'I don't know you either,' he pointed out crisply. 'So why would I want to drop you down a cliff, especially with a television camera trained on me? Or hadn't you noticed they're filming you right now?'

'Of course I've noticed! Why do you think I'm whispering?'

Tilly's arms were aching with the effort of holding on to him. Her feet were braced just over the lip of the cliff, but she could feel gravity pulling her weight backwards.

And, let's face it, it was a substantial weight to be pulled. Why, oh, why hadn't she stuck to any of her diets? Tilly wondered wildly. This was a punishment to her for not subsisting on lettuce leaves for the past thirty years.

Campbell glanced at the distant cameras in disbelief. 'They're miles away! Of course they can't hear you, but they can see you.

They've got a socking great zoom on that camera and it's pointed straight at you so, for God's sake, pull yourself together!' he told her sharply. 'You're making yourself look ridiculous.'

And him by association.

'Better to be ridiculous than splattered all over the bottom of this cliff!'

A muscle was jumping in his cheek and his jaw looked suspiciously set. 'For a start, this is not a cliff,' he said with the kind of restraint that suggested that he was only hanging on to his temper with extreme difficulty. 'It's barely twenty feet to the bottom there and, as I keep telling you, you're not going to fall. You're on a secure rope, and you can let yourself down slowly. Even if you did lose control, I've got hold of the rope and I'd stop you dropping.'

'You might not be able to,' said Tilly, not at all convinced. 'That rope's awfully fine. I can't believe it'll hold my weight.'

'Of course it will,' he said impatiently. 'This rope could hold a hippopotamus.'

'Now, I wonder what made you think of a hippo,' Tilly said bitterly.

She wished Campbell hadn't mentioned the zoom on that camera. It was probably trained on her bottom right now. Unsure of quite what 'a day in the hills' involved, but fairly sure it would mean getting cold, she had squeezed herself into her old skiing salopettes, bought in a burst of enthusiasm soon after she had met Olivier and was at least two sizes smaller. Now her big red bottom would be filling the screen down there, and the television crew would all be having a good laugh.

Tilly had a dark suspicion that had been the idea all along.

'Who thought up this show in the first place?' she demanded, fear and humiliation giving her voice a treacherous wobble, but at least talking took her mind off the void beneath her.

'God knows,' said Campbell, thinking that a deep longing to be elsewhere was probably all that he and Tilly had in common.

'I bet they were sitting around in some bar or wherever television types congregate, and someone said, "Hey, I know, let's make a programme where we make fat people look absolutely ridiculous!"'

'If that were the case, all the contestants would be fat and, in fact, none of us are,' he pointed out impatiently.

'*I* am.'

'Not noticeably,' said Campbell, although now she came to mention it, the figure clutching him was definitely on the voluptuous side.

He had been too focused on the task in hand to notice at first, which was perhaps just as well. Under other circumstances, he would have enjoyed the situation. He was only human, after all, and he certainly wasn't going to object if a lush-bodied woman chose to press herself against him. Sadly, however many points Matilda Jenkins might score on the physical front, she was losing a lot more with all this carry-on about a simple abseil.

'Your theory is nonsense, in fact,' he told her. 'None of the other novices are the slightest bit overweight.'

Tilly thought back to the meeting that morning, where they had met their three rival pairs who had also made it through from the first round. Much as it might go against the grain, she had to admit that Campbell was right.

Leanne had a perfect figure, for instance. Tilly had noticed her straight away as a possible kindred spirit. She was the only other contestant wearing make-up and looked about as happy to be there as Tilly was. It turned out that Leanne was a beautician, blonde and very pretty, and, almost as much as her figure, Tilly had envied her partner, a gregarious outdoor sports instructor called Roger who had all the latest equipment and was friendly and reassuring. The opposite of Campbell, in fact.

Leanne definitely wasn't fat, and nor were the other two girls. Defying the usual stereotypes, one of them was a capable-looking outdoorsy type who had been teamed with a medieval art historian raising money for the restoration of some cathedral's stained glass, and even he was downright skinny.

'Well, perhaps they thought it was funny to make us *all* look ridiculous,' Tilly conceded grudgingly, reluctant to let go of her theory completely. She managed a mirthless laugh, no small achievement when you were teetering on the edge of a sheer drop—and she didn't care what Campbell said about twenty feet, it felt like the side of the Grand Canyon to her. 'Ha, ha.'

'More than likely,' said Campbell tersely, 'but, since we've all agreed to take part, we're not in a position to complain about it now.'

Further along the rock face, he could see his three competitors preparing their partners for the abseil. There were three other beginners in Tilly's position, chosen for their complete lack of experience with anything remotely connected with outdoor activities, but they seemed to be getting on with what they had to do without any of the drama Matilda Jenkins seemed determined to wring from the situation.

He blew out a breath. There were better things to be doing on a bright, cold Saturday in the Highlands. A brisk wind was pushing the clouds past the sun, sending shadows scudding over the hills around them, and the air smelt of peat and heather. It would be a great day for a climb, or just to walk off the restlessness that had plagued him so often recently.

Instead of which, he had a hysterical woman on his hands. Campbell didn't care how lush her body was, how appealing her perfume. He would rather be behind enemy lines again than cope with a scene of the kind Matilda Jenkins was evidently all too capable of creating.

Why had he ever let Keith talk him into this? Good PR, indeed! How the hell could it be good PR for Manning's Chief Executive to be seen being strangled by a panicky woman at the top of a drop so short you could practically step down to the bottom?

And this was only the beginning, Campbell reminded himself darkly. He had to get the bloody woman down this rock face, across the hill, into the valley and across the river at the bottom before the others, or they wouldn't get through to the next round, and if they didn't do that, they wouldn't win the competition.

And Campbell Sanderson didn't do not winning.

Tempting as it was to just push her over the edge and lower her to the bottom, Campbell reluctantly discarded that option. He was prepared to bet that Jenkins had a scream that would be heard across the border in England. The noise would be appalling, and she had a surprisingly strong grip, too. He wouldn't put it past her to try and drag him back with her, and they would end up wrestling and making themselves look even more ridiculous than they did already.

No, he was going to have to talk her down.

Drawing a breath, Campbell forced patience into his voice.

'Come along, Jenkins, you're losing your grip here,' he told her. 'The way I see it, you've got two choices. You can let me pull you back on to the top here and admit defeat, sure, but are you really prepared to let down the charity you're doing this for in the first place? They're going to be pretty disappointed when you tell them that you bottled out because you were too chicken to do a simple abseil. They'll be counting on you winning lots of money for them. What is your charity, anyway?' he asked casually.

'The local hospice,' Tilly muttered. She wished he hadn't brought that up. Of course she ought to be thinking about the hospice and everything they had done for her mother, and for Jack. She set her teeth.

'Great cause,' he commented. 'There'll be lots of people rooting for you to do well, then.'

'Oh, yes, pile on the emotional blackmail, why don't you?' she said bitterly.

'I'm just telling it like it is,' said Campbell with a virtuous air. 'One option is to disappoint all those people, not to mention the television company who have set up this challenge. The other is to take your arms from round my neck, lean back against the tension of the rope and walk slowly backwards down the rock face. It'll be over in a minute, and you'll feel great once you've done it.'

Tilly doubted that very much. More than likely, she wouldn't be in a position to feel anything ever again.

'Isn't there another option?'

'We could spend the rest of our lives up here with our arms around each other, I suppose, but I don't imagine that's an option you want to consider.'

'Oh, I don't know…' said Tilly, playing for time.

The worrying thing was that it wasn't actually *that* unappealing an option. Obviously, she hardly knew him, and he did seem rather cross, but on the other hand there were worse fates than spending the rest of your life holding on to a body like Campbell Sanderson's. He might not be the friendliest or best-looking man she had ever met, but Tilly had to admit there was something about that cold-eyed, stern-mouthed, lean-jawed look.

If only he wasn't so determined to make her lean back over the void. Why couldn't he be intent on whisking her away for a fabulous weekend in Paris instead?

'Come on, Jenkins, make up your mind.' Impatience was creeping back into Campbell's voice. He glanced along to where the other contestants were almost at the bottom of the rock face. 'We haven't got all day here. It's time to stop messing around and just get on with it.'

Tilly sighed. Obviously he wasn't keen on the clinging together for eternity option. She couldn't really blame him. If

Campbell Sanderson was going to spend the rest of his life with anyone, it certainly wouldn't be with a panicky, over-weight cook.

'You'll be absolutely fine,' the production assistant had re-assured her when breaking the news that her original partner had had to drop out. She'd lowered her voice confidentially. 'Campbell Sanderson is ex-special forces, I heard,' she'd whispered enviously. 'You couldn't be in better hands.'

Tilly looked at Campbell's hands on the rope. They were strong and square and very capable. The sort of hands that would ease the strap of a sexy nightdress off your shoulder with just the right amount of *frisson*-inducing brushing of warm fingers. The sort of hands that under any other circumstances it would be a real pleasure to find yourself between, in fact.

More importantly, the sort of hands that wouldn't drop or fumble with a rope when you were dangling on the end of it.

'Jenkins…' he said warningly, and Tilly dragged herself back to the matter in hand.

'All right, all right…'

She was going to have to do it, Tilly realised. She had to do it for her mother and for everyone who needed the care she had had, but Tilly's stomach still turned sickeningly at the prospect.

Trust me, Campbell had said. She risked a glance into his face and saw him in extraordinary detail. The pale green eyes, the dark brows drawn together in a forbidding frown, that mouth clamped in an exasperated line… Funny how she hadn't noticed him in the same way when they'd been introduced.

Then, he had simply struck her as taciturn. Now, he seemed cool, competent, unsmiling. She could just see him in a bala-clava, parachuting behind the lines to blow up a few tanks before tea. He clearly wasn't the type to fool around. Unlike some males of her acquaintance, Campbell Sanderson wouldn't pretend to drop her for a lark, just so he could chortle at her squeals of terror. No, he would do exactly what he said he would do.

In return, all she had to do was lean back, walk down the cliff. And trust him.

Tilly drew a breath. She was going to have to do *something*.

Very, very cautiously, she loosened her hold on Campbell's neck.

'If I do it will you stop calling me by my surname?' she asked.

'Whatever you want,' said Campbell, one eye on the other competitors, who were already packing up and getting ready to head down the hillside. 'Just do it.'

'OK,' said Tilly bravely. 'Let's get on with it then.'

In spite of her best resolution, it took a couple of attempts before she had the nerve to let go of his neck completely and put her hands on the rope instead.

'Good,' said Campbell, and she was ashamed of the tiny glow of warmth she felt at his approval.

He explained what she needed to do. 'Off you go, then,' he said briskly.

Tilly inched her way back to the edge. 'You won't let me fall?' Her voice was wavering on the verge of panic again and Campbell looked straight into her eyes.

'Trust me,' he said again.

'Right,' said Tilly and, taking a deep breath, she leant backwards over the empty air.

It would be too much to say that she enjoyed her abseil, but the hardest part was that first moment of leaning into the void, and once she was making her way down the cliff, gradually letting out the rope, it didn't seem quite so terrifying. Campbell was at the top, letting out the rope as she went, and very quickly, it seemed, her feet touched the grass and she was collapsing into an untidy heap.

The next moment, Campbell had abseiled down in two easy

jumps and was gathering up the equipment. 'Come on,' he said briskly, barely sparing a glance at Tilly, who was still sprawled on the grass and recovering from the trauma of her descent. 'We're behind.'

Reluctantly, Tilly hauled herself upright. Her legs felt distinctly wobbly but when she looked up at the rock face, she could see that it wasn't in fact that high. Campbell had been right, damn him.

'What now?' she asked.

'Now we have to get down and across the river, and we have to do it before the others, or we can't be sure of getting through to the next round.' Campbell coiled the last rope and stowed it away in his rucksack. 'Come on.'

He strode off, leaving Tilly to trot after him. 'Are you sure you're going the right way?' she asked a little breathlessly, and pointed over her shoulder. 'Everyone else has gone that way.'

'Which is why we're going *this* way,' said Campbell, not breaking his stride in the slightest. 'It's a tougher route, but much quicker.'

'How on earth do you know that?'

'I looked at a map this morning.'

Tilly stared at his back. 'Boy, you really do want to win, don't you?' Her father was the only person she knew with that kind of drive to win at any cost.

'Why are you here if you don't?' he countered. Just as her father would have done.

'I was tricked into it.' Tilly's blue eyes sparkled with remembered indignation. 'My twin brothers decided that it was time for me to get out of my rut and entered me in the competition. The first I knew of it was when people who work at the hospice started coming up to me and telling me how thrilled they were that I was taking part and what wonderful things they would be able to do with the money if I won. So I could hardly turn round then and say it was all a terrible mistake, could I?' she grumbled.

Campbell glanced down at her. Her heart-shaped face was pink with exertion and she was vainly trying to stop the breeze blowing the mass of curly brown hair into her eyes. She looked cross and ruffled and vibrant in her red ski-suit. It seemed a bizarre choice to wear for a weekend walking in the hills, but at least there was no chance of her getting lost. You could see her coming a mile away. Perhaps the television people had told her they wanted her to be noticeable—although it was hard to imagine *not* noticing her.

'Why not?' he asked. 'If you didn't want to do it, you could have just said so.'

Of course he *would* say that, thought Tilly. It was easy for people like Campbell Sanderson and her father, who only ever focused on one thing. They didn't worry about what other people would think or whether feelings would be hurt. They just said what they thought and did what they wanted and it never occurred to them to feel guilty about anything.

'It would have seemed so selfish,' she tried to explain. 'The hospice is a really special place. It was so awful when we knew my mother was dying. She was in pain, my brothers were very young, my stepfather was distraught... I was trying to hold things together but I didn't know what to do.'

The dark blue eyes were sad as she remembered that terrible time. 'I was so afraid of Mum dying,' she said. 'I don't know how any of us would have got through it without the hospice. It wasn't that we were any less bereft when she did die, but when she was there we were all calmer. They were so kind, not just to Mum, but to all of us. They helped us to understand what was happening, and accept it in a way we hadn't been able to do before.

'It was the same when my stepfather died,' said Tilly. 'It was

still terrible, but we weren't so scared. I owe the hospice so
much that I can't just back out. They were all so thrilled about
the prospect of me taking part for them! If we win, they'll get
the prize money, which would mean so much to them. They're
building a new wing, so that other families can have the help
and support we had. How could I turn round and say I wasn't
going to try and help them after all?'

'There must be other ways of helping them,' Campbell
pointed out.

'I volunteer in the shop,' said Tilly, 'but that isn't much of
a sacrifice, is it?'

'It's more than most people do.'

'Maybe, but most people don't get a chance to win a huge
donation to the charity of their choice either. If an opportunity
like that comes along, it's virtually impossible to turn it down.
I'd have felt worse than a piece of poo on your shoe if I had—
as Harry and Seb no doubt worked out.'

'Harry and Seb?'

'My twin brothers,' Tilly told him without enthusiasm. 'This
whole thing was their idea. They found out about the programme and took it upon themselves to enter me on my behalf.
They sent in a photo and some spurious account of why I was
so keen to take part—and then made sure everybody knew that
I'd got through to the first round before I did so they were all
lined up to lay on the emotional blackmail when Seb and Harry
finally broke the news.

'At least, they didn't mean it as emotional blackmail,' she
amended, wanting to be fair. 'Everyone at the hospice thought
I wanted to take part and had just kept quiet in case I wasn't
picked. So of course when my brothers told them that I was
going to be on the programme, they were all delighted for me
and kept telling me how proud Mum would have been if she
knew what I was doing, which she would have been, of course.'

Tilly sighed. 'I *couldn't* disappoint them by telling them it was all a mistake, could I? It would have felt like letting Mum down, too.'

Campbell frowned as he headed across the hillside, cutting down from the track so that they had to leap between clumps of heather. At least, Tilly did. Campbell just carried on walking as if he were on a pavement. Tilly had never met anyone as sure-footed. There was a kind of dangerous grace about the way he moved, and it made her feel even more of a lumbering walrus than she did normally.

He was obviously incredibly fit, too. Look at him—he wasn't even out of breath, thought Tilly, aggrieved, while she was puffing and panting and tripping over heather and generally making it obvious that she was extremely *un*fit.

'Why were your brothers so keen to get you on the programme?'

'They've got this bee in their bonnet that I'm in a rut,' puffed Tilly, struggling to keep up with him. 'I was thirty earlier this year and you'd think I was about to cash in my pension the way they're carrying on about my missed opportunities!'

'*Are* you in a rut?'

'If I am, it's a very comfortable one,' she said with an edge of defiance. 'I'm perfectly happy doing what I'm doing, and I haven't got time to worry about ruts. The boys only think that because they've been away at university, and they've got this idea that Allerby is boring—although I notice they don't mind coming back when they're short of money and in need of some good square meals,' she added tartly.

Of course, Campbell would probably think an attractive market town in North Yorkshire was boring, too. He didn't look like a provincial type. He would stand out like a tiger amongst a lot of fat, pampered pets in Allerby, for instance.

On the other hand, he didn't look like a true townie either. Tilly couldn't imagine him going to the theatre or sipping a cappuccino. His military background probably explained that slightly dangerous edge to him, but then what was he doing here?

There was one easy way to find out.

'So what are *you* doing here? You don't seem the kind of bloke who does things he doesn't want to do.'

'I seem to have ended up doing this,' said Campbell sourly. 'I'm Chief Executive of Manning Securities.'

'The sponsors of the show?'

'Exactly,' he said, without once breaking pace. 'Keith, my PR Director, convinced me that the show would be good for our image. Personally, I'd have thought it was more effective just to give the money to charity, but Keith was adamant that this would have a greater impact. It fitted with our ethos of corporate social responsibility and, as I didn't think I'd have to be involved myself, I gave the go-ahead.'

'You look pretty involved now,' Tilly commented, and he grunted a reluctant acknowledgement.

'Not out of choice. This is Keith's fault. He rang me yesterday morning, saying that one of the contestants had had to withdraw because he'd broken his leg and that the production team were desperate for a last-minute replacement with survival skills.'

'That was Greg,' said Tilly. 'I met him last week when I learnt I'd got through to this round. They said he was an experienced Outward Bound instructor and a vegan, so I suppose they thought he would make a good contrast with me. He seemed a nice enough guy, but I can't tell you how relieved I was when I heard he'd broken his leg. I thought I'd have the perfect reason to withdraw, and then they partnered me with you!' Her expression was glum.

'Glad I was such a nice surprise!' said Campbell with a touch of acid.

'Well, you can't pretend you're exactly thrilled at being stuck with me for the next couple of days,' she pointed out.

'I'm not thrilled to be doing this at all,' he said. 'I'm moving to a new job in the States in a few weeks, so I've got better things to do than mess around with television challenges. But Keith is very committed to the project and, as he knows that I used to be in the forces, he was piling on the pressure to get me to agree to help out.'

'If you didn't want to do it, why didn't you just say so?' Tilly was delighted to be able to quote Campbell's words back to him. 'Aren't you military types trained not to give in to pressure?' she added innocently. 'You could have stuck to name, rank and serial number.'

Campbell shot her a look. 'Keith was a little cleverer than that. He talked a lot about how the programme wouldn't work if they didn't have the right number of contestants, and what a shame it would be if my last few weeks at Manning were re-membered for a failure.'

'Sounds like he knows just how to press all your buttons,' said Tilly, full of admiration for the unknown Keith. It was clear that he had his boss sussed. She had barely known Campbell for more than an hour, but even she could see that he was driven by the need to be the best. Any suggestion that he might be associated with failure would be like a red rag to a bull.

'He said it would just be a weekend with an amateur in the Highlands,' Campbell went on, darkly remembering how he had been misled. 'I didn't realise quite how much of an amateur you would be, I must admit.'

'Look at it from the television producers' point of view. Where's the fun if both of us know what we're doing? If you ask me, they want scenes like the one at the top of the cliff.'

'What cliff?'

'The one I abseiled down!'

'That little drop? You could have practically stepped down it!'

Tilly eyed him with dislike. 'So what's your charity?'

'What do you mean?'

'Everyone who's taking part is doing it for charity. So I'm doing it for the local hospice, and I think Greg was hoping to raise money for mountain rescue dogs or something. You must have some incentive to win.'

Campbell shrugged. 'Winning's enough for me,' he said. 'But I tell you what. My prize money will go to your hospice if we win, so they'll have a double donation.'

Double the money. Tilly thought about what that would mean to the hospice. 'Really?' she asked.

'Only if it gives *you* some incentive to hurry up,' he said astringently.

'I *am* hurrying,' said Tilly, miffed. 'I'm not used to all this exercise. I suppose that's why they picked me,' she added with a glum look. 'They thought I'd be just the person to hold you back.'

'Then I hope you'll be able to prove them wrong,' said Campbell, pausing on a ridge to look down at the river below.

His eyes scanned the valley. A television crew was waiting on the other side of the river, but there was no sign of the other contestants yet. They had taken the straightforward route, which meant that his gamble had paid off.

Tilly puffed up to stand beside him. 'Where next?'

Campbell pointed to the river. 'Down there.'

'But how…?' Tilly's heart sank as she peered over the edge at the precipitous drop.

'This is more like a cliff,' Campbell conceded.

'Oh, no…' Tilly started to back away as she realised just what he had in mind. 'No! No, absolutely not. There's no *way* I'm hanging off that rope again. Don't even think about it!'

CHAPTER TWO

TEN minutes later, Tilly was standing at the bottom, watching Campbell do his SAS act. Sliding down the cliff in one fluid action, he made it look so easy, she thought resentfully.

'There, that wasn't that bad, was it?' he said to her as he unclipped himself and began briskly coiling ropes.

'Yes, it was,' Tilly contradicted him sulkily, although it hadn't, in fact, been *quite* as bad as the first time. 'I'm going to be having nightmares about today for years,' she told him, unwilling to let him get away with his unashamed bullying that easily. 'I can't believe I was glad when I heard Greg wouldn't be able to take part! He would have been much nicer to me. I'm sure he would never have told me to stop being so wet or made me throw myself off the edge of a cliff,' she grumbled.

'I'm sure he'd have been perfect,' Campbell agreed. 'But he wouldn't have got you to the river ahead of everyone else.'

'He'd probably think there were more important things than winning,' said Tilly loftily.

Campbell looked at her as if she had suddenly started talking in Polish. Clearly it had never occurred to him that not coming first might occasionally be an option.

'Then why would he have been participating?'

'Perhaps he was the victim of emotional blackmail, like me.

This might come as news to you, but some of us think that it's enough to take part.'

'Tell that to the people hoping for a bed in the new hospice wing,' said Campbell brutally.

Tilly winced. He was right. She mustn't forget about why she was doing this, but if only there was some other way of raising money that didn't involve her being stuck in these freezing hills with the ultra-competitive Campbell Sanderson!

'Your company's sponsoring this whole show,' she said a little sulkily. 'Why don't you just hand out a few cheques instead of making everyone jump through all these hoops?'

'I couldn't agree with you more,' he said, to her surprise. She would have bet money on the fact that they would never agree about anything. 'I would much rather write cheques than spend a weekend messing around like this, but PR isn't my forte.'

'*No?*' said Tilly, feigning astonishment. 'You amaze me!'

Campbell shot her a look. 'Keith tells me programmes like this one are the way forward, viewers want to be engaged in the process of giving money, blah, blah, blah. The long and short of it is that I pay him a good salary as PR Director to know about these things and he assures me this is what will work best for Manning Securities.

'If it's the best thing for Manning, it's what I'm going to do,' he told her, 'and if I'm going to do it, I'm going to win it. In order for me to win, you've got to win, so you might as well get used to the idea. Any more questions?' he finished with one of his acerbic looks.

Tilly sighed and gave up. 'Did they say anything about lunch?'

For a moment Campbell stared at her, then the corner of his mouth quivered.

'No, but I imagine there'll be something to eat at the check-point across the river.'

Tilly looked away, thrown by the effect that quiver had had on her. For a moment there, he had looked quite human.

Quite attractive, too, her hormones insisted on pointing out, in spite of her best efforts to ignore them. That body combined with the undeniable *frisson* of a mysterious and possibly dangerous background was tempting enough, but if you threw in a glint of humour as well it made for a lethal combination.

She could do without finding Campbell Sanderson the slightest bit attractive. This whole weekend looked set to be humiliating enough without lusting after a man who would never in a million years lust back. That whole hard, couldn't-give-a-damn air gave him a kind of glamour, and Tilly was prepared to bet that there would be some lithe, beautiful, stylish woman lurking in the background.

Tilly could picture her easily, pouting when she heard that Campbell would be spending the entire weekend with another woman. *Don't go*, she would have said, tossing back her mane of silken hair and stretching her impossibly long, slender body invitingly. *Stay and make love to me instead.*

Of course it would take more than a sultry temptress to deflect Campbell's competitive spirit, but it would have been easy for him to reassure her. *There's no danger of me fancying the woman they've paired me with*, he would have said dismissively when she'd threatened to be jealous. *The television people have deliberately picked someone fat and dowdy to give the viewers a good laugh.*

Tilly could practically hear him saying it, and she scowled. No, she wouldn't be gratifying Seb and Harry by finding Campbell Sanderson attractive.

Well, not very attractive, anyway.

'Let's go, then,' she said. Campbell wasn't the only one who could do a good impression of don't-give-a-damn. 'I'm starving.'

She followed him down to the river's edge, where he walked up and down for a while, sussing out the situation while she eyed the river with some misgiving. It was wider than she had imagined, and the water was a deep, brackish brown and fast-flowing. It looked freezing.

If Campbell hadn't trailed the possibility of lunch on the other side, she would have been tempted to have given up there and then.

'Now what?' she asked as he prowled back. 'Surely they're not expecting us to throw up a pontoon bridge?'

She was joking, but Campbell seemed to think it was a serious suggestion. 'That'll take too long,' he said. 'Let's try further up.'

Still boggling at the idea that anyone would know how to build a pontoon bridge, let alone how long it would take, Tilly trotted after him.

'Where are you going?'

'To find a better crossing place.'

Perhaps lunch might not be such a distant possibility after all. Tilly brightened. 'Do you think there might be a bridge?'

'Not exactly,' said Campbell. He stopped abruptly as they skirted a bend and his eyes narrowed. 'Ah…that's more like it,' he said with satisfaction.

Tilly stared at the river. 'What is?'

'There,' he said. 'We can cross here.'

She stared harder. All she could see were a few boulders just peeking out of the rushing water. 'How?'

'Stepping stones,' he said. 'Couldn't be better.' He jumped lightly out on to the first boulder. 'We don't even need to get our feet wet.'

Leaping nimbly on to the next stone, he stopped and looked back to where Tilly was still standing on the bank. 'Aren't you coming? The sooner you get across, the sooner you get lunch.'

Did he think she couldn't work that out for herself?

'I'm *terribly* sorry.' She offered a sarcastic apology. 'Didn't they tell you I can't actually walk on water? I've been practising and practising, but I just can't get the hang of it somehow!'

'Look, it's just a step,' he said, impatience seeping into his voice once more.

'It's a step if you've got legs that are six feet long, which I haven't, in case you hadn't noticed.'

'OK, it's a jump, but you can do it easily.'

'I can't.'

'That's what you said about the abseil, and you did that.'

'Well, I really can't do this,' said Tilly crossly. 'I'll fall in.'

Muttering under his breath, Campbell stepped back on to the bank. 'Look, it's really not that far between each stone. Why don't I take your pack? You'll find it easier to balance without that.'

Tilly had to watch him stepping easily from stone to stone with an ease your average mountain goat would have envied before dumping both packs on the far bank and making his way back to her while she was still trying to formulate an excuse.

'Now it's your turn,' he said, waiting on the first boulder and stretching out a hand. 'All you need is a little jump and I'll pull you the rest of the way.'

'Oh, yes, I can see *that* working!' scoffed Tilly, with visions of her taking his hand and promptly pulling him into the water with her.

'Or shall I come and carry you across?'

'Don't even think about it!'

Out of the corner of her eye, she could see a cameraman approaching on the far bank. The crew had obviously spotted their approach from an unexpected angle and were hurrying to catch some entertaining moments on film. What a terrific shot it would make: Campbell trying to lift her, staggering under her weight, collapsing into the water with her. Ho, ho, ho. *How* everyone would laugh!

Over Tilly's dead body.

'All right,' she said quickly, seeing Campbell getting ready to come and fetch her if necessary. 'I'll jump.'

Without giving herself time to change her mind, she launched herself off the bank and Campbell only just managed to grab her and haul her on to the boulder with him. Tilly teetered wildly, only seconds from toppling backwards into the icy water before his arm clamped round her and pulled her hard against him.

He was steady as a rock and incredibly reassuring. Throwing pride to the chilly Scottish wind, Tilly clung to him.

'We must stop meeting like this,' he said dryly over the top of her head as she burrowed into him.

Aware of how ridiculous she must look but not daring to let go, Tilly did her best to play it cool. She kept her voice casual, as if she hadn't even noticed how strong and solid he was, or how good it felt to be held against a male body like his. Given that she was stranded in the middle of a freezing Scottish river, it was amazing that she was noticing anything about him at all.

'I usually like to get to know a man before I start hugging him,' she said, teeth chattering with a mixture of cold and nerves. 'You know, have a cup of coffee together or something first.'

'Our relationship does seem to have progressed quite quickly,' Campbell agreed over the top of her head. 'We'd hardly met before you were flinging your arms around my neck, and now this. I feel I should at least have sent you roses.'

There was a thread of amusement in his voice that only succeeded in flustering Tilly more.

'Roses will be the least I deserve if I survive today,' she said.

'Well, if we win, you can have a dozen,' said Campbell, looking for a way to get her to move on. Not that he wasn't appreciating having a soft feminine body squashed up against him, but the minutes were ticking by.

'Make that bars of chocolate and you're on,' said Tilly.

It would be too much to say that she was hot, stuck as she was on a rock in the middle of a freezing river with a chill wind whipping round her, but that was definitely warmth tingling in the pit of her stomach. This was one hell of a time for her hormones to start acting up.

'Do you think you're ready to try the next one then?'

She groaned a little. 'God, must I?'

'There's a camera trained on us right now,' Campbell pointed out. 'It must be getting a little boring for the cameraman, just the two of us entwined on a rock.'

If her hormones had their way it wouldn't be at all boring, Tilly thought. It could be extremely interesting, but knowing that a camera was pointing straight at her rather took the edge off any piquant little fantasies. Everyone knew that a camera added at least two sizes, and she didn't want to look any more ridiculous than she did already.

'OK, let's do it, then.'

Boulder by boulder, Campbell helped her across the river until there was just one last jump on to the bank. He went first and, the moment she let him go, Tilly started teetering. Her arms windmilled wildly and she took a wild leap for the bank before she fell back into the water.

Unprepared for her sudden jump, Campbell had no time to turn and catch her, and she missed her footing as she landed flat on her face, half on top of the bank, half down it. For a moment she lay stunned and splattered with mud before realising that she had provided the cameraman with his perfect action shot.

Excellent. She was *so* glad she was going to provide so much light entertainment for the viewers tucked up in their nice warm houses.

Tilly lifted her face from the mud. 'I want to go home,' she announced.

'You can't go home now. You're in the lead,' said Campbell, putting a hard hand under her arm and lifting her to her feet as easily as if she were a size six. It wasn't often that Tilly got to feel like thistledown, and she would have appreciated it more if she hadn't been spitting out mud. 'You're doing fine,' he told her.

'I am not doing fine. I'm making a prize prat of myself,' said Tilly bitterly, even as she bared her teeth in a smile for the camera which was zooming in on her.

'The viewers will love you,' soothed Campbell, helping her on with her backpack.

'Do you want to try that one again?' she enquired with a touch of acid. 'I think you'll find that the correct reply there was, *No, of course you're not making a prat of yourself, Tilly.*'

The corner of his mouth quirked. 'Would you believe me if I said that now?'

'Obviously not,' said Tilly crisply as she tried to quell her fickle senses, which were fizzing at the mere hint of a proper smile.

'Then I'll save my breath. Come on, we're nearly at the end of the first section. You'll feel better when you've had some lunch.'

Lunch wasn't very exciting, but at least it was provided. As she plodded after Campbell to the checkpoint, a horrible thought occurred to Tilly. What if they were expected to take survival skills to the extreme? She wouldn't put it past the television crew to make them catch their own rabbit or dig up worms for a quick snack.

In the event, the flaccid cheese and tomato sandwiches were a huge relief and Tilly devoured all of hers before Campbell, who had been in discussion with the producer, came over.

'What happens now?' she asked, her heart sinking at the sight of the map under his arm.

'We were first across, so we're definitely through to the next round.'

'Fabulous.' Tilly sighed.

Why couldn't she have been paired with a loser? He would have been much more her style, after all, and she could have been waiting for the bus home right now, which would have suited her fine.

Then she remembered the hospice, and what it had meant to her mother, to all of them, and immediately felt guilty. She shouldn't be wishing they could lose just so she could go home and get warm and comfortable.

'What do we have to do now?' she asked Campbell to make up for it.

'We have to get ourselves to the top of Ben Nuarrh.'

'Where's that?' Already Tilly knew that she wasn't going to like the answer.

It was even worse than she had feared. Campbell squinted into the distance and pointed at a jagged hill just visible in the purplish grey haze on the horizon. 'That's Ben Nuarrh.'

'But that's *miles*!' she said, aghast.

'It's a fair trek,' he agreed.

'We'll never do that this afternoon!'

'No, we'll have to camp. They've given us a tent and supplies.'

'A *tent*?' This was getting worse and worse. 'Nobody said anything to me about camping!'

'You must have been told you'd be away all weekend, weren't you?'

'Well, yes, but I thought we'd be staying in some lovely hotel. A baronial hall or something, with antlers in the library and a fire and deep baths and clean sheets...' Tilly trailed off. 'I should have known.' She sighed. 'My fantasies never turn into reality.'

Campbell lifted an eyebrow. 'What, never?'

Well, there had been Olivier. He had been a dream come true, at least at first, Tilly remembered, but the rest of her fantasy hadn't come to anything, had it? It had been so lovely, too. Olivier would look at her one day and the scales would fall from his eyes. *You're beautiful, Tilly*, he would say. *Marry me and share my life for ever.*

No, that fantasy hadn't lasted, she thought a little sadly. Not that there was any need to tell Campbell Sanderson that. A girl had to have some pride.

She lifted her chin. 'Hardly ever,' she said.

'Maybe you need to have more realistic fantasies,' he said.

'Like what?'

'Like a tent that doesn't leak, or a dry sleeping bag…or a bar of chocolate to have halfway there.'

Tilly was unimpressed. 'The chocolate sounds OK,' she conceded, 'but otherwise that's not really the stuff my fantasies are made of.'

'What about the fantasy of winning this challenge?'

'That's your fantasy, not mine,' Tilly objected, but she got to her feet, brushing the crumbs from her lap. 'Still, may as well try and make your fantasy come true at least.'

'That's not an offer a man gets every day.'

His mouth was doing that infuriating, tantalizing half-smile again. Tilly averted her gaze firmly and tried not to think about what other fantasies he might have that would be a lot more fun to help him with than traipsing up and down bloody mountains.

However, winning seemed to be all Campbell was interested in right then. 'We've got a good forty-five minutes on the others,' he told her with satisfaction as they went to collect the extra equipment. 'We'll be well ahead by the end of the day.'

He put the tent and most of the food in his own rucksack, deftly packing everything away.

'I'll take the chocolate,' Tilly offered generously, but Campbell only sent her an ironic glance.

'I think I'd better keep it,' he said. 'I may need it to get you up that mountain.'

'It'll take more than chocolate.' She sighed, thinking of the long afternoon ahead of her.

'It's a challenge,' he reminded her, handing her the lighter rucksack.

'I've been challenged enough today,' she grumbled, but she put the pack on. 'I've abseiled—twice!—and forded a river, and walked for *miles*… It's only lunchtime and I'm exhausted! I don't need any more challenges.'

Campbell tsk-tsked. 'That's not the right attitude, Jenkins. You're supposed to be thinking positive.'

'Don't call me Jenkins,' said Tilly crossly as she jerked the straps into place. 'It makes me feel as if I should be doing press ups and shouting *sir!*'

Ignoring her, Campbell turned to the producer, Suzy, who had come over to give them their final instructions before they set off.

'You know where you're going, and where the final checkpoint is?' she asked.

'All under control,' Campbell told her.

'Have you got everything you need?'

'A lift home would be nice,' muttered Tilly before Campbell frowned her down.

'We're fine.'

'Roger and Leanne were second across, so they'll be racing you to the top and back,' said Suzy. 'Roger's got GPS,' she added. 'That'll give them an advantage, but we've got it here, and I can give it to you, too, if you like.'

'What's GPS?' asked Tilly.

'It's a satellite navigation gizmo,' said Campbell dismissively. 'Some people can't get from A to B without them.'

'Is that what Roger had on his watch?'

Tilly remembered Roger showing Leanne his watch and explaining loudly how it would not only tell him where he was but could measure altitude, barometric pressure, temperature and even his heart rate.

It wasn't just his watch that was top of the range either. Roger's jacket was apparently a wonder of technology, his boots were cutting edge and his thermal underwear had been tested under polar conditions. He had the gear for every eventuality.

Next to Roger, Campbell had cut an unimpressive figure. He had no fancy watch, no smart jacket, not even a plastic cover to stop his map getting wet. His trousers were tucked into thick socks and old leather boots, and he wore a thick blue Guernsey—oh, and a contemptuous expression, although Tilly couldn't see why he was sneering at Roger. Roger was younger than Campbell and much better looking.

He smiled a lot, too, unlike some people who couldn't manage much more than a twitch at the corner of their mouths, she remembered with a darkling glance at Campbell.

If GPS told you where you were, it sounded a very good thing to Tilly. 'I think we should take one, just in case,' she said, but was overruled by Campbell.

'We've got a map,' he said with finality. 'That's all we need.'

'I'm surprised you're even deigning to take a map,' Tilly grumbled. 'I'd got you down as one of those men who refuses to even look at a map. I bet you think you can get wherever you're going by some kind of primeval instinct, as if you've got some universal A to Z encoded in your genes. I'm right, aren't I? How many times have you driven round and round for *hours* rather than give in to the woman sitting beside you who's bleating, "Why don't we stop and ask for directions?"'

Campbell opened his mouth to make a cutting reply, but Suzy

got in first. 'That's great!' she said enthusiastically. 'There's real chemistry between you two. The viewers will love it!'

'What viewers?' said Tilly blankly.

'This is a television programme,' Suzy reminded her. 'That's why we've been filming you.'

'What, just now?' Tilly cast a hunted look around. Sure enough, one of the cameramen was filming them from a few feet away. 'I thought it would be just when we were doing stuff,' she whispered, hurriedly turning her back on him.

'The interaction between you is just as interesting as how you get down a cliff or across a river,' Suzy explained patiently. 'The winners won't necessarily be the ones who get to the end first. They'll be the ones the viewers vote for, the ones they like and feel they can identify with. That reminds me,' she said and dug in her bag. 'You'll need this.'

She produced a smart little video camera and handed it to Campbell.

'What's this for?'

'You'll have to film yourselves at the top of Ben Nuarrh, and then of course you'll have to keep a video diary.'

'*What?*' Campbell's brows snapped together and Tilly stared, united for once in their consternation.

'The viewers aren't just interested in whether you can rise to these challenges or not,' said Suzy. 'They want to know your reactions, too. Video diaries are a great way to get insight into what people really feel, and of course they're very visual, too. People tend to treat them like a confessional. There's nobody asking questions. It's just you talking to the camera on your own, and it's much harder to pretend somehow when you're alone. People say things they wouldn't dream of admitting in front of anyone else.'

Campbell was appalled at the very idea. He had got through life perfectly well without ever talking about his feelings and he had no intention of starting now. They could whistle if they wanted anything interesting out of him!

'We don't both have to do them, surely?'

'Of course you do.' Suzy was firm. 'We're interested in how you react to each other. For this part of the challenge, you're the one who knows what he's doing, but for the next part, it'll be Tilly who's in charge.'

'What next part?' asked Campbell with foreboding.

'When Tilly teaches you how to make and decorate a wedding cake.' Suzy's smile faltered as she saw his expression. 'Didn't Keith tell you?'

'No.' His voice was grim. 'He omitted that part.'

No doubt because Keith had known exactly how Campbell would react! He'd thought it would just be a question of getting Tilly to the last checkpoint before anyone else. Physical challenges, he could deal with. A race was no problem, but making a *cake*? What a ridiculous waste of time!

'I'm not sure I can do that,' he said.

'Oh, come now,' said Tilly, who had been watching his expression and reading it without any difficulty. 'That's not the right attitude, Sanderson,' she quoted his words back at him wickedly. 'You're supposed to be thinking positive.'

The look he shot her promised vengeance but, with the camera still trained on them, he had to refrain from the murder that was clearly on his mind.

Tilly didn't care. This was the first time she had enjoyed herself all day. Let Campbell Sanderson see what it was like to be made to do something completely alien! Suddenly she could see the point of the programme. She would be able to get her own back when he was in her kitchen. All she had to do was survive Ben Nuarrh.

'I'm thinking about *timing*.' Campbell frowned at her before turning to Suzy to explain. 'I'm leaving Manning very soon and moving to a new job in the States. Obviously, I've got a lot to do before then.'

Suzy was dismayed. 'If you can't do the second part of the challenge, we'll have to cut you,' she said. 'That would be such a shame! We've got some great footage of you two already. Roger and Leanne are doing well, too. If you drop out, it'll probably mean a walkover for them, and then the competition would lose any tension. You know, it could be worse than a wedding cake,' she added in a wheedling voice. 'Roger's got to learn to do a pedicure.'

'Plus, they'll all think we dropped out because we were losing,' said Tilly, knowing Campbell would hate the very thought. It wasn't that she cared about winning, but she wanted her revenge for today's humiliations.

Campbell sucked in an irritable breath. He had a fairly clear idea of why Tilly was so keen for them to continue. She might look sweet with that rosy, heart-shaped face but there was an intriguing tartness to her, too. She would no doubt be hoping that it would be his turn to make a fool of himself next.

Let her hope. Campbell had no intention of indulging her. If he pulled out now, there would be no question of winning and, having got this far, he was loath to give up. How hard could it be to make a cake, after all? It wouldn't take long, and if he needed to make more time, he would just delegate a few things to Keith. Serve him right for getting him into this mess in the first place.

'But if we're carrying on with the competition, we're going to win,' he warned Tilly as they said goodbye to Suzy and set off towards Ben Nuarrh. 'That means no more dawdling!'

He set a punishing pace and Tilly was soon struggling. 'Can't we stop for five minutes so I can get my breath back?' she pleaded at last.

'You can have a rest when we get to the top.'

When she finally clambered up to where Campbell was waiting, Tilly was wheezing and bright red in the face.

'God, this is killing me!' She collapsed on to a rock while she struggled for breath. 'If this is just a hill, I'm never going to get to the top of that mountain.'

'You're very unfit,' he said disapprovingly.

Tilly scowled. 'Why not come right out and say I'm fat?'

'I would if that's what I thought,' he retorted. 'You're screwed up about your weight, clearly, but you don't look fat to me. You *do* seem unfit. Don't you take any exercise?'

'Not if I can help it,' said Tilly, only slightly mollified. 'I'm too busy.'

'Making cakes?' Campbell didn't bother to hide his disbelief.

'Yes, making cakes,' she said evenly. She was used to men pooh-poohing what she did for a living. 'It's my business.'

Campbell unscrewed a water bottle and passed it over to her. 'Doesn't that get boring?'

She shook her head as she drank gratefully. 'I love it. And every cake I make is different. It's not just piping endless icing roses for traditional wedding cakes. Every one I make is unique. I spend a lot of time talking to my clients so that I can come up with an individual design for their special occasion.'

'Like what?'

'It was some guy's fortieth birthday the other day, and he'd always dreamt of having a Porsche. His wife couldn't afford one of those, obviously, but she got me to make a cake in the shape of a Porsche 911, down to the last detail. Or I quite often make shoes or bags for girls' twenty-first birthdays—they're always fun.'

Campbell's eyes rested on her face. She was recovering from her breathlessness and her colour was fading, but she still glowed pinkly. Her eyes were a dark and rather beautiful blue, he found himself noticing, and the lush mouth curved in re-membered enthusiasm.

He wished he hadn't noticed quite how warm and soft and inviting it looked.

He looked away.

'I've never thought of cakes as fun before,' he said.

'I've never thought of climbing hills as fun either,' said Tilly frankly. She blew out a breath and pushed her hair back from her face. 'I suppose they put us together because we're so incompatible.'

'That was the general idea,' said Campbell.

'I wonder if Roger and Leanne found anything in common?'

Campbell snorted. 'Roger could always use his GPS. He says he can find anything with that.'

They glanced at each other, then suddenly both began to laugh, although Tilly was so startled by the effect a smile had on Campbell's expression that she almost stopped. Who would have thought a laugh could make such a difference? A mere crease of the cheeks, a simple curve of the mouth, a brief glimpse of strong white teeth? That was all it was, really.

The cool green eyes were lit with amusement as they met hers, and Tilly felt her heart give an odd little skip that left her almost breathless. It was as if a switch had been flipped, brightening the light so that she could see him in extraordinary detail—the pores of his skin, the dark ring around his pale irises, every hair in the thick brows—and she was abruptly aware of him as a powerful male animal, all muscle and leashed strength.

The image made Tilly blink and sent heat flooding through her, reaching places that hadn't tingled in quite that way for a very long time. Jerking her gaze away from his, she took a long glug from the water bottle, aware that her cheeks were burning.

Well, she would be hot, wouldn't she? She had just climbed a huge hill.

CHAPTER THREE

SHE hoped that was the reason, anyway.

There wasn't much point in finding man like Campbell Sanderson attractive, she reminded herself glumly. He was out of her league.

Friends would be furious if they knew she was thinking like that. Cleo was always urging her to forget Olivier and boost her ego with a quick fling. 'You need to feel good about yourself again,' she would insist to Tilly. 'You don't need to fall in love again just yet. You just need some fun. Find someone attractive and have a good time for a while. Think of it as a transitional relationship.'

The idea sounded good in principle but, as Tilly had discovered, it was a lot harder to put into practice. Even if her confidence had been up to it, attractive single men were in short supply in Allerby.

Anyway, Campbell wouldn't be single, she decided. He must be in his late thirties, and even SAS types surely fell prey to a committed relationship of some kind somewhere along the line. He had probably been snapped up by someone slender and beautiful and—even worse—really nice long ago.

There was no sign of a wedding ring, of course, but macho men like him wouldn't wear anything that remotely smacked of jewellery. So he *might* be married.

Or he might not.

Studying him covertly, Tilly drank some more water and wondered if she could ask him outright. It might seem a bit obvious, especially when they were going to be sleeping together in a tiny tent.

Sleeping together. Hmm. What was *that* going to be like?

Cleo would have told her to make the most of the opportunity but, like all of Cleo's ideas, that was easier said than done. Tilly only had to look at Campbell to know that *he* certainly wasn't fizzing with anticipation at the thought of sleeping close to her. He probably hadn't given the issue of sleeping arrangements a moment's thought.

He wouldn't care *what* happened as long as he won this stupid race.

Tilly sighed inwardly. That was just her luck. She had finally stumbled across an attractive man only to discover that, even given the remote off-chance that he might be available, he was far too competitive to let himself be distracted by the possibilities of a man and a woman in a small tent.

Look at him now—totally focused, glancing at his watch, determined to keep her moving.

'Let's get going,' he said.

Tilly groaned but hauled herself obediently to her feet. 'How much further is it?'

'We could do another three hours at least.'

'I'm not sure my feet will last that long,' she said, wincing as she wriggled her toes in her boots.

'Mind over matter,' said Campbell briskly. He threw his pack on to his back and adjusted the straps with deft movements. 'The trick is to keep thinking about something else.'

'Like what?'

'Like what you'd really like to find at the top of the next hill.'

'That's easy,' said Tilly, securing her own pack into place and trudging after him. 'Can you please make sure there's a fabulous bathroom, with a deep, scented bath piled high with bubbles? I'd like candles and a glass of champagne waiting for me on the edge of the bath…oh, and a little plate of nibbles, too. Smoked salmon, probably,' she added reflectively. 'Or nuts? No, smoked salmon,' she decided. 'Little roulades stuffed with prawn mousse and soft cheese.'

'I'll see what I can do,' said Campbell in a dry voice.

He was taken aback by how vividly he could picture Tilly sinking into the water with a sigh of pleasure. Her skin would be pink and pearly and wet, her hair clinging in damp tendrils around her face, her breasts rising out of the bubbles as she tipped back her head and dropped smoked salmon into that lush mouth…

Campbell had to give himself a mental shake, and he picked up his stride. He felt almost embarrassed, as if someone had caught him peeking round the bathroom door.

Tilly was still fantasising. 'While you're at it, can you arrange for a wonderful meal to be cooking so that the smell comes wafting up the stairs? No niminy piminy nouvelle cuisine, though, not after the day I've had. I want something hot and tasty. It doesn't have to be fancy.'

'A roast?' Campbell suggested, drawn back into the scene she was creating in spite of himself.

'Yes, a roast would be very acceptable, especially if you can lay on all the trimmings, too. Or a really good casserole with creamy mashed potatoes.' Tilly was beginning to salivate now. She could practically taste that first mouthful. 'Or—I know!—steak and kidney pudding…mmm, yum, yum… Even a—'

Glancing at Campbell just then and catching his fascinated gaze, she broke off. 'What—you don't have fantasies?'

'Not about food.'

'What *do* you fantasise about then?' she demanded grouchily, embarrassed at having revealed quite how greedy she was. Why couldn't she be the kind of girl who hankered after a green salad or a mug of nice herbal tea?

Campbell lifted an eyebrow in response, and she tutted. 'Not *that* kind of fantasy,' she scolded as if he had spoken, although actually she wouldn't have minded knowing that at all. 'A fantasy you can share with a nice girl like me!'

'I'm not sure any of my fantasies are suitable for nice girls.'

There was just the faintest thread of amusement in his voice and Tilly was sure that he was mocking her.

'All right, imagine being really relaxed,' she challenged him. 'What?'

'Just do it,' she insisted. 'Close your eyes—or, on second thoughts, you'd better not, you might trip—and picture yourself happy.'

Campbell sighed and prepared to indulge her. At least it might stop her whingeing about her feet for a while longer. He thought for a moment.

'OK.'

'Have you an image of yourself relaxed and happy?'

'Yes.'

'Where are you?'

Tilly hoped that he wasn't going to say that he was in bed. That would make it very hard to concentrate. She waited for him to say *standing on top of a mountain* or *skiing down a black run*.

'I'm sitting in a comfortable chair in front of the fire.'

It was so unexpected that she actually gaped at him. *Sitting?* Wasn't that a bit tame for a man like Campbell?

'What are you doing?'

'Reading.'

The defensive note in his voice made Tilly grin. 'You make it sound like you're confessing a dirty secret! What are you reading? Nothing illegal or immoral, I hope.'

'Roman military history.'

Campbell practically bit out the words, and this time Tilly really did laugh.

He scowled at her. 'What's so funny?'

'I'm sorry. It was just so unexpected,' she tried to explain.

'What, marines aren't allowed to read?'

'It's not that. It's just that you seem such a macho action man that it's hard to imagine you poring over ancient history, that's all.'

'I don't want to spend all day doing it. You asked me to imagine myself relaxed,' said Campbell almost crossly. 'That was just a picture that came into my mind. Obviously I should have said some kind of extreme sport instead!'

'That wouldn't have been as interesting, though,' said Tilly, meaning it, but Campbell clearly thought that she was joking.

'I've had the mick taken out of me for years,' he said in a resigned voice. 'Anyone would think I had some bizarre fetish. It's only military history, for God's sake.'

'But why the Romans?'

He shrugged. 'I like their logical approach. Their sense of order. They were great engineers. Great strategists.'

'And successful,' Tilly reminded him, sure that was the key to their appeal for him. 'The Romans were winners, too.' She caught his look. 'Hey, I did history at school. Roman history may not be my bedtime reading, but I'm not completely ignorant!'

She studied him from under her lashes as she toiled on beside him. She hoped he wasn't regretting telling her. She rather liked the idea of him sitting quietly and reading by the fire, and was touched by the fact that he seemed faintly embarrassed by it, as if he had confessed some weakness.

'So…have you got a fantasy meal cooking in the background while you read your book?'

'I'm afraid I'm not someone who spends a lot of time

thinking about food,' he said. 'I eat what's put in front of me. I'll have some of your roast.'

Tilly wished he hadn't said that. It was enough to conjure up an instant cosy domestic scene. There she was, upstairs in the bath, and there was Campbell by the fire. Any minute now he would look at his watch, put his book down and go and check on the roast, then he would come upstairs and sit on the edge of the bath.

I've turned the potatoes, he would say, topping up her glass. If you were going to have a fantasy, Tilly believed, you might as well make it a really good one. *Will you be much longer?*

And Tilly would sip her champagne and ask him to wash her back while he was there. She could almost feel his warm, firm hands soaping her, and obviously he wouldn't stop at her back...

'That must be some bath.'

Campbell's voice jerked Tilly out of her daydream. 'What?' Disorientated, she looked around her to find that she had somehow made it to the top of the hill without even realising it.

'You haven't said a word for the last mile. I'm impressed by the power of your fantasising!'

If only he knew.

A guilty flush stained Tilly's cheeks and her eyes slid away from his just in case an ability to mind-read was something else he had forgotten to mention, along with a knowledge of ancient military history.

Now that she had snapped out of it, she was appalled at herself. What had she been *thinking*? Harry and Seb had been right. She had been on her own too long. It was time she found another man.

At least she knew she was over Olivier. He had been the focus of her fantasies for quite a while, most of them involving him crawling back and confessing that he had made a terrible mistake. Satisfying in their own way, but nowhere near as erotic as the one that had carried her up the hillside.

'Perhaps I can make one of your fantasies come true,' said Campbell, digging in his rucksack.

For a blanket? Tilly wondered wildly and gulped. She must get a grip.

'Which one?' she asked, appalled to hear that her voice came out as barely more than a croak.

'Chocolate,' he said, and produced a bar. 'You can have a rest for ten minutes, too.'

Tilly didn't know whether she was disappointed or relieved. 'Great,' she said weakly.

The light was already going from the sky and the air was cooling rapidly as she perched on her pack. Unwrapping the chocolate, she broke the bar in half and offered part to Campbell, who shook his head.

'You have it,' he said.

He was fast becoming a fantasy man in reality, thought Tilly ruefully. A man who gave you chocolate and insisted you ate it all without sharing.

Unaware of the trend of her thoughts, Campbell was unfolding the map that he had shoved carelessly into his pocket.

'Isn't it a bit late to be looking at that now?' said Tilly through a mouthful of chocolate. 'I hope you're not about to tell me that we've climbed the wrong hills?'

She almost wished he would so that she could go back to feeling cross with him. It would be a lot easier than this unnerving awareness. See what happened when you let your fantasies get out of control?

'No, we're in the right place. I'm sure Roger's GPS would tell us exactly the same thing.'

'Then why aren't they here with us?'

'We had a head start, remember? And Roger may well take a different route to Ben Nuarrh.'

'I bet it's an easier one!'

'This is quicker,' said Campbell firmly.

He passed Tilly the map. 'We're here,' he said, pointing, and Tilly found her eyes riveted on his hand. The one that had done such incredible things with the soap in her fantasy...

'Concentrate, Jenkins!' Campbell's peremptory tone made her jump. 'You're fading out, there.'

'Oh...um, yes...sorry...I'm just a bit tired.'

A frown touched his eyes as he glanced at her. 'I thought we'd camp there,' he said, moving his finger on the map. 'Do you think you can make it, or will you need a new fantasy to get you there?'

Tilly swallowed. 'I think I've done enough fantasising for today!'

'Are you ready to get on, then? I can't promise a bath or a bed, but we'll have something to eat and you'll be able to sleep.'

'That'll be enough for me,' said Tilly.

It was a mistake to have stopped. She found the last leg a real struggle. The threatened blister had become a reality, and her feet were killing her. She was stiff, too, and tired and cold.

Seeing her hobbling, Campbell took her pack for her and managed to walk just as easily with two. He stayed beside her, encouraging her up the last steep slope, and refusing to let her stop when she threatened to collapse.

Tilly couldn't have done it without him, but she was vaguely distrustful of his motives all the same. It was all very well being Mr Nice Guy *now*. She might appreciate his help, but she knew quite well that he was only doing it because he wanted to get to the top of Ben Nuarrh first.

Her father was just the same—determined to get his own way whatever happened. If charm was the easiest way to get what he wanted, he would lay it on with a trowel, but he would never lose sight of his goal. Tilly had learnt early to distrust men who'd do anything to win, but it was still hard not to warm treacherously at the approval in Campbell's voice as he practically carried her the last few yards.

'Well done.'

It was almost dark by then, so Tilly couldn't see much. They were somewhere high on the flank of Ben Nuarrh, that much she knew, and Campbell seemed to have found a sheltered hollow where a peaty burn ran between granite outcrops and there was enough flattish, if somewhat soggy, ground to set up the tent.

He lowered her on to one of the outcrops and she sat, numb with exhaustion, and watched as he put up the tent with an efficiency that didn't surprise her in the least. Unrolling the bedding, he backed out and held open the flap.

'Why don't you get in?' he said to Tilly. 'You can take off your boots and do your video diary while I make the stew.'

'Stew?' She gaped at him, wondering how on earth he was going to conjure a casserole out of his pack.

'Don't get excited. It's a dehydrated pack—add to boiling water and stir, which is pretty much my level of cooking. It won't be your fantasy, but it'll be hot and filling.'

'I suppose that's better than nothing,' she said, getting up stiffly and hobbling to the tent.

It was very small. She bent and peered inside. 'Is there going to be room for both of us?' she asked doubtfully.

'It'll be tight, but that's a good thing. We won't be wasting body warmth,' said Campbell. 'But don't worry,' he added ironically as she straightened. 'We've separate sleeping bags.'

Tilly wasn't sure how to respond to that. She couldn't decide whether to make it clear that she was relieved, or play it cool, as if she took the prospect of sharing sleeping bags in her stride the whole time.

Or perhaps this was a good opportunity to find out a bit more about him?

'Still, it's going to be very cosy,' she said. 'Are you going to have some explaining to do when you get down?'

'What do you mean?' Campbell glanced up from where he was setting up a portable gas ring with his usual deftness and economy of movement.

'Well, if I discovered that my husband or boyfriend had spent the night with another woman in a tent this size I wouldn't be very happy about it.'

'Oh, I see,' he said, returning his attention to the gas. 'No, there's no one I need to explain anything to, and that's the way I like it.'

'You're not married then?'

'Not any more.'

'I'm sorry.' Tilly hesitated by the tent entrance. 'What happened?'

Campbell sighed and sat back on his heels, looking up at her with a sardonic expression. 'Does it matter?'

'God, you can tell you're a man who's been trained to withstand interrogation,' grumbled Tilly. Talk about trying to get blood out of a stone! 'Don't they teach you the art of conversation in the Marines? I just thought it would be nice to find out a bit more about the man I'm going to be sleeping with,' she told him with a huffy look and then, to her fury, blushed when he lifted one amused brow at her choice of words. 'In a manner of speaking,' she added stiffly.

'Lisa left me for another man who could give her more than I could. We got divorced. She's married again and lives in the States now. End of story.'

'Do you have any kids?'

'Nope.'

Tilly sighed. 'I was about to say that must make it easier because that's what people always say when a relationship breaks down. *At least there weren't any children.* As if it helps somehow,' she remembered with a bitter edge to her voice. 'When someone leaves you, it doesn't hurt any less just because you haven't got children.'

'Sounds like you're speaking from experience,' Campbell commented.

'I am.'

'Well, you don't need to feel sorry for me,' he told her, ignoring the opportunity to say that he felt sorry for *her*, Tilly couldn't help noting. 'It was a disaster from the start. I should never have married her.'

'Then why did you?'

He shrugged. 'Why? Because Lisa was—is—the most beautiful woman I've ever seen. She's absolutely dazzling. The moment I saw her, I had to have her.'

Tilly tried—and failed—to imagine a man ever saying that about her.

'You must have loved her.'

'Are you going to take your boots off?' Campbell made it plain the conversation was over by getting to his feet.

Clearly *not* a man who believed in talking things through.

Resigned to the fact that she wasn't going to get any more out of him, Tilly applied herself to the problem of actually getting into the tent. She was so tired that she was afraid that once she was in she would never get out again. Campbell had managed to make it look a perfectly simple business—he would—but she was reduced to kneeling down and then attempting an undignified dive inside between the entrance flaps.

Once in, she had to wriggle around until she was in a

position where she could sit up and take off her boots—no easy task in itself. Campbell had set up a light near the entrance, which she had managed to knock over twice during her ungainly entrance, but at least it meant she could see what she was doing.

Pulling off the second boot with a gusty sigh of relief, Tilly collapsed back on to her sleeping bag and stared up at the weird shadows the light cast on the orange roof of the tent. She couldn't remember ever being so tired, or so cold.

'I don't think I'll ever be able to move again,' she shouted out to Campbell, who had been to the nearby stream and boiled some water in the time it had taken her to sort herself out. 'I'm going to have to spend the rest of my life here. They'll find me in five thousand years, frozen like that prehistoric hunter guy in a glacier, and use my body to find out about twenty-first century society.'

Tilly rather liked the idea of scientists of the future poring over her body and speculating about her life. 'They'll decide I lived and worked up here, and that red salopettes were the height of fashion.'

Outside the tent, she could see Campbell shaking his head in disbelief. 'You have the most extraordinary imagination,' he said.

'All that research,' said Tilly, too carried away by her idea to care what he thought, 'and none of them will know that I was only stuck up here because my loathsome brothers thought I should get out of my rut!

'This is all their fault,' she went on bitterly. 'They'll be sorry when I'm not there to cook for them and show them how to use the washing machine and be nice to their girlfriends! *If only we hadn't been so stupid*, they'll say to each other. *What were we thinking? Dear Tilly could still be with us instead of stuck up on that mountain.*'

'Dear Tilly will be back with them by tomorrow night,' said Campbell, unmoved by her story. 'I'm not going to leave you here.'

'You would if you thought you could win without me,' said Tilly sulkily.

'Fortunately for you, I can't.'

Ducking into the tent, he handed her an enamel mug of black tea. 'Have this to warm you up while I get the stew going.'

'Warm? Warm? What's warm?' She shivered but took the tea gratefully. 'The only trouble with stopping is realising how cold you are.'

Campbell tsk-tsked. 'Stop complaining,' he said 'Have one of your fantasies instead—or, better still, do the video diary.' He dug around in his rucksack for the camera.

'Why do I have to do it?' grumbled Tilly as he held it to the light so that he could see how it worked.'

'Because you'll be better at that than me.'

'I won't. I'd feel a complete idiot talking to a camera,' she protested. 'I wouldn't know what to say.'

'Just carry on wittering the way you've been doing all day,' suggested Campbell with a touch of acid. 'Tell them one of your fantasies—that should win a few votes!'

'I'm not going to do that!' She flopped back down on to the sleeping bag. 'Why don't we pretend we forgot about the video diary business?'

He shook his head firmly. 'We can't do that. The diary is part of the challenge.' Propping the camera on top of his rucksack, he bent down to peer through it and check that it was pointing at Tilly. 'You heard what Suzy said. We're going to be judged on the video diary and film clips as well as on who gets back down from Ben Nuarrh first.'

'If you care so much about winning, you do it,' said Tilly crossly.

'I've got to make the stew.' Campbell moved the lamp so that the light fell on her. 'Look, just talk for a minute and then it's done. You don't even have to get up. I promise I won't listen, so you can be as horrible about me as you want.'

He pointed at a button on top of the camera. 'I'll set it going. Just press this when you've finished.'

'Hang on!' Tilly started to struggle up in protest, but he was already crawling out of the tent, leaving the red light beckoning encouragingly.

Tilly's video diary:
[Staring at camera with a hunted look] Oh, God, I suppose I'll have to say something... Um... [Long pause] OK, here I am, halfway up a Scottish mountain with a man I'd never met before this morning. It's funny to think that this time last night I'd never even heard of Campbell, and now it seems as if I've known him for ever. And tonight we're going to sleep together...well, not sleep together, except of course we will be sleeping...oh, you know what I mean. Can whoever's watching this edit that bit out? [Yawns hugely] I'm so tired, I can't think straight!

Where was I? Oh, yes, Campbell... Well, he was a terrible bully this morning. You should have seen him making me abseil down that cliff—two cliffs! Talk about competitive! And he's not exactly chatty. I've never met a man who talks so little about himself, to be honest. His middle name must be Clam. Campbell the Clam Sanderson. [Giggles]

At least they'd never have to worry about him blabbing operational secrets. I bet he was in one of those special units, you know. No point in asking him, though. He'd just say he could tell me, but he'd have to kill me. He probably would, too. Still, I'm sure Suzy's assistant is right. He's got that steely-eyed thing going that's quite exciting when he's not pushing you down a cliff [Pauses, looks doubtful] Actually, could you cut that bit, too?

[Yawns again, belatedly covering mouth] Anyway, he wasn't so bad this afternoon. In fact, he was really quite nice, especially the last few miles. [Pauses again, remembering] Yes, surprisingly nice. And now he's making me supper. I'm not sure what this stew is going to be like, though. Dehydrated doesn't sound very nice, but I'm so hungry I'll eat it. I ought to offer to help, but I really don't think I've got the energy to get out of the tent. [Slides out of view of camera] Perhaps if I just closed my eyes for a moment, and then I'll go and give him a hand...

Campbell looked up from the pot he was stirring, suddenly alert. He could hear the wind whistling around the crags, the canvas flapping, the hiss of the gas, but when he listened, he realised there was something missing.

No Tilly. How long was it since he had heard her voice?

'Tilly?'

He bent down to peer into the tent. She had crashed out over both sleeping bags, and appeared to have simply toppled from where she had been sitting talking to the camera and was sound asleep.

Shaking his head, Campbell turned off the camera.

Tilly was still fully dressed apart from her boots, and he contemplated her slumped form with a slight frown. How was he going to get her into her sleeping bag? He had no intention of undressing her, but she would be better off without her jacket. Its stiff fabric was digging into her face as it was. It would certainly be uncomfortable if she did wake up and, besides, she would need the jacket as an extra layer to put on in the morning.

'Tilly?' he tried again, but she was dead to the world and didn't even stir when he lifted her up to pull her arms out of the sleeves and get rid of the jacket.

It was like dealing with a very large floppy doll, although he imagined dolls weren't usually that warm and soft. Not having had even a sister, Campbell's experience of dolls was negligible, but he was fairly sure they didn't smell faintly of...what was it? He sniffed. Some flower. Roses, perhaps? He had never been very good on flowers but something about the fragrance of Tilly's hair reminded him of his mother's garden on a summer evening long ago.

The thought made Campbell frown. He wasn't supposed to be thinking about things like that. Unzipping one of the sleeping bags, he manoeuvred Tilly inside it, not without difficulty. Quite a bit of manhandling was required and he was very aware of her lush body even through the layers of clothing. It was all very well staying focused but it was hard not to be distracted by the fact that, whatever else Tilly might be, she was all woman.

An exasperating one, Campbell reminded himself. At least she was quiet now that she was sleeping. He had never met anyone quite so chatty. Lisa had been mistress of icy silence, and he wasn't at all sure which was worse.

Tilly stirred and mumbled something as he tucked her legs into the sleeping bag and zipped her up. The next moment she was turning and snuggling down like a child with more unintelligible mumbling and some smacking of her lips before she sank back into a deep sleep.

Campbell sat back on his heels and watched her for a moment. It was the first chance he had had to look at her properly, he realised, and without that challenging blue gaze fixed on him he could see that she had lovely creamy skin and beautiful eyebrows. The heart-shaped face was slack with sleep, but her generous mouth still had a humorous curve to it, as if she were on the point of smiling.

Even now, sound asleep, there was something *disorderly*

about her, Campbell decided. She was all softness and curves and curls, and it made him twitchy. There were no straight lines with Tilly, no logic, no control. She talked the whole time and her imagination was so vivid he wasn't sure whether she was talking nonsense or not half the time.

His eyes rested on her mouth almost unwillingly. Tilly might be high-maintenance, but there was a warmth and a sweetness about her, too, offset by an intriguing tartness and a stubbornness that had kept her climbing all day. No wonder she was tired!

Without quite realising what he was doing, Campbell reached out to smooth the tumbled hair from Tilly's cheek. The silkiness of her curls and the smoothness of her skin were like a physical shock, and he withdrew his hand sharply.

Better have that stew, he told himself.

He took the video camera with him as he backed out of the tent. God only knew what Tilly had been saying to the camera before she had fallen asleep. Knowing her, it might have been anything! He had better make sure there was something sensible on there.

Campbell finished the stew, cleaned out the pot and his plate, and turned his attention to the camera. Clicking it on, he cleared his throat.

'This is Campbell Sanderson. We're camped on the shoulder of Ben Nuarrh, so if we leave at zero six hundred tomorrow morning we should be in a position to make it to the summit in good time. It's been a successful day, after a slow start. I didn't feel that Tilly was taking things very seriously to start with, but she's done well this afternoon. Very well, in fact.'

There, that ought to do it. Campbell decided that he had been concise, accurate and generous. He hadn't said anything about how long it had taken to coax her down the abseil, or about the stupid fuss she had made about jumping over a few stones to cross the river. He had carefully refrained from commenting on her lipstick or on how unfit she was. He had said nothing about her bizarre flights of imagination.

And nothing about her smile, nothing about the teasing humour in her dark blue eyes, or her infectious laugh.

Nothing about her enticing softness as she'd pressed up against him on one of those boulders.

No, he wouldn't be saying any of that. Campbell switched off the camera with a sharp click.

CHAPTER FOUR

'OLIVIER?' Tilly struggled out of a deep sleep to find herself pressed up against a solid male body.

It was pitch dark. Disorientated, she tried to prop herself up on one elbow and her stiff muscles screamed in protest, jerking her properly awake with a gasp.

Campbell was instantly alert. 'What's the matter?'

That wasn't Olivier's voice. Tilly blinked at the darkness for a moment until her brain kicked in and she remembered where she was, and just who she was cuddled up against.

Campbell Sanderson.

'Ouch!' Her sore muscles pinched again as she moved hastily away from him. Between her stiffness and the sleeping bag, it was hard to move at all.

'It's you,' she said, dismayed.

'I'm afraid so.'

Tilly was attempting to disentangle herself from her sleeping bag. The wind was howling and shrieking around the tent and she could hear an ominous drumming on the canvas. Rain. Just what you wanted when you were camping.

'What time is it?' she asked blearily.

'Two-fifteen.'

'How on earth do you know that?' She had seen no tell-tale

luminous watch face and there was no way he could have seen the time without a light.

'I just do.'

Her silence was obviously eloquent with disbelief, for he sighed and switched on a pencil torch, pointing it at his watch. 'Satisfied?'

Tilly peered at the watch face. 'Two-sixteen,' she read.

'It was two fifteen when you asked me.'

His calm certainty riled her. 'I bet you were checking your watch under the sleeping bag just before I woke up.'

'Of course. I've spent all night awake in the hope that you would wake up and ask the time so that I could trick you.'

Her lips tightened at his tone. 'Well, how did you do it, then?'

He shrugged. 'I've got a clock in my head. It's years of training. There are times when you need to know the time but can't afford to switch on a light.'

Tilly tried to imagine what it would be like to be in a situation where you couldn't risk putting on a light. She would never be able to cope. She was a terrible coward.

'Presumably nobody is going to ambush us up here, so can I have the torch again?' she asked as she wriggled awkwardly out of her sleeping bag at last.

'Where are you going?'

'I thought I'd pop out and get a DVD.'

'*What?*'

She sighed. 'Where do you think I'm going?'

'Oh.' He sounded exasperated. 'Can't you hang on until morning?'

'No, I can't. My bladder hasn't had years of training. I'll never be able to get back to sleep until I've been.' She groped around for her boots. 'Can you point the torch while I put these on?'

With a long-suffering sigh, Campbell directed the beam of light. 'You'll need a jacket, too. It's raining.'

'What did I do with it?' wondered Tilly, patting the end of her sleeping bag. It was hard to see anything with just a fine pencil beam of light. 'I was so tired I can't remember taking it off.'

'You didn't. I undressed you last night.'

It was Tilly's turn to do a double take. 'You did *what*?'

'Don't worry,' said Campbell dryly. 'I didn't even enjoy it. You were dead to the world and I'm not into necrophilia. I stopped at your dungarees. I thought they might be a bit tricky to take off without some cooperation from you.'

Tilly flushed in the darkness, imagining him grunting with effort as he manhandled her out of her clothes. No wonder he had stopped! The poor man had probably been exhausted.

That was the story of her life, she thought glumly. An attractive man undressed her and she wasn't even awake to appreciate it.

She didn't bother to lace her boots. It sounded like a wild night out there and she wasn't planning on being very long.

Yelping at her sore muscles, she took the torch and struggled out of the tent only to find herself staggering against a gust of wind that slashed rain across her face. Straightening as best she could, she saw that it was very dark, and she began to wish that she had hung on after all. There might not be enemy soldiers lurking behind the outcrops, but it took her imagination no time at all to sketch out the beginning of a horror story. The sooner she got back into the tent, the better.

Tilly did her business as quickly as she could, which wasn't very fast, given that her fingers were numb with cold. The skiing dungarees might be warm, but she had forgotten just how long it took to unfasten them. It was all right for Campbell, with his no doubt highly trained bladder.

She was wet and shivering by the time she scrambled back into the tent and zipped up the entrance once more. Then she

had to go through the whole business of taking off her jacket
and boots again. She put the torch on the sleeping bag where
the beam was promptly buried until Campbell picked it up and
held it for her so that she could see what she was doing. Tilly
was grateful, but very conscious, too, of how close he was. It
felt very intimate, being together in such a confined space,
and, although she did her best to stick to her sleeping bag, it
was impossible not to touch him.

'I can't believe people do this kind of thing for fun,' she
grumbled through chattering teeth. 'Who'd want to camp when
you could be tucked up in an nice, cosy B and B? God, I'm
freezing!'

'Your hair's wet,' said Campbell. Incredibly, he had a
smallish towel in his hand. 'Turn round and I'll dry it for you.'

'Where on earth did you find that?' Tilly asked to distract
herself from his nearness as he rubbed her hair vigorously.

'In my pack.'

'That's not a pack—ouch!—that's a bottomless pit!'

'I came prepared for the conditions,' he said. 'I knew there
was a good chance we'd get wet somewhere along the line.'

'Pity you didn't bring a hot shower,' muttered Tilly. 'You
seem to have everything else in there.' Her ears were sore and
she tried to pull her head away, but Campbell kept a firm grip
on her. 'Ow!' she protested. 'That hurts—and God knows what
my hair's going to look like in the morning.'

'It's more important that you don't go to sleep again with
wet hair,' he pointed out, giving her hair a final rub before
tossing the towel aside. 'There. Get back in your sleeping bag
and you'll soon warm up.'

Shuddering with the cold, Tilly clambered back into the bag
and pulled the covers tight under her chin. 'How soon is soon?'
she asked, unclenching her jaw after a few moments. 'I don't
suppose you thought to bring a hot-water bottle?'

She heard a sigh through the darkness, and the next moment Campbell had rolled over and was pulling her bodily towards him, sleeping bag and all, making her squeak with surprise. 'You'll have to make do with body heat,' he said. 'You can't beat it when you're cold.'

He shifted to make himself more comfortable and put an arm over her, tucking her firmly into the curve of his body. 'Now, have you quite finished fidgeting?' he asked, his astringent tones at odds with the warm reassurance of his hold.

'Yes.' Tilly's voice was huskier than she wanted.

'Then perhaps we can both get some sleep?'

Sure, but how could she be expected to sleep when his arm was heavy over her and she could feel his breath stirring her hair? Even through two sleeping bags, she was desperately aware of his solid male warmth.

In spite of her exhaustion, Tilly had rarely felt less like sleeping. All her senses were on high alert and fizzing away as if they had had ten coffees apiece. She could hear the rain drumming overhead while the wind plucked angrily at the canvas. The tent smelt of canvas and hillside and wet jackets.

It was strange to be lying next to a man again, and Tilly was surprised at how right it felt with Campbell's arm around her. There had been no one since Olivier.

Olivier… How desolate she had been when he had dumped her! Tilly had done her best to hide her humiliation behind a bright and breezy exterior and she thought she had done a good job of convincing everyone that she was over him, so it had come as something of a shock to realise that even her brothers, never very perceptive when it came to emotions, had realised how miserable she was inside.

'You need to meet someone new,' they had told her. 'It's time you got out there and started looking instead of hiding away in your kitchen.'

'I'm not hiding away! I've got a business to run, and it happens to involve a lot of time in the kitchen, that's all.'

Even her friends had started. 'Olivier wasn't the one for you. The right man is out there somewhere, Tilly, but you won't meet him stuck at home. You've got to go out and find him.'

Tilly hadn't believed them. She knew none of them had liked Olivier particularly, but she had been so in love with him, so utterly convinced he was The One. What was the point of looking for Mr Right when she had already found him, and discovered that she couldn't have him? Tilly hadn't wanted to meet someone new. All she'd wanted was for Olivier to come back and tell her that it had been a terrible mistake, that he did love her after all. That was all she had dreamed about for months now.

The odd thing was that now when she closed her eyes, she couldn't picture him clearly. Tilly frowned into the darkness. Oh, she remembered what he looked like, of course she did, but his image was strangely two-dimensional, like a photo in a magazine. When she tried to bring it into sharper focus, all she could see was Campbell: Campbell looking exasperated, Campbell shaking his head in disbelief, Campbell smiling that unexpected smile that made her pulse kick just remembering it.

Perhaps the boys and all her friends would shut up now, Tilly hoped. They had got their way. Between them, they had bullied her out of the kitchen and halfway up a Scottish mountain, and sure enough she had met someone new, even someone available.

But Campbell was no Mr Right, and even if he had been looking for Ms Right, which she doubted very much, it was clear that Tilly wasn't at all what he would have in mind.

How could she be? She had known him for less than twenty-four hours, but it took a lot less than that to realise that he was a man determined to have the best of everything. She hadn't been at all surprised to hear that his ex-wife was dazzling. Campbell Sanderson would never accept that anyone else could do better than him. So any woman on his arm would have to be the most beautiful, the wittiest, the cleverest, the best-dressed.

Tilly was none of those things. No way would a man like Campbell ever want someone who muddled through life and looked a mess most of the time while she was doing it. Olivier hadn't wanted her either.

No, she should just accept that she was never going to be a woman men desired or cherished. She was resigned to being good old Tilly now—the good friend, the one men went out with if they wanted a break from adoring their high-maintenance women and needed an evening of fun with no strings attached.

Not that Campbell would even want that. He was too chilly and driven to relax with a jolly evening in the pub. He wasn't the type to want a shoulder to cry on either. Look at how he had clammed up the moment she had suggested that he might have loved his wife.

How he must have hated losing her to another man. Of course, anyone would find it devastating, but it would be the losing that would really rankle with a man as competitive as Campbell. He wasn't the type to shrug his shoulders and accept a situation. He certainly wasn't the type to make do with second-best, Tilly decided, and that was the most she could ever be. Frankly, she would be lucky to make second-best. Those keen green eyes missed nothing, and she wouldn't be at all surprised if she had ranked as a non-starter.

Well, that was OK, Tilly told herself. He didn't have anything *she* wanted either.

All right, maybe that wasn't *quite* true. He had a great body and an unexpectedly attractive smile, but any Mr Right of hers would need a lot more than that. Tilly had no intention of humiliating herself any further by not reaching Campbell's impossible standards. She had never matched up to her father's, had failed to meet Olivier's, and she was sick of feeling inadequate, she decided. There was only so much rejection a girl could take.

No, if Harry and Seb thought their plan to drag her out of the kitchen would lead her to Mr Right, they were in for a disappointment.

Tilly was prepared to admit that she found Campbell attractive, but that was as far as it went. She wouldn't be letting her defences down or getting her expectations up.

On the other hand, since she was here, being held tight against that hard body, it would be silly not to enjoy it, wouldn't it? Tilly closed her eyes and snuggled closer to Campbell. She might as well make the most of it.

'Time to get up.' Campbell touched Tilly on the shoulder to wake her, but she only groaned and turned away from his hand to bury her face in her sleeping bag.

He shook her harder. 'Come on, wake up. We've got a mountain to climb.'

Tilly groaned louder. 'Climb it yourself,' she mumbled.

'Unfortunately, I can't do it without you,' said Campbell. 'Come on, get up. I've made you some tea. You can drink it while I'm packing up the tent.'

Tilly was tempted to tell him what he could do with his tea, but Campbell was already rolling up his bag and stuffing it into his pack. Clearly he wasn't going to let her rest until she was up and out.

Grumbling, she climbed blearily out of the tent and straightened, only to freeze as she found herself staring at a view that was literally breathtaking. The rain had stopped some time in the early hours and the chilly wind had blown away all the clouds, leaving a pale luminous sky suffused with sunrise. Great golden brown hills rolled away into the purple distance, without a single sign of human habitation. No roads, no telegraph poles, no electricity pylons. Just rocks and heather and a lone bird calling somewhere above them.

'Oh,' she said.

'Quite something, isn't it?' Campbell poured tea into an enamel mug. 'Now, aren't you glad you got up?'

'Ecstatic,' said Tilly sourly, grimacing as she tried to straighten her back. Awe-inspiring it might be, but it would take more than a view to improve her mood. 'I love being bullied awake at the crack of dawn and dragged outside to drink tea in the freezing cold halfway up a mountain when I'm so stiff I can't even stand up straight! I mean, it's the perfect way to start a day. Who wants to wake up in a big, wide bed with sun striping the crisp white sheets as some gorgeous man brings in a tray laden with fresh coffee and croissants and apricot jam when you could be here?'

Campbell handed her the mug of tea with a mixture of incredulity and amusement. 'You've only been awake two minutes, woman! It's too early for fantasies.'

'It's never too early to fantasise about food,' she told him. 'Especially when you missed supper. Is there any breakfast? I'm starving.'

'Well, I can't provide coffee and croissants, but otherwise I can fulfil all your fantasies,' said Campbell, and Tilly looked hopeful.

'*Really?*'

'Here.' He produced a cereal bar from his pocket and offered it to her.

She took it suspiciously. 'What is it?'

'It's a high energy bar. You'll need it to get you up to the top.'

Unwrapping it, she took a cautious bite. 'Disgusting,' she pronounced, chewing madly.

'Hey, you wanted breakfast, I gave you breakfast.'

'You're going to have to work on the fantasy thing,' said Tilly, still chewing.

'I will if you'll work on the getting going thing,' said Campbell pointedly. 'Roger and Leanne are probably already on their way.'

'I bet they're not. I bet Roger is being nice and letting Leanne have a lie in after walking so far yesterday.'

'More fool him.' Campbell bent back to the tent and hauled the two packs outside before starting to pull out the tent pegs. 'He'll never win by being nice.'

'No chance of catching *you* making that mistake,' Tilly said acidly, and he looked up at her with a fleeting grin.

'I never make that mistake,' he said.

Jarred anew by the effect of a smile on that wintry face, Tilly looked away. She almost wished he wouldn't do it, especially not when she had just decided that he was impossible and how glad she was that she wasn't his type.

She busied herself looking in her pack for a toothbrush instead, and took her empty mug to the burn so that she could clean her teeth. She felt a little better after that, at least until she found a tiny folding mirror.

Aghast at her reflection, she went back to Campbell, who was dismantling the tent poles with his customary efficiency. 'Why didn't you tell me I looked like a dog's breakfast?'

He glanced up briefly. 'What's the problem?'

'Look at my hair! That was you messing it up last night,' she accused him. 'And my face!'

Dismayed, she peered into the mirror once more, hoping that the red welt across her cheek might have miraculously disappeared. She had obviously been lying with her face pressed against the zip of the sleeping bag. It didn't make for a good look, particularly not when combined with eyes that were piggy with tiredness and hair that resembled a straggly bird's nest. There were probably things nesting in there already.

And the final touch—a smear of mud left over from her splat landing on the river bank. She rubbed at it grouchily but that only seemed to make it worse.

'It doesn't matter,' said Campbell, not knowing what all the fuss was about. She looked fine to him. A little tousled, maybe, but he thought that dishevelled, just-fallen-out-of-bed look suited her.

Unfortunately, his attempt to sound soothing didn't appear to have worked. 'It does matter!' Tilly was scrabbling in her pack for a hairbrush. 'There'll be cameras at the other end. I don't want to go down in posterity looking like this!'

Campbell sighed. 'Can we worry about that when we get there? Look, I promise you can have a primping stop on the way down, but let's just get to the top first.'

Forcibly removing the hairbrush from her hand, he made her put everything away again. By the time she had finished, the tent was neatly folded up and stowed away in his rucksack. He picked up her pack, helped her into it and adjusted the straps for her as if she were a child.

'OK,' he said and pointed up to the summit that loomed above them. 'Let's get up there.'

Tilly craned her neck to follow his finger and her heart sank. 'I'll never be able to do it! I can hardly walk!'

Campbell swung his own pack on to his back. 'You'll feel better when you get going.'

Annoyingly, she did. It was steep going, though, and they had to scramble up the last bit.

'I can't do it,' Tilly kept wailing, her breath coming in ragged gasps as she clung to a rock or clutched at a clump of heather, but Campbell wouldn't listen.

'You can.'

And, in the end, she could. It was an amazing feeling as she climbed the last few feet and stood on the summit, looking down at the magnificent hills spread out at her feet. Tilly felt her heart catch with awe.

'Wow,' was all she could say.

Campbell was watching her face. He had deliberately waited so that she would get to the top first. 'See what you can do when you try?' he said as he joined her.

'It's amazing!'

It was. It was like discovering yourself poised on the edge of a brand new life—one you never imagined you could have. A smile spread over her face and she stretched out her arms as she spun slowly, savouring her achievement. 'I can't believe I did it!'

'And you got here first,' he reminded her.

'Unless Roger and Leanne have been and gone?' Tilly suggested. She looked innocent, but the blue eyes were dancing with mischief.

Campbell didn't rise to the provocation. 'They're still on their way up,' he said with satisfaction, and pointed down to where they could make out two tiny figures toiling up the slope.

'Looks like Leanne got a lie in after all,' said Tilly. 'We should wait and say hello.'

'We'll do no such thing,' said Campbell. 'We haven't won yet. We'd better get something on camera to prove we were here, and then we're on our way down.' He got the camera out and checked it. 'Ready?'

'Hang on, just let me put some lippy on…'

He rolled his eyes. 'For God's sake, Jenkins!' he said impatiently. 'We're on top of a mountain. This is no place for lipstick!'

'It is if I'm going to be on film.'

Tilly peered into her mirror, squinting so she didn't have to look at her hair or the smudges of mud, and carefully outlined her mouth with her favourite cherry-red. It was extraordinary what a bit of bright lipstick could do for the morale. She had always wanted to be able to do the natural look but the fact was that she suited bright colours.

Campbell had been setting up the camera on an outcrop and was squinting through it while he waited impatiently for her to finish. 'If we sit on that rock, it'll get us both in. Might be a bit of a squash, but it'll be quicker than two separate sessions.'

They perched together on the rock, and Campbell put his arm round her to keep them both in frame. 'Smile!' he muttered out of the corner of his mouth. 'And say something for the camera.'

Burningly aware of his arm, Tilly smiled. 'Here we are on the top of Ben Nuarrh and it feels as if we're on top of the world,' she told the camera and gestured around her. 'It's the most beautiful morning.'

She drew a deep breath. 'I can't believe that we got here at last,' she confessed. 'I feel incredible! I never believed that I could do it, and I probably wouldn't have done if Campbell hadn't bullied me all the way,' she said with a glance at him. 'I'm glad you did,' she added almost shyly.

'That's not what you said this morning!'

'No, well, I was tired this morning,' said Tilly with dignity. 'I hardly slept at all.'

Campbell pretended to gape in astonishment. 'You most certainly did!'

Forgetting the camera, she turned to look at him. 'I didn't snore, did I?' she asked anxiously. She had been worried about that.

'I wouldn't call it a *snore*, exactly. There was quite a bit of snuffling and grunting and smacking of lips. It was like sharing a tent with a rather large hedgehog.'

'Charming!' Tilly made to thump him but she was laughing, elated by the morning and the mountain top and the fizzing awareness of his presence.

'Other than that,' he said, 'I very much enjoyed sleeping with you.'

That was when she made the mistake of looking into his eyes. They were the same pale, piercing green but alight with humour and something else that made Tilly's laugh falter suddenly.

She moistened her lips. 'Do you think that's enough for the camera?' she asked, and Campbell's gaze held hers for a moment longer.

'I think it probably is.'

For the umpteenth time, Tilly rearranged the wooden spoons by the hob and then snatched back her hand with an exclamation of annoyance. 'Oh, for heaven's sake!' she said crossly. She was driving herself mad!

The television crew were due any minute. Tilly told herself she was just worried about having cameras in the house, zooming in on all the undusted mantelpieces, but deep down she knew that the prospect of seeing Campbell again was the real reason she was feeling so jittery.

It was three weeks since they had stood on the top of Ben Nuarrh. Campbell had marched her down the mountain in record time to make sure that they won the first stage, so they were ahead on points. Winning, however, was by no means a foregone conclusion. He still had to complete his challenge first, and then the viewers would have a vote after seeing clips from the video diaries and filming, so they wouldn't learn the final result until a grand awards ceremony later in the year.

Remembering Campbell's frustration at realising how much depended on the vagaries of the viewers' reactions, Tilly smiled wryly. He was so obviously a man who liked a clear goal, a definite mission that he could go out and accomplish. Want a bridge blown up? A hostage rescued? A mountain climbed in record time? Campbell was your man. But all this waiting to see what people thought and felt was not for him. Having started, though, he was committed to finishing now or it really would feel like failure.

And failure wasn't something Campbell Sanderson was prepared to contemplate, that was clear.

So he would be arriving any minute now to learn how to design and make a wedding cake, and he would be determined to succeed, however little he might enjoy it.

Well, she hadn't enjoyed abseiling, Tilly remembered, or crossing that river. *Or* being bullied up and down that mountain! It had been wonderful at the top, of course, and she was very glad that she had done it in the end, but she wasn't at all anxious to repeat the experience. She had been very happy to come back to her cosy kitchen—or rut, as Harry and Seb would call it— and she was looking forward to being the one who knew what she was doing this time.

How was Campbell going to react to *that*? Tilly didn't see why she should make it too easy for him. He had made her suffer, after all.

After the elation of making the summit, he had been brisk on the way down, and clearly couldn't wait to tie up the formalities at the end and get away. Tilly had been a little hurt by that, even though she knew it was silly. It wasn't as if either of them had wanted to be there. Nothing had *happened*.

It was absolutely ridiculous to be missing him, in fact.

'So, what was he like?' her best friend, Cleo had asked, brushing aside details of Tilly's traumatic abseil and homing straight in on the man assigned to partner her. 'Attractive?'

Tilly thought about the glint in Campbell's green eyes, about his mouth and that smile and the strength in his hands. She had barely known him forty-eight hours, and it was vaguely disturbing that she could still picture him in quite such detail.

She decided to downplay all that, though. Cleo would never

let her forget it if she thought Tilly had found herself alone in a tent with an attractive man and done absolutely nothing about it.

'Quite,' she said, deliberately casual. 'In an I-could-show-some-emotion-but-then-I'd-have-to-kill-you kind of way.'

'Ooh…' Cleo brightened. 'He sounds gorgeous!' Her eyes sharpened. 'Available?'

'He's divorced,' Tilly admitted reluctantly.

'I think you should go for it.'

Tilly felt oddly ruffled. 'I wouldn't stand a chance. Besides, he wasn't really my type. He wasn't anything like Olivier.'

Which was true. Olivier had been dark and passionate, while Campbell was all cool containment. It was hard to imagine two men more different, in fact.

'All the better,' said Cleo, who hadn't liked Olivier. 'Someone not like Olivier is exactly what you need.'

'I don't need Campbell Sanderson,' said Tilly definitely. 'I've never met anyone so competitive—unless it's my father! All men like that care about is winning,' she went on with a touch of bitterness. 'Never mind whose feelings they might be trampling on their way to success.'

'You don't need to spend the rest of your life with him, just have a bit of fun. Boost your confidence after that toad, Olivier.'

Tilly shook her head so the brown curls bounced around her face. 'I can't imagine anything *less* likely to boost my confidence,' she said frankly. 'Campbell is someone who has to have the best of everything, including women, and I don't see me falling into that category, do you?'

'You are the best,' said Cleo loyally. 'You're funny, generous, warm, caring and sexy, if only you'd admit it. And you're a fabulous cook. What more does a man want?'

'A size six with legs up to her armpits?'

Cleo clicked her tongue. 'You are so screwed up about your weight, Tilly! Listen, you are *not* overweight, you're just curvy.

That's the way women are meant to be, and that's how most men like them if the truth be told. Why do you think their tongues hang out whenever they spot a cleavage? You're never going to be a stick insect, true, but you shouldn't just accept that, you should celebrate it!'

'Maybe I would if I could just lose a stone,' said Tilly, reaching glumly for the biscuits. 'Anyway, don't get your hopes up about Campbell Sanderson. He's hung up on his ex-wife, if you ask me, and I don't want to get involved with that again. I had enough of being a consolation prize with Olivier.'

'Then why not think of Campbell as *your* consolation prize?' Cleo suggested.

The more she thought about it, the more Tilly had begun to wonder whether Cleo might have a point. She was overdue a good time, after all. She deserved a treat, and it wasn't as if she would have any expectations. A brief affair to boost her ego and make her feel good about herself again—was that so much to ask?

Then Tilly would catch a glimpse of herself in a mirror and she would catch herself up, appalled at her presumption. What was she *thinking*? There was no way Campbell would be interested in her, even if she laid herself out on a plate for him.

Anyway, she was probably building him up in her mind, she reassured herself. When she saw him again, she would probably wonder what she had made all the fuss about and be very glad that she hadn't made a fool of herself.

CHAPTER FIVE

EXCEPT it didn't work out like that. The moment Campbell came through the door, Tilly's heart gave a sickening lurch into her throat, where it lodged, hammering so hard she could hardly speak.

He was exactly as she remembered him, but somehow more so. Everything about him seemed very definite, and she was aware of him in startling detail, down to the buttons on his shirt, the fine hairs on his wrist, the faint line between his brows as he watched the crew bustling around the kitchen, talking about light and angles.

Momentarily sidelined with him, Tilly cleared her throat and forced her heart back into position. 'How have you been?'

'Busy,' said Campbell succinctly. 'I'm moving to the States in three weeks, and there's a lot to do before then.'

So he clearly wasn't going to have time for a little seduction on the side.

Tilly told herself that it was just as well. Her confidence was so low that he would be boarding his plane before she got up the nerve to try a little light flirtation. She had never been any good at that.

Anyway, look at him, so cool, so detached, so self-contained. It was all very well for Cleo to talk about having fun, but how could she have fun with a man like Campbell? It would be like trying to have fun with a granite rock.

No, forget it, she told herself. Just do the programme. Think about Mum and what this could do for the hospice. Teach him how to make a cake and don't for one second let him think you might even have considered the possibility of fun!

There was a pause. It didn't seem to bother Campbell but the silence made Tilly uncomfortable. 'Where are you staying while you're here?' she asked, hating how inane she sounded. The two of them had shared a tiny tent. They had laughed on top of a mountain. She had clung to him and begged him not to let her go. And now she was treating him as if he were a stranger she had met at a cocktail party.

If Campbell noticed the incongruity of it, he made no comment. 'In a hotel,' he said. 'The Watley…' He twiddled his hand to indicate that he had forgotten the rest of the name.

'The Watley Hall.'

'You know it?'

'Everyone here knows the Watley Hall, even if we can't afford to eat there. It's the best hotel in Allerby.'

She might have known that was where he would be staying.

'It's not very enterprising of you,' she commented tartly. 'I thought you would be pitching a tent in the garden!'

Campbell glanced at her. His face was perfectly straight but there was a glimmer of a smile at the back of his eyes, and her heart tipped a little, as if she had missed a step.

'Sorry to disappoint you, but I'm just a boring businessman nowadays, wanting a place to work.'

'I thought you were supposed to be learning how to make a wedding cake?'

'During the day,' he agreed. 'I will need to catch up with work in the evenings, so a hotel will suit me rather more than a tent. And you'll no doubt be glad to know that I'll be out of your hair once the baking lesson is over for the day.'

The baking lesson. Tilly didn't miss the dismissive note in Campbell's voice, and her eyes narrowed. He obviously thought cake-making was a trivial business, easily mastered. A token few minutes in the kitchen every day and then he would be planning to head back to his hotel room to deal with real man's business!

They would see about that.

Campbell was looking around the kitchen. He had somehow imagined Tilly living in a muddle, but although the room certainly had a relaxed feel to it, with a couple of comfortable old armchairs at the far end, he was relieved to see that it was clean and very well-organised. From what little he had seen of it so far, the whole house had a friendly, welcoming air.

'This is a nice house,' he commented. 'There must be more money in cakes than I thought.'

'Sadly not,' said Tilly dryly. 'This was my stepfather's house. My mother and I moved in here when I was seven. Mum died when I was twenty, and Jack the following year, so the mortgage was paid off. We spent quite a lot of time at the hospice over those couple of years,' she explained with a little sigh. 'I suppose that's why it means so much to me.'

'How old were your brothers then?'

'Only twelve,' she told him. 'Jack made me their guardian before he died so I could keep this as a home for them. We'll have to decide what to do with it when they reach twenty-five. If they ever settle down, Harry and Seb may want to sell so they can buy their own places, but there's no sign of them doing anything remotely sensible yet, so until then I'm happy to stay here.'

Campbell was watching her with a slight frown in his cool eyes. 'Don't you get a say?'

'It's not my house. Seb and Harry aren't going to throw me out in the street, so it's not as if I'm going to be destitute or anything.'

'Still, it seems strange not to have made any allowance for you,' said Campbell, surprised at how concerned he felt on her behalf. 'I know you were just a stepdaughter, but presumably Harry and Seb are your half-brothers. You're family.'

'Don't blame Jack,' said Tilly loyally. 'At the time it was the reasonable thing to do. My real father is still alive and has much more money than Jack ever had. Of course Jack assumed that I would be well provided for.'

'And you're not?'

Tilly looked away. 'I asked my father for help after Jack died. We had the house, but most of Jack's money was tied up in trust for the boys' education, and I didn't know how I was going to manage with day-to-day expenses.'

'Surely your father didn't refuse to help you?'

'No, not exactly,' she said. 'He offered me a home, college fees if I wanted them and even an allowance, but he wasn't prepared to take on the twins. I don't think he ever forgave my mother for being happy with Jack,' Tilly went on thoughtfully. 'Even though *he* was the one who left *us*, for a new wife more in keeping with his oh-so-successful image,' she added with a touch of bitterness. 'Mum wasn't supposed to be happier than he was after that.'

Campbell's brows contracted. 'So he made you choose?'

'That's right. I could be his daughter or I could be the twins' sister, but I couldn't be both.' She smiled wryly. 'At least it wasn't a difficult decision to make!'

'Wasn't it?' he said. 'Not many twenty-one-year-olds would turn their back on financial support in favour of looking after two boys.'

'What was I supposed to do? Walk away and leave them to bring themselves up?'

'They must have had other family who could have looked after them.'

'There was Jack's sister, Shirley, but she was much older than Jack, and she'd never had any children. I'm not sure if she would have been able to cope with the twins, and it would have been awful for them, too. She was very strict and used to get terribly anxious about noise and mess, two things you can guarantee a lot of with twelve-year-old boys around!

'They'd lost so much,' Tilly remembered sadly. 'First Mum, and then Jack. I was all they had. I wasn't going to abandon them.'

She was watching the television crew moving around the kitchen, but the deep blue eyes were sombre and it was clear that she was lost in memories. Campbell found his gaze resting on her face, on the dark sweep of her lashes and the curve of her cheek. She had beautiful creamy skin, the kind you wanted to touch, to see if it was as warm and soft and lush as it looked.

He had thought about her much more than he had expected over the last three weeks. The oddest things would trigger a memory and he would be back on that hillside with Tilly. Campbell had been surprised at how vividly he could picture her, how precisely he remembered the scent of her hair, the feel of her squashed against him, the curve of that generous mouth and the sound of her laughter.

Most of all, he remembered how he had felt when he was with her. Her sparkiness had made him uneasy, and he had been torn between exasperation and feeling reluctantly intrigued by the contrast between her warm, sensuous body and her tart humour.

Looking at Tilly now, Campbell realised that there was a stubbornness and a strength to her, too. He could imagine her squaring her shoulders and bearing the burden of her young brothers' grief as well as her own. It couldn't have been easy looking after the two of them.

'You were very young for that kind of responsibility,' he commented.

Tilly shrugged, her eyes still on the cameraman. 'Lots of girls are mothers before they're twenty-one,' she reminded him.

'Not of twelve-year-old boys.'

'Maybe not, but I just had to get on with it. People deal with a lot harder things every day.'

Yes, stronger than he had thought.

'Still, it must have been hard. At twenty-one you should be off exploring the world, enjoying yourself, finding out what you really want to do with your life.'

She smiled slightly at his determination to feel sorry for her. 'I know what I really want to do,' she said. 'I'm doing it now.' She gestured around the kitchen. 'I worked in an office for a few years. It was a dull job, but it paid the bills and meant I could make a home for Harry and Seb while they were at school, but when they went to university I could suit myself, and that's when I decided to set up Sweet Nothings.'

Campbell was looking dubious. A cake-making business was all very well, but she was clearly an intelligent woman.

'You didn't want to do something more…?'

'More what?'

'More…' He searched for the right word, and failed to find it. '…challenging?' he suggested at last.

As soon as the word was out of his mouth, he knew he had blundered. Tilly was smiling, but there was a flinty look in her eyes.

'No,' she said levelly. 'I love what I'm doing. How can one ask for more than that?'

Fortunately Suzy came over just then. 'I think we're ready,' she said. 'Tilly, can you show Campbell the kitchen and explain what he's going to have to do for the camera, then we'll leave you to get on with it. Have you arranged about the wedding cake, by the way?'

'Yes, a friend of mine called Cleo has agreed to let Campbell make hers. She's got a good sense of fun and she won't be traumatised if it's all a disaster.'

'When's the wedding?'

'A week on Saturday.'

'Perfect. We'll come and film you both with the cake then. It should make a great scene!'

Campbell was expressionless as Tilly showed him round the kitchen and then opened her portfolio of designs. She had made cakes in an extraordinary range of designs, from Manolo Blahnik shoes to giraffes to a golfer driving off a tee.

'As you can see,' she said for the benefit of the camera, 'here at Sweet Nothings we make whatever the customer wants. It's important that they feel that their cake is unique, so I spend quite a lot of time talking to them first, about who the cake is for, and what exactly they want to celebrate.'

She turned a page and the camera zoomed in over her shoulder, missing the real story, which was the tightening of Campbell's jaw as he realised just what he was getting into.

'Some people want a fun cake, perhaps to fit in with the theme of a party, or with a particular interest. You'd be amazed what some people are interested in, so you need to be adaptable. So if you had to make a cake for someone with a really strange hobby—an interest in Roman military history, say—' she said, unable to resist the dig at Campbell, 'you'd have to do some research to see what a soldier in the legions might have worn, for instance.'

Campbell was looking wooden, and Tilly suppressed a smile. 'Fortunately, there aren't too many odd-bods like that around,' she went on innocently. 'Most people are normal.'

That would teach him to sneer at baking.

For the benefit of the camera, she turned a few more pages. 'Some customers prefer a more traditional cake, but they still want the personal touch. The main thing to remember is that I'm making the cake they want, not the cake I think they should have. You'll have to bear that in mind when you make Cleo's wedding cake.'

Campbell managed to unclamp his jaw. 'Has she decided what design she wants yet?'

'No, she's coming in tomorrow to talk to you about that. You can discuss it together.'

Campbell couldn't see *that* conversation lasting long. He didn't have the slightest interest in wedding cakes, as Tilly clearly knew only too well. How the hell was he supposed to come up with a design for a wedding cake? There hadn't even been a cake at his own ill-fated wedding to Lisa.

He eyed Tilly suspiciously, wondering if she was deliberately setting him up, and when she pulled a pink apron emblazoned with 'Sweet Nothings' from a drawer, he was sure of it.

'You'll need to wear this when you're baking and decorating,' she told him, and he recoiled, his expression everything Tilly had hoped for.

'I'm not wearing that!'

'I'm afraid you'll have to,' she said sweetly. 'Health and safety regulations.'

'Do put it on,' Suzy urged from behind the camera. 'The viewers will love it!'

Campbell opened his mouth to tell her in no uncertain terms what she could do with her viewers when he caught sight of Tilly's face. Her eyes were alight with laughter.

'You planned this!' he muttered out of the corner of his mouth.

'Only in the way you planned that river crossing,' she whispered back.

'It'll win you so many votes,' Suzy promised. 'Roger was none too happy about putting on a special uniform to do the pedicure either, but the viewers do love a good sport.'

'Does Roger have to wear pink?' Campbell asked sourly, but he tied the apron round him. This whole experience was going to be humiliating enough without letting Roger outdo him. It would take more than an apron to beat him.

Folding his arms, he glared at the camera. There was a long moment of utter silence while Tilly, Suzy and the cameraman all looked at him, and then there was a muffled snort as Tilly broke first.

She couldn't help it. Campbell looked so ridiculous, glowering over the pink pinny. On a man who would be utterly at home in camouflage and a black balaclava, the apron looked positively bizarre and his expression was so forbidding that she started to laugh.

A moment later Suzy joined in, too, and then the camera was shaking as Jim, the cameraman, succumbed as well. They laughed and laughed while Campbell regarded them with a jaundiced expression, not at all amused.

'I didn't realise you were making a comedy,' he said caustically.

'Oh, dear.' Suzy wiped her eyes and made an effort to control her giggles. 'I'm sorry, but this is just perfect! The contrast between you two couldn't be better!' She sighed happily. 'This is going to be *such* a great programme. All you've got to do is make that cake now, Campbell—oh, and don't forget your video diaries again!'

'Boy, that Suzy knows how to manage you,' said Tilly as they waved the producer and cameraman off at last.

Campbell scowled as he snatched off the apron. 'What do you mean?'

'She knows she just has to dangle the prospect of Roger winning in front of your nose and you'll do anything to beat him, even if it means wearing a pink apron!'

'I'm certainly not going to make myself look ridiculous unless I *do* win,' said Campbell trenchantly.

'Campbell, has it ever occurred to you that you might lose?' Tilly asked, folding her arms and studying him curiously. 'Someone has to.'

'Not me,' he said. 'I never lose.'

'Your ex-wife might not agree about that,' Tilly couldn't help retorting. 'You don't have a very good success rate when it comes to relationships.'

He shrugged that aside. 'Relationships are different.'

And clearly a lot less important than winning as far as Campbell was concerned.

Tilly remembered Cleo's advice to have a little fling and sighed. Campbell was far too focused on winning this competition to waste any time on her. She could stand on the table and do the dance of the seven veils until she was stark naked, and Campbell would be telling her to stop wasting time, they needed to get on. He was only here now because he couldn't win without her.

'Come on,' she said, resigned. 'If you're going to win, we'd better get on with teaching you how to make a cake. Have you ever done any baking before?'

Campbell was still fuming about the apron episode as he followed her back to the kitchen. 'No, but surely it's just a question of reading some instructions?' he said irritably.

'Oh, good point.' Tilly paused and put her head on one side as if struck by his good sense. 'I never thought of that. Well, that'll save us some time. Why don't you go ahead and make one, then, and I'll put the kettle on? We probably won't need to bother with the rest of the week. We'll just have half an hour on icing tips before the wedding, and you can spend the rest of the time working.'

He eyed her for a moment, certain that she was testing him

somehow, but then again, how difficult could it be? It was only a cake, for God's sake!

'All right,' he said, accepting her unspoken challenge. Unconsciously, he squared his shoulders. Not only would he make a cake, he would make the best cake she had ever tasted. If she thought mocking his interest in the Romans and dressing him in pink would put him off his stroke, she would soon discover that she was mistaken!

'Don't forget your apron,' she reminded him.

Setting his jaw, Campbell retrieved the apron and looked around for a recipe. The dresser held a whole range of cook books and he had no idea where to start. Only the knowledge that Tilly was just waiting for him to admit that he could do with some advice made him pull out a book at random.

Favourite Cake Recipes… Just what he needed. Campbell turned the pages determinedly, although his heart sank as he was presented with yet more choices. Who would have thought that there were that many different kinds of cake?

Eventually he settled on a chocolate sponge cake with butter icing. It looked like the ones his mother had used to make when he was a boy and she had knocked them out in no time.

'I'll do this one,' he said, showing Tilly the picture.

'Great,' she said. 'I love chocolate cake. You'll find cake tins in that drawer there, dry ingredients in the larder—over there—and everything else in the fridge. Off you go, Sanderson!'

He looked at her, suspicious of her enthusiasm. 'What are you going to be doing?'

'Oh, I'll be here working on a few designs,' she said, plonking herself down at the table. 'Feel free to ask if you can't find anything.'

Campbell set about his task with grim determination. Working his way down the list, he managed to assemble all the ingredients, but the eggs were cold, the butter hard and he had obviously dismissed the difference between caster and granulated sugar as irrelevant. Tilly could practically see him thinking *flour is flour is flour* before deciding that plain flour would do just as well as self-raising, and he picked out a cake tin at random without any thought for its size or whether or not it needed to be lined.

It was odd that a man so focused, so competent, so coolly logical, should have such a cavalier approach to baking, she thought. But then, Campbell wouldn't see cooking as important, would he?

Still, she had to give him marks for perseverance. He got points for tidying up, too, after he had put the cake in the oven. 'There,' he said at last, laying the cloth out to dry on the edge of the sink at a precise right angle. 'That's done.'

Realising that he was still wearing the stupid apron, he wrenched it off and tossed it aside.

Tilly was sitting at the end of the table, idly turning the pages of a magazine, and he eyed her sardonically.

'Working hard?'

'I am, as a matter of fact,' she said equably. 'I'm researching. I've got clients coming in to choose a twenty-first birthday cake for their daughter, so I want to be able to give them some fun ideas. I do a lot of bags and shoes, but I'm wondering if I might do a complete outfit like this one.' She turned the magazine so Campbell could see the photograph she was considering.

He looked at it uncomprehendingly. 'Why don't you just make her a nice chocolate cake?'

'Because anyone can do that—even you, apparently! I'm offering something different, and I can't do that unless I've got a real sense of the person the cake is for. Actually, making the cake is the easy part. You need to be able to talk to people, and listen to what they tell you.'

She fixed him with a stern gaze. 'That means when Cleo

comes in tomorrow you can't just fob her off with a traditional three tier cake. You need to find out what kind of wedding she's planning, what sort of cake she really wants, and come up with some ideas for her. Cleo's my friend, and she's agreed to let you do her cake as a favour to me, so you've got to make it really special for her.'

'You'll be there, too, won't you?' Campbell asked with a touch of unease. He couldn't imagine having much to say to an excited bride full of wedding plans. 'I'm not very good at talking at all, let alone about that kind of stuff.'

'I wasn't any good at abseiling, but I still had to do it,' Tilly pointed out tartly. 'Yes, I'll be there, just as you were at the top of the cliff, but I can't do it for you. This time it's your challenge.'

Campbell sighed. 'Why does it have to be so complicated? A cake is a cake!'

'When you were in the army, were all operations the same?'

'I was in the Marines, but no, they weren't.'

'And now you're in business, is every deal exactly the same?'

'No.'

'Well, it's the same with cakes.'

Tilly could see that he wasn't convinced. 'Every time I make a cake, I'm making it for different people, and a different situation. Even if they choose exactly the same cake, the way I mix it and bake it and decorate it is all different. If it wasn't, my customers might as well go to a supermarket and buy one made in a factory.'

'The next time I'm negotiating an important deal I'll think of you and remind myself that it's just like a cake,' said Campbell dryly.

Tilly couldn't help warming to the idea that he might be thinking about her in the future. 'Will you have to do much of that in your new job?'

'Negotiating? I imagine so. This will be my most challenging job yet. I'm going to a global corporation that's been on a downward slide for some time. I've been appointed to turn it round, but it won't be easy.'

'Oh, but surely it's just a question of reading some instructions?' Tilly murmured provocatively.

Campbell looked at her sharply. She met his gaze blandly, but the dark blue eyes gleamed and, in spite of himself, he laughed.

'It would be nice to think that there would be some instructions to read!'

Tilly found herself smiling back at him, even while wishing that she hadn't made him laugh. It was so obvious that Campbell thought that making cakes was beneath him that she had been doing a good job of disliking him again, and now he had gone and spoilt that by smiling.

All at once she was tingling with awareness again and, instead of thinking about how arrogant and disagreeable he could be, she was thinking about the fact that the two of them were alone in the house, and trying not to notice how tall and lean and tautly muscled he was, how out of place he seemed in the cosy kitchen with that air of tightly leashed power.

Looking at him in that pink apron, Tilly had the unnerving sensation that she had tied a bow around a kitten only to realise that it had turned into a fully grown tiger, complete with swishing tail, and she only just stopped herself from gulping.

She pushed back her chair so that it scraped on the tiles. 'Tea?' she asked brightly.

'Thanks.'

Campbell sat down at the table and pulled her sketchbook towards him. As he flicked idly through it, his brows rose. Her designs were quick and clear, and she had somehow captured each idea in a few clever lines.

'These are good,' he said, unable to keep the surprise from his voice.

Tilly switched on the kettle and turned to lean back against the sink, determinedly keeping her distance.

'It's not exactly turning round a global corporation, is it?'

Campbell turned another few pages. 'I'm beginning to wonder if that might not be easier than coming up with ideas like these.'

'Well, that's why you're a hotshot international executive and I'm the provincial cake-maker,' said Tilly. 'If you think about it, we don't have a single thing in common, do we?'

Campbell looked at her standing by the kettle. Her nut-brown curls gleamed with gold under the spotlights, and he remembered how soft her hair had felt under his cheek as they had lain together in the tent up on the Scottish hillside. Funny to think they had only spent a matter of hours together. She seemed uncannily familiar already. Campbell wasn't a fanciful man, but it felt as if he had known the glint of fun in her eyes, the tartness of her voice, the gurgle of laughter, for ever.

'No, I don't suppose we do,' he agreed, his voice rather more curt than he had intended.

And they didn't. Tilly was right. They had absolutely nothing in common.

It hadn't taken Campbell nearly as long as he had expected to adjust to civilian life. He had always been too much of a maverick to fit that comfortably into naval life, even within an elite unit. An unorthodox approach and a relentless drive to succeed at whatever cost came into their own on special operations, but were less of an advantage in the day-to-day routine.

He hadn't regretted leaving all that behind. Lisa hadn't intended to change his life for the better when she'd walked out, but he was grateful to her in an odd way for making him so determined to prove that he could make twice as much money as her new husband that he had gone into business. It had turned out that he was made for the ruthless cut and thrust of corporate life. Campbell didn't do emotions, or talking or any of the things women thought were so important, but he knew how to make money, and that was what counted.

When it came down to it, Campbell believed that everybody was motivated by money at some level. Tilly wouldn't agree, he was sure. That was *another* thing they didn't have in common.

'We just have to get along for a fortnight with nothing in common,' he said. 'Then I'll be gone.'

Thanks for the reminder, Tilly thought, piqued in spite of herself. It was all very well deciding not to get involved with him, but quite another thing to be hit over the head with the fact that he was planning to leave the country soon. She had a nasty feeling he had done it to make sure that she got the message that he wasn't available. Why didn't he just hang up a sign saying 'don't bother'?

Not that she had any intention of letting him know that she had even *considered* the possibility of getting involved. That really *would* make him laugh.

'Of course, you're moving to the States, aren't you?' Tilly was Ms Cucumber Cool as she carried the teapot over and found two mugs. She could do couldn't-care-less as well as anyone, even Campbell Sanderson. 'Where exactly are you going?'

'New York.'

'Is that where your ex-wife lives now?'

Campbell looked at her, startled. 'How do you know that?'

'Well, you said she lived in the States, and you don't seem the kind of man who lets go easily. I wondered if you were going there because you wanted to see her.'

'Not at all,' he said sharply. 'It just happens that's where the head office is.'

Infuriatingly, though, Tilly's words had made him pause and examine his own motives for the first time. 'Of course I've considered the chance that I might bump into her,' he went on after a while. 'New York is a big city, but Lisa's new husband is in a similar line of business, so it's not beyond the bounds of possibility that we'll meet.'

'Gosh, I hope he's not more successful than you,' said Tilly, only half joking, and Campbell smiled grimly.

'Not any more,' he said.

CHAPTER SIX

TILLY poured the tea. She could just imagine how Campbell would have been driven to out-perform the man who had taken his wife away from him. It would have hurt anyone, but to a man like Campbell the implication that she had left him for someone more successful must have been an extra dose of salt in the wound.

'What will it be like, seeing her again?' she asked.

He shrugged, and she rolled her eyes as she pushed a mug across the table towards him.

'Come on, you must have thought about it! I've spent the last eighteen months practising what I would say to Olivier if I ever saw him again—not that I've had the chance to say any of it,' she added ruefully. 'It's probably just as well.'

'Olivier?'

'The beat of my heart for two years,' she said, blue eyes bleak with memory.

And presumably the man who had taught her that the absence of children didn't make a break-up any easier. Campbell was remembering now.

'Ah,' he said. Were commiserations in order? These kinds of emotional conversations always made him uncomfortable. He couldn't understand why women insisted on talking about this kind of stuff the whole time.

'What *would* you have said?' he asked at last, opting for a practical approach.

Tilly thought about it. 'It depended on the mood I was in,' she said. 'Sometimes I was determined to make him realise just what he'd lost, so I was going to pretend to have a fabulous new lover and carry on as if I'd almost forgotten him. At other times I wanted him to acknowledge how he'd hurt me, but either way I would be very cool and calm.

'In reality, of course, if I *had* bumped into Olivier, I would have burst into tears and begged him to come back, and then none of my friends would ever have spoken to me again!'

Campbell studied her across the table. Her generous mouth was twisted in a self-deprecating smile, but the blue eyes were wistful, and he wondered what Olivier was like. Campbell didn't like the idea of him at all. He didn't like the idea of anyone hurting Tilly.

She wasn't beautiful, not like Lisa. Her features were too quirky for that, but there was something alluring about her all the same, he realised. She had warmth and wit and a charm that Lisa had never had, and in a strange way she was sexier, too.

The thought was startling, but Campbell decided it was true. Lisa was slender and elegant and perfect, but she was a woman most men admired from a distance. Tilly was quite different— all soft curves and luminous skin—and there was something irresistibly *touchable* about her. Any man's fingers would be twitching with the need to reach out and slide through her hair, to smooth and stroke and explore that warm, lush body, and then he would want to take that mouth and see if it tasted and felt as good as it looked…

Alarmed by how quickly his thoughts had drifted out of control, Campbell slammed on the brakes and gave himself a mental slap.

He drank his tea, feeling jarred and vaguely uneasy. Tilly was the one with the vivid imagination, not him. Campbell Sanderson was famous for his coolness under pressure, for his single-minded pursuit of a goal. He wasn't a man who let himself get distracted, especially not by a woman. The last time that had happened, he had ended up married to Lisa, and look what a mistake that had been! No way was he doing that again.

'If you cried, there really would have been no chance of getting him back,' he said caustically to make up for the fact that while his mind was firmly back under control, his hands were taking rather longer to catch up and were still tingling at the idea of touching Tilly.

Scowling at the sign of weakness, Campbell gripped them firmly around the mug.

'I know.' Tilly sighed. 'What is it with men? Look at you. You're happy to jump off a cliff but show you a woman in tears and I bet you'd run a mile!'

This was unfortunately so true that Campbell could only glower. 'I like dealing with facts,' he said. 'Emotions are messy.'

Tilly stared at him and shook her head. 'How on earth did you ever manage to get married in the first place? You must have had to succumb to a teensy little emotion then, surely!'

'The attraction between us was a physical thing. It was never about hearts and flowers and all that stuff. Lisa's not like that. She's like me in lots of ways. She knows what she wants, and she goes after it, and she gets it. And for a time,' he said, 'she wanted me.'

Campbell paused, remembering. 'It's hard to resist a woman who looks the way she does. You'd have to see her to understand,' he said, catching Tilly's sceptical expression.

'I can't see you being pushed into doing anything you didn't want to do, let alone marriage,' she said. 'You're not the passive type.'

'No,' he admitted. 'I did want to marry her.'

'Because you loved her, or because you could show her off, prove that you had a more beautiful wife than anyone else?'

A very faint flush stained Campbell's cheekbones. 'I suppose there's some truth in that,' he acknowledged. 'But marriage was Lisa's idea. I'd never imagined myself as a marrying type, but she wanted a wedding, and I was mad for her. I didn't care what happened as long as I could have her. I should have known it wouldn't last.'

What would it be like to be so beautiful you always got your own way? Tilly wondered. What would it be like to be desired so much by Campbell that he would do whatever you wanted?

'How long were you married?' she asked instead.

'Just three years,' said Campbell. 'There was great sexual chemistry but not much else going for the marriage. I was away on operations most of the time, and Lisa wasn't prepared to sit at home waiting for me. She liked to have fun, and she liked money, and it didn't take her long to get bored and start to want something more glamorous. Arthur offered her the lifestyle she wanted, so she took it.'

He shrugged, but Tilly couldn't believe that he was as non-chalant about the failure of his marriage as he pretended. It must have been a huge blow to his pride.

'Are you hoping that if she sees how successful you are now, she might come back to you?'

Campbell stared at her for a moment, then pushed the mug abruptly aside. 'No,' he said instinctively, and then, honestly, 'I don't know.'

So what were you thinking, Tilly? Tilly asked herself. That he might say, *Of course not, how could I possibly want my beautiful ex-wife with whom I shared such incredible sexual chemistry when I could have you for a brief fling?*

'I was angry when she left,' he said unexpectedly, almost as if the words had been forced out of him. For a long time all I thought about was seeing Lisa again, and making her regret the choice she had made. I probably did hope that she might change her mind then.'

'And now?'

'Now...now I think I want her to see what she could have had if she had stuck with me. Beyond that, I really don't know. I probably won't know until I do see her again.'

Well, she had asked and he had answered. Tilly couldn't complain that he hadn't been honest. She was very glad that she hadn't done anything silly, like taking Cleo's advice. Campbell was like a dog with a bone that it had tired of until the moment someone tried to take it away. Losing Lisa to another man would smack too much of failure for a man like him. Consciously or not, Tilly was prepared to bet that his life since then had been focused on getting his wife back.

Perhaps that was how it should be, she thought, but it was hard not to feel a little disconsolate. No one would ever feel that way about *her*. Olivier certainly hadn't, she remembered with a trace of bitterness. Even if she had been the one to dump him, he would probably just have been relieved that she had saved him the trouble. He wouldn't still be hankering after her four years down the line.

She should just face up to the fact that she wasn't the kind of girl men got possessive or obsessed about, Tilly decided glumly. She had better just stick to baking.

And, talking of which...She sniffed delicately and looked across at Campbell, who was staring into his tea with a brooding expression.

He glanced up as he felt her eyes on him. 'What?'

'How long has your cake been in?'

'The cake!'

Campbell leapt to his feet and yanked open the oven, only

to cough and splutter as smoke billowed into his face. Grabbing a tea towel, he pulled the tin out, swearing as he burned his fingers and let the tin fall with a clatter on to the work surface.

When the smoke cleared, he could see that the cake was not the perfect chocolate cake he had intended to make. Instead, it was burnt, hard and flat. It didn't take a Michelin starred chef to see that it was going to be inedible.

Only the tiniest of smiles dented the corner of Tilly's mouth as she went into the larder and found a banana cake she had made a couple of days earlier. She put it on the table and sat down again, very carefully saying absolutely nothing.

'All right!' snarled Campbell as if she had been shouting accusingly at him. 'All *right*! It's not just a question of reading the instructions, OK? I admit it! Happy now?'

He looked so chagrined at his failure that Tilly had to bite her cheeks to stop herself from laughing out loud.

'Actually, it *is* just a question of following a recipe,' she tried to placate him, 'but you have to know how to read it first. I can teach you that.' She cut him a slice of cake. 'Here, try a bit of this.'

Campbell took a bite. It was a revelation—moist and light and delicious, its flavours and textures perfectly balanced. He felt as if he had never eaten cake before. He finished the slice without speaking and then looked straight at Tilly. 'That was the best cake I have ever tasted,' he said simply.

She laughed, pleased. 'That's one of the easiest cakes to make. You can try one for yourself tomorrow if you like.'

'I suppose there's some secret ingredient you keep to yourself to make sure no one else makes a cake as good as yours.' Campbell looked at her accusingly, but Tilly held up her hands in a gesture of innocence.

'I promise you there isn't. Pleasure in food is for sharing, not keeping to yourself.'

'There must be something special you do.'

'Oh, there is,' she agreed. 'I make all my cakes with love. Do you think you'll be able to do that?'

There was a tiny silence as their eyes met across the table.

Campbell was the first to look away. 'Will determination do instead?'

'If that's the best you can offer, we'll have to hope it's good enough for Cleo's cake.'

Cleo was dark and vivacious and she eyed Campbell with un-disguised interest when she arrived to discuss her wedding cake the next day. Right at home in Tilly's kitchen, she plonked herself down at the table and proceeded to cross-examine him with all the subtlety of a sledgehammer while Tilly made coffee.

Campbell wasn't doing a bad job of deflecting her questions, Tilly thought as she put a plate of biscuits she had made earlier on the table between them, but if he had hoped to deter Cleo he was in for a disappointment.

'Biscuits…yummy…and Tony's favourites, too! Can I take some home for him?'

Without waiting for an answer, Cleo turned back to Campbell.

'Tilly's a fabulous cook! Well, you probably know that already, Campbell.' She leant confidingly towards him. 'Tony was wild with envy when he heard you were going to be spending a couple of weeks here. He's always angling for an invitation to dinner and then he spends weeks after-wards asking me why I can't be a domestic goddess like Tilly.'

Ignoring Tilly's warning kick under the table, she sat back and warmed to her theme.

'Lucky she's such a special person or I'd really hate her. As it is, everyone loves Tilly,' she told Campbell. 'She's the best friend anyone could have. She's the one we all go to when we need looking after. I don't know what I'd do without her, and I certainly don't know what Harry and Seb would have done without her. She brought them up, you know. She's a born mother, I think, and she's going to make some lucky guy a perfect wife one day.'

Tilly sighed and gave up on trying to be discreet. It was way too late for that now. The only thing she could do now was to brazen it out. 'Why not come right out and offer Campbell fifty camels if he'll take me off your hands?' she asked acidly. 'You'll have to forgive Cleo,' she said to Campbell as she handed out mugs of coffee. 'Wedding bells have gone to her head. Just because she's getting married, she thinks everyone else should be, too. She's desperate to get me attached to some poor unsuspecting man and she doesn't care who she embarrasses to do it! Just ignore her.

'And you, Cleo,' she added, pointing a stern finger at her friend, 'stop it! Campbell is here to make your wedding cake, and that's it. He isn't attracted to me and I'm not attracted to him.'

Cleo was quite unabashed. 'We wouldn't have to embarrass you if you ever made the slightest effort to find someone new. You just hide yourself away in this kitchen and nobody ever knows what a lovely person you are. Honestly, it's a crime! *Tell* her, Campbell.'

'I am not hiding away!' said Tilly, exasperated, before Campbell had a chance to reply. She dropped into the chair next to him. Right then, he seemed to be her only ally. 'Nobody seems to understand that I'm trying to run a business here! Tell *her*, Campbell!'

Campbell looked from Tilly's heated face to Cleo's amused one, and his lips twitched. He had, it was true, been a little taken aback by Cleo's blatant matchmaking, and wasn't at all sure how he should react, but Tilly's intervention had dispelled any awkwardness.

She was right, of course. He *wasn't* attracted to her. Interested, perhaps. Amused, even intrigued, but not attracted.

Not really. Not the way he had been attracted to Lisa, anyway, and the two women were such polar opposites that it would be bizarre to find them both attractive. Still, Tilly's bluntness had stung a little. She had made him feel a fool for being so aware of her the day before.

When he had taken himself back to his hotel at the end of the day, Campbell had told himself that he was relieved, but the truth was that his room had seemed cold and empty and sterile somehow after Tilly's house. He had opened his laptop determinedly and tried to concentrate on work but his famous ability to focus had completely deserted him. He'd found himself reading emails without taking in a word, while his mind had drifted back to Tilly moving around the bright kitchen.

In her own context, her movements were graceful, her hands quick and competent. Campbell had found it strangely restful to watch her. Alone in his hotel room, he had pictured her in disconcerting detail, pushing her hair back from her face, rolling her eyes, smiling her crooked smile. She had a way of running her tongue over her lips when she was thinking. It was quite unselfconscious, and Campbell wondered if she had any idea how sexy she was, or how it made him think about what it would be like to lose himself in her warmth and her softness and her light.

'Campbell?' Tilly waved a hand in front of his face. 'This is Earth calling! Do you receive?'

Campbell snapped to, aghast to discover that he had been lost in his thoughts and that Cleo and Tilly were staring at him. He was supposed to be trained to be alert at all times. He could just imagine his Commanding Officer's scathing comments if he had caught him sitting there daydreaming about a woman! A faint flush of embarrassment crept up his cheeks.

'Sorry,' he said gruffly, remembering what he was supposed to be doing. 'I think it's probably better if I don't get involved. That way you can both carry on believing you're right.'

'A little weasely, but tactful, I suppose,' said Tilly in a dry voice. She pushed the biscuits towards her friend. 'Have one of those and give up on the matchmaking! And now that's sorted, let's get down to business.'

'I thought we were doing just that,' said Cleo, who had been watching Campbell's face with amusement.

'Your *cake*,' Tilly reminded her, exasperated. 'That's why you're here, in case you've forgotten! This is supposed to be a business meeting. Have you had any thoughts about it? Or have you been too busy meddling in the lives of all your single friends?'

'No, I've been thinking about it and I've even consulted Tony,' said Cleo with a grin. 'The wedding service and the reception immediately afterwards are going to be traditional—it wasn't worth fighting Mum on that one—but we want the party in the evening to be fun. What do you think about an Antony and Cleopatra theme?' She looked hopefully at Campbell. 'Could you make a cake like that?

Campbell glanced at Tilly for help, but she just looked blandly back at him. 'Antony and Cleopatra?' he repeated carefully.

'Yes, you know, like the Shakespeare play. I mean, how can we resist? My name really is Cleopatra, can you believe it? I don't know what my parents were thinking of!' Cleo shook her dark head, but her eyes twinkled. 'It's just chance that I fell in love with an Anthony, but it's a cool coincidence, don't you think?' She struck a melodramatic pose. 'Another pair of legendary lovers!'

'Correct me if I'm wrong, but don't Antony and Cleopatra

die at the end of the play?' said Campbell dryly. 'It doesn't seem much of a precedent for a wedding cake.'

'Details, details.' Cleo waved that aside. 'We just want all the fun bits. Egypt, eyeliner, bathing in milk, you know the kind of thing.'

Eyeliner? Ye gods. Campbell had to resist the urge to bang his head on the table.

'None of that sounds very suitable for a cake,' he told her austerely, and Tilly dug a finger into his ribs.

'What did I tell you about listening to the client?' Her voice was bubbling with suppressed laughter. 'If Cleo wants an Antony and Cleopatra cake, that's what she can have.'

She turned to Cleo. 'I can't believe I've never made the connection between Tony and Anthony before! I think it's a brilliant idea, Cleo. I did the play for A level and loved it. There's no reason why we—Campbell, I mean—can't make a cake for you. It could be the alternative version: Antony and Cleopatra, happy ever after.'

'That's what I thought.' Cleo nodded eagerly. 'Antony and Cleopatra going off on their honeymoon, perhaps?'

'On their barge…wasn't there a barge in the play?'

Cleo clapped her hands together. 'Oh, yes, of course. The barge!'

'And they could have tin cans tied on the back, and a card saying "just married"!'

'And our names and the date of the wedding along the side.'

'*Yes*. This is going to be great!' Tilly gave Campbell another prod. 'Are you noting all this down, Campbell?'

Campbell felt as if he were at a tennis match, his eyes shifting from side to side as he tried to follow the ideas bouncing backwards and forwards between them.

He looked at the notebook in front of him. 'You want me to make a *barge*?'

'An ancient Egyptian one. You're bound to be able to find a picture on the Internet somewhere. Antony was a Roman so you'll be able to do him OK, and Cleopatra will be easy—give her black hair, big fringe, lots of eyeliner.'

And he was supposed to make all this out of *cake*?

Campbell listened as Tilly and Cleo carried on sparking ideas off each other, talking at dizzying speed, laughing and egging each other on. 'We mustn't forget the asp!'

He couldn't help comparing this with the business meetings he was used to, where he told people what he wanted done and they did it. The meetings he chaired were much more controlled, much more efficient.

Much less fun.

'What do you think, Campbell?' Tilly had been drawing a quick summary in her sketchbook and she twisted it round so that he could see. He leant closer, trying not to notice the summery scent of her hair.

'Very clever,' he said. 'I would have just stuck a couple of figures on top of a cake.'

'Yes, well, that wouldn't have won you many votes, would it?'

Campbell straightened. He had forgotten about the competition there for a while. Which was odd, given that winning it was the only reason he was here.

'They're bound to be impressed by this, if you can do it,' said Cleo. 'It does look a bit complicated, though. Would you rather we came up with a simpler design, Campbell?'

'No, that's fine,' he said, unable to admit that he didn't have a clue where to start with it, but was determined to succeed at this the way he succeeded with everything else. 'Tilly promises her clients that they can have whatever cake they want, so if this is what you want, Cleo, this is what I'll make you.'

'Wonderful!' Cleo beamed as she got to her feet. 'It's going to be such fun! You will stay for the party after they've filmed the cake, won't you, Campbell? Once they've gone, you and Tilly can relax and enjoy yourselves—separately if you want,' she added, rolling her eyes in such exaggerated resignation at Tilly's expression that Campbell couldn't help laughing.

Normally the thought of a wedding made him run in the opposite direction, but Cleo was so friendly that he didn't want to hurt her feelings. Besides, he had to go anyway to deliver the cake. It would be his last evening with Tilly.

'Thanks,' he said. 'I'd like to come.'

'I'm sorry about that,' said Tilly as she came back from seeing Cleo off. She dropped into a chair with a sigh. 'I hope Cleo didn't embarrass you. She certainly embarrassed me! Sometimes I feel like disowning all my friends!'

'I liked her,' said Campbell. 'And she's obviously very fond of you.'

'I know.' Tilly dragged the hair back from her face with both hands. 'She's a good friend, but she's got it into her head that I need a man. And it's not just Cleo! It's a conspiracy,' she complained. 'Even my brothers are in on it, so be warned. Seb and Harry are both coming home for the weekend and, as neither of them know the meaning of subtlety, you'll probably find yourself tied up and forced into bed with me!'

A tiny smile tugged at the corner of Campbell's mouth as her regarded her. 'I can think of worse fates.'

Dark blue eyes flew to meet his for a fleeting moment before she looked away and coloured. 'You don't need to be polite,' she muttered.

'I'm not. You're an attractive woman. You must know that,' he said with a frown as Tilly goggled at him.

She swallowed. 'It's not how I think of myself, no,' she said at last.

'Why not?'

'Isn't it obvious?'

'I don't understand why you're so hung up about your

weight,' said Campbell with a touch of exasperation. 'OK, so you're not the thinnest woman I've ever met, but you look absolutely fine to me. Some women aren't meant to be thin, and you're one of them. It's only women who get worked up about what size they are. Men don't care.'

'I notice they all like to go out with thin women, though,' said Tilly waspishly as she got up and began clearing away the mugs. 'I bet your ex-wife is slim, isn't she?'

'She ought to be. She never ate anything. It was a waste of time taking her out to dinner,' Campbell remembered.

'I wish I could be like that!'

'But then you wouldn't have had your fantasies about meals to get you up Scottish mountains,' he pointed out. 'You wouldn't be you.'

'No, I might be slender and elegant and controlled.'

There was no mistaking the bitterness in her voice as she turned and began rinsing the mugs at the sink.

Campbell looked at her back. 'That sounds very dull,' he said carefully, forgetting that Tilly's chaotic quality had once made him uneasy, too. 'Who on earth would want you to be like that?'

'Olivier did.' Tilly was still clattering mugs and wouldn't turn round. 'That's why he broke off our relationship in the end. I couldn't be the kind of person he wanted me to be. I was too much for him.'

'Too much what?'

'Too much everything, I think. I ate too much, laughed too much, talked too much, loved too much...' Her back was still firmly turned and, even though she was clearly trying to keep her voice light, Campbell could still hear the undercurrent of pain.

'Surely those are the reasons he would want to be with you in the first place?'

'I don't think it was like that for Olivier. Cleo's theory was that I was a kind of project for him. Perhaps he saw me as some kind of challenge. Maybe he thought it would be interesting to see if he could shape me into something different, someone cool and controlled who would blend with his stylish décor.

'But of course I never could blend in,' Tilly went on, setting the mugs on the draining rack and turning at last. 'Now I feel ashamed for trying to, but I loved him so much, I was desperate to please him. I'd have done anything he wanted, but I just couldn't be that different. I'm just not like that.'

Her throat was tight with remembered hurt, and she couldn't bear to meet Campbell's eyes. She reached for a tea towel instead and wiped her hands very carefully.

'In the end, I think Olivier found me disgusting,' she said with difficulty, her gaze on the tea towel. 'It was awful. The more I tried to please him, the more he withdrew. It was as if he couldn't bear me near him.'

Campbell heard the crack of pain in her voice and anger closed like a fist around his heart. 'Who was this guy?' he demanded furiously.

'He's an architect. A very good one. He's moved to London now. I think Allerby was too provincial for Olivier.'

'Or maybe he was too affected for Allerby,' Campbell suggested. 'What can you expect with a poncey name like Olivier?' he demanded. 'I suppose his real name is Oliver and he wanted to make himself more interesting.'

Tilly couldn't help feeling touched that he was so angry on her behalf, but habit drove her to defend Olivier.

'His mother's French,' she told him. 'That's why he's Olivier and not Oliver. Actually, the name suits him. He's very dark and good-looking and…oh, *glamorous*, I suppose,' she remembered with a sigh. 'He was always out of my league. He's not just handsome, he's clever and witty and artistic and good at everything he does.'

'He certainly did an excellent job of destroying your self-confidence,' said Campbell acidly.

Tilly smiled a little sadly. 'I don't think I've ever had much of that, not when it comes to men, anyway.'

Her hands were as dry as they were ever going to be. She made herself hang the tea towel back on its hook and opened the fridge to look for butter and eggs. When in doubt, Tilly always baked. There was something about the process that soothed her. She had made an awful lot of cakes in the months since Olivier had decided she was never going to match up to his standards.

Campbell pushed back his chair to watch her. 'Why not?'

'Cleo blames my father, but then Cleo would. She's an amateur psychologist. She says that I'm "replicating a pattern of loving men I can't trust".' Tilly hooked her fingers in the air to emphasise the quotation.

'And are you?'

She shrugged as she searched for sugar, flour and sultanas in the sliding larder.

'I don't know about that, but whatever it is I do, I'm not doing it again,' she said. 'It wasn't just Olivier. Before him it was Andrew, and before *him*, Simon. They weren't quite as demanding as Olivier, but I'm sick of not being quite good enough. I'm sick of having my heart broken.'

Carrying the dry ingredients over to the table, she started to set them down and looked at Campbell at last. 'I know my friends mean well. I *know* they just want me to be happy. They think I shouldn't let Olivier put me off men for life, and that I should just get back out there and start dating again, but I don't dare. I'm too afraid I'll just end up getting hurt again.'

She stopped, the packet of sultanas still clutched against her chest. 'Funny, I've never admitted that to anyone else,' she said, a puzzled crease between her brows. 'I must feel safer with you than I thought.'

'I'm not sure that's very good for my ego,' said Campbell wryly, and she flushed a little, belatedly realising that she had spoken her thoughts aloud.

'I just meant...because you're only here for a week,' she tried to explain. 'You're not just leaving Allerby, you're leaving the country soon, so even if we did find each other attractive, a relationship would be out of the question.'

CHAPTER SEVEN

RIGHT, and he needed to remember that, Campbell told himself that night. He was surprised at how much he had hated seeing how hurt Tilly had been by Olivier—and he didn't care what she said about him being half-French, it was still a damn fool name.

What a sinful waste that she should have cut herself off from men. Alone and restless, Campbell scowled up at the ceiling through the darkness. He badly wanted to show Tilly that she was wrong, that she was quite beautiful and sexy and desirable enough as she was.

But how could he do that without hurting her himself?

Tilly had told him that she was afraid, and he didn't have time to win her confidence. Even if he did, what then?

He was moving to the States, Campbell reminded himself. Taking over a company with a global reputation like Mentior's would be the culmination of his business career. There would be no stopping him now. He was going to take that firm and turn it round and make it the best in the world again, and he was going to do it where Lisa couldn't fail to note his success.

Ever since Lisa had left him, he had been focused on proving to her just how big a mistake she had made. He would never have a better chance than this. There was no question of not going.

And that meant there was no question of convincing Tilly

that she was a desirable woman. She was absolutely right. It was best for both of them if they kept their relationship firmly on a friendly basis. Tilly had made it very clear that was all she wanted.

He needed to be realistic, after all, Campbell told himself. They were only together because of the television programme. As soon as Cleo's wedding was over, and he had made that cake, they would go their separate ways. They would meet up at the awards ceremony for one last filming and, if they had won, as Campbell fully intended they would, they would hand over their cheques to the hospice that meant so much to her, and that would be that.

It was impractical to even think about anything else.

Unfortunately, that didn't stop Campbell thinking about it anyway. It was hard not to when he and Tilly were spending so much time together.

Campbell hadn't expected to enjoy his time learning to make cakes. He had expected to be bored and impatient to get back to the office. He checked his email regularly, and his PA had strict instructions to ring him if there were any problems, but they all seemed to be managing perfectly well without him, and Campbell found himself thinking about work less and less and about Tilly more and more.

Never having given it any thought, he had been surprised at quite how much was involved in making cakes for a living. As Tilly explained, it wasn't just a question of baking. She had long interviews with each client to find out exactly what they wanted, then the cake had to be designed and decorated and delivered on time. She sourced recipes, shopped for ingredients and priced each cake, but what she was best at was talking to people.

Inclined to be dismissive at first, Campbell came to recognise her ability to make connections for the skill it was. He watched clients relax as they sat at Tilly's table and told her about who or what they wanted to celebrate with a special cake, and he watched their faces when they saw what Tilly had made for them.

There were almost always gasps of pleasure and admiration when the cake was unveiled, and he could understand why. Campbell was amazed at what she could do. The day after Cleo's visit, she had made a football pitch complete with players in the correct strips for a nine year-old boy who was a Manchester United fan. Campbell had helped her deliver it to the birthday party and would have enjoyed the whole experience if he hadn't had to drive a van with 'Sweet Nothings' painted on the side.

A *pink* van.

Campbell had told Tilly she needed to work on her corporate image, but she'd just laughed at him. 'Everyone loves the pink van,' she said. 'It's fun.'

'I just hope to God nobody I know sees me in it,' he grumbled and Tilly slid him a mischievous glance.

'Perhaps you're the one who needs rebranding,' she suggested. 'You could tone down all that macho man and get in touch with your feminine side!'

The look Campbell sent her in reply made Tilly laugh out loud.

'OK, there *is* no feminine side. That would explain why you're finding it so hard to make a cake!'

And Campbell had to admit that he was struggling on that front. Tilly made it look so easy, but when he'd tried to make even a basic sponge it was a disaster.

'Look, it's not a competition,' Tilly said to him, watching him square up to his ingredients for yet another practice cake. 'It's not about winning, or beating the ingredients into shape. It's magic.'

She let some caster sugar run through her fingers, caressed a speckled brown egg. 'It's about taking all these different ingredients and turning them into something that looks wonderful and smells wonderful and tastes wonderful. You're too aggressive,' she scolded him. 'You're treating cooking as a battle, with you as Julius Caesar and the ingredients as the poor old Britons! Don't think of the recipe as a series of manoeuvres. Think of it as helpful advice to create something beautiful.'

But, frustrated by his inability to master baking the way he had mastered every other obstacle in his way, Campbell was too brisk, too impatient for results, to do anything of the kind. He didn't know what Tilly meant when she said it wasn't about winning. Why else would he be making a fool of himself like this?

He was much happier sorting out her office for her and criticising her accounting system. He fixed wobbly shelves and changed the light bulbs she couldn't reach. He checked the oil in the van and filled up the windscreen wash. He set up a special business email account for Sweet Nothings.

'If you carry on like this, I'm not going to want you to leave,' Tilly said.

Leave. Campbell was jolted by the reminder. Of course he would be leaving. He would be getting on a plane and flying off to the States, where there would be no Tilly humming tunelessly as she moved around the kitchen. No Tilly endlessly teasing him about his military approach or his interest in Roman history. No Tilly there rolling her eyes, wearing her bold bright lipstick, leaning forward with an animated face, encompassing everyone she talked to in her warmth and her light.

But he would be in New York. He would be successful. He would look Lisa in the face and show her everything that she had lost.

'Careful!' Tilly cautioned him as he lifted the cake out of the back of the van. 'This one's very fragile.'

Campbell looked down at the cake, decorated to look like a bed complete with pink frills, scatter cushions and a teddy bear. It was covered with cosmetics, a chick flick DVD and a sparkly top.

'Is this a birthday cake?'

'It's for a sleepover party.'

To Campbell the house seemed full of shrieking, giggling girls who flocked around them, exclaiming at the cake and tossing back their hair as they cast sidelong glances at him under their impossibly long lashes while Tilly carried on an in-depth conversation with the birthday girl's mother.

'Phew!' He let out a long breath when he finally managed to extricate her and made an escape. 'I'd rather parachute into enemy territory than do that again.'

Tilly rolled her eyes in a characteristic gesture. 'Honestly, they were just a few little girls!'

'They weren't little, and they were terrifying. You could have warned me!'

'I didn't realise that it would be quite such a traumatic experience for you,' she said, grinning as she unlocked the van. 'You certainly weren't much back-up support!'

'Hey, I got you out of there, didn't I?'

'I'm not sure grabbing me by the wrist, telling Jane that we had to go and dragging me to the door really counts. You might try a more diplomatic approach next time.'

'There's going to be a next time?' said Campbell, his horror only half feigned.

'Perhaps I'd better make it solo missions if there's any girly stuff involved,' said Tilly, laughing at him over the roof of the van. 'I hope this never gets back to the mess. The day Campbell Sanderson panicked when confronted with six twelve-year-old girls!'

'I did not panic,' he said, trying to suppress an answering grin. 'I merely made a strategic retreat. I was thinking of you, in any case,' he added virtuously as they got into the van. 'It's been a long day.'

Tilly stretched and sighed. 'It has. At least that's it for today.' She reached for her seatbelt. 'Do you want me to drop you back at the hotel?'

'If you'll let me buy you dinner,' said Campbell on an impulse and when she froze with her seat belt halfway across her, he held up his hands in a gesture of innocence. 'Don't panic, I'm not planning to make a move on you! You made your feelings clear enough about that,' he told her. 'I was just thinking that you'd done enough cooking today, and I'm sick of eating in a restaurant on my own.'

Tilly hesitated. Far from panicking, she was perversely miffed that Campbell had made his lack of intentions so obvious. It didn't help that she was perfectly aware that it was her own fault. She *had* told him that she didn't want to get involved, so she shouldn't complain that he had taken her at her word.

She should be glad, in fact. Her heart couldn't take another break. It would just shatter and there would be nothing left of it at all. She didn't dare let her guard down, Tilly reminded herself. It would be so easy to let Campbell in, but how could he not hurt her? He might amuse himself for a while, but he wouldn't stay for ever, and why should he? Look at her—overweight and screwed up and stuck in her rut. What could she possibly have to offer him compared to an incredible new job and a beautiful ex-wife who clearly would only have to crook a perfectly manicured finger to have him back?

No, face reality, Tilly, her mind told her firmly. *Campbell is not for you.*

The trouble was that her body hadn't quite got the message.

Instead of listening to what her head was saying, her body was simmering with awareness of him. All Campbell had to do was turn and smile and every nerve she possessed seemed to suck in its breath.

Tilly couldn't take her eyes off his hands, his mouth. She couldn't stop remembering how lean and hard his body had felt, couldn't stop wondering what it would be like to unbutton his shirt, to run her hands over his powerful muscles, to press her lips to his skin. To forget about her poor, broken heart and let him bear her down on to a bed, a couch, the floor—*anywhere*— as long as he made love to her.

That was the point where Tilly had to stop herself. Wasn't it Campbell who had accused her of having a vivid imagination? It wasn't always a good thing, she decided, not when it left you with a thudding heart and a dry mouth and your insides roiling and writhing with desire.

And if she was like this during the day, what sort of state would she be in sitting across a table from him, where the lighting would be soft and intimate and she would only have to move her hand a matter of inches to be able to touch him?

No, the sensible thing would be to go home and put herself firmly out of temptation's way.

On the other hand, Tilly's body argued back, it would be nice to have a meal someone else had cooked, and it wasn't fair to leave him on his own every night. There was no point in being silly. It was just a meal with a friend. What could be the harm in that?

'Dinner would be nice,' she said firmly. 'Thanks.'

They arranged to meet a couple of hours later at a restaurant in the centre of Allerby. That gave Tilly enough time to jump in the shower and then work herself into a frenzy of doubt about what to wear.

She didn't want to look as if she were trying too hard, or as if she were expecting anything more than a friendly dinner, but it would be nice to show Campbell that she didn't always look a mess. She dressed for comfort when she was cooking, and her shoes were always practical and flat. It wasn't exactly a glamorous look. As for what she had worn on that Scottish hillside, Tilly didn't want to think about what she had looked like then!

In the end she settled on a clinging wrap-over top in a lovely deep violet with a swirly black skirt which looked good with her favourite shoes. They had perilously high heels with cutaway sides and peep toes and Tilly felt a million times better about herself the moment she put them on. Really, she ought to wear them the whole time, she decided, and to hell with teetering around the kitchen all day or throwing out her back.

Even the shoes couldn't stop her feeling nervous as the taxi stopped outside the restaurant. Tilly knew it was stupid, but her heart was thumping ridiculously and her entrails were fluttery.

'Please, please don't let me make a fool of myself,' she prayed as she paid off the taxi and turned for the entrance. The restaurant was reputed to be the best in Allerby and Tilly had been doubtful that they would get a table at such short notice, but she should have known a little thing like the restaurant being full wouldn't stand between Campbell and getting what he wanted.

Taking a deep breath, she pulled open the door. The *maître d'* glided towards her, but Tilly had already seen Campbell. He rose from the table at the sight of her, and their eyes met across the restaurant.

Campbell had showered and shaved and, in his beautifully cut suit, he looked lean and cool and more than a little ruthless. He looked devastating. Tilly's knees felt as if they were about to buckle, and she swallowed hard.

See? her mind was nagging. *I told you this was a bad idea. Now how are you going to resist him?*

She pushed the thought aside. This was just a friendly dinner. But her mouth was dry as, oblivious to the *maître d'*, to anything except the man waiting for her, she walked over to join Campbell.

'Hi,' she said. The queen of sparkling repartee that was her.

Campbell felt as if all the oxygen had been sucked out of his lungs at the sight of her walking towards him in a tight top and a skirt that skimmed her gorgeous curves and shoes so sexy they practically left scorch marks on the floor.

Without thinking, he reached out to touch her. He couldn't help himself. He had a hand at her waist and was drawing her towards him before the red alert siren went off belatedly in his head. He wasn't getting involved, right?

Right.

So yanking her into his arms and kissing her, pulling her towards him and exploring all that tantalising warmth and softness, making it his, right there in front of everybody, was probably *not* a good idea.

His senses screamed in protest as he regained control at the very last moment and dropped a chaste kiss on the corner of her mouth instead.

Just breathing in her perfume, feeling the softness of her skin, grazing the alluring curl of her lips was enough to make Campbell's head reel, and he had to jerk his head back before he did something really stupid.

He had to clear his throat before he could speak. 'You look wonderful,' he managed at last and winced inwardly at the croak in his voice. Whatever had happened to cool Campbell Sanderson, famed for his focus and control?

'Thanks,' said Tilly. 'You brush up nicely yourself.'

She was surprised at how ordinary her voice sounded. The brief brush of his lips had been like an electric jolt and she had to sit down before her legs gave way. Her face was throbbing where his mouth had touched her, her waist tingling where his hard hand had held her.

She picked up the menu with hands that weren't quite steady and made a show of reading it.

'Hungry?' Campbell asked.

'You know me, I'm always hungry.'

But she wasn't, not really. Tilly couldn't concentrate. The words wavered before her eyes, and it was impossible to focus on them when every sense was fixed on Campbell on the other side of the table. His lashes were lowered over the keen eyes as he read his own menu. His fingers were drumming absently on the cloth, and his mouth was set in the cool, quiet line that made her heart turn over whenever she looked at it.

Tilly was hardly aware of what she ordered. The wine waiter appeared as soon as the waitress had gone and tried to discuss wine with Campbell, who simply closed the wine list and handed it back. 'Whatever's good,' he said brusquely. 'And whatever you can find most quickly.'

'You'll probably get the most expensive wine in the restaurant,' Tilly warned him as the wine waiter, disappointed, took himself off.

Campbell shrugged. 'I'd rather pay for it than endure a lot of poncey talk about it.'

Olivier had been a wine buff. He had spent ages perusing the wine list before every meal, and Tilly couldn't help thinking that it would be a nice change to have a meal out that wasn't punctuated with exhaustive lectures on grapes and vineyards and bouquets and aromas.

The wine waiter took Campbell at his word and came back almost immediately with a bottle. Evidently deciding they weren't worth any flourishes, he opened the bottle, poured two glasses and left.

Tilly lifted her glass. 'Here's to you surviving your latest dangerous mission!'

'All those giggling girls?' Campbell's laugh was rueful. 'I'd rather do just about anything than face a gaggle like that again!'

'My hero!'

'You mock,' he said severely, although there was a hint of a smile about his mouth, 'but I'm not used to girls—or not twelve-year-old ones anyway.'

'You don't have a sister, then?'

'No, it was just me and my brother growing up. Girls were an alien species for a long time.'

'We're not *so* different, you know,' said Tilly. 'You'd learn that soon enough if you had a daughter.'

The smile vanished abruptly. 'God forbid!' he said, horrified at the thought. 'I wouldn't know where to start dealing with a girl.'

'Oh, I wouldn't worry. She would deal with you,' Tilly reassured him. 'She'd have you wrapped round her little finger in no time! It's always the same with you macho men. You're putty in the hands of a little girl.'

'It's just as well I never had any kids then,' said Campbell dryly.

'Did you ever think about having children when you were married?'

He shook his head. 'No, babies weren't part of Lisa's plan, and I've never even considered it. I don't think I would have been a good father.'

Tilly put down her glass with a frown. 'Why do you say that?'

'I'm afraid I would have turned out like my own father.' He straightened his cutlery without looking at her. 'I suppose he loved us in his own way, but I never remember having fun with him, or doing the stuff other boys do with their fathers.'

'That's a shame,' said Tilly, remembering how her stepfather had been with Harry and Seb. 'He missed out on a lot.'

'We all did. I know you think I'm bad at expressing emotion, but you should have met my father. He was an army officer, a very moral man in lots of ways, but he had rigid standards that my brother and I never met. We used to try and outdo each other in a bid to please him but nothing we did was ever quite good enough. It didn't matter how well we did, he never praised us. I think he thought it would spoil us or something.'

'What about your mother?'

'She died when I was nine.' Campbell sighed. 'To be absolutely honest, I don't remember her that well. Looking back, I wonder what kind of life she had, married to my father. I suspect that any spirit she may have had was crushed out of her early on. And after that we were packed off to boarding school, which sounds heartless, but we liked it more than being at home with our father.'

Poor little boys, Tilly thought, her heart twisting with pity. She had seen what losing their mother had done to her own brothers at not much older than Campbell had been. At least she had been there for them, but Campbell had had no such softening influence against his joyless, demanding father.

'I see now why you're so competitive,' she said, as lightly as she could, and he gave her a crooked grin.

'My brother is a barrister now. He's worse than me!'

'Your father must have been proud of you both, even if he didn't show it. You've both been very successful.'

Campbell shrugged. 'He died when I was in the Marines. Since trying to please him hadn't got me anywhere, I'd started to rebel and I was heading off the rails. I was lucky the Marines took me,' he confessed. 'God knows where I would have ended up otherwise, but I was too much of a maverick to make a successful career in the forces like my father did. I'm not sure even that would have been enough for Dad.' His mouth twisted in self-mockery. 'Lisa used to tell me I was still trying to prove myself to him.'

You didn't need to be married to him to guess that, Tilly thought waspishly. She wasn't going to give Lisa any points for insight.

Absently, she crumbled a piece of bread, imagining Campbell as a boy, growing into a wild young man, his mother dead, his father distant, driven always by the need to succeed. No wonder he wasn't good at talking about emotions. Being abandoned by his wife wouldn't have helped either. Underneath that surface cool, was he as lost as the rest of them?

Her heart cracked for him, but she knew better than to offer pity.

'My father is disappointed in me, too,' she offered. 'He doesn't think making cakes is a proper job. It doesn't make enough money, and that's his only measure of success.'

Campbell wasn't sorry to change the subject. 'Have you seen him since your mother died?'

'We keep in touch,' said Tilly. 'We have lunch every now and then, but it's never very successful. I think it's because we're so different, but *he* thinks it's because I've never forgiven him for leaving Mum. There may be some truth in that, although I know Mum was much happier with Jack than she would have been if Dad had stayed with us.'

'How old were you when your parents divorced?'

'Nearly seven,' she said. 'My mother kept telling me that my father still loved me, and that his leaving was nothing to do with me, but I didn't believe her. If he'd loved me, he wouldn't have left.'

She stopped and cocked her head, as if listening to what she had just said. 'Hmm, that sounds bitter, doesn't it? Maybe Dad's right after all!'

Campbell wasn't fooled by her bright smile. 'You stayed with your mother, then?'

'Yes, I had occasional weekends with Dad, but he was always busy. He got married again, and his new wife went perfectly with the smart, super-successful life he'd always wanted. Unfortunately a tubby little girl who reminded him of his old life just didn't blend with his décor!'

'It was always a relief to go home,' Tilly remembered. 'I loved Jack. He was calm and steady and safe, and I was so happy when my mother married him. Once the twins arrived, it felt like the perfect family.'

She smiled wistfully. 'I suppose I always hoped that I would meet someone like Jack myself. Instead, as Cleo is always pointing out, I seem drawn to men like Olivier, who are much more like my father. That's all going to stop, though.' She put on a resolute air. 'From now on, I'm only interested in nice, kind men.'

Well, that ruled him out, Campbell thought. No one would ever describe him as nice or kind. It was on the tip of his tongue to tell Tilly that she was much too exciting to be content with merely nice and that she would be bored rigid after a week, but he stopped himself just in time.

It wasn't his business. He was leaving.

Focus on the new job, he told himself. Focus on Lisa and what it's going to be like seeing her again. But all he could think about was Tilly—warm, desirable, messy Tilly, with the candlelight glowing in her dark blue eyes and the mouth that made his mind go blank.

Campbell had never met a woman so easy to talk to. He liked her spiky, self-deprecating wit and the animation in her face. He liked the smile that lit her up from inside, the glint in her eyes as she teased him. She was never still. She fiddled with the wax dribbling down the candles, or traced invisible patterns on the cloth with her glass. She sat back, and leant forward, folding her arms on the table and just about giving Campbell a heart attack as her cleavage deepened.

'Let's get you a taxi,' he said gruffly when they at last came to leave. Not trusting himself to touch her, he shoved his hands deep into his pockets and walked beside her to the taxi rank in silence.

At least they didn't have to wait. Campbell wasn't at all sure what that would have done to his self-control. He should have gone with Tilly to see her home himself, but there was no way he could manage sitting in the back seat in the dark without reaching for her.

He leant through the window of the taxi at the head of the rank and handed the driver a note that would more than cover Tilly's fare. 'Make sure she gets safely in,' he said as the driver pocketed it quickly, unable to believe his luck.

'There's no need for that,' Tilly protested. 'I can get my own taxi.'

'I know you can, but I'm getting this one.'

Tilly opened her mouth to argue, then shut it again. Campbell's jaw was set at an angle that suggested she could argue all night and it still wouldn't make any difference.

'Well…thank you,' she said awkwardly instead. 'And thank you for dinner. It was lovely.' At least she assumed it had been. Too fixated on trying to keep her gaze from crawling all over Campbell, she could barely remember what she had eaten. Never had she paid less attention to food.

'I'll see you soon then.' Campbell's voice was brisk, but when their eyes met, the air shortened alarmingly between them.

'Yes,' she managed on a gasp.

'Goodnight, Tilly,' he said.

'Goodnight.'

Tilly's heart was pounding and her legs felt as if they were about to buckle. She badly needed to sit down. *Get in the car*, her mind screamed at her. *Get in the car—now! You'll regret it if you don't, you know you will.*

So it wasn't as if she didn't know what she should do, but somehow Tilly couldn't move. She couldn't even drag her eyes from his, so there was no way later she could claim that she had been caught unawares, as her mind was pointing out in no uncertain terms. *This is* so *not a good idea*, her mind scolded, but it was too late to back away now and, anyway, Tilly didn't want to. Her mind might be backing away and moaning *no, no, no*, but her body was screaming *yes, yes, yes!*

And her body won.

As if in slow motion, she saw Campbell lower his head towards her, and then his mouth captured hers and sensations Tilly hadn't even known existed exploded inside her. She parted her lips on a gasp that was part thrill, part alarm at the dizzying loss of control as she felt herself submerge beneath a rush of response. Every cell in her body was clamouring to press closer, taste more, touch again and again and again...

Her arms went round his waist and she leant into him, giddy with the feel of him. His lips were warm and sure as they explored her mouth, his tongue teasing, his hands hard and insistent. He smelt wonderful, tasted better, and she clung to him almost feverishly. He was her solid anchor, her safe harbour, the one point of certainty in a world that was unravelling with electrifying speed, and she kissed him back, oblivious to the waiting taxi, oblivious to anything except the gathering need and the deep, dark pulse of desire inside her.

And then, abruptly, it was over.

Campbell stepped back and opened the taxi door. His jaw was set and a muscle jerked in his cheek, but Tilly was too dazed to take much else in. Somehow she got herself into the back seat of the taxi. Campbell closed the door without a word and the taxi drove off, leaving him standing on the pavement and cursing himself for a fool.

CHAPTER EIGHT

TILLY fumbled with the seat belt. Her body was raging with disappointment and frustration. Why had he stopped? She had no idea now of how long the kiss had lasted. Could it really have been just a brief goodnight kiss?

But then why would it mean any more to Campbell? Tilly asked herself disconsolately. He must have picked up on the vibes she had tried so hard to suppress all night, and realised that all she could think about was touching him. Maybe he had thought to himself, why not? Or, worse, had decided to indulge her.

Body still thumping, she scowled miserably out of the window. *I told you so*, her mind said smugly. *I knew you'd regret it.*

But she didn't, not really. She had had to know what it felt like to kiss him, to hold him. The trouble was that now that she did, she wanted it again, she wanted more. Tilly had never had much time for the saying that a taste of honey was worse than none at all, but it was starting to make more sense.

Perhaps she *could* have more. The daring thought slid into her mind and she sat up straighter, as if shocked at her own presumption.

If she made it clear to Campbell that she had no expectations of any relationship, if she could convince him that it would just be a physical thing as far as she was concerned, would he be prepared to kiss her again? To make love to her? To share a night where they could shrug off the past and the future, where they could put aside hopes and fears, and not think at all, where nothing would matter but touching and tasting and feeling and the heady swell of pleasure?

Tilly's mouth was dry, her heart hammering at the mere thought of it. A single night... Would it be worth it? *Yes,* her body shouted. *Yes, yes, yes!*

What about your poor heart? her mind countered immediately, the way Tilly had known it would. *What if Campbell breaks it?*

She wouldn't let him break it, Tilly decided firmly. She would keep her heart intact. There would be no question of loving him. It would just be...sex.

She could suggest it, and see what Campbell said. She was a grown woman, he was a man. Surely they could talk about sex without embarrassment. He could only say no. It would be perfectly simple.

Or would it?

Tilly's confidence, ever fragile, faltered whenever she imagined facing Campbell with her proposition. *Campbell, about Friday night,* she could begin, but she couldn't decide what to say after that. *Could we try that again,* she might suggest, *but next time, don't stop and put me in a taxi.*

Perhaps it would be better to be more upfront. *I was wondering how you felt about a brief affair before you go?* Somehow Tilly couldn't see herself carrying that one off.

She couldn't decide whether she was glad or sorry that she wouldn't see him the next day. The arrangement had been that the participants in the competition would have the weekend off, presumably so that they could go home if necessary, but when Campbell had indicated that he wouldn't be going back to London it had seemed only polite to invite him for Sunday lunch.

Seb and Harry were coming home for the weekend on Saturday, and Tilly had been pleased at first. She had thought that her aching awareness of Campbell would be easier to handle if the boys were there to dilute the atmosphere, but now she wished they were staying at their respective universities and partying too hard the way they usually did. She loved Harry and Seb dearly, but she could hardly propose an affair in front of her younger brothers.

As it turned out, Seb and Harry were both still in bed nursing hangovers when Campbell arrived on Sunday. Having practised exactly what she would say if the opportunity arose, Tilly promptly forgot every word when she opened the door. The sight of him was like a fist thumping into her stomach, driving the breath from her lungs and leaving her reeling with a strange mixture of shock and delight.

Somehow she'd expected him to have changed since that kiss, but he looked exactly the same as always: cool, contained, faintly austere. It was hard to believe that only thirty-six hours ago he had held her hard against him and kissed her, that the stern mouth had been warm and sure and exciting on hers.

Campbell's expression gave nothing away. The pale, piercing eyes were guarded, Tilly thought, and her entrails churned. It was all very well deciding to be cool and upfront, but it all seemed a lot harder when you were faced with six feet of solid, detached male.

Flustered, she led the way to the kitchen and explained about Seb and Harry in far too much detail.

'They should be down any minute now. Would you like a coffee while we're waiting?'

'No, thanks. I'm fine.'

He might be fine, but she needed something to do to distract herself from the memory of that kiss that reverberated in the air between them. Tilly busied herself checking the meat, and tried to ignore the silence yawning around them.

This was ridiculous, she told herself, exasperated. She was being pathetic. It was just Campbell, for heaven's sake. She had been able to talk to him perfectly easily before, so she should be able to now. Taking off the oven gloves, she turned from the oven with a deep breath.

'About Friday night,' she began, exactly as she had planned. She even sounded calm, which was quite something given that her nerves were jumping and jittering and jangling in a way that that made it hard to think, let alone string a coherent sentence together.

She didn't get a chance to say any more. Campbell held up a hand to stop her.

'It's OK,' he said. 'You don't need to say any more.'

'Er...I don't?'

'I need to apologise,' he said stiffly. 'I was out of order on Friday night. I didn't mean to kiss you, I was just...I wasn't thinking,' he confessed. 'All I can say is that I'm sorry, and that it won't happen again. I'll keep my hands to myself in the future.'

Ah.

How was she supposed to respond to that? Tilly wondered. Clearly Campbell regretted the kiss and had no intention of re-peating it, so she could hardly force herself upon him now. Her heart twisted at the realisation, but the only thing to do was put a good face on it.

At least it wouldn't be difficult. She had years of experience of being 'good old Tilly' who could be relied upon to dispel any potential awkwardness with a smiling face.

'It must have been that wine,' she said lightly. 'I don't think either of us was thinking clearly on Friday evening. That'll teach you to leave the choice up to the wine waiter!'

There was no mistaking the relief in Campbell's expression. He had obviously been dreading a scene, or that she might do exactly what she had been planning to do and throw herself at him.

'It's good of you to take it like that,' he said. 'I'd be sorry if I had spoiled things between us.'

'There's no question of that,' said Tilly, keeping her bright smile firmly in place.

'I was afraid I might have jeopardised our chances on the programme.'

Of course, the programme. Tilly had almost forgotten about that. It was telling that Campbell hadn't. He might be momentarily distracted by a kiss, but he would never lose sight of his ultimate goal.

'The only thing that will really jeopardise them is if you can't make Cleo's cake,' she told him and he grimaced.

'I know. It's harder than I expected,' he admitted.

Convincing herself that it was all for the best was harder than Tilly had expected, too. No matter how fiercely she reminded herself that he was leaving soon, or that he was still hung up on his ex-wife, disappointment still twisted painfully inside her. She made herself remember how much it had hurt when Olivier had gone, of how much better off on her own she would be in the long run, but none of it helped.

There was nothing to be done but keep the smile on her face, but it was feeling fixed by the time first Seb and then Harry appeared, yawning and rubbing their rumpled hair. In spite of their hangovers, they brightened considerably at Tilly's suggestion that they take Campbell to the pub while she finished getting lunch ready.

Campbell was all set to demur. 'We can't leave you alone to do all the work,' he protested.

'Honestly, it's better if we do,' Seb confided, and Harry

nodded vigorous agreement. 'She'll just get ratty if we hang around.'

'We could help,' Campbell suggested, but they only looked at him as if he had sprouted a second head.

Tilly rolled her eyes. 'Their idea of "helping" was to send me off for a weekend in the Highlands and look where that got me! No, you go,' she told him. 'Seb's right, you'll all just get in the way. There's not much more to do, in any case.'

She was desperate to get rid of them and have a few minutes to herself so that she could stop putting on a front.

Seeing that she was serious, Campbell let himself be persuaded, and the three men walked down to the local pub together. Tilly's brothers were very young but engaging company, and they were obviously very fond of their sister.

Over a beer, they told him all about Olivier. 'What a tosser!' said Harry dismissively. 'I'm glad Tilly isn't with him any more, but she was really cut up about him. She deserves better.'

Seb nodded. 'I mean, we give her a hard time, of course, but she's done everything for us. She stayed in Allerby and worked so that we could have a home and now we've gone we think it's time she got out and had a life for herself. That's why we put her up for this television thing. We thought it would be good for her. Left to herself, she'd just stay stuck in her kitchen and the truth is we don't like to think of her being on her own.'

'No,' his twin chimed in. 'Tilly needs someone to love, and she's not going to find anyone if she doesn't go out and look. The trouble is, she's got lousy taste. Knowing her, she'll just end up with another loser like Olivier!'

That made Campbell feel even worse about kissing her the other night. He had acted purely on instinct, and he had been taken aback by how sweet she had tasted, how good it had felt to hold her in his arms—how *right* it had seemed.

It had been a huge effort to make himself stop but, if he

hadn't, there was only one way it could have ended. Rather late in the day, Campbell had remembered how honest Tilly had been about not wanting to get involved. She had been badly hurt, he had *known* that, and she deserved better than a Friday night fumble.

He should have had more control, Campbell blamed himself austerely. He didn't like to think about how thoughtless he had been. It wasn't like him to lose sight of what was what. Perhaps Tilly was right, and the wine was to blame?

Whatever the reason, he had felt stupidly nervous about seeing her again today. He'd been afraid that she would have been embarrassed about the kiss, and awkward about telling him that she didn't want a repetition—as she clearly didn't. At least he had got in first with his apology to save her having to find the words. It had seemed the least he could do.

It was all sorted, anyway. He had taken evasive measures, a potentially difficult situation had been resolved, and all he had to do now was make that damn wedding cake. Then he could leave to get on with the rest of his life. It was the right thing to do for both of them.

So why didn't it feel right?

Campbell's video diary:
[Clears throat] I've been reminded to record this tonight, as there's only one more day to go. Tomorrow I've got to make Cleo's wedding cake, assemble it, decorate it and get it to the hotel in time for the party in the evening. I've planned much more difficult missions in my time, but I've got to admit this is the one I feel most nervous about. Cleo wants lemon sponge cake, so it has to be made fresh, and that means I don't get a trial run. But I'm sure it will be fine. I've been practising. Tilly has showed me how to cut the cake into blocks and then assemble them in the right

shape, and I've learnt how to ice and use a piping bag—which I have to say I never thought I would hear myself say! Tilly is a good teacher. Very good, in fact.

There's much more to the cake-making business than I realised. I've seen how Tilly makes a real connection with people, not just when it comes to the design and what's likely to be suitable, but when she's delivering the cakes. [Relaxing as forgets camera and pursues own thoughts] I think her brothers may be wrong about her being stuck in the kitchen. It seems to me that Tilly is out all the time and that she knows a lot of people.

Yesterday, for instance, we went to the hospice she'll donate her cheque to if we win. It was quite an experience. I'd never been anywhere like it before. I expected it to be a depressing place, to be honest, but it wasn't. It felt bright and light and peaceful and I felt... [Pause, searching for the right word] ...well, I suppose I was moved. Yes, moved.

Tilly was quite at ease there. She seemed to know everyone, but she told me afterwards that she didn't. I think people respond to her warmth. There's a kind of brightness about her ...[Abruptly recollects camera] Anyway...well, I can see how much winning would mean to the hospice, so I'd better make Cleo a good cake tomorrow and make sure we get the maximum number of points.

I can't see why we shouldn't. I've done a bit of research and got a picture of an ancient Egyptian barge and the costumes and so on. I even had a look at the play. Tilly drew up a design and kept it as simple as possible, but it's still going to be tricky. I'll be glad when tomorrow's over.

[Stops, realises that hasn't sounded very sure] Yes, of

course I will be. I need to get back to work. I've got things to do. I want the cake to be a success tomorrow, but then it will be time to say goodbye.

Tilly's video diary:
[Pushes hair tiredly from face] I can't believe it's almost over. Campbell has just gone back to his hotel for the last time. He'll be back tomorrow to make Cleo's cake, but then he's leaving. It's funny to think how much has changed since the last time I recorded this diary. Campbell's changed—or maybe it's just that I've got to know him better. Or maybe I'm the one that's changed.

The kitchen won't be the same without him. I mean, he can be really irritating. He insists in clearing up im-maculately—and I mean immaculately—*every five minutes, which I know is a good thing, and I should do that, too, but sometimes when you're doing a tricky bit of piping you don't want someone asking, 'Have you finished with the sugar because I'll put it away if you have?' or, 'If you just stand away from the table a minute, I'll wipe up the extraordinary mess you've created'. The worst thing is, I think I'm going to miss it. [Sighs]*

Anyway...he's learnt how to make a sponge. The thing about Campbell is that he's really focused. If he decides he's going to do something, he'll do it. He'd never admit it, but I think he might be a bit nervous about Cleo's cake. It's a difficult design. Too difficult for a beginner, but he's determined to get it right. I hope he does. I'm not supposed to have anything to do with it, but I'll be around to give advice until I have to go to the wedding ceremony at three. There's a small reception afterwards, but the cake is for the party in the evening, so I'll come back after that and hopefully the cake will be all ready to go.

And then that'll be it. It's going to be…strange. But of course, Campbell has got his new job to go to, and I've got a business to run. [Stops, swallows] It'll be for the best, I know, but I hate saying goodbye.

'You won't forget the asp, will you?' It was the morning of Cleo's wedding, and Tilly was supposed to be getting ready for the ceremony, but she kept popping down to the kitchen where Campbell was making cakes with military precision.

'Stop flapping,' he said, exasperated. 'I'm the one that's supposed to be nervous here! It's all under control. Look!' He waved the time plan he had plotted minute by minute at her and checked his watch. 'Right now cakes five and six are supposed to be in the oven, and there they are, see,' he said, pointing at the oven. 'I'm going to take them out at thirteen ten.'

'I don't like all this precision,' Tilly fretted. 'This isn't a mission that can be planned down to the last second. The cakes will be ready when they're ready. Remember what I told you about the skewer? Keep an eye on them rather than the clock, that's all I'd say.'

Campbell wished she would go away. Quite apart from the fact that she was casting doubt on his plan, of which he was secretly very proud, she was far too distracting standing there in a faded towelling robe, with her hair wrapped up in a towel and her face clean and rosy from the shower.

She smelt of baby powder. It was all too easy to imagine pulling her towards him by the belt of her robe, shutting her up with a kiss while he untied it in one easy move so that he could slide his hands beneath the material to explore her lush body. She would be warm and sweet and clean.

Snarled up with longing and frustration, Campbell wished she wasn't standing between him and the sink. He could do with putting his head under the cold tap. As it was, he would have to pass her to do that, and he couldn't trust himself that close.

Ever since that kiss, he had been achingly aware of her. Again and again he had had to remind himself of all the reasons why he shouldn't touch her, but the reasons were sounding thinner with every day that passed.

He did his best to concentrate on the future, on the challenge of his new job and the move to New York but whenever he tried to imagine what it would be like, all he could picture was life without Tilly, quiet and cold and empty.

It was absurd. What was he thinking? Campbell demanded, exasperated with himself. That he should give up his career, his plans, the chance to turn round a company and make it a global leader again? Drop out of the race just before the finishing line? Of course he couldn't do that, and if he wouldn't contemplate any of that, it would hurt Tilly.

And that was something Campbell wasn't prepared to do.

'Shouldn't you be getting ready?' he asked her pointedly.

'Yes, I'd better go and dry my hair.' She looked anxious. 'Are you sure you're OK?'

'Everything's fine.'

If only it were, Campbell thought as she whisked out of the kitchen and he could let out a long, very careful, breath at last. Right then everything felt as if it might slip out of control any minute, and that wasn't a feeling he liked at all.

Squaring his shoulders, he turned his attention back to his time plan. Focus, that was all he needed to do. It had always worked for him in the past and in a lot more difficult situations than this. It would work now.

It was hard to focus, though, when Tilly reappeared at last, spilling out of a deep aqua-blue suit. A bag was wedged under her arm while she fastened her earrings.

'OK, I'm off,' she said, her face intent as she fiddled with the second stud.

Her outfit wasn't particularly daring. It had a cropped jacket, nipped in at the waist, and a lacy camisole gave modesty to the plunging neckline. A flippy skirt ended at the knee. Her shoes were precipitously heeled, true, with ridiculous bows. Otherwise, it was the kind of outfit you would expect a woman to wear to a wedding.

So there was no reason for Campbell to feel as if his head was reeling. He actually had to close his eyes.

'What's the matter?'

He snapped them open to find that Tilly had sorted out her earrings and was watching him. 'Nothing,' he said tightly. 'Nothing at all.'

She wasn't satisfied, but made matters worse by coming closer and peering at him. 'You look as if you're in pain.'

If only she knew! 'I'm fine.' Campbell managed a controlled smile. 'Just thinking about what needs to be done.'

Like take a cold shower.

'Well, if you're sure…' Tilly checked her bag. 'Now, you've got the design?'

'Yes, yes,' he said impatiently.

'And you haven't forgotten about piping the names on the side of the barge, the way we discussed? Make sure you spell them right, too. It's all noted on the design. Do you think I should check it quickly?'

'No,' said Campbell. 'I think you should go. You'll be late.'

Tilly looked at her watch and squeaked with dismay. 'God, yes, I will be…' Grabbing the keys to the van, she hurried to the door. 'I'll be back later,' she called on the way out of the room. 'Good luck!'

By the time she returned, Campbell had himself well under control. He just had to keep his hands to himself for a few more hours. He could do that. Look, he had even made a wedding cake, and if he could do that, he could do anything!

He had to admit that he was secretly very proud of the cake. It looked just like Tilly's sketch. Sitting on top of the cake base was the cake Cleopatra's cake barge, complete with a cake Antony, dressed as a Roman general, and even a cake asp, curled ironically in a corner. Authenticity had suffered with the tin cans trailing off the back and the large sign with 'just married' iced carefully on to it, but all in all it was pretty damn impressive, Campbell thought.

He could hardly believe that he had made it himself.

He was changed and ready to go as soon as Tilly got back. That was what you could do when you stuck to your time plan.

Tilly's face when she came into the kitchen and saw the finished cake was everything Campbell could have hoped for.

'Oh, Campbell, it's *fabulous*!' she cried. 'Well done! I know we talked about it but it's so different when you see it made up. Wait till Cleo sees it! She's going to be so thrilled,' she said as she walked round the table to inspect the cake more closely. 'This is bound to win!

'It's incredible to think that a fortnight ago you didn't even know how to make a basic sponge,' she told him admiringly. 'I'm so *proud* of you! This is going to be the highlight of the party tonight and—'

She stopped.

'What?' asked Campbell.

'The names on the side of the barge,' she said in a hollow voice.

'What about them?'

'You've spelt Anthony wrong.'

'I have not!' Campbell was outraged at the suggestion. 'I made a point of checking.'

'Not against my design.' Tilly snatched up the sketch-book and thrust it at him. 'How is Anthony spelt there?'

'With an "h".'

'Yes, and it's spelt with an "h" because that's how Anthony spells his name, so why have you spelt it without one?'

'Because that's the correct spelling,' said Campbell, sure of his ground. 'I even rang up a mate of mine who's a lecturer in English and specialises in sixteenth-century drama, and he told me Shakespeare's Antony definitely doesn't have an "h".'

'Maybe not, but Cleo's Anthony *does*,' said Tilly, exasperated.

Campbell was seriously put out. He had gone to a lot of trouble to make sure that everything was right. 'What was the point of finding out what Cleopatra's barge might have looked like and exactly what Antony would have been wearing, if you're not going to get his name right?' he demanded crossly.

'Because it's Tony and Cleo's wedding cake, not an academic treatise! Why do you have to be such a pedant? I know you like to be precise, but this is ridiculous! The whole point is that it's *their* names because it's *their* wedding!' She threw the sketch-book on to the table, furious with him for spoiling things when everything else looked so perfect. 'We're going to have to change it.'

Campbell was equally irritable. 'Who's going to notice?'

'Tony will, for a start. And his parents. Cleo says his mother is the queen of nit-pickers and is always moaning about missing apostrophes and the misuse of commas. She's the kind of person who sends back thank you letters with the spelling mistakes corrected! She's *bound* to comment. If there's one thing you ought to be able to get right at a wedding it's the groom's name, after all!'

A muscle was working furiously in Campbell's cheek. 'There isn't time to change it now,' he pointed out. 'It'll mean taking off all that icing.'

'There is if we do it together.' Tilly tossed an apron to him and tied on another over her wedding outfit.

The television cameras would be there again tonight. She didn't want them filming Cleo's new mother-in-law complaining that Campbell had made a mistake. She might be livid with him herself, but he had worked so hard on the cake and it looked fantastic. Trust him to mess everything up by insisting on being right!

Part of Tilly wanted to pick up the cake and crown him with it, but another part was already working out how to fix things. The cake had to be perfect for Cleo, and there was the competition to think of, too. Campbell might be the biggest nit-picker on the planet, but winning was important to him, and there was no way Tilly was going to let a little icing stand in the way when they were this close to victory.

'You make up some more yellow icing for the timbers,' she told him, 'and I'll do some white for the lettering. Then we just need to scrape off what's there, retouch it a bit and pipe on the new names.'

Campbell looked at his watch. 'We're supposed to be there in less than half an hour.'

'It takes ages for a party to get going.' Tilly was already shaking out icing sugar. 'Better for us to be a bit late than spend the whole evening being told we've spelt Anthony's name wrong! Come on, let's get going.'

Of course it took longer than expected, and in the end Tilly piped on the names as they couldn't afford to make the slightest mistake.

'We're cutting it very fine,' Campbell warned, anxious to make up for his blunder with the name. But how the hell was he supposed to have known that when Tilly had said spell a name correctly she had actually meant spell it wrong?

'We'll just have to hope there's not too much traffic. You drive,' Tilly said, tossing him the keys. 'You'll be faster than me. I'll hold the cake.'

They were in such a hurry by then that they didn't even stop to take off their aprons. Campbell took off with a squeal of brakes and drove with a nerveless skill that had Tilly clutching the cake box.

She didn't tell him to slow down, though. If they didn't get there before the television crew, she was sure they would lose points for being late, and she was determined now that they should win. It would be good to be able to give the money to the hospice, of course, but more than that she wanted to win because it mattered to Campbell.

The party was being held at a country house hotel some ten miles outside Allerby.

'We'll take the dual carriageway,' said Tilly as they screeched to a halt before yet another red light. 'We'll never get there if we have to stop at all these lights and get past all these stupid people dithering around looking for somewhere to park.'

She directed him out to the ring road, where at last Campbell could put his foot down. The pink van wasn't exactly powerful, but it responded valiantly, shuddering at the unfamiliar speed as they shot down the outside lane.

'It's not the next roundabout, but the next one,' said Tilly. 'We don't want to miss the turning. What is it?' she asked as Campbell glanced in the rear-view mirror and stamped on the brake, swearing under his breath.

'Police,' he said curtly.

'Please tell me you're joking!'

But Campbell had rarely felt less like joking and the next moment Tilly saw for herself as a policeman on a motorbike came alongside and flagged them, pointing over to the hard shoulder.

Campbell had little choice but to obey. He wound down his window as the officer approached.

'Would you get out of the car, please, sir?'

Rigid with frustration and temper, Campbell got out, remembering too late that he still had his pink apron on.

The policeman eyed him for a moment, and then read the side of the van. 'Let me guess,' he said. 'You're Mr Sweet, are you, sir? Or would that be Mr Nothing?'

Campbell set his teeth. 'Neither,' he said tersely, struggling to get rid of the apron so that he could dig in his back pocket for his wallet and driving licence. He couldn't have a sensible conversation wearing the stupid thing. This was all Tilly's fault for insisting that he wear one.

The policeman inspected the driving licence. 'Were you aware that you were exceeding the speed limit?'

'I can explain, officer. We've got something of an emergency.'

'This isn't the way to the hospital.'

'It's not that kind of emergency.' For a wild moment Campbell wondered whether he should pretend that Tilly was about to give birth, but presumably few mothers stopped to put on high heels and make-up when they went into labour. 'We've got this cake,' he began.

'Cake?' the policeman repeated expressionlessly.

'Yes. It's for a wedding.'

Campbell trailed off, realising how absurd it must sound but before he could say any more, Tilly had emerged from the van, having set the cake carefully on the seat. She had had the foresight to remove her apron, which gave the policeman a splendid view of her cleavage, Campbell noted.

'I'm afraid it's all my fault, officer.' Her eyes were huge and dark as she gazed limpidly at the policeman, who was clearly finding it difficult not to stare at the plunging neckline with its tantalising glimpse of lace below.

'It's my best friend's wedding,' she went on in a breathy voice that Campbell had never heard her use before, 'and I promised *faithfully* that I would have this cake ready for when she got to the party, but we had all sorts of problems, and now we're late and Cleo's going to be *so* disappointed, and it's her wedding day and I can't *bear* to think of letting her down so I was making Campbell drive fast...'

Campbell watched in reluctant admiration as words tumbled breathlessly from her, befuddling the policeman with their speed and intensity.

'It's really not his fault, officer. He wouldn't normally *dream* of speeding, and I know you're just doing your job and of course you must, but could we please, please, just get the cake to the wedding first and then we'll report to the police station or whatever you want.'

Taking the policeman's arm, she dragged him over to look through Campbell's open window. 'Look, you can see we're telling the truth. There's the cake, and it's so beautiful. Cleo will be devastated if we don't get it there in time, and we're already so late! I'll never forgive—'

Bemused by the flood of words, or possibly by the allure of Tilly's cleavage, the policeman backed away from the van. He had evidently given up trying to make sense of it all and simply held up a hand to stop Tilly in mid-sentence.

'Where is this wedding?' he asked gruffly.

'At Hammerby Hall. It's—'

'I know where it is.' He waved them back to the van. 'If I catch you speeding again, I won't be so lenient,' he warned them, 'but I'll make allowances for today. We don't want to disappoint the bride, do we?'

Climbing on to his bike, he kicked up the stand and switched on the flashing light. 'Follow me.'

CHAPTER NINE

CAMPBELL pulled out after the policeman, who was already speeding ahead along the dual carriageway, siren blaring, to clear the traffic out of their way, and for a good minute there was utter silence in the van.

Then they both started to laugh at the same time.

'I can't believe you got away with that!' said Campbell, still laughing but trying to sound disapproving. 'I've never seen such a revolting display! *I'm so sorry, officer,*' he mimicked her breathy voice. '*Please look down my cleavage instead of writing a speeding ticket.*'

Tilly wiped her eyes. 'It worked, didn't it? It's not as if you were getting far.' She burst into giggles again. 'I wish you could have seen your face when he asked if you were Mr Sweet!'

Campbell snorted and shook his head. 'That was your fault for making me wear that stupid apron!' he said but his attempt at disgust was short-lived in the face of Tilly's infectious laughter, and in the end he gave in and laughed too as they sped after the policeman.

Thanks to their escort, they arrived bare moments before the bridal party. Waving a grateful farewell to their policeman, Tilly and Campbell hurried in and were just lifting the cover off the cake when the television crew turned up, all ready to record Cleo's reaction.

She didn't disappoint, squealing with delight when she clapped eyes on the cake and throwing her arms around Campbell's neck.

'It's *so* fabulous! You clever thing!' she exclaimed as she planted a resounding kiss on his cheek. 'Thank you so much, Campbell. It's the best wedding cake ever! I'm never going to be able to cut it. Oh, I think I might be going to cry, it's so perfect.'

Alarmed at the prospect of tears, Campbell patted her gingerly and rolled his eyes over her shoulder at Tilly in a silent plea for help.

'Cleo, what do you think of Antony's costume?' she asked, coming to his rescue. 'Campbell researched it down to the last detail. He's even got the shoes right!'

To Campbell's relief, Cleo let go of him and bent to examine the cake in more detail. 'It's incredible. I can't believe you've learnt to do this in just two weeks, Campbell! Tony, come and look at this.'

Fortunately for Campbell, her groom restrained himself from hugging, but he was equally complimentary. 'This is really impressive,' he said to Campbell. 'I can see a hell of a lot of research has gone into it.' He walked round the cake, inspecting it closely. 'Isn't Cleopatra's Antony spelt without an "h", though?'

Tilly met Campbell's gaze across the cake. A definite smile was tugging at his mouth, and the sight of it unlocked something deep in her chest, releasing a disquieting tingle that seeped slowly along her veins.

'Could we have a quick interview?'

Suzy's voice at her elbow startled Tilly out of her thoughts. The producer drew her and Campbell away from the crowd gathering round the cake and beckoned Jim, the cameraman, over.

'It's certainly a wonderful cake, Campbell,' Suzy began. 'Is it really all your own work?'

'Yes,' said Tilly, as Campbell said, 'No.'

Suzy looked from one to the other.

'I had to have Tilly's help in the end,' he told her. 'I'd made a mistake, and Tilly put it right.'

'Why did you say that?' Tilly demanded crossly under her breath while Suzy was conferring with the cameraman. 'Now we'll lose points! I thought you wanted to win.'

'I do, but I'm not going to cheat to do it. The rules were clear. I had to make the cake entirely myself.'

'You did that! It was perfect.'

'It wasn't perfect. I spelt the name wrong, and you had to put it right.'

Tilly chewed her lip. 'No one would ever have known it wasn't you. You'd done it exactly the same, just without the "h".'

'I would have known,' said Campbell. He looked at her curiously. 'You've changed your tune, haven't you? I thought you didn't care whether we won or not?'

Tilly couldn't meet his eyes. She couldn't tell him that she only wanted to win for his sake. 'We've gone to all this effort,' she said. 'It just seems a shame to blow it now.'

'We've done what we can,' he said carelessly. 'It's down to the viewers now. One way or another, it'll be over soon.'

Tilly looked away. Yes, it would all be over soon, and that was probably just as well. The tension over the last few days had been almost unendurable, erupting at last in that stupid row over how to spell Anthony. She had been torn between not wanting their time together to end and wishing that it would so that she wouldn't have to live any longer with the breathless churning that gripped her whenever she looked at Campbell.

She was going to miss him so much, but there would be a certain relief in not having to fight the attraction any more. She had to think about that, and not about how empty the kitchen was going to be without his solid, straight but somehow steadying presence. She couldn't allow herself to think about how the severe expression relaxed when he was amused, crinkling the corners of his eyes and deepening the creases on either side of his mouth.

His mouth...she definitely couldn't afford to let herself think about that. *Or* his hands. Or the whole lean, muscled length of him.

It was extraordinary how a man so austere and restrained-looking on the surface could have reduced her to a state of feverish desire where the most casual brush against each other left her boneless, a smile would stop the breath in her throat and the touch of his hand was like a jolt of electricity.

Campbell wasn't romantic, he wasn't passionate, he wasn't any of the things Tilly yearned for in a man. He was tough and terse and acerbic, and she wanted him in a way she had never wanted anyone before.

But she couldn't have him. He was leaving. Remember that, Tilly?

She wished now that she had ignored his reluctance and told him how she felt after that kiss. At least they could have had a week together and she would have had some memories. But it was too late now. Tomorrow he would be gone.

There was no point being miserable about it, Tilly decided, forcing her shoulders back and fixing on a bright smile. She had made a choice and now she had to live with it. In the meantime, it was Cleo's wedding, and Cleo would want her to enjoy herself.

She threw herself into the party spirit with a touch of desperation, and it wasn't, after all, that hard. She knew lots of people and there was a very happy atmosphere, especially after Cleo and Tony performed a dance routine for all their guests. This seemed to involve Cleo pushing Tony around the floor and hissing exasperated instructions at him. Clearly, he didn't have a clue what he was supposed to be doing, and their audience was soon laughing uproariously.

Campbell looked at Tilly beside him. She was almost doubled over, helpless with laughter. Her face was alight, her eyes glowing, and he was seized by the urge to touch her, to hold her, to draw her warmth and her light around him.

So strong was the impulse that he had to make himself move away, but the more he tried to concentrate on making conversation with the other guests, the more aware he was of Tilly, scintillating, sparkling, in the background. She was talking and laughing, smiling, hugging friends, kissing acquaintances on the cheeks, and Campbell was gradually consumed by the longing to stride over, take hold of her and pull her away, outside.

To make her smile at him. Touch *him*. Kiss *him*.

By the time Tilly danced over to him at last, he was in no state to be sensible. He couldn't remember why resisting her had ever seemed like an option, let alone a necessity, and every stern resolution evaporated as she stopped in front of him. Buoyed up by champagne and the party atmosphere, she was attempting to belly dance but succeeding only in looking faintly ridiculous and yet incredibly sexy at the same time.

'Come on, Campbell,' she cried over the throb of the music. 'Show us what you're made of!'

And Campbell gave in to the terrible temptation that had been tormenting him all evening and took her by the waist.

'How can I refuse an invitation like that?'

At the touch of his hands, Tilly abruptly lost her rhythm. She stumbled and would have fallen if he hadn't been holding her and instinctively she put her hands on his arms to balance herself.

And then she was lost.

The feverish gaiety that had swept her through the evening evaporated without warning, sucked away with the music and the laughter and the other guests behind some invisible barrier where everything was muted, leaving the two of them stranded and alone, while the space shrank around them, shortening the air and making her heart boom and thump and thunder in her ears.

It felt as if an insistent hand in the small of her back was pushing her towards Campbell, and it was a relief to give in, to let herself lean against him with a tiny sigh, knowing there was nothing else that she could do, that there was something more powerful than either of them forcing them together, insisting on balancing his hard strength and solidity with her softness and her warmth.

And, once she *had* given in, it felt so wonderful that Tilly wondered why she had ever believed that she ought to resist.

Afterwards, she could remember nothing about the music they danced to that evening. She knew only that she was holding Campbell at last, that he was holding her, and that they were dancing together.

Her arms slid up to his shoulders, savouring the feel of the powerful muscles beneath his jacket. Her face was almost touching his throat. She could see the pulse beating below his ear, and she breathed in the scent of clean skin and clean shirt and something that was purely Campbell.

Close to him, she felt light and shimmery, lit by the glow spreading through her, a glow that was burning brighter and brighter the tighter he held her. They were barely dancing, barely swaying, but his lips were against her hair, drifting downwards, and Tilly's mouth curved expectantly. They would reach her cheek soon. They would graze her jaw, would nuzzle the lobe of her ear until she gasped and arched, and then she would turn her head and they would kiss, and that glow would ignite into a flame, a *fire*…

Adrift in anticipation, Tilly didn't realise that the music had stopped until Campbell straightened slowly. His hands fell from her, but he held her still with his eyes, eyes that could look deep inside her and could surely see the desire beating there.

'Shall we go?' he asked, his voice deep and low, and Tilly nodded.

Still snared in the magic of the dance, she sat wordlessly beside Campbell as he drove the van back to the house. It seemed a long time since they had driven in the other direction, laughing helplessly as they'd followed their police escort.

Campbell was silent, too. They hadn't spoken at all, as if something stronger than both of them had them in its grip, but perhaps she had it wrong? The headlights from passing cars swept over them, illuminating the austere profile, and Tilly's stomach hollowed.

It won't happen again, he had told her after that one devastating kiss, and she knew instinctively that he would keep that promise. If she wanted him, it would be up to her to tell him that. Did she dare?

Careful, her heart reminded her. *Remember how much it hurt last time. You don't have to do this if you don't want to.* The choice was hers.

But with every sense, every cell in her body, clamouring for his touch, it didn't feel like much of a choice to Tilly. She had gone too far to turn back now. The best she could do was protect herself as best she could.

Just one night... What harm could there be in that? Her heart was on guard, so if she could just keep her emotions in check and make it clear to Campbell that she wasn't looking for anything more than a night together, surely that wouldn't be risking too much?

Campbell turned into her drive and parked outside the front door. He cut the lights and turned off the engine, plunging them into darkness and utter silence. For a moment, they both sat completely still, staring straight ahead through the windscreen.

It was up to her, Tilly remembered.

She moistened her lips. 'Do you remember being on that mountain?' she asked. She wanted to sound cool, but of course her voice came out thready and wavering.

'Ben Nuarrh?' Campbell turned to look at her, his expression impossible to read in the darkness, but she thought she detected an undercurrent of amusement. 'How could I forget?'

'Do…you remember how we talked about fantasies?' Tilly made herself persevere.

'Yes,' he said cautiously.

She took a deep breath. 'I've got a fantasy now.'

'Does it involve food?'

That was definitely a smile in his voice. Tilly wasn't sure whether that was an encouraging sign or not.

'Not this time.' She hesitated. 'It involves you.'

Campbell stilled, and this time when he spoke the laughter had vanished. 'Tell me.'

And, suddenly, it was easy after all.

'Well, in my fantasy we're here, like we are now, in the dark, but there's no future, no plans, no responsibilities, no being sensible. There's just the two of us and one night together.'

She swallowed. 'In my fantasy, you reach out and lay your palm against my cheek,' she said, and Campbell lifted his arm slowly and caressed her face.

The warmth of his hand made Tilly suck in a breath. 'You tell me that you're leaving tomorrow, but you want to spend tonight with me.'

'I want to spend tonight with you.' His voice was so low, it seemed to reverberate down her spine. 'I haven't been able to think about anything else for weeks now.'

'Hey, this is my fantasy,' said Tilly shakily. 'No improvising.'

'Sorry.' Even in the dim light she could see the quiver at the corner of his mouth, and she felt her bones liquefy.

'Then you tell me you haven't been able to think about anything else for weeks now.'

The quiver deepened. 'Then what?'

'Then...then you kiss me.'

There was a pause, then Campbell let his hand drift down to her throat, where it curved beneath her silky hair so that he could pull her with a breathless lack of speed towards him. Very, very slowly, he bent his head until their mouths met.

'Like this?' he murmured.

His lips were gentle at first, tantalising and persuasive, until Tilly leant into him with a tiny sigh as she parted her own and wound her arms around his neck to pull him closer.

It was so delicious to be able to kiss him, to taste him, to feel his hand at her knee, sliding insistently under her skirt as they kissed and kissed and kissed again—deep, sweet kisses that grew harder and hungrier with every moment.

'Yes, like that,' she said unsteadily, tipping back her head as Campbell's lips trailed down her throat, and his free hand flicked open the buttons on her jacket. 'Exactly like that.'

She gasped as she felt him smile against her skin, and his fingers tightened possessively on her thigh.

Kissing his way lazily back up to her earlobe, Campbell let his hands continue their delicious exploration. 'Do I get to tell you my fantasy yet?' he whispered in her ear and it was Tilly's turn to smile.

'What's yours?'

'You beg me to take you inside, right now, and make love to you all night.'

'I'm not sure I like the idea of begging,' Tilly managed and a laugh shook his big frame.

'It's my fantasy now,' he pointed out. 'Fair's fair.'

'How about if I ask nicely instead?'

'How nicely?'

She laughed, intoxicated with his touch. 'Very nicely,' she said. 'I'll ask very, very nicely.'

Pushing him back into his seat, she clambered into his lap so that she was straddling him, and took his face between her palms, covering it with teasing kisses, tickling him with her tongue.

'Please,' she whispered, kissing her way down his throat in her turn. 'Please, Campbell. Please take me to bed and make love to me all night.'

'That's *quite* nice,' said Campbell in a ragged voice. 'Ask me again.'

He was pushing aside her jacket, tugging up her silk camisole, and Tilly shuddered and writhed with pleasure as his hands closed on her bare skin.

'Please,' she gasped again. 'You don't need to pretend anything. It's not about love. It's not about forever. It's just you and me and one night together. Make love to me, please.'

'Well, since you asked so nicely…'

Somehow they got out of the van, but they couldn't bear to let go of each other, couldn't bear to stop kissing. For long, mindless minutes, Campbell pressed her against the driver's door and Tilly didn't care that the handle was digging into her hip, cared only that she could hold him and touch him and kiss him back.

At last they made it to the front door. There was a short delay while Tilly fumbled for keys, distracted by Campbell kissing her shoulder and the nape of her neck, as his hot, hungry hands explored beneath her open jacket. Her fingers shook as she inserted the key impatiently and they practically fell through the door, still kissing.

Unheeded, Tilly's bag fell to the floor, closely followed by the jacket Campbell was peeling from her shoulders. He pushed her back against the door and she arched beneath his touch, gasping his name as she clutched her fingers in his hair, incoherent with desire.

'What happens in your fantasy now?' Tilly asked shakily when he raised his head at last, and Campbell took her by the hand and tugged her towards her bedroom.

'I'll show you.'

Tilly mumbled and brushed at something on her face before rolling over to bury her face in a pillow.

'Wake up, Jenkins. It's breakfast time.' Campbell's voice, warm and threaded with laughter, slowly penetrated her sleep and she stirred, opening sleep-clouded eyes to find him sitting on the edge of the bed, tickling her cheek with a finger.

He smiled at her. 'I thought I'd make your fantasy come true.'

Tilly pulled herself blearily up on to the pillows. She felt boneless with pleasure still, as if she had been drenched in honeyed delight, and the colour rose in her cheeks as the memories of the night before flooded back.

'I think you've already done that,' she said, and he smiled.

'This is a different fantasy. You told me all about it on Ben Nuarrh. Don't you remember? You wanted to wake up with coffee and croissants.'

Brought by a gorgeous lover. Tilly did remember, and the fact that he did, too, made her heart turn over.

'Look,' said Campbell as he laid the tray on the bed. 'The sun's even shining.'

There was a ridiculous lump in her throat. Tilly swallowed. 'So it is.' Leaning forward, she made a big deal of breathing in the smell of coffee. 'Mmm,' she murmured appreciatively and unfolded a tea towel to find the promised croissants. They were even warm.

She lifted her eyes to his green ones and wondered how she could ever have thought of them as cold.

'Where did you find these?'

'At the shop on the corner. You were dead to the world so I thought it would be worth a trip.' He nodded down at the tray. 'I realise the orange juice wasn't specified in your fantasy. That's my own innovation.'

Tilly was overwhelmed. Nobody had ever done anything like this for her before.

Last night, he had made her feel beautiful and desirable; this morning, instead of being desperate to leave, as she had half expected, he had gone to all this trouble to make her a special breakfast. He had *remembered* something she had once said and acted on it to make her feel special.

He made her feel loved.

If you were talking fantasies, this one was hard to beat.

'Hey, stop that!' she said, deciding that her only option was to make a joke of it. It was that or cry. 'It's not fair to start being thoughtful and perfect now you're about to go!'

'You could come with me.'

'What, to the States?' she asked, keeping the smile fixed on her face and assuming that he was joking as well.

'Why not?'

Her smile faded as they looked at each other. He couldn't mean it.

Tilly didn't want to think that making love had been a mistake, but she was afraid that it probably had been. Now she was going to have to live with the memory of the heart-stopping rapture, of the consuming pleasure and the heady delight of touching and being touched, of the fierceness of the passion they had discovered together. Night after night, she would have to lie in this bed and remember and know that she would never feel that again. She would never hold him again, never kiss him again.

She would have to say goodbye and it would hurt.

She was a fool, in fact, but Tilly couldn't regret it. Just one night, they had agreed, and what a night it had been.

And now Campbell was suggesting—seriously?—that she wouldn't need to say goodbye after all.

There was no point in denying that she was tempted, but deep down Tilly knew this was just another fantasy. Maybe fantasies could come true for a night, even for a morning, but how could they endure day after day, in the harsh realities of life?

She couldn't go to the States with Campbell. Her business was here, her friends were here. And what would he do with her over there? He was a high-powered businessman, she was a homely cake-maker. Their lives would barely coincide. Tilly had seen what different aspirations had done to her parents' marriage.

No, she had ignored her sensible side long enough. This was no time to believe in fantasies. It could never work. Campbell was driven by the need to win. His priorities were different, his life was different.

And he had an ex-wife to get out of his system.

Tilly had forgotten Lisa for a while, but now she remembered the way Campbell had talked about her. He might not love Lisa any more, but there was definitely some unresolved business there, and Tilly had no intention of being a distraction until he found out what he really wanted. She had been that for Olivier, and she wasn't doing it again.

'I don't think that would work,' she told Campbell, choosing her words carefully.

'Because…?'

'Because we're too different. Last night was wonderful, but perhaps it was wonderful because it was just one night,' she tried to explain. 'We both got what we needed without having to think about the consequences.'

Campbell eyed her thoughtfully. 'Did we? What did you get?'

'I got Olivier out of my system,' she told him, lifting her

chin slightly. It was the truth, but not the whole truth, as they said. 'My friends have had this theory that I'd never get over him properly until I had a fling with someone to restore my confidence. And I've done that now,' she finished.

There was a tiny pause. 'I'm glad I was able to help,' said Campbell with a touch of acid.

'You know what I mean,' said Tilly. 'I mean, come on, Campbell, you know I'm right. You're leaving the country, we've got completely different lives. How could it ever be more than a night?'

All right, maybe she *was* right, thought Campbell. The trouble was that it didn't *feel* right. It felt all wrong.

But what could he do? He could hardly force her to go with him. He wasn't sure where the idea that she could go to the States with him had come from. The truth was that he had been almost as surprised by his suggestion as Tilly had been. The words seemed to have come from nowhere, and yet once they were out, they made perfect sense and Campbell had been taken aback by how badly he'd wanted Tilly to agree, how disappointed he had been when she'd said no.

Of course she was right. There was no way it could work. It was madness to even think about it. He would leave here and go to his new life in the States, and he would be grateful then that she had saved them both a lot of awkwardness by rejecting his impulsive offer.

'OK,' he admitted, 'you're right. It was just a night, but it was a great one.'

Smiling, Tilly relaxed back against the pillows. 'Yes, it was,' she said softly, 'and now you've brought breakfast, it's a wonderful morning.'

'Then let's make the most of it,' said Campbell, leaning across the tray to kiss her. 'It's not over yet.'

That had been a mistake, too, he realised much later as he watched the taxi draw up outside the house.

Had they really thought making love again would make it easier to say goodbye? Breakfast had been ruined, of course, but neither of them had cared. They had made fresh coffee eventually and reheated the croissants and ate them together, neither of them wanting to think about the minutes ticking away.

Now the moment they had both been dreading all morning had arrived.

Tilly came outside to the taxi with him. She watched as he threw his bag into the back and then turned to her.

'Well, I guess this is it,' he said.

'Yes.' Her throat tightened painfully. 'But I'll see you at the ceremony when they announce the winners. You are coming back for that, aren't you?'

'Of course,' he said, thinking that was not for another three months.

Once he would have been impatient to find out whether he had won. Now all he could think was that it meant three months without Tilly.

And, after that, the rest of his life without her.

It would be fine, he told himself. Once he was in New York, there would be so much to do, he wouldn't have time to miss her. He would be making a new life, being even more successful than before. He would be relieved that Tilly had been sensible.

He wouldn't feel the way he did now.

He looked for the last time into Tilly's dark, beautiful blue eyes, knowing that he could never tell her how he felt. So he reached for her instead, and she melted into him and they kissed, a bittersweet kiss that went on and on because neither could bear to let the other go.

'I'm glad Keith pushed me into taking part in this stupid programme,' Campbell confessed against her hair at last. 'I'm glad Greg broke his leg.'

'I'm glad you were the one who got to push me down that cliff,' said Tilly.

'I'm glad about last night, too.'

Tilly was terribly afraid that she was going to cry. She couldn't do that, not after being so brave all morning. 'Me, too.' She swallowed, hard. 'Now, get in that taxi and go before I start getting all sloppy!'

'All right,' said Campbell.

He held her tight against him for one last hard kiss and then he let her go. 'Goodbye, Jenkins. Don't go fulfilling any more fantasies without me.'

Tilly's determined smile wobbled. 'Don't call me Jenkins,' she managed with difficulty.

Her heart was cracking, tearing, as she watched him get into the taxi. 'Goodbye,' she said, but it was barely more than a whisper.

Campbell leant forward to tell the driver to take him to the station, then he looked back at Tilly and lifted a hand in farewell. She waved back, barely able to see through her tears, and then the taxi was pulling away, turning on to the street, and he was gone.

Tilly took a fortifying gulp of champagne. She probably shouldn't have ordered a glass in her room, but she badly needed something to steady her nerves. In a few minutes, she would have to go downstairs and see Campbell again, and she had no idea how she was going to handle it. For three months now, she had longed to see him, but now the moment was almost upon her she was terrified that she would simply go to pieces.

The programme had been screened the week before. Suzy

had done a good job and it had been very cleverly edited, with a fair balance between all the contestants at each stage and good coverage of their chosen charities.

Expecting it to be hidden in the daytime schedule some-where, Tilly had been taken aback at how popular the pro-gramme had proved, and she had been overwhelmed at how many viewers had voted. Perfect strangers had come up to her in the street and told her that they hoped she would win, and the hospice had reported a flood of donations since they had been featured.

Tonight was the final ceremony when they would announce the winners, and the charities who would receive the winning donations. Tilly knew she ought to be nervous about the results, but all she could think about was seeing Campbell.

It had been three months. Three months of telling herself it was all for the best. Three months of trying to forget the night they had spent together.

Three months of missing him.

'That's what comes of forcing people out of their ruts,' she had raged to her brothers. 'I was perfectly happy until you made me do that stupid television programme.'

'We were only trying to help you get over Olivier,' they protested.

'Well, don't help any more!'

The kitchen was so empty without Campbell, her bed so lonely. It wasn't just a physical ache either. Tilly hadn't realised how alive she had felt in his presence, how everything had seemed to click into place when he'd been there. She missed talking to him, arguing with him, laughing with him… She even missed being exasperated by him. That was how bad it was.

Time and again, she'd tried to convince herself that she didn't really know Campbell at all. They had spent a matter of days together. She knew nothing about his life, his home, his friends. It was silly to build one night into such a huge deal. Much better to treat it as the brief fling she had insisted it was.

But deep down, she was convinced that she *did* know him. She knew the way the crease at the corner of his mouth deepened when he was amused. She knew exactly how he turned his head, how his brows contracted, the way he would look at her and shake his head in exasperated disbelief. There had been so many times when she'd wanted to turn to him and tell him her thoughts, and she'd always known exactly how he would reply—usually irritably, of course, but Tilly wouldn't have cared if only he had been there to reply for himself.

All the participants had been sent a copy of the final programme in advance. Tilly had watched it with Cleo and Tony, although she'd longed to be able to see it on her own so that she could freeze the picture whenever Campbell was on the screen.

Most of the shots were of the two of them together. There she was, clutching Campbell's neck at the top of that wretched cliff, falling on to the muddy river bank, playing the fool on the mountain top.

Tilly's throat had ached as she'd watched herself. She remembered it all so clearly. She could practically smell the air and feel the breeze in her face. It was as if Campbell were still beside her, making her tingle with the astringency of his presence, the touch of his hand, the heart-twisting quiver of amusement at the corner of his mouth.

There were clips from the video diaries, too. She rambled and Campbell was cool and concise. Everyone laughed at Campbell in the pink apron, but the most telling scene was at Cleo and Tony's wedding when the camera caught Tilly looking at Campbell with her heart in her eyes.

Cleo had turned and fixed her with an accusing expression. 'Why didn't you tell me you were in love with him?' she demanded.

Tilly squirmed, but couldn't deny it. 'Because there's no point in loving him,' she tried to explain. 'Nothing's going to change. Campbell's living in the States now. Even if his ex-wife doesn't want him, there'll be any number of single women in New York waiting to snap him up.'

'You should tell him how you feel,' said Cleo, but Tilly shook her head.

'It's too late for that.'

She had heard from Suzy that Campbell would only be in the country for a couple of nights. He would come to the awards ceremony, but then he had some important meeting to get back to. They wouldn't have time to do more than say hello. There was no use expecting anything else.

That didn't stop Tilly from hoping, of course. Oh, she wasn't stupid. She knew nothing lasting could come of it, but that one night had been so special, she couldn't help wanting it again. If Campbell was still single, she had decided, she was going to suggest it to him. She was staying in the hotel where the ceremony was taking place. She would have a room, if he wanted to share it with her.

CHAPTER TEN

JUST one more night. Was that so much to ask?

Tilly didn't think it was, but she wasn't sure she would have the nerve to suggest it. She had been hoping the champagne would give her Dutch courage, but it didn't seem to have had much effect yet.

Draining the glass, she put it down on the dressing table with a sharp click and regarded her reflection for a doubtful moment. She was flushed with a mixture of excitement, champagne and nerves. Her hair tumbled to her shoulders, her eyes were dark and dubious.

Cleo had insisted that she buy a new dress, and Tilly was glad now that she had. It was a lovely midnight-blue, in a flattering cut that left her shoulders bare. She picked up a gossamer-fine shawl spangled with sequins and draped it over them. She was going to feel vulnerable enough asking Campbell to make love to her one last time without feeling half naked while she did it.

After all the agony of waiting, Tilly dithered so long getting ready that she was one of the last to arrive in the ballroom where the ceremony was to take place. There was to be a champagne reception first, followed by dinner, and then some excerpts from the programme would be screened before the final winners were announced. All the participants would be there, along with representatives from the charities they supported, and Suzy had promised a good turnout from the celebrities who had been invited, too.

The room was crowded by the time Tilly arrived, but she had eyes for only one man.

Hesitating in the doorway, she let her eyes travel slowly around until they locked with a pair of familiar green ones, and her heart seemed to collide with something hard and unyielding as all the oxygen was sucked instantly from the huge room.

Campbell.

He looked amazing. He was wearing a dinner jacket that only made him look leaner, tougher and more devastating than ever.

Unsmiling, Campbell walked towards her. 'You're late, Jenkins,' he said, and then he smiled into her eyes. 'But you look wonderful.'

Tilly stammered some reply. She wanted to throw her arms round him and pat him all over like a dog to make sure he was real. Had he really said she looked wonderful?

She should ask him now, in case he had meant it, and before her mascara smudged and her lipstick wore off and she spilt something down the front of her dress. *Would you like to come to my room later?* she could say and get the question out of the way, but she hesitated too long. Maybe it *was* a bit crass to come straight out with it, before they had even had a token conversation.

The trouble was that it was difficult to have any kind of conversation when she was overwhelmed by his nearness. There was so much she wanted to ask him, so much to say, but Tilly was tongue-tied with nerves, and when a waiter passed with a tray of champagne she grabbed a glass and practically downed it in one.

'Aren't you drinking?' she asked Campbell, seeing that he was holding a glass of orange juice.

'Not yet.'

'Keeping a clear head for your winning speech?'

The dent at the corner of his mouth deepened. 'Something like that.'

There was a pause.

'So…how are you?' Tilly tried to get things going again.

'Good. And you?'

'Oh, fine, fine,' she lied. 'Is the new job going well?'

Campbell nodded. 'I'd say so. We're poised to win back a major contract, and if we can pull that off, then we should be able to start turning things round. Unfortunately, the meeting is on Monday, so I'll have to fly back tomorrow.'

'It must be important.'

'It is. It could be make or break.'

'For you or for the company?'

'Both,' said Campbell.

Tilly looked around the crowded ballroom. 'It's a long way to come for one night,' she commented.

'Some things are worth coming a long way for.'

Winning would always be worth the effort for competitive types like Campbell, Tilly remembered. 'Beating Roger and his GPS?' she enquired, and he smiled then.

'Not just that,' he said.

Tilly wanted to ask what else would matter enough to him to make it worth crossing the Atlantic for a night, two at best, but before she had a chance they were joined by Maggie, director of the hospice. She had been invited with some of the nursing staff and representatives of patients' families, and they were all much more excited about the result than Tilly was.

'You both came over wonderfully,' Maggie told them, talking about the programme. 'I do hope you'll win, and not just for what it will mean to us. Thank you so much for everything you did, especially you, Tilly.'

'That's what I always want to say to you,' said Tilly, embarrassed. 'I'll never forget what everyone at the hospice did for Mum, and for Jack. Besides, the competition turned out to be fun, so I got more out of it than anyone. I loved every minute of it.'

Campbell arched a brow. 'What, even the abseil?'

'Well, not those few minutes,' she said, making a face at him, 'but just about everything else.'

I loved being with you, she wanted to tell him, but there never seemed to be an opportunity. People kept coming up and saying how much they had enjoyed the programme. Keith, Campbell's old PR Director, ribbed him about the pink apron, Suzy wanted to talk about what would happen when the winners were announced... Couldn't they see she just wanted to be alone with Campbell?

Tilly was so jittery with frustration and nerves that she didn't notice quite how often her glass was being refilled until the wooziness hit her with a vengeance. She was badly in need of some food to mop up the champagne, but it was already half past nine and there was no sign of dinner.

She had better try and clear her head a little or she would never make it through to the announcement of the winners.

Murmuring an excuse, Tilly slipped outside. The night air was cool and quiet after the hubbub of the ballroom and she took a deep breath. How was she ever going to get Campbell on his own with all these people around? Perhaps part of her had hoped that he would follow her, but there was no sign of him. Instead, she saw Jim, the cameraman, sneaking out for a smoke.

Jim was a chatty type and, if he noticed her, he would be bound to come over and talk. It wasn't that Tilly disliked him, but there was only one man she wanted with her right then, and she made a show of digging out her mobile as if she was about to make an important call.

Out of the corner of her eye, she saw Jim veer away but,

having got that far, she thought she might as well switch the phone on. Cleo had said that she would text her to wish her luck, and Seb and Harry might remember what a big night it was for her, too.

Sure enough, there was a text message from Cleo, and another informing her that she had a message on her voicemail. Feeling virtuous without a glass of champagne in her hand, Tilly dialled up the service to listen.

It was Harry, and all thoughts of champagne were promptly driven from her mind. Horrified, she listened to his message and looked wildly round, instinctively seeking Campbell.

Campbell saw her hurry back into the ballroom and one look at her face had him striding towards her. 'What is it?' he asked sharply.

Tilly grabbed at him. 'Oh, thank goodness I've found you! It's Seb,' she said, her voice threaded with panic. 'I've just had a message from Harry. There's been an accident and Seb's in hospital... Harry said something about operating and needing me as next of kin.'

Her eyes were huge as she stared up at him. 'I don't know what to do. I know I should stay for the hospice, but I need to go to Seb. What if he's really hurt? What if he's...?'

Her voice broke, unable to finish the sentence, and Campbell gripped her firmly by both arms. 'Tell me exactly what Harry said,' he said, and Tilly drew a steadying breath as she felt the strength of his hands holding her, calming her, sending reassurance seeping through her.

'Listen to his message,' she said, holding out the phone, and Campbell put it to his ear. Harry was rambling rather than incoherent. He sounded shaken, but not desperate, and he had even ended by telling Tilly she wasn't to worry. Campbell almost smiled at that bit. Harry clearly didn't know his sister very well. There was no way Tilly wasn't going to worry after a message like that.

'Which hospital does he mean?' he asked her, hoping to get her to focus on details rather than the unknown.

'The local one in Allerby. They were both back this weekend to see friends. There was some party…' Tilly ran her hands distractedly through her hair. 'They'll all have been out playing the fool…you know what boys that age are like.'

'How are you going to get back?' Campbell asked and she looked at him, grateful that he wasn't going to waste time trying to dissuade her.

'I suppose it's too late to get a train… It'll take too long to get to the station from here. I'll have to drive,' she decided wildly. 'I'll hire a car.'

'You've been drinking.'

'Taxi, then,' she said with a touch of desperation.

'I'll drive you,' said Campbell. 'I've got a car for the couple of days I'm here, and I've been on orange juice all evening. You go and get your things.'

She stared at him, longing to put herself in his capable hands but horribly aware that she shouldn't. She should be looking after herself.

'You can't,' she said, fresh problems rearing their ugly heads. 'What about the announcement?'

'I'll explain to Maggie. If we win, she can accept the cheque for us. This whole thing has been about the hospice anyway, so I can't see there'll be a problem. I'll have a word with Suzy, too.'

'But it'll take hours to drive to Allerby from here!' With a strangely detached part of her mind, Tilly noticed that she was actually wringing her hands. 'You'll never get back in time for your flight tomorrow.'

'There will be other flights,' Campbell said.

'What about your meeting, though? You said it was really important.'

'It's not as important as getting you to Seb. Now, I'm not

going to tell you not to worry,' he went on without giving her time to react, 'but you don't need to panic. We'll get on our way and you can ring Harry and find out what's happening. You'll feel better when you've got more information.'

Tilly let herself be persuaded. She knew she shouldn't be relying on Campbell like this, but he was exactly what she needed. He was calm and competent and he was going to take her to Seb.

He dealt with all the practicalities, which meant that all she had to do was to bundle her things into her bag and hurry down to where he had the car already waiting. In a fever to get to the hospital, she hadn't even taken the time to change and was still in her blue ball gown.

At first, Tilly sat rigidly staring ahead, too tense to think about anything except what might be waiting for her at the hospital, but, as the miles passed, she gradually succumbed to the quiet reassurance of Campbell's presence and leant back inch by inch until she could relax into the luxurious leather seat.

Only then did she let herself think about the man beside her. Campbell hadn't wasted time changing either. Like most men, the severe lines of a dinner jacket suited him beautifully. Tilly eyed his profile from under her lashes, and something about the angle of his cheek made her ache.

Be careful what you wish for. Wasn't that the saying? She had longed to be alone with him, and now here they were, driving through the dark in the quiet, powerful car, but she was too consumed by anxiety to be able to say any of the things she had wanted to say to him. There would be no invitation to her room, no last night of passion, no kiss goodbye.

Tilly's heart twisted at the opportunity lost, but then she immediately felt guilty. How could any of that matter when Seb was injured?

Campbell's car was fast and comfortable and he drove it the

way he did everything else, with an austere competence and utter control. He let Tilly sit quietly when she wanted to, and when she wanted to talk about her brothers, he listened.

'They were always trouble, even as little boys,' she remembered with a wobbly smile. 'It's not that they're bad boys. They can be lovely, but they can be thoughtless and irresponsible like a lot of young men, too, and they egg each other on, just the way they used to do when they were toddlers.

'You'd think they'd be growing out of it now.' She sighed. 'They're twenty. I keep hoping they'll settle down when they graduate and have to get jobs…' Tilly trailed off as she remembered that Seb might never graduate and fear clutched at her afresh.

'It's not just Seb I'm frightened for,' she confessed in a low voice. 'It's Harry, too. They've always been so close. If anything happens to Seb…' She swallowed hard. 'Harry won't be able to bear it, I know he won't.'

She was twisting her fingers in her lap, and Campbell reached out and covered them with one big, warm hand. It felt incredibly reassuring.

'Harry will be with Seb now,' he said. 'His phone will have to be switched off in the hospital, and that's why you can't get through, but at least that means they're together.'

Tilly often wondered afterwards how she would have got through that night without Campbell. He was a fast driver, but even so it took over four hours to get to the hospital. They stopped once to fill the car up, and he bought her some coffee and chocolate biscuits, which steadied her a little, and he didn't try to tell her everything would be all right.

When they finally drew up outside the hospital, he let Tilly out so that she could run inside while he found somewhere to park. They still hadn't been able to contact Harry, and Campbell hoped he would be there or Tilly would be frantic with worry about him, too.

Fortunately, Harry was where he was supposed to be for once. Campbell eventually tracked Tilly down to a waiting area linking three wards, and found her sitting with her brother on the kind of rigid seats he always associated with airport departure lounges—the ones specially designed to discourage you from getting comfortable at all, let alone lying down.

Tilly was looking crumpled and tear-stained, but she jumped up when she saw Campbell and came instinctively towards him with her hands held out.

Campbell gripped them between his own, afraid of what the tear stains might mean. 'Seb?' he asked tensely.

'He's going to be OK.' Tilly pulled her hands away so that she could search for a tissue. 'He's sleeping, but I've seen him, and the nurse said everything went well. I'm so relieved, I can't stop crying. It's stupid, isn't it?'

'Here,' said Campbell, producing a clean handkerchief, and she took it with a watery smile and blew her nose.

'Thank you,' she said gratefully.

'Tell me what happened.'

'I haven't heard the full story yet, but it sounds as if they were all messing around at some party, and walking along walls. Seb fell badly, and broke his arm and his ankle, which will teach you not to be so silly,' she added with a darkling glance at Harry. 'It's lucky you're not both in hospital!'

Belatedly realising what all the crying must have done to her make-up, Tilly used the handkerchief to wipe under her eyes. Sure enough, it came away with great black streaks. Now not only did she look like a panda, but she had ruined Campbell's handkerchief.

'Apparently his arm had a particularly nasty fracture, so they had to reset it under anaesthetic, but he should be fine.'

'I *told* you not to worry,' said Harry defensively. He turned to Campbell. 'I can't believe she dragged you all the way up here! Seb'll be furious when he finds out.'

'It was no problem.' Campbell intervened quickly before a full-blown argument developed. 'I was glad to help.'

'I'm afraid it *was* a problem,' Tilly said ruefully when Harry had gone off to pass on the good news about Seb, and probably to continue partying, as she had observed with a sigh.

'You've missed the ceremony, your flight and your meeting,' she reminded Campbell. 'I feel terrible now. I've dragged you all the way up here for a broken arm! I'm so sorry,' she said, scrubbing absently at her face with the handkerchief. 'I should have found out more before I panicked.'

Too tired to think what to do next, Tilly dropped back down on to the bench seating under a framed print of some anonymous seaside scene. Someone had done their best, but it was a depressing place. A selection of tired-looking magazines lay on the low table with a couple of discarded plastic cups of coffee from the vending machine down the hall. At this hour of the night, the wards around them were quiet, the lighting dim.

After a moment, Campbell sat down beside her. 'You needed to be here,' he said, 'and I needed to be with you.'

'You had much more important things to do,' she said, balling the handkerchief between her hands, but Campbell shook his head.

'No,' he said, his voice quiet and firm. 'Nothing could be more important than this.'

Tilly looked at him then, her eyes dark and blue and puzzled, and something she read in his expression made her heart begin to thud.

He was tall and solid and *close* beside her and, despite her exhaustion, the receding anxiety about Seb was being replaced by a breathless awareness of Campbell, who had driven through the night for her, who had been there for her when she'd needed him.

She looked around the waiting area, at the discarded cups and uncomfortable seats. Her dress was creased and crumpled and there was a stain down the front where she must have spilt some coffee in the car. The champagne she had drunk what seemed like a lifetime ago had left her with a dull headache. Wiping the handkerchief under her eyes once more, Tilly sighed.

'This wasn't how I imagined tonight.'

'What did you think it would be like?' Campbell asked her quietly. He wasn't touching her, but she could feel his eyes on her face.

'I thought we'd be drinking champagne with a lot of glamorous people,' she said, not looking at him. 'I bought this dress specially.' She rubbed at the stain with a rueful expression. 'I wanted to look nice. I imagined us listening for the winners to be announced together, hearing our names and going up to collect the cheque for the hospice.' She smiled wistfully. 'I thought it would be great.'

'It would have been,' Campbell agreed.

Tilly nodded slowly. 'And then I imagined us celebrating together,' she went on, and she turned her head to look straight into his eyes while she told him the truth.

'I was going to suggest we go to my room so we could be alone,' she told him. 'I was going to tell you I hadn't been able to stop thinking about the night before you left. I was going to ask if we could spend one last night together.'

Campbell was sitting very still, staring at her, and she bit her lip. She might as well know the truth. 'What would you have said?'

A smile had started at the back of his eyes, giving her hope, so she wasn't expecting his answer. 'I would have said no,' he said.

'Oh.'

Tilly looked blindly away, a stricken expression in her dark blue eyes.

Very gently, Campbell reached out and laid his fingers along her jaw, turning her head back to make her face him again.

'I would have said no, I didn't want it to be a last night,' he told her softly. 'I'd have said I didn't want to say goodbye the next morning, the way we did before. If we were going to spend the night together, Tilly—and you have no idea how much I wanted that!—I wanted it to be a beginning for us, not an ending.'

Unable to speak, still reeling from that 'no', Tilly could only stare uncomprehendingly at him, and he smiled crookedly.

'This isn't how I imagined this evening either, Tilly,' he said. 'The reason I wasn't drinking earlier was because I was nervous.'

She found her voice at that. 'You? Nervous? I don't believe it!'

'It's true. But it wasn't about whether we won or not. I didn't fly all this way to hear whether the viewers thought my cake was worth more than Roger's GPS. I came to tell you that I've missed you.'

His voice was very deep as he released her face, tossed the handkerchief she was still clutching aside and took both her hands in his warm grasp.

'I came to tell you that I've thought about you every day. There I was in New York, living in a penthouse, surrounded by everything I could possibly want, and all I could think about was you, and how I wished you were there with me.

'I thought about that last night we had, too, Tilly,' he went on. 'I kept remembering what you said about it just being a fling to get over Olivier. You were so definite about us having different lives and not wanting part of mine, and I told myself that I had to respect that, but then they sent me the advance tape of the programme.'

He paused, remembering. 'I watched you on the screen, and you were so gorgeous and funny and I saw myself and it was blindingly obvious that I'd wanted you right from the start. It made me realise that I had to try and persuade you to change your mind.

'You weren't the only one with plans to say something tonight,' he told Tilly with a half smile. 'All I could think about was getting you alone somehow so I could tell you how I felt. I was going to tell you that I love you and need you, that life's no fun without you now. I was going to ask you to marry me,' said Campbell. 'Is it any wonder I was nervous?'

Tilly was struggling to take it all in. This had to be a dream, she thought. That would explain everything. She had drunk too much champagne and fallen asleep and any minute now she would wake up and her heart would break to realise that none of it was real.

But Campbell *seemed* real. This awful waiting room seemed real, and so did the biscuit crumbs in her skirt and the unmistakable hospital smell.

'If I had had the chance to say all that, Tilly, if I had been able to ask you to marry me,' said Campbell quietly, 'what would *you* have said?'

Maybe it *was* real. Tilly's heart quivered, ballooning with hope, and her eyes were huge as she looked back at him. If this were a dream, this was the point when she would fling her arms around him, laughing with delight, when she would tell him that she loved him, too, and that of course she would marry him.

But if it wasn't, if this was real after all, she would have to remember all the real reasons she hadn't told him that she loved him before.

'I think,' she said slowly at last, 'that I would have asked you if you were sure that you were over your ex-wife.'

Campbell nodded. 'That would have been a good question,' he said seriously. 'I saw Lisa in New York. I needed to see her again.'

His fingers twined around Tilly's, warm and strong. 'I hated it when she left me, but you made me realise that I hated losing more than I hated losing *her*. We weren't right together, and I know now that was as much my fault as hers.'

He paused, wondering how to explain the relief of meeting Lisa and realising that he felt nothing. 'Lisa's happy now. She's found someone who's right for her, and I'm glad for her. I wish in lots of ways that I'd faced up to seeing her again, but maybe I needed to meet you before I could understand that she did the right thing when she walked away. You taught me a lot.'

'Me?' Tilly was astonished. 'I only taught you how to make a sponge cake! I don't know how to do anything else.'

'You know more than that,' said Campbell. 'You're the one who taught me that success isn't always about what you have, or what you achieve. It's about how you live your life. You've always known that. You look after your brothers and you care for your friends, and they love you in return. You live where you want, doing a job you enjoy. You do what's right, and you do it with warmth and laughter. In the things that matter, you're the most successful person I know, Tilly.'

Tilly gulped, tried to speak and failed utterly. Nobody had ever said anything like that to her before.

Smiling at her expression, Campbell tightened his hold on her hand. 'So, no, this isn't how I imagined tonight,' he said. 'I imagined I would tell you all of that without making a fool of myself, or stumbling and stuttering too much when I asked you to marry me. I'd even let myself imagine you'd say yes.'

His smile twisted. 'I thought we would be in bed by now, loving each other, instead of which we're sitting here in this crummy waiting room, and you're tired and worried and we're both miles away from where we should be, but I don't care. I don't care what happens as long as I'm with you.'

Tilly's heart was beating so loudly by then that she was afraid it was going to burst right through her ribs. She so badly wanted to believe him…but how could she?

'But look at me,' she said helplessly. 'I'm a mess! I'm fat and piggy-eyed and my hair's a disaster and my dress is ruined!'

'You're not a mess,' he said. 'You're beautiful.'

'Don't make fun of me!'

'I'm not. God, Tilly, you have the self-confidence of a shrimp!' said Campbell, sounding almost his old exasperated self. 'Who cares if your dress is creased or your mascara's run? You're still gorgeous. Why won't you believe me?'

'Because…' Tilly gestured helplessly.

'Because that moron Olivier convinced you you weren't thin enough or smart enough or perfectly groomed enough for him?'

'I suppose so,' she muttered.

'And because your father made you think the same thing when you were just a little girl?'

'Probably.' She wouldn't meet his eyes.

'Come here,' said Campbell, pulling her on to his lap and holding her firmly with one arm while his free hand smoothed her hair away from her face. 'Do you remember that abseil?'

'Yes,' said Tilly cautiously, not quite ready to believe him, but wrapping her arms around his neck anyway. It seemed rude not to and, anyway, what else could she do with them when she was trapped on his lap like this?

'You didn't trust me then,' he reminded her. 'You begged me not to let you go.'

'I was terrified!'

'*Did* I let you go?'

'No,' she admitted.

'Did I tell you you could make it to the top of that mountain?'

'You did.'

'And was I right?'

A smile tugged at Tilly's mouth. 'I see where you're going with this,' she told him.

'Go on, admit it.' He grinned. 'I was right.'

She rolled her eyes. 'Yes, you were right.'

'I'm right about this, too,' said Campbell, and his smile

faded. 'You're gorgeous and sexy and warm and funny and I adore you and, if you'll marry me, I'll spend the rest of my life trying to make you happy.'

And then, because talking didn't seem to be getting him anywhere fast, he kissed her.

Tilly was lost the moment their lips met and she sank into him, giving back kiss for kiss, while happiness poured like liquid sunshine along her veins. 'I love you,' she confessed, mumbling between kisses. 'I love you, I love you.'

'At last!' Campbell pretended to grumble, holding her hard against him. 'I thought I was never going to get you to say it! *Now* will you marry me?'

'Do you promise not to let me go?'

'I promise,' he said gravely.

'In that case, I will,' she said, and he kissed her again.

'It's lucky you said that,' Campbell said when he came up for air at last. He dug around in the inside pocket of his jacket. 'I can give you this now.'

He produced a little box. 'I promised you roses once if we got through the competition,' he reminded her, 'but I'm hoping you might like this instead.'

Tilly's eyes widened, and he watched anxiously as she opened the box and drew a sharp gasp. Nestled in the velvet padding was a band of exquisite diamonds bracketing a deep, square-cut sapphire.

'It's the colour of your eyes,' he said.

For a long moment Tilly couldn't say anything. Her heart was too full to speak, and her eyes when she lifted them to his were shimmering with tears. 'Campbell…' was all she could manage.

The tears made Campbell nervous. 'Maybe you would rather choose it yourself?' he said hurriedly. 'We can change it if you want.'

'No.' Tilly stopped him with a kiss. 'It's perfect,' she told him with a shaky smile. 'I'm only crying because I'm so happy.'

Campbell let himself relax a little. 'Are you sure you like it?'

'I love it…almost as much as I love you, in fact!'

'Try it on.' Picking up the ring, he made Tilly hold out her left hand.

'I hope it's not too small,' she said, bracing herself for humiliation, but it slid on to her finger as if made for it. 'Oh, Campbell, it's beautiful,' she told him, her eyes starry as she kissed him again. 'Now I know you really *do* want to marry me,' she said. 'You had it planned down to the last detail!'

Campbell laughed with relief as he pulled her close. 'It didn't work out exactly as I'd planned, or we would be somewhere a lot more comfortable than this where I could make love to you the way I've been thinking about making love to you for the past three months.'

Tilly allowed herself a last kiss and slid off his knee. 'In that case,' she said, 'I think we should go home.'

'I was thinking I could give up my job in the States and come back here,' said Campbell as they walked down the quiet hospital corridors. 'I know you're happy here in Allerby, and I could find another role somewhere round here.'

Tilly thought about it while they waited for a lift. 'No,' she decided eventually. 'Not unless you have to find another job after missing that meeting!'

'I'm not going to miss it,' he said confidently. 'I'll get myself back there in time for it somehow, and then I'll come back and be with you.'

'I think I should go to you,' said Tilly. 'Harry and Seb have been going on at me to get out of my rut, so that's what I'll do,' she said bravely. 'I can make cakes in America as well as here.'

They walked hand in hand across the silent hospital grounds

to where Campbell had left his car. 'I'm nervous about the idea of a penthouse, though,' she admitted. 'I bet it's immaculate.'

He smiled down at her. 'We can buy a messy house if you like.'

'It's not the house, it's the kind of life you live.' Tilly hesitated, chewing her lip. 'I think I might be losing my nerve already! We're so different.' She looked anxiously at him. 'Do you really think if we get married we'll live happily ever after?'

Campbell stopped and turned to face her. 'I don't know,' he said honestly. 'We're bound to argue about stuff, and maybe things will be difficult sometimes, but we'll have to work it out together.'

Pulling her in to him, he rested his cheek against her hair. 'There are no guarantees, Tilly, but if you love me and I love you, and if we trust each other, I think we'll make it. I know it's a risk, but this time,' he said, 'we're going over the cliff together.'

Tilly smiled as she remembered that first morning and how terrified she had been at the end of that rope. What was it she had said to him then? She pulled back slightly so she could put her arms around his neck and draw his head down for a kiss warm with promise.

'Let's get on with it then,' she said.

Enveloped in a haze of delight, they were almost back at the house before they remembered the competition. Tilly switched on her phone to find a message from Suzy, the producer.

'Oh,' she said, and glanced at Campbell, hoping he wasn't going to be too disappointed. 'Apparently it was very close, but Roger and Leanne won in the end. There's a message from Maggie, too…'

She listened closely, then closed the phone. 'Maggie says she's really sorry we didn't win, but she wants to thank you for matching the winner's cheque with a donation to the hospice.'

Reaching across, she laid a hand on his thigh and smiled. 'That was generous of you.'

Campbell drew up outside Tilly's house and switched off the engine. 'For the record, I would have done it for Roger and Leanne's charities as well if we'd won,' he said with a shrug. 'The competition was just to make the programme more interesting for the viewers. I didn't want any of those good causes to miss out on money that could make a real difference.'

Leaning across the handbrake, he kissed her. 'I even arranged a donation to mountain rescue dog training.'

'Whatever for?'

'It turns out that was Greg's chosen charity, and I felt it was the least I owed him for breaking his leg and making it possible for me to meet you. It seems a bit unfair on the poor bloke, but I'll always be glad that he did!'

Tilly laughed as she got out of the car, but her expression was doubtful as they walked to the front door. 'Are you *sure* you don't mind that we didn't win?'

But Campbell, Mr Competitive, only smiled and put an arm around her. 'I'm here with you and we've got the rest of our lives together,' he said simply. 'I think we *are* the winners, don't you?'

When he put it like that, Tilly could only agree. Smiling, she found her keys and unlocked the door. 'Much as I hate to admit it, I think you're right about that, too!'

* * * * *

Mission:
Mountain Rescue

AMY ANDREWS

Dear Reader,

I'm honoured that *Mission:Mountain Rescue* has been chosen to be a part of this fabulous *Loving Our Heroes* collection along with two of my favourite authors India Grey and Jessica Hart. I've been reading up on Help for Heroes and have been amazed at their achievements. I'm so excited that Mills & Boon® are supporting this very worthy charity.

My grandfather was a WW2 digger. That's what we call them here, in Australia—diggers. There are multiple theories as to how this term originated, but it definitely stemmed from the battlefields of WW1 and we've been proud of it ever since. But I digress... He fought against the Japanese in New Guinea along the now infamous Kokoda Track—a 96 km, single-file, remote highland trail. He died when I was a little gir,l but the enduring image of the Aussie digger battling the enemy in the mud and filth of a New Guinea jungle has not only been ingrained on the Australian psyche but that of a proud granddaughter.

The digger in *Mission:Mountain Rescue* is an army medic. Medics, more so than nurses and doctors, have been on the front lines of conflict since wars began. They were there in New Guinea too. And so were the Fuzzy Wuzzy Angels—PNG nationals, still essentially living a highland tribal existence, who assisted and escorted injured Australian troops back down the Kokoda track. They nursed, fed, carried and sheltered. No known injured soldier that was still alive was ever abandoned by the Fuzzy Wuzzy Angels, even during heavy combat, and there is no doubt that our fatality count during that campaign would have been much higher without them.

Help for Heroes does wonderful things for injured servicemen and women. This November 11, along with remembering those who've given their lives in wars around the world and those still serving, I'll be remembering Help for Heroes and the incredible work they do. Please give them your support.

And enjoy the book.

Love,

Amy

As a twelve-year-old, **Amy Andrews** used to sneak off with her mother's romance novels and devour every page. She was the type of kid who daydreamed a lot, and carried a cast of thousands around in her head. From quite an early age she knew that it was her destiny to write. So, in between her duties as wife and mother, her paid job as Paediatric Intensive Care Nurse and her compulsive habit to volunteer, she did just that! Amy Andrews lives in Brisbane's beautiful Samford Valley with her very wonderful and patient husband, two gorgeous kids, a couple of black Labradors and six chooks.

To Private Roy Underwood, 2nd/9 Battalion Australian
Army.
My grandfather.

And to the Fuzzy Wuzzy Angels.

PROLOGUE

HOLLY briefly scanned the elegant room. Her eyes quickly assessing each male occupant. A glance at the creepy little man approaching fast made her search all the more desperate.

A man entered her peripheral vision and sauntered towards the bar. His short black hair, lightly streaked with grey was rumpled and his tie askew. He looked tired but there was an unmistakable air of authority about his tall erect frame. She felt a silly little flutter in the region of her heart. Richard.

'There you are, darling.' Her tone one of accusation. 'We must have had our wires crossed. I've been waiting for you in the other bar.'

A frown furrowed his forehead. Holly launched herself into his arms and he grabbed her shoulders to steady her from the clumsy impact. She pressed a kiss against his lips and he felt his surprise give way to stupor.

His lips remained immobile. He wanted them to move. After all, it had been a long time since she had kissed him with such blatant appreciation. A whole month since she had kissed him at all. And, heaven knew, he'd missed it like crazy. But he seemed to have developed a short circuit between his brain and the nerves to his face. In fact, his entire face seemed to be stricken by some weird kind of palsy.

As she released his lips, he saw disappointment and accusation in her eyes and, despite knowing how pointless it was, he wanted to rectify it immediately. It was easy to figure out what was happening. Some guy was trying to hit on her and she needed him.

'Sweetheart.' He smiled a dazzling smile and pulled her to him again, giving her the kind of kiss he should have given her before. The kind of kiss that had made their tempestuous relationship so addictive. So hard to walk away from. When he pulled away they were both slightly out of breath.

Oh, man! She had missed his kiss. Holly stared at him and he stared back, a smile touching his full lips. She felt the familiar zing between them and her gut told her it couldn't possibly be over.

Her pursuer cleared his throat and she dragged her eyes away from Richard. Time to ditch the Leech, who had suckered up to her half an hour ago and who she just couldn't shake.

'And who's this darling?'

'Oh, just some nice man who kept me company in the bar.' She could afford to be gracious now. No need to hurt the Leech's feelings altogether.

'So, you really are meeting someone?' His nasal voice crawled along her spine. 'You must be Holly's fiancé?'

'That's right,' Holly supplied, quickly squeezing Richard's hand, imploring him to play along and not blow her story. 'Richard.'

She felt his hand tense in hers, his body still, his spine straighten, and he gave her a hard look.

'Darling?' She shoved him gently with her shoulder. Do this for me, just this one thing, her eyes begged him.

'Er, hmm, yes.' He cleared his throat. 'Thanks for looking after my girl. You never know what predators are out there these days.' And then he turned them around and walked her to the bar.

Holly sat down next to him and could feel his hostility.

'Thank you, Richard. He was such a creep, he just wouldn't take the hint.'

'What are you doing here, Holly?'

Just like Richard to cut straight to the chase. 'I just wanted to say goodbye.'

'I thought we did that a month ago.'

'Please, Richard,' she pleaded. I will not cry. 'You're leaving for Africa tomorrow. Can't we at least have a farewell drink?'

Richard sighed and looked into her lovely young face and the urge to leave the bar with her right away and say good bye properly was almost overwhelming. 'Chardonnay, Pollyanna?'

Holly smiled despite the wretchedness wrought by the familiar nickname and memories of their first-ever meeting in this very bar two years before he swamped her. She had plonked herself next to him after a particularly horrible day at work and he had taken pity on her and offered to buy her a drink. She remembered it as if it had happened yesterday.

'You sure you're old enough to drink?'

'Of course.' She smiled. 'Why? How old do you think I am?'

'Twelve,' he said, sipping at the froth on his beer, not even looking at her.

She giggled. 'I'm twenty-one.'

'Egad.' He clapped his hand to his forehead theatrically. 'All grown up.'

'How old are you, then?'

'Way older than that.'

'Oh, come on, Methuselah.' She nudged his arm. 'Spill the beans.'

'I'm thirty-six.'

'Oh, no!' she gasped, mimicking him. 'Practically in your dotage.' And she giggled again. 'That's only fifteen years' difference.'

'*Forget it. I'm way too old for you, babycakes.*'

'*Oh, pish!*'

'*Pish?' He shook his head. 'Your parents should have named you Polly instead of Holly. Short for Pollyanna.*'

Holly laughed, finding the idea outrageously funny.

'*I rest my case,' he said derisively.*

They sipped at their drinks for a few moments. 'So, old man, what do you do?'

'*I'm a soldier.*'

She whistled. 'Impressive.'

'*Pollyanna.' He rubbed his hands through his hair in exasperation. 'How do you know I didn't just tell you a big, fat lie?*'

'*Why would you lie?*'

He shrugged. 'Get you into bed.'

She laughed again.

'*You can laugh. Lots of women want to sleep with men in uniform.*'

'*Well, rest assured, Richard, I wouldn't sleep with you because you were a soldier.*'

'*Good for you.' He raised his glass to her and took a swig.*

'*I'd prefer to sleep with you because you're the sexiest man I've ever met.*'

Richard swallowed his mouthful of beer hard and stared at her.

'*Sorry.' She said, smiling, looking at his shocked face. 'Not a very Pollyanna-like thing to say, huh?*'

'*Not the Pollyanna I remember.*'

'Fiancé?' he said after the barman had paced her drink in front of her and she had taken a sip.

Holly came back from the past. 'Fiancé's are always much more threatening than boyfriends.' And a girl could dream, right?

They drank in silence for a few minutes.

'You will be careful over there, wont you?' Holly felt nauseous every time she thought about him in the middle of a war zone.

'It's a UN humanitarian mission. It's perfectly safe.'

His dismissal of her fears were typical. In retrospect he had always treated her as a bit of a kid, dismissing her opinions and telling her only what he'd thought she'd needed to know. Holly had known for a while that she wanted more. To be treated like an equal. Like an adult. To get married and start a family.

'I've seen the television footage. It looks terrible.'

He took another mouthful of beer.

'It's not too late to back out,' Holly said softly.

'Yes, it is.' He put his glass, down and turned to her. 'And even if it wasn't, I'd still be going. This is what I do, Holly. I put on my uniform and I go where and when my country tells me. These people need us. I can help them.'

'And what about me? I need you, too.'

Richard felt her words go straight to his groin. She was incredibly appealing...too appealing. And she was also wrong. She didn't need someone fifteen years older who was married to his job. She needed someone who had a joy and zest for life to match her own. She was twenty-three for heaven's sake. She needed to get out in the world and explore it. See other countries, taste other cuisines, be with other men.

'No. You need a direction in your life, Holly. A purpose.'

'I did have a purpose in my life.' I wanted to marry you and have your babies. Was that such an awful thing?

'Other than me.'

'You know me, Richard,' she said sipping her wine, 'I've always been a little between things.'

'How nice for you,' he said, his voice laced with derision. Her easy-come, easy-go attitude had always been at complete odds to his. In fact, in some perverse kind of way it was what had intrigued him. And irritated him the most. Nice to know he and his kind would keep her world safe while she was 'between things'. 'You want something to do? There's a whole screwed-up world out there, Pollyanna. I'm sure you'll find some way to decorate it.'

His dismissal of her rankled. 'You always did think I was kind of frivolous, didn't you?'

'No, Holly,' he sighed, rubbing his fingers through his hair, messing it further. 'Look, I told you at the beginning this would never work.'

'Because of my age?'

'Yes, amongst other things. I am too old for you, Holly. We are at different stages in our lives. We're too different.'

'Would those other things have anything to do with your emotionally stunted upbringing? Or your unhealthy dependency on your job for validation of your life?' She was trying not to be bitter.

When she said it like that it made him seem so emotionless. So cold. But he had warned her he wasn't good at relationships. He'd had no yardstick in his life worth a damn.

'I've always been up front with you, Holly.'

'Please, Richard.' She faced him and placed her hand on his. 'Don't shut me out. You're going away? So go. I know I can't stop you but I can be waiting here for you when you get back.'

He looked into her earnest face and thought how much he desperately wanted to take her up on it. Having Holly to come home to would be nice. But, face it, after the initial high of frenzied sexual activity wore off they'd be back at square one. Chemistry had never been their problem. She wanted things he wasn't prepared to give. She needed to move on and he was not used to needing anyone.

He removed her hand. 'We've been through this, Holly. Don't make it harder than it is.'

Holly blinked hard and nodded. She wasn't being fair. 'Then take me home and make love to me one last time.' Holly threw away her last shred of dignity, but she needed to be held by him now more than her next breath.

Richard swallowed hard. Being with Holly one last time sounded like heaven. But he knew once he started he wouldn't want to stop, and he'd never want to get out of bed in the morning and leave.

And she'd look at him with those eyes and he'd feel terrible walking away from her. He didn't need that, going to a war zone. He figured life in general would probably be pretty crappy for the next six months, even without a guilt trip from Holly. He'd made the break. He needed to keep it clean.

'I can't, Holly.'

Of course he couldn't. Richard was an honourable man. Twenty-one years in the military had seen to that. Tears rose in her throat but she swallowed them. She'd laid herself bare enough today. She would not disgrace herself completely by sobbing over his shirt in a public bar.

He drained his beer glass and pushed himself off the stool. 'Goodbye, Holly. Take care.'

'Wait,' she said, whipping the pen out of his shirt pocket and desperately scribbling on a bar napkin. 'It's my new number. Call me when you get back.'

'No.'

'Please?' she asked, returning his pen to his pocket along with the napkin.

'It's over, Holly.' He reached into his pocket, his fingers stilling as she placed her hand on his.

'Please, Richard, keep it. Let at least part of me be close to your heart.'

He rolled his eyes at her girlish sentimentality but relented because he had been harsh, and he could see the shine of unshed tears she was bravely holding in check. 'I won't call you.'

'Yes, you will.' She sounded more confident than she felt. Surely after six months in a war zone he'd need a bit of female company?

'No, Pollyanna.' He picked up her hand and kissed her knuckles gently. 'I won't.'

CHAPTER ONE

Two years later…

Holly hadn't expected this morning to be quite so gruelling. But then anything, even sitting and listening to a series of boring lectures was hard going in the stifling humidity of Tanrami. She felt her enthusiasm begin to wane.

She listened to the army officer drone on and let her eyes wander to the view outside their green tented shelter. The sides had been rolled up to allow as much air to circulate as possible, but still everyone seated around her were fanning themselves with the pages of written material they had been handed this morning.

She looked at the leaden sky hanging over Abeil, the capital, and wondered if it did actually rain, whether it would help or not. Hot she was used to, Australia was hot, but this? At the moment, unacclimatised, it felt like she'd moved to hell.

She couldn't believe she was finally here. Her thoughts drifted to Richard, as they still too often did, and she couldn't help but wonder what he'd have thought of her ending up in a sweltering, typhoon-ravaged country. He had so often accused her of frivolity…well, look at me now, Richard. Look at me now.

After his parting barb she had determinedly knuckled down to her nursing career, still smarting from his damning summation of her life. But it just hadn't been fulfilling. Deep down she hadn't felt like she had been making a difference in anyone's life. Modern medicine was all so rush and hurry. So the opportunity to come here and really make a difference had appealed to her immensely.

Who could not be touched by the news reports night after night? The images of so many people killed or displaced, their homes and infrastructures totally destroyed, were heartwrenching. Super-typhoon Rex had cut a path of destruction through the hundreds of islands in the group but Tanrami had borne the brunt. Their plight had called to her. She'd felt…compelled. There was no other way to describe it.

These were people who needed help and she wanted to be part of it. Maybe Tanrami was a place where she could finally get back to the basics of health care. Fundamentals like looking at the patient as a whole instead of a body part to be fixed. Embracing individual cultures and beliefs and understanding that sickness and illness were multi-factorial. And that you couldn't afford to treat a patient in isolation to these factors.

The sky rumbled, interrupting her thoughts, and Holly wondered how much more moisture those black clouds could support. She yawned and sank lower in her chair, shutting her eyes as she fanned herself. At least being seated right at the back she could snooze unobtrusively.

Another khaki-kitted boffin was introduced and started talking to them about more safety issues. Enough already, Holly wanted to stand up and bellow in an I'm-hot-and-bothered voice. It's dangerous. We get it. There's a civil war going on and there are rebels and landmines and diseases and mosquitoes. But we came anyway. We want to help. Just let us get to it.

They'd been briefed and briefed and briefed! It had been mandatory to attend lectures by the recruiting agency and the aid agency and the Foreign Affairs department before being allowed to depart, and now it had been made clear that in order to begin working they also had to attend the army briefing.

Most of the meetings dealt with the security situation in the country. She'd heard a thousand times about what dangerous criminals the rebels were. She'd heard it so much she almost felt sorry for them. In fact, she'd been following the political situation in Tanrami closely since deciding to volunteer. It seemed to her that the rebels were freedom fighters wanting to liberate their country from colonial roots.

Holly's excitement at finally making it here was being tempered by the heat and the repetitive, boring lectures. She just wanted to get on with it. The process had been too long as it was, a flood of volunteers overwhelming Aid agencies. Everyone had wanted to do their bit. Even with her nursing background it had taken three long months to place her at the orphanage.

The speaker finished and there was a smattering of polite applause. Next up was a mosquito talk and Holly, her eyes still shut, swallowed the urge to scream. How long would that take?

Richard was thinking the same thing as he took the podium. How many of these things had he attended since his deployment here three months ago? He looked at his notes and wondered why he'd bothered bringing them. He could certainly give his spiel verbatim.

Not that he disagreed with briefings. In fact, a lot of civilian aid workers were totally green when they arrived and they needed to be briefed extensively. It was just that he had so much work on back at the lab.

Now that the initial lifesaving stuff that they'd done in the first days and weeks of the disaster had been dealt with, a backlog of non-urgent tests had to be cleared. Not to mention the research he had been carrying out to monitor mosquito populations and test the effectiveness of the eradication plan he had spearheaded on his arrival in Tanrami.

Looking out at the sea of faces he could tell he wasn't going to hold their attention for long. They looked hot. And bored. Two major stumbling blocks to retention of information. He decided to ignore his notes and instead talk to them about his project. At least it was interesting and still managed to educate them about the dangers of malaria.

The speaker opened his mouth and uttered some words of introduction. Holly's eyes flew open. She'd know that voice anywhere. She'd dreamt about it and its owner so often in the last two years its timbre was instantly recognisable. It was Richard!

Suddenly the heat didn't matter, or the hours of boring talks—nothing mattered. Her eyes sought his face and drank the sight of him in greedily. She sat a little straighter. He'd changed. Even sitting right at the back she could see the differences.

He seemed harder somehow. Leaner. The grey streaking his hair more noticeable. The planes and angles of his face more pronounced. The way he held himself, more erect. Dressed in his uniform, dark sunglasses hiding his eyes, he looked completely without emotion. Like a machine. A military robot.

Sure, he'd always looked tough and forebidding but it was more than that now. His camouflage fitted him superbly, the red cross stitched to his shoulder denoting his status as a medic. His body seemed even more honed than previously. The uniform had always been a huge turn-on but today it seemed to create distance rather than invite her to touch. With his eyes shaded by reflective lenses, he epitomised the military image. From the way he carried himself to the authority in his deep voice, it screamed soldier.

He looked so…alone. So untouchable. What had happened in two years to make him appear even more unreachable than before? Holly felt her traitorous heart pick up its tempo.

Oh, no. No way! She was well and truly over Richard. She wasn't going down that track again. Particularly not with the new Richard. The old one had been hard enough to love. Her days of beating her head against a brick wall were over.

Still, the urge to call out to him, to have him look at her and fix her with one of those 'hey, babe' smiles was almost overwhelming. She shimmied down in her chair. She would not do that. She was here to help, not rekindle a relationship with someone who'd always been a bit of an unwilling partner in the first place.

And something told her he'd be none too impressed with her presence. It was best to just sit quietly and unobtrusively and sneak away at the end. After all Tanrami was a big place. There was no reason to think that they'd even cross paths. She should be able to finish her three-month stint without him even knowing she was here.

He talked on, oblivious to her turmoil. About his research and collecting specimens and the data he'd amassed about the mosquito populations in Tanrami. Also about malaria and its symptoms and treatment and the importance of taking prophylactic medication. The silky timbre of his voice slid over her skin and she was reminded of the times when he had laughed and teased. Looking at him today, she wondered if those times had actually happened or if she'd merely dreamt them.

Someone in front of her raised their hand and Holly tuned back into the content. She realised for the first time since sitting down with her fellow volunteers over two hours ago that they actually seemed interested in what the speaker was saying. Richard had engaged them which had been a big ask after hours of information delivered in a way that made it as interesting as watching paint dry.

'Yes, potentially specimen collecting is dangerous but probably more so out in the villages than in Abeil,' said Richard in answer to the question Holly hadn't paid any attention to. 'Most of my earlier work involved the villages further away and required more stringent security measures, but in and around

Abeil I generally go out by myself. Enemy forces are more likely to be a problem in the less-populated areas.'

Enemy forces? OK, enough already. Holly sat up a bit more. She'd sat through a whole morning of lectures about the protracted civil war and the bias was appalling. She felt her hackles rise further. Not Richard, too! Richard who, despite being a soldier, had always had a moderate, almost philosophical view of the world. It looked like more than just his physical appearance had changed. What had happened to him?

'Enemy forces? That's a bit extreme, isn't it?'

Everyone turned and looked at her and she realised that she must have spoken aloud. Oh, crap! So much for being unobtrusive!

'I'm sorry,' said Richard, pausing in mid-sentence and removing his shades. 'What do you mean?' He searched the back rows to locate the identity of the voice. It had been a while but its familiarity was ringing bells. Surely not?

As people in front and beside her parted he pierced her with a direct look from his black eyes and all her thoughts and feelings on the subject fled. Wow! She'd forgotten how impressive his eyes were! If nothing else, at least she had forced him to remove those damn sunglasses. She saw his eyes narrow as a flash of recognition streaked through them and then a very subtle flinch as his jaw clenched.

Oh, hell! Holly. Pollyanna was sitting in an army tent in Tanrami being briefed by him. What the hell was she doing in the middle of a disaster zone? Holly of the 'between things' fame. He remembered how harsh and dismissive he had been of her the last time he had seen her and couldn't believe she'd turned up here.

Silly girl! Didn't she realise these situations involved a lot of hard work and were potentially dangerous? That they weren't places you could come and play for a while as you flitted through life? That you saw things which could be traumatic and damaging?

'I mean that just because they hold different views from the general establishment, it doesn't make them the enemy.' She realised everyone was waiting for an answer and she managed to find her voice, swallowing to moisten her suddenly dry mouth.

Her voice was the same as he remembered. High with a sweet girly lilt. It was fresh and full of promise and…flirty. He remembered her saying she'd sleep with him because he was the sexiest man she had ever met and felt the familiar pull in his groin.

He suppressed the urge and focused on what she'd said, not how she'd said it. She was more Pollyanna-like than he'd given her credit for. Was she really that naïve? People who chose armed rebellion and took advantage of the chaos wreaked upon them by one of the world's worst natural disasters to further their cause were dangerous.

'Maybe not. But it does make them dangerous and not to be underestimated,' he said bluntly, placing his sunglasses back on his face.

He had retreated again. The machine was back and Holly was more than aware of the meaning behind his actions. Me soldier. You civilian. Me right. You wrong. How often had he taken that tone with her? Could she goad him back out of his glasses? 'Or maybe it just makes them misunderstood?'

Richard assessed her from behind his lenses. He didn't have the time or the inclination to go into the decades-old history of the civil war that had ravaged and held Tanrami back for too many years. A war older than Holly herself. All he knew for sure was the rebels were shaping up to be more of a menace than any of the international forces now stationed in Tanrami had bargained for.

Between hostage taking, stealing aid parcels meant for the poorest villages and hampering attempts to reach the most sick and injured, the forces had their collective hands full. Worse still was the nuisance of their landmines planted decades before and displaced by the massive storm surges that had swamped the area when Rex had hit during a king tide.

And Holly had just put herself amongst it. He felt the familiar urge to protect her rush through him and wondered how he was ever going to rest easy with her being so close.

'There are more effective ways to further your cause than armed conflict.'

'I agree,' she said, trying to stare him down despite the glasses. 'But when the other ways don't work, I guess they're left with little choice.'

He had underestimated her naïvety. His view of her as young and impulsive was confirmed. In true Pollyanna style she had added two and two together and come up with five. Even now at twenty-five she was seriously misguided.

'There is always a choice.'

She felt her stare being returned even though she couldn't see it, and quashed her dismay. Had he become some kind of military hard-liner? Or, worse, a mindless drone who accepted whatever his superiors fed him?

No. She refused to believe Richard didn't have a mind of his own. He had always been strong and sure and decisive. He'd never dithered or sought permission from anyone. Blind loyalty just wasn't him.

'Anyway...I think we've got ourselves off track,' said Richard.

He continued for a while longer and Holly was relieved to lose the attention of everyone else in the tent. She shook herself mentally. He was entitled to his opinion but it rankled and his obvious dismissal of hers found her in the midst of familiar emotions. How many times had she battled the fifteen-year age gap? Battled Richard's ingrained opinion that she was a mere child?

Holly stood at the end of Richard's talk, grateful that the briefing was over and they could finally go to their allocated jobs. Seeing Richard had been a complication she hadn't bargained on and the inequity that had existed in their relationship seemed even more glaring with two years' distance.

Refreshments were served in the tent and army personnel mingled with the new recruits. Richard made his excuses and slipped out. He had work to do and didn't have time to play benign soldier today. And seeing Holly again had disturbed him more than he wanted to admit.

From the moment she had burst into his life she'd always been difficult to ignore. How was he going to concentrate on his job knowing she was so near? Knowing she'd signed up for a dangerous role? He had to leave now before he sought her out and insisted she go home. She was a big girl and it was none of his business.

He rounded a corner and ploughed straight into her.
They apologised simultaneously as they disentangled themselves.

'Richard.'

Her voice floated towards him and he felt the same grab in his groin as before. 'Holly.'

There was silence for a few moments while they looked at each other. Their history faded from her mind as she took him in. Up close the changes were more evident. His hair had greyed considerably. There were frown lines on his forehead and around his mouth and a shuttered look to his eyes. It took someone who knew him intimately to see past the barriers. To see the damaged soul.

How was it was at all possible that with all these negative changes he was sexier than ever? His nearness reminding her of why she'd been so attracted to him. The solid broadness of his chest told her he was all man. Her previous boyfriends had paled in comparison. They had been mere boys.

'What are you doing here, Holly? It's dangerous.' Maybe he could make her see sense.

'I can handle it,' she said quietly.

'I thought you were between things? You should be out enjoying life. That's what young people are supposed to do. Not risking your pretty neck in a disaster zone.'

'A lot's happened in two years, Richard. I came to help. I need to help.'

'Don't be silly, Holly. Tanrami has plenty of helpers. Go be young while you can. Travel, buy nice clothes, sleep with lots of men—'

'I already own nice clothes,' she interrupted, dismayed that he was still treating her as a child. 'And if this isn't travelling then I don't know what is. As for sleeping with men, well, I think I've definitely come to the right place.' She couldn't help but goad him. 'Can't go wrong with five hundred soldiers just up the road.'

Richard scowled at her, appalled by the idea.

'Holly, you could see things here that are really very unpleasant. You're too young, too…happy. Go home before it damages you.' He couldn't bear the thought of her becoming jaded and cynical. Like him.

'I'm a nurse, Richard. I think I've already seen my share of unpleasant. And, besides, I think the Tanramans could probably do with a bit of happy.'

'I'm serious, Holly. This isn't a place you come to find yourself.'

Holly tried not to flinch as his blunt words fell between them. 'I've come to help, not to find myself. I've come to make a difference.'

She brushed past him, the moisture dewing her eyes a good match for the humidity. She had to get away from him. Her joy at seeing him again was suddenly crashing down all around her.

'Holly,' he called after her, immediately sorry for his harshness. She turned to face him and he was proud of the brave front he could see she was putting on. 'I'm sorry…it's just that you're too…'

'Young. Yeah, so you said.' And with as much dignity as she could muster, she turned on her heel and left him standing by himself.

Holly bustled through the back streets, cursing the heat and humidity. She felt the sweat trickle between her breasts and run down her abdomen. It was hot, it was humid and the air was rancid with months of waterlogged, decaying rubbish. All it needed now was to rain and her day would be complete, she thought. A warm, fat drop of water fell from the sky onto her face. Right on cue.

Walking around the devastated capital, she could see there was still so much to be done. Abeil, sitting right on the coast, had been a sitting duck for the fury of nature. Half of the city had been swamped and flattened by the massive storm surges that had thrown a good deal of the ocean at the city's primitive infrastructures.

Much had been accomplished in the time since. Rebuilding had begun but there was so much that remained to do. Large areas of debris in outlying areas had still not been cleared and bodies were still being found. Many had perished. Many more had died since as a result of disease, starvation and homelessness. And many children had been orphaned.

Which was why Holly was walking the streets of Abeil. She'd only been here for a fortnight but knew the routine backwards. Every morning two of the orphanage workers would walk into what remained of the old city of Abeil, follow an established route and pick up any orphaned children at designated checkpoints.

The locals knew the system and would be waiting for them along the way. Initially there had been many but the numbers had slowed to a trickle. A few times Holly had completed the two-hour journey empty-handed but on one occasion she had felt like the Pied Piper, a scraggly bunch of urchins trailing behind her.

Holly had separated from Glenda, one of the other aid workers, as they always did, to help shorten the route. She would meet up with her again at the ruins of the old Catholic church where they would continue for another half an hour before walking back to the orphanage.

But for now, as a tropical downpour appeared from the sky as if someone up there had flipped a switch, Holly sought shelter in an alley where the rickety construction of houses on both sides caused them to lean towards each other, reducing the torrent of rain from the heavens. She found a doorway to shrink even further into and managed to stay reasonably dry.

It wasn't such a bad position actually, she thought as she listened to the rain beat down on the tin roofs all around her. The noise was deafening, like a million drummers striking their instruments simultaneously. A breeze blew down the alley and her nostrils filled with the earthy smell of rain hitting dirt.

It was amazing how much the precipitation relieved the heated atmosphere and Holly revelled in the cool air on her face. It felt so good she was almost tempted to strip off her clothes and stand in the rain in her bra and knickers. Almost.

She pulled her baseball cap off, held it out, allowing it to half fill with water and plonking it back on her head. The water drenched her short fine hair, cascaded down her face, neck and shoulders and soaked into the fabric of her long-sleeved T-shirt. She looked down at the wet patch spreading from her neckline to her waist and sighed blissfully as the water cooled the sweaty skin beneath.

As quickly as it had begun, the rain ended, and Holly waited until she could no longer hear any pattering before she stepped out of the doorway. A noise further down the alley caught her attention and curious, she went to investigate. Maybe it was a child—lost and frightened and alone.

Like so many of the residential streets that made up Abeil, one alley led to another which led to another. The back streets were a maze of dingy alleys and dirt tracks formed around a mish-mash of lean-tos, huts and baked mud shelters.

She could hear voices now, muffled and speaking in the native tongue. She rounded a corner and stopped abruptly. The noises weren't coming from hungry children searching for food. They were coming from a gang of four boys who looked no older than fifteen. They appeared to be kicking at something on the ground.

It was a person! The inert form lay still as the youths continued their assault, oblivious to her presence. Holly felt temporarily paralysed as her mind tried to compute what her eyes were seeing. Her heart beat was loud in her ears. She felt sick listening to the dull thud of boots striking flesh. And scared and angry. They had to stop.

She strode forward on shaking legs, summoning the courage to help. She couldn't just stand there and let them kick a defenceless human being. She moved into the fray and felt her heart slam in her chest and hoped she could pull it off. Hoped they couldn't tell she was scared out of her mind.

'Stop that,' she said, advancing toward the scuffle. 'Stop it right now,' she demanded.

The youths stopped and turned to face her. A tall one with greasy hair and bad acne took a couple of paces towards her. He appeared to be the ringleader. After a few seconds he started to laugh. His mates joined him, a little hesitantly.

Holly felt chilled by their callousness. She didn't know the circumstances of what had gone on here in the alley and she didn't care, there were no excuses for such cruelty. Holly could now see it was a man on the ground and he still hadn't moved. Was he dead? The nurse in her demanded that she help him but the female was more than a little frightened of these brash, callous young men.

The leader advanced further towards her with a smile on his face that was far from reassuring. Holly swallowed nervously and held her ground. Great! Now what? She glanced over at the man on the ground again and was relieved to hear him moan and then cough. The youth said something in his own language and the rest of the gang sniggered.

Just then Holly heard whistling coming from where she had entered the alley and almost sagged in relief. 'Help,' she yelled in a loud voice, keeping her eyes on the leader who hesitated slightly. 'I need some help.'

Richard hitched his pack closer and kicked on some speed, sensing the desperation in the plea for help he had just heard. He rounded the corner at top speed and saw a tall youth startle as he burst on the scene. Richard's snap assessment of the situation stirred his ire. A gang of youths were menacing a woman. She was lucky he'd been in the vicinity.

'What the hell is going on here?' growled Richard, striding past Holly. The leader was tall but Richard was taller and meaner and trained in unarmed combat—he'd teach these boys to threaten a women.

The youths didn't hang around for their lesson. They disappeared quickly and Richard chased them for a short distance but stopped, knowing that his first priority was the safety of the civilian female he had rescued. The gang members had looked sufficiently petrified to think twice about doing that again.

Holly knew it was Richard the instant he'd spoken. Her relief at being rescued from a situation that hadn't been going well was tempered by the irony of who her rescuer was. Yet another sticky situation he had saved her from! Oh, well, beggars couldn't be choosers, and at the moment there were more pressing matters.

Holly rushed to the injured man's side. He was lying on his back and blood trickled from his nose and a wound near his temple. She felt for his carotid pulse and was alarmed by his stertorous breathing and the bluish tinge of his lips.

'Hey, mister, wake up,' she said, opening his eyes and noting his pupillary constriction to the bright light now filtering into the alley.

The man moaned in pain and coughed again, spluttering bright frothy blood on her shirt. That wasn't good, Holly thought as she hiked the man's shirt up and inspected the damage to his ribs. Definitely not good. The bruising was already coming out and Holly noted in alarm the flail segment of broken ribs on his left side.

She looked up when Richard ran back towards her and was so relieved he was by her side she almost forgave him their last meeting.

'Richard! Thank God. We have to get this man out of here and back to your hospital now.'

'Holly?'

Holly? He had rescued Holly? She wore baggy fatigues that hid her body and her cap covered her hair but it was definitely pixie-faced Holly. He felt his heart give a couple of loud thuds at what could have happened to her if he hadn't come along and wanted to yell at her and then shake her for good measure. This was exactly what he had feared.

The man on the ground coughed yet again and Richard felt his feelings ebb as concern for the stranger took over. Where the hell had he come from?

'What happened?' he demanded, kneeling on the other side of the patient, opposite Holly. His eyes met hers and he realised she had purple eyes. Purple eyes? Holly always did like to accessorise.

'Those boys were kicking him half to death when I found them. I think his ribs bore the brunt. He's got a flail segment.'

Flail? He dragged his gaze from her face and opened his pack, having noted the depressed section of ribs that was moving in and out completely asynchronous to the rest of the chest wall. It was severely impeding the man's ability to breathe.

Richard threw Holly some gloves and as he was putting his on, she reached for his stethoscope.

'Absent air entry on the left,' she said, pulling the stethoscope out of her ears with gloved hands.

Alarmed by the man's increasing dyspnoea and rapidly developing cyanosis, Richard assessed the man's neck veins. They were bulging.

'He's developing a tension pneumo,' Holly said. Richard didn't have time to be impressed by Holly's clinical skills as right before his eyes the stranger's lips lost their colour and his trachea slowly deviated to the right, shifting from its midline position.

'Get me a fourteen-gauge needle,' barked Richard as he tore the man's shirt right up the middle. 'He's got mediastinal shift, he'll be in real trouble soon if we don't decompress his chest, stat.'

She quickly located the large-bore needle and passed it to Richard, knowing that their patient's damaged lungs were leaking air into his chest cavity. His respiratory system was enormously compromised and his cardiac function would be next.

Richard methodically palpated the second intercostal space, running his finger to the mid-clavicular point, and plunged the needle through the man's skin and into the pleural cavity. There was no time for sterility, for preparing the skin with an antiseptic wash or even a local anaesthetic. The patient needed the air drained from his chest cavity so his lung could reinflate—now!

The effectiveness of the treatment was instantaneous. As quickly as it had deviated, the trachea moved back to its normal position. The patient's lips lost their cyanotic tinge and pinked up. He dragged in some deep ragged breaths.

Holly let out her pent-up breath. They'd done it. Their patient's condition had drastically improved. She started to feel shaky as reaction to the events sank in and the adrenaline surge ebbed.

She watched as Richard did a head-to-toe examination of the man, his capable hands running over the patient's body, thoroughly checking for any other areas of concern. She felt absurdly like crawling over, sitting in his lap and burrowing her head into his chest.

What would have happened if he hadn't come along when he did?

CHAPTER TWO

TWENTY minutes later an army ambulance carried the injured man back to the field hospital. Richard had radioed HQ and they'd stabilised him, padding his flail segment and inserting two IVs. Holly was acutely aware of Richard's arm brushing lightly against hers as they watched the vehicle until it disappeared from sight.

Without speaking, he marched back into the alley where all the excitement had occurred. Now it was all over he knew that if he opened his mouth she would feel the sharpness of his tongue.

Holly trailed after him. He was packing up his equipment and she knelt down beside him and silently helped. She passed him the stethoscope and as their hands brushed she tried to quell the familiar rush of sensation because they were in a dingy alley, in a foreign land, and it just didn't seem appropriate.

Richard's hand stilled as the contact reminded him of how tactile their relationship had been. He looked at her closely despite every cell in his brain telling him not to.

'You have purple eyes,' he said, because it was the first thing that popped into his head.

Holly had forgotten about the contacts she had put in that morning. The kids at the orphanage had loved them! 'Oh, yes...' she said. 'Just because I'm in a disaster zone doesn't mean I still can't look good, right?'

And she did. She really did. He stared at her for a few moments, a familiar heat building and invading every part of his body. He shook his head to clear the fog, remembering where he was and why he was there. He pushed himself up from the ground. He had to put some distance between them.

'We'd better get moving,' said Richard.

He picked up his pack and set off at a brisk pace. Holly practically had to run to keep up with his long-legged stride.

'So what were you doing out here?' asked Holly, trying to make conversation when it became obvious he wasn't going to talk to her.

'Collecting specimens,' he said.

'Mosquito water?' she asked.

He nodded briefly. 'Pleased to see you were listening the other day.'

She opened her mouth to compliment him on his lecture but almost as if he sensed her intention to talk he kicked on some more speed. While she was running to catch up she admired him from behind. His salt-and-pepper head bobbed with each footfall, his army camouflage pants pulling taut across his buttocks and his khaki T-shirt stretching across his wide back. His six-four frame was achingly familiar.

'I always listen,' she said, finally catching him up.

'Not that well, obviously. If you had, you'd know it's dangerous…a woman wandering around by herself.' He relived the awful moment when he'd realised that it was she he had rescued and the things that could have happened to her. It made him sick thinking about it. Just because they weren't in a relationship any more, it didn't mean he didn't care for her.

'I wasn't alone, we're not allowed. Glenda came with me, we just separated temporarily to shorten the trip.'

'So you were alone.'

'Well, technically…yes.'

'No technically about it. You were alone and that is not only dangerous, it's downright stupid. Do you have any idea what could have happened to you today?'

'I had to stop them beating him, Richard.'

'What?' Was she telling him she'd approached them?

Holly filled him in on what had happened. He shook his head. Just as he'd feared, she was going to get herself killed.

'Are you crazy?' he demanded. He opened his mouth to deliver another lecture on safety and her complete unsuitability for Tanrami but stopped abruptly when she squeezed his arm.

'Richard. Don't say it. I know that today could have ended very badly and I promise not to take any more risks. Please, just spare me the lecture. I'm OK. Nothing happened.'

'But it could have.'

'But it didn't. Got my own tough-guy soldier looking out for me,' Holly said, smiling at him.

Richard looked at her in exasperation. 'Holly, what happens next time…when I'm not around?'

'Cheer up Richard, it'll probably never happen.' This time she shot him a wicked grin because the conversation was getting kind of old. She'd been sufficiently scared to take heed.

Holly checked her watch. 'Shit, I'm late. Glenda will be worried.'

Richard smiled despite himself at her expletive. 'You work in an orphanage now, Holly. Language like that will see you go straight to hell.'

She cast her eyes around at the waterlogged city, the leaden sky, and drew in a deep breath of foetid air. 'Too late, Richard, I'm already here.'

She sighed and enjoyed the difference even a slight smile made to his face. It dimpled his cheeks and softened the planes and angles and the deep black of his eyes. It even made the dark stubble on his chin less military. It reminded her of the Richard she had first known and loved.

They found a very worried Glenda pacing outside the meet-

ing point a few minutes later. Holly introduced them and
Richard escorted them back to the orphanage. He listened to
their idle chatter and made a mental note to talk to the CO about
sparing someone each day to accompany the workers into the
city on their orphan runs. He'd sleep easier if he knew a soldier was accompanying them. Not that he slept well at the best
of times.

Richard plodded along behind them, trying not to ogle
Holly's cute backside or the seductive sway of her hips. Even
in baggy clothes she had a great strut. His mind wandered to
how good she looked naked and then he shook his head, disgusted at himself.

Honestly, having her here was just the living end! He was
here as part of an Australian Defence Force humanitarian mission. To monitor and eradicate mosquito populations. To treat
cases of malaria and dengue and provide public health services and education. Not to pick up where he'd left off with a
girl nearly half his age.

They reached their destination and Holly watched Glenda
walk into the sturdily constructed stone building that had miraculously survived the typhoon and had been commandeered
in the early days for use as an orphanage. All around them were
the temporary buildings of various aid agencies, part of the massive international humanitarian response which had poured in
after the devastating news had circulated the globe.

She could see the khaki tents in the distance that was
Richard's field hospital and, further beyond that, myriad mul-
ticoloured tents stretched as far as the eye could see, a city full
of displaced people, refugees in their own country, awaiting the
agonisingly slow rebuilding process.

She looked at Richard who was looking anywhere but at her.
He seemed to be finding the bustle of activity all around them
particularly riveting. She also allowed the hubbub to distract her
from her thoughts and the sudden awkwardness between them.

'Look, I'm sorry about before. While I think you took an un-acceptable risk, what you did, confronting those boys was very brave,' said Richard.

He was a great believer in giving praise where it was due, and he had to admit her actions had surprised him. He knew from experience that a bug usually sent her into the vapours, and yet she had taken on a gang of violent teenagers.

Holly blinked, startled by the reluctant compliment, and felt stupidly happy. It had obviously cost him a lot if his serious face was anything to go by. She had the sudden urge to see him smile again. 'And me being so young and everything,' she sighed dramatically.

He gave her a grudging smile. Aha! That was more like it. 'I'd better go,' she said. 'I guess I'll be seeing you around.'

He watched her hips sway as she walked away from him. Watched until she disappeared inside the orphanage. Not if I can help it, Pollyanna. Not if I can help it.

Three days passed. Three days that lulled Richard into a false sense of security. He didn't see her, he didn't talk to her. He was beginning to think having Holly less than a kilometre away wasn't going to be a problem. Wrong.

'Sergeant,' said Gary Lynch, an army doctor, entering the lab area of the army hospital.

'Yes, sir,' said Richard, lifting his eyes from the microscope.

'I have customers waiting for you outside. Five children from the orphanage need malarial screening. I've just done physicals—they're all undernourished but remarkably well otherwise.'

And that's when his sense of security came to an abrupt halt. He just knew that Holly was out there also.

'Roach!' he called, returning his eyes to the microscope where he was examining mosquito larvae.

No one answered and he looked around the empty lab with

a sinking feeling. He was going to have to do it himself. He made a mental note to have Private Roach flogged and reluctantly left his desk.

He stood at the flap that separated the lab area from the outpatient section and looked through the clear plastic panel. There she was, with a bunch of rag-tag kids sitting patiently on the chairs provided.

Holly nursed an infant on her lap, one hand resting on its back. She was absently rubbing her face back and forth through the babe's soft downy hair. The child's hand rested on Holly's T-shirt-clad breast and had its head snuggled in her cleavage. It was a touching scene and Richard felt a pang somewhere in the region of his heart.

She looked up as he pushed the flap aside and smiled at him her purple eyes twinkling.

'Hello, Richard.'

'Holly.'

He stared at her for a bit longer. Everything about her was delicate, from her slender ankles to her heart-shaped face. Her blonde pixie-cut hair, feathering around her face, completed the picture. It emphasised her age, and Richard suddenly felt very old.

The child on her lap stirred, lifting its head up and swapping cheeks, pressing the other side to Holly's bosom. Richard couldn't keep his eyes off it as the child's hand settled back to rest gently on Holly's breast.

He looked back at Holly and realised she'd been watching him all along. Their eyes locked momentarily and it was suddenly as if they were the only two people in the world.

Private Roach brushed passed him and almost tripped as he did a double-take when he saw Holly. He stopped abruptly.

'You were looking for me, sir.'

Roach smiled at Holly and she smiled back at him and

Richard saw the gleam in the young private's eyes. He made a further note to use a cat-o'-nine-tails when Roach was flogged.

'I've left some slides under the microscope. Can you continue the classification process for me?'

Roach dragged his gaze away from Holly with difficulty, about to protest, but thought better of it when he saw the look of steel in his superior's eyes.

'Yes, sir,' he said, leaving reluctantly and shooting Holly another dazzler for good measure.

'Through here,' he said, and indicated for Holly to follow him.

She smiled at the children and stood and they followed her in their silent serious way. Holly had never met more solemn children. They had been through so much and her heart broke to think of how deep their sorrow must be.

'Up here,' said Richard, and patted an examination bench. The children stared at him with their big brown eyes. Apart from the baby, the youngest looked about three and the oldest around six. None of them moved.

Holly smiled. She was used to this blank, silent routine. It wasn't recalcitrance, just a mixture of a huge language barrier and powerlessness.

'Come on, my darlings,' she said, and smiled and nodded at them reassuringly. 'It's OK. *Jup, jup,*' she clucked, thankful that she was learning enough of the native language to get by.

Still they didn't move and her heart went out to them even more.

'What do we do now?' Richard asked, a smile playing on his lips.

He was wearing the same uniform as the other day and Holly tried not to be distracted by the broadness of his chest or the covering of dark hairs on his perfectly muscled arms.

'I'll sit up with them,' she said, and he helped her climb up onto the bench. She was still holding the infant, who was clinging to her.

The children watched the new development silently.

'*Jup, jup,*' she said again, and patted the space beside her. She turned back to him. 'Richard, you'll need to help them up.'

'OK, then, chickadees,' he crooned, crouching down to their level. 'Whose gonna be first? Who wants to sit next to Holly?'

Holly almost fell off the bench at the change in Richard as he spoke to the wary children. So he did have a soft side.

'I know,' he said. 'Who likes balloons?' He stood and drew a trolley closer that held various things, boxes of gloves amongst them. He pulled a few out, grinned wickedly at the kids and blew in the open end of a glove which he had narrowed into a neck with his finger and thumb.

The glove blew up just like a balloon except it had a bizarre udder shape to it as the five fingers inflated to their full length. Richard tied a knot in it and then turned it the other way round. Now it looked like a head with spiky hair and Richard completed the look by drawing a face on it.

One of the little girls giggled nervously and soon they were all laughing. He gave one to each child, lifting them onto the bench behind them as he did so. Suddenly they were chattering to each other and to Holly in their native language.

'Thank you,' she whispered, and hugged the now squirming baby to her breast. He wanted in on the act too and Richard handed him a glove balloon with a crazy face and earned himself a toothless baby grin.

While the noise of happy children filled the air, Richard told Holly what he was going to do.

'It's just a finger-prick,' he explained, 'I drop it onto the test strip and it reads in seconds. Like a urinary preg test. Think they'll be OK?'

'Not sure,' she admitted. The five kids had only come to the orphanage over the last couple of days and they still had trust issues.

'You're a nurse. You could help me. They might trust you more.'

'Oh, no. No way. Sorry, but I need to earn these kids' trust and I won't do that by sticking a needle into their fingers. Sorry, but you get to be the bad guy today.'

Richard could see her point but took up her suggestion that he run a test on her so they could see it wasn't going to hurt them. She held out her finger dutifully and he smiled to himself as the laughter died and five pairs of eyes focused on what he was doing to Holly.

Holly held her breath and tried not to flinch, both at the unexplained eroticism of Richard's gloved hand rubbing her finger and as the lancet pierced the tip. He squeezed out a drop of blood onto the test strip and then gave Holly a cotton-wool ball to blot the blood. He showed the kids the strip and they watched as the pink test line appeared.

'You're safe,' he teased in a low voice as the second line, indicating a positive result, didn't appear. He picked up her finger again, removed the cotton-wool ball, wiped off the smear of dried blood and covered the puncture site with a sticky plaster.

And then, because he couldn't help himself and he had an audience, he kissed her finger. 'All better now,' he murmured.

The children giggled and clapped, but Holly hardly registered them at all. Her finger felt hot, burning hot, as hot as the colour darkening her cheeks, and she sat pole-axed, momentarily stunned by his action.

'OK, who's first?' he asked the little ones.

The eldest girl held out her hand and he repeated the test on her. She didn't make a murmur when her finger was pricked and Richard knew that the others would be fine. These kids had been through so much more pain and suffering than a simple finger-prick. They were tough. Survivors.

'All done,' he said to the first girl, but she shook her head and thrust her finger back at him. 'It was good.' He nodded and smiled. 'All clear.' He nodded again, curling her fingers into her palm and placing them in her lap.

She shook her head again and thrust it back.

'I think she wants you to kiss it,' Holly suggested, coming out of the sexual haze his tiny kiss on her finger had caused.

Richard looked at her doubtfully and she shrugged at him. The little girl held her finger out solemnly. He sighed and pressed a kiss to it, sure that this went against every protocol he could think of. Still, the same went for kissing Holly but that hadn't stopped him.

The girl beamed at him, a huge smile of such utter happiness that Richard immediately forgot about the rules. The other children clapped again and Richard laughed and clapped with them.

He finished the other children in no time. The baby was more difficult and cried a bit when the needle pierced his skin but was easily placated by Holly. All the kids were clear and Richard was helping them down when an army nurse stuck her head through the flap.

'Sergeant, helicopter ETA fifteen minutes. Troops hit a land-mine in their Jeep. Four critical. Sergeant Lynch wants you to stock up on fresh blood.' And then she was gone.

'I'll get out of your hair,' said Holly, rounding up her charges.

Richard waved the kids goodbye and then forced himself to turn away and not watch the sway of her hips and the wiggle of her cute bottom. He had a job to do.

CHAPTER THREE

HOLLY was outside, playing hopscotch with a group of children, when Richard passed by.

'Hey, where are you going?' she called out to him, and watched as he slowed then stopped and turned around.

He sighed heavily.

'Ignoring me isn't going to make me go away, Richard.'

'I wasn't ignoring you,' he lied.

'Oh, so you just…didn't see me.'

'That's right,' he said, swallowing another lie.

Holly wasn't fooled for a minute but she let it pass. 'Where are you going?' she repeated, walking further down the fence line so she was nearer him because he obviously wasn't going to come closer to her.

'Collecting some more specimens.'

'Pack looks kind of heavy.'

'I'm used to it.' He shrugged.

'Can I come with you?' she asked hopefully.

'No.'

'I can help you collect your specimens.'

'I don't need any help.'

'Have you ever, Richard?'

'I've been self-sufficient all my life, Holly. I don't need anybody.'

Apparently so!

'Which area are you going to?'

'The eastern side. You're not coming.'

'Cool. We haven't been to that sector for a while. I'll just let Kathleen know.' She turned away to head inside.

'I'm not waiting for you.'

'That's fine, I'll catch you up.' She shot him a dazzling smile as she disappeared out of sight.

Right. Like he was going to let her go wandering into the eastern side of the city all by herself.

'Oh, you waited,' she said innocently, reappearing a few minutes later.

Like she didn't know he would be waiting for her. He was pleased to see she'd got out of her scuffs and had put on some boots and thick socks. With her three-quarter length cargo pants and modest black T-shirt she looked kind of military and Richard tried not to go there. Women in uniform and all that.

'Shouldn't you have another worker with you?' he asked.

'Nah. Got a big tough-guy soldier by my side.' She grinned as she pushed open the gate and joined him.

Her purple eyes twinkled at him. He turned away abruptly, setting off at a killer pace.

'Are we trying to set a world record?' she asked, her short legs unable to keep pace with his.

'You wanted to come,' he said in a clipped voice, staring straight ahead, 'so keep up. Don't complain and definitely do not sprain an ankle or anything else typically female.' He couldn't bear emotional, scatty women who used their wiles instead of their heads. Way before Holly had come on the scene he had nearly married one and still felt blessed by his lucky escape.

She daren't ask what came under the typically female banner. She had a feeling he was talking about his mysterious fiancée that he'd alluded to on a couple of occasions when they'd been together but had steadfastly refused to talk about.

AMY ANDREWS

41

Whatever—he was letting her come so she scurried along, determined not to ask him to slow down. So what if she practically had to jog to keep up? She was fit, she would manage. 'So, talk to me about mozzies,' she said.

Richard relented and slowed his pace a little at the breathy hitch in her voice. 'What do you want to know?'

'Well, today, for instance, what's the purpose of collecting the specimens?'

'We're entering a critical stage at the moment. Any real problems with malaria and other mosquito-borne illnesses are going to explode if we don't monitor the situation and stick to our strategic plan.'

'Why now?'

'Well, it's been three months since the typhoon, right?' He looked at her and she nodded. 'Now what happened back then was that there were these huge storm surges, where the wind was so strong it whipped up massive waves and hurled them at the shore. And because Rex chose the worst possible time to hit, during a king-tide, the result was much more catastrophic. As these surges inundated the land they cleaned out all the mosquito breeding areas, just sucked them right back into the ocean, and all the fresh-water habitats that mozzies need to breed in were washed away and replaced by salt water.'

He stopped to see if she was following and she nodded at him again. 'It takes about three months for the salt to evaporate from these puddles and ponds and waterways and make them mosquito-friendly again. Plus with the monsoon season just getting into full swing, all the fresh water from the sky helps to quicken the process by flushing out salinity and leaving plenty of puddles and pools and even man-made receptacles for mosquitos to breed in.'

'What do you mean, man-made?'

'Oh, anything that will hold water. Things like buckets, bowls, discarded tyres, even empty coconut shells that the locals leave lying around fill with water in the rain. A lot of my job is public health education. Going into the areas where the locals are living and talk to them about not creating opportunities for mozzies.'

They reached an area that, even for Abeil, was exceedingly dingy. It had been the poorer section of the city but had survived remarkably well. It certainly wasn't anything to do with the construction of the dwellings because the whole area reminded Holly of a shanty town. It was pure economics. The more affluent you were, the more you were able to afford a home closer to the sea. So the eastern side through sheer distance alone had survived reasonably well.

'This'll do,' said Richard, pulling a map out of his pack and consulting it.

'Why here?' she asked, looking around and then trying to make sense of his map. 'What are all those shaded areas?'

'They're areas I've already collected specimens from.'

'So what do the specimens tell you?' she asked as she accepted the handful of yellow-lidded pots he gave her.

'It basically tells me if our earlier eradication programme has been successful. As I said earlier this is the most critical time to assess that. We look for, one…' he held out a finger '…if there are any larvae in the water specimens and, two, if any, what sort of mosquitoes they are. That way I can map mosquito populations and keep an eye on their progression and change or alter our strategic plan accordingly.'

'When did you become such an expert?'

She lifted an old discarded tin to find a pool of trapped rain water. She'd been watching Richard poke around in the rubble and rubbish and figured he'd tell her if she was doing something wrong. She opened the lid of a pot and scooped some of the water in. She handed it to Richard and he wrote on the label.

He shrugged. 'I've been working in malarial research for

about a decade now and had lots of field experience in Timor and Bougainville.'

Holly stopped mid-scoop. He'd been to Timor and Bougainville? Why had he never told her these things when they had been together? He had never talked about his job other than to impress on her his total dedication to it.

'You sound married to the job,' she said, stopping to observe his concentration as he made some notes in a notebook.

'I am,' he said, looking up and fixing her with a knowing stare, the lid of his pen still between his lips.

'Sounds lonely,' she said quietly.

'Nothing wrong with that, Pollyanna.'

She was about to object, tell him he was missing out on all the good things in life, when he turned away and continued his foraging. She sighed and shook her head. She'd had the conversation with him a million times already.

Holly returned to the job at hand in silence for a little while. But the quiet soon got the better of her and she had just opened her mouth to ask another question when a noise from behind stopped her. She was turning around when a low voice told her to stop. The request was backed up by the cold metal of a gun being pushed into her neck and a hand jerking her by the arm into an upward position.

'Tell your friend to throw his gun on ground,' the low voice spoke again.

'He hasn't got a—Yow!' she yelped as her captor twisted her arm behind her back.

It didn't even raise an eyebrow from Richard, who had wandered a little distance away and was staring intently into a dark hole.

'Ah, Richard,' she said, her heartbeat thundering in her ears so she was actually unable to hear herself say the words.

'Hmm?' he said, not turning around, not looking up from what he was doing.

'Richard!' she said louder, more insistent as the gun was pressed harder against her neck.

He looked up and, if the situation hadn't so serious, the look on his face would have been comical. Now she had his attention!

'What the—?'

'Stay where you are. Throw your gun on the ground. One false move and I'll kill her,' the man stated.

'OK, mate. Take it easy,' said Richard in a steady voice.

'Gun. Now!'

Holly jumped as the demand ricocheted around her ear canal. Her denial that he didn't have a gun died on her lips as he pulled something that looked like a pistol out from behind his back and tossed it a short distance away.

'Kick it to me.'

Richard did as he was told. The man said something in his native language and Holly watched as three men came from somewhere behind her and were suddenly all over Richard, patting him down then forcing him to kneel on the ground.

'Stop!' she said frantically, suddenly very frightened that they were going to execute him right in front of her. Her heart pounded in her chest. 'What are you doing? He's an Australian soldier, a medic, he's here to help the people of Abeil. Stop it! Let him go.'

The man holding her captive marched her over beside Richard and forced her to kneel, too.

Faced with her own mortality, Holly suddenly felt very angry. And scared. She was about to launch into an angry diatribe when she felt Richard's hand seek hers and squeeze. Was it for reassurance or a warning?

'What do you want from us?' Richard demanded.

Holly was amazed his voice sounded so calm. So in control. And for whatever reason he had held her hand, it had given her a measure of calmness as well.

When he got no answer Richard ploughed on regardless. He

felt fear but his priority to remove Holly from danger overruled everything. He had been in some hairy situations in the past, but he had skills and training and knew when it came down to it he could defend himself. But Holly? She hadn't signed up for this.

'Whatever it is, you don't need both of us. She's an aid worker. A volunteer. Let her go. You have me, you don't need her.'

Holly felt a lump lodge in her throat and decided right then and there, kneeling in the dirt of a foreign land, a gun pressed to her head, that if she died there today, she couldn't think of anyone she'd rather be with. Just his mere presence gave her courage in the face of such dire odds.

It was ironic on so many levels. That the man who had hurt her the most was the one she was going to draw her last breath with, and that somehow it seemed kind of…fitting. And it shouldn't. After all, the man in question still continued to dismiss her as being young and frivolous and it looked like she was never going to get a chance to prove to him otherwise. It just didn't make any sense to feel like this.

But holding his hand as she stared death in the face, she realised lots of things didn't make sense in this world. Not typhoon Rex, not kneeling in an alley, awaiting her death, and certainly not their convoluted relationship.

'Shut up and listen!' said the man who appeared to be the ringleader. 'We are soldiers from the Abeil Freedom Movement and you are prisoners of war.'

And then everything went black.

CHAPTER FOUR

THE dark sacks that had been placed over their heads were impossible to see out of and air flow wasn't great. It was stuffy and suffocating but Holly knew she could live with that. She was still alive and that was the most important thing.

Their hands were bound behind their backs and Holly could feel the pulses throbbing through her hands as the tightness of the rope constricted the flow of blood. They were yanked off the ground and forced to walk a short distance, stumbling and tripping because of their blinded state.

They entered some kind of dwelling where they were forced to sit on the ground next to each other while a heated conversation took place around them. Soon after they were manhandled to their feet again, the person 'helping' Holly letting his hand linger on her hip. She suppressed a shudder and refused to think about all the things they could do to her. There was no point dwelling on the what-ifs.

They were led outside again and then someone picked Holly up and placed her none too gently on her back against a hard metal surface and ordered her to lie still. She felt Richard beside her and quelled her rising panic. If he was with her, she could get through anything.

She remembered his earlier comments about typical females and guessed he didn't need to cope with histrionics from her.

It was a golden opportunity to prove to him she wasn't the young superfluous girly that he had pegged her as. If she could show him that she could be brave and level-headed and mature, then maybe, if they actually got through this ordeal alive, he would realise she was a woman. Not a child.

She heard an engine start and realised they were in a vehicle. They were being transported somewhere. Was that good or bad? She took a deep breath and tried not to think about what lay ahead.

She felt her ankles being tied together and for a brief moment she witnessed the grey, leaden sky as the sack was removed from her head. She took the opportunity to drag in some deep breaths of fresh air and orientate herself. They were lying in the back tray of a utility truck. Where were they going? A black tarp was secured quickly into place above them and once again they were effectively blinded.

'You OK?' Richard asked as they felt the vehicle start to move.

Holly could just make him out as her eyes adjusted to the gloom. A thin sliver of light shone into the space from where the tarp hadn't been fully secured at the tailgate end. It was tied back slightly and allowed fresh air to circulate.

Holly nodded because she didn't quite trust her voice.

'See if you can get out of your ropes,' he said as he worked away at his. 'Let's try and get out of here before we get too far out of Abeil.'

Holly nodded again because she was pleased that he was thinking about ways to get them out of the situation. She battled with her bonds for a while but it was no use.

'Richard,' she said into the silence.

'Hmm?' he said, still concentrating.

'Are they going to kill us?'

Richard stopped the frustrating activity and heard the note in her voice that said she was scared but trying to be brave. He marshalled his thoughts. He needed to keep her positive and focused on their freedom. 'If they'd wanted to kill us, they would have already done it.'

Richard's reasoning sounded sensible. 'Why are they doing it, then?' Holly just couldn't work it out. She'd been a good person all her life. Why the hell was this happening to her?

'What's the matter? Holly,' he said as he worked at his ropes. 'Losing faith in the misunderstood? Still think the rebels aren't the enemy?'

She stopped trying to free herself and gritted her teeth. He wanted to goad her into a political debate now? 'I still think that they have reason to be angry. Don't you? Or do you just blindly swallow the government line?'

'No, I don't. As it happens, I have a lot of sympathy for their cause. But I have absolutely no tolerance for their tactics.'

Yeah, well, she didn't have a whole lot of tolerance for their tactics at the moment either. It still didn't stop her from recognising that they had been wronged and feeling for their struggle. 'Have you ever thought that maybe they're driven to these tactics and that maybe they're not endorsed by all of their followers? Do you think we should tar them all with the same brush?'

Richard sighed and cursed himself for derailing his attempt at focusing her. 'Look. I'm sorry. OK? Maybe you're right.'

Holly didn't hear much conviction in his voice. They were both silent for a few moments, reflecting on each other's words. 'I suspect they're probably going to hold us for ransom,' he said into the silence.

Holly felt momentarily cheered by the thought and their apparent value to these people. And then she remembered that her government didn't negotiate with terrorists and certainly didn't pay ransoms. How long would they be held for before the rebels got trigger-happy?

'And when our government refuses to talk with them?'

'Hopefully we'll be long gone.'

He grinned at her and despite their predicament and disagreement she felt encouraged by his confidence.

Richard gave up on his ties and looked at the tailgate that was just beyond his feet. He wriggled down until they were touching and then he kicked with all his might. The utility looked fairly old and rusty from the inside so maybe the catch would loosen.

He kicked at it repeatedly, striking it with both of his feet simultaneously. Nothing. It didn't budge. He tried again. And again.

'I don't think it's going to work,' she said when he stopped for a breather. The noise produced by his efforts had been deafening and Holly was glad of the respite.

Richard kicked it once again out of sheer frustration. There had to be a way out of this. Think, damn it! Think!

The ride started to get really bumpy and Holly knew as she was bounced around that she was going to be covered in a million bruises come tomorrow.

'Where do you think they're taking us?' she asked.

'Into the mountains is my guess. It's their stronghold.'

Confirming Richard's supposition, the utility started to tilt as if going up an incline and she heard a gear change.

Into the mountains? Holly remembered seeing them in the distance from the back of the orphanage. They'd always looked so majestic, jutting from the earth in all their emerald glory. But seeing them, admiring their beauty and actually being among them were different things. Holly shivered. They had always seemed so isolated and she felt fear slide down her spine.

Richard saw the worry etched on her pixie face and sensed her apprehension.

'It's going to be all right, Holly. I promise.'

She swallowed the rush of emotion that rose in her throat and nodded. His confidence gave her hope. She gave him a half-smile. She would be brave.

He shuffled over to where she lay because she was a lousy

actress and her body betrayed her doubt, and he desperately needed her to believe in him. To believe that he would keep her safe at all costs. He needed her to trust him and to do anything and everything he asked of her to get them out of this alive.

He could do nothing at the moment but lend her some comfort and if that's what it took to allay her fears and forge some trust then that's what he would do.

'Roll on your other side,' he said.

'Why?' she asked, eyeing him suspiciously.

'Because you're scared, and if I had the use of my arms I'd hug you but as I don't we can spoon instead. It's not ideal but it might help.'

'You want to spoon me?' she asked. Half of her was incredulous at his request the other half found it, given their dire circumstances, absurdly funny.

'Yes.' He smiled.

'What, no flowers, no champagne?' She smiled back.

'I'm a fast mover.' He shrugged.

Holly laughed but did as he'd requested. A cuddle to calm the nerves sounded like just the right medicine at the moment. And let's face it, she thought, they could do little else.

It was a tricky process, changing positions while lying down with your hands tied behind your back in a moving vehicle, but she accomplished it with reasonable dexterity.

Once she was over she shuffled back and finally their bodies came into contact. She shuffled around a bit more, fitting herself to the shape of his body before she settled and relaxed.

Of course, that put her hands in the wrong spot altogether. Oh, dear, here she was, abducted by rebels, and all she could think about was how close to his groin her hands were nestled.

'Don't even think about it.' His low voice held unmistakable humour and she gave a half-laugh. The rasp of his chin stubble grazed her neck slightly and she felt her nipples stiffen at the erotic sensation.

'Maybe I'm a fast mover, too,' she said.

He heard the corresponding humour in her voice and chuckled. 'What? No flowers? No champagne?' And they laughed together.

They fell into silence for a few minutes. Holly squirmed a bit more because the ropes were chafing her ankles and biting into her wrists and it was difficult to find a comfortable position.

'For God's sake, Holly, can you stay still?' Bad predicament or not, he was just a man. One who could remember how good they were together as if it were yesterday.

'Sorry.' She ceased her struggle and found a position she could live with.

Richard was conscious of how big he was around her. She fitted against him perfectly, emphasising her smallness. Her head fitted snugly under his chin and he had to suppress the urge to rub it against her soft hair. How many times had they lain together like this?

Holly couldn't believe in their desperate situation she could feel so calm, but the familiarity of their position took her back to happier times. Snuggled into him, her naked flesh hot against his as they'd waited for the next inevitable surge of desire to choreograph their frantic coupling.

Richard could feel her trembling lessen and felt pride swell inside him. She had to be scared out of her mind and to her credit she hadn't cried once. She was doing a great job but lying this close to her soft body her frightened state was obvious and he needed her to continue to be brave and strong.

He cast around for something to say. 'So, tell me about what you've been doing these last couple of years.'

Holly filled him in on her nursing career, her midwifery, her work at the hospital and her growing disillusion with medicine. He listened without interrupting and Holly realised how much she had missed their conversations. Maybe he hadn't always treated her as if she were two.

The ute banged over a hole in the road and Holly felt her hipbone smash against the metal floor. She winced as the truck lurched and the movement flung them to one side, Richard's weight pinning her against the side.

The road smoothed out again and Richard eased back slightly.

'You OK?' he asked.

'No. I'm sure I'll be black and blue tomorrow.'

They settled back against each other again.

'What about you, Richard? How was Africa?'

'Hot.'

Holly felt his body tense around her. 'Something happened to you there, didn't it?'

Richard spent a good part of his waking life trying not to think about Africa and most of his sleeping life right back there again. Her intuition surprised him. Did it show?

'Africa is in the past. I prefer to think about the future.' And the only future he was interested in at the moment was their immediate one.

'And what's in your future, Richard?'

'Getting through this ordeal.'

His abruptness brought their situation back into sharp focus again. But it also seemed to intensify her curiosity. They were both living on borrowed time, surely he could open up a little?

'I mean if we get out of this. Is there a special person on the scene? Any little Richards running around?'

She held her breath suddenly afraid he would say yes.

'I think you know me better than that. I don't need a family, remember?'

Unfortunately she remembered only too well. Holly heard the utter conviction in his voice. So some things hadn't changed. Did he truly believe he could go through life totally alone? Completely isolated? What a chilling thought. She snuggled her body closer to his instinctively seeking his warmth and hoping, somehow, to convince him he was wrong.

'Everyone needs family,' she said wistfully.

'The army is my family.'

She'd heard that come out of his mouth so often yet still it horrified her. This was what she'd been up against. A man who was the product of a broken home that he wouldn't talk about. He had been offered a safe haven, a refuge in the ranks of the military. A man who felt indebted to an organisation who had offered him the closest thing to a family he had ever known. A man consequently married to his job. 'Oh, very personal.'

'A family has never been on my list of priorities, Holly.'

'Your priorities suck,' she said quietly, appalled at his callous dismissal.

'My priority at the moment is getting you and preferably me out of here alive. I cannot, I will not think about anything else.'

The engine cut out abruptly and there was no time for any more idle chit-chat. Holly felt hot acid burning her throat as fear slammed into her again. 'I'm scared, Richard,' she said in a quiet voice.

'I know, Holly, but you've got to be strong. It's going to be tough but you can do it. Just watch me and follow my lead at all times. You have to be prepared to make a break for it at any time, OK?' he whispered frantically, before their captors came for them. 'I need you to trust me and do anything I ask. I don't care how strange it seems at the time, OK?'

She nodded and then they heard car doors open and voices getting closer and the tarp was pulled back, flooding the tray with bright light. Richard and Holly screwed their eyes shut. Their captors dragged them from the vehicle and they stumbled and swayed until their eyes became accustomed to the light.

Behind the car a dirt road led back down a relatively gentle gradient through the foothills and eventually back to Abeil. Ahead was a narrow track, disappearing upwards into apparent jungle.

'Where are we?' said Richard stalling.

'The hills, Sgt Hollingsworth,' said the leader.

'And you are?'

'You can call me…John,' he said, and laughed, obviously amusing himself.

Holly felt a chill slide down her spine at the coldness of his laugh. John, or whoever the hell he was, had creepy written all over him. His age was hard to gauge but Holly thought he looked about fifty.

He had small piggy eyes and greasy slicked-back hair. His thin lips seemed to have an almost permanent sneer and his teeth were yellowed. A thin, hand-rolled cigarette hung from the corner of his mouth and Holly noticed he had matching nicotine stains on his fingers. He looked…evil.

'Where are we going?' Richard demanded.

'Up,' he said.

Holly looked at the mountain before her. OK, it wasn't Everest but it was quite a climb.

'Why have we been abducted?' he demanded.

'An Australian army medic and an aid worker? Come, now, Sergeant, you'll fetch a pretty penny,' John taunted softly.

Richard curled his fingers into a fist behind his back. John would pay for his smugness. 'Our government won't pay and you will be tracked down and brought to justice.'

Holly stared agog at Richard's defiance as John chuckled loudly, joined by his brothers in arms. Way to go, Sarge! Goad them into shooting us now. Good plan.

John turned to one of his crew and issued an order. The younger man scurried quickly away, going to the car and bringing back a digital camera.

'Say cheese,' said John, and he pointed it at them, snapping a quick photo, the flash somewhat out of place in the primitive jungle setting.

John nodded to the same man and he took the camera back to the car, got in, started up the engine and took off like a bat out of hell. They watched the car disappear and then John barked another order and two men undid their ankle ropes.

Next they untied her hands and Holly rubbed at her chafed wrists as she felt the blood rush back to her fingers in a wave, gritting her teeth at the painful hot prickling sensation as feeling returned.

'Let's go,' said John, and Holly felt a gun prod her in the back.

'Untie my hands,' said Richard, refusing to move.

'Sorry Sergeant, I'd be a fool to do that. You will remain restrained and one false move from you and I will shoot your friend without thinking twice. Now move.'

Richard ignored the painful jab of the rifle in his ribs and dug in his heels.

'You're right, Sgt Hollingsworth. We don't need you both. I could just shoot her now,' said John, cocking Richard's pistol and pointing it at Holly's chest.

Richard saw Holly pale and close her eyes, preparing to die. He waited for her to wail or beg or scream abuse at him, but she stayed bravely silent. Slowly Richard began to move and John smiled triumphantly.

They walked in single file up the narrow mountain track. Two rebels led them, their rifles slung over their shoulders. The one at the front wore Richard's pack on his back. Holly came next, then Richard, then John, followed by two more armed rebels.

After an hour of solid walking up the steady incline Holly's legs were screaming for mercy. She was relatively fit but this mountain goat routine was testing her limits and the track stretched ever upwards. Were they going right to the top?

Her muscles protested another increase in the gradient. How were they going to be tomorrow? All providing she was alive then, of course. She couldn't believe how blasé she was becoming where her life was concerned. Although when John had pointed Richard's gun at her it had been a different story. Her heart still hadn't settled from the rush of adrenaline.

Mind you, the climb wasn't helping her heart rate. All they needed now was for it to rain. Looking at the sky and glancing at her watch, Holly figured it was just about time for the mid-afternoon monsoonal downpour.

Richard had been planning and plotting like a man on a mission, the view of Holly's back keeping him focused on his goal—to get the hell off this mountain. Alive! The further up they went the more out of his control the situation became. John was clearly very clever and Richard knew he'd have to stay alert to outsmart him.

Richard was certain an opportunity would present itself. He just had to be ready. He noted the many side tracks that ran off the main route down either side, like narrow tributaries snaking off a big river. Were they just formed from soil erosion during the monsoon or were they alternate pathways, short cuts even, that the rebel forces used when needed?

'So, John,' said Richard breaking the silence, 'you speak remarkably good English.' He may as well try to get as much information as possible.

Holly startled. Birds and insects had been the only sounds until now. She noted the distinct lack of puff in his voice. Maybe the man really was a machine?

'Thank you, Sergeant.'

'May I ask where you learnt it?'

'Australian schools are excellent Sergeant, but I guess you know that already.'

Richard was far from cheered by the leader's generosity in sharing information with him. He had expected to gain nothing useful—after all, John was too clever to give away important identifying facts. Unless…he already knew their fate. Richard's mouth set into a grim line. Not without a fight, Johnno. Not without a fight.

'I'm surprised an educated man would be party to such futile, thug tactics,' Richard goaded.

'Desperation can bring out the thug in us all, Sergeant. There has never been a better time to promote our cause. The whole world has witnessed Abeil's tragedy. We would be foolish to not take advantage of the free publicity.'

'Surely your cause is better promoted through political means. You must know you will only get the world off side through abducting us.'

'It is difficult to seek a political compromise when we are considered criminals and dismissed out of hand. Forty years of struggle and still a free state of Abeil remains elusive, Sergeant. We grow weary of the wait.'

'I still don't understand what you hope to gain from holding us hostage. As I've already said, our government doesn't negotiate with terrorists.'

'So, now we are terrorists. So much name calling.' Richard didn't have to turn around to see the smile on John's face. He could hear it.

'You are much more valuable to me than you know, Sgt Hollingsworth. It's not just the price we can put on your head.'

About to query the cryptic comment, Richard was cut off by a sudden deluge from the heavens. He was drenched in seconds. They all were. The noise of the rain was thunderous and drowned out all other sounds for the half-hour it lashed down around them.

Holly was just visible in front of him, struggling against the storm, slipping often on the track as dirt quickly turned to mud. She was doing so well. Much better than he'd expected a woman to be doing. She still hadn't cried or had a tantrum. She hadn't even broken her ankle.

If Holly had found it hard going before, it was almost impossible in the rain. The ground was slippery, making the route suddenly treacherous. Visibility was bad and she was frightened she'd stumble and plummet right off the edge down the sheer drop on either side. Her clothes weighed a ton and her boots and socks felt like they were made of lead. Her thighs and calves ached.

She wanted her mother. And a cup of tea. And a warm bed. She wanted to close her eyes and for this all to be a bad dream. So she did the only thing she could do in this sort of situation. She cried.

Oh, she was quiet about it. She didn't beat her chest and shake her fist at the heavens, which was exactly as she felt like doing. She felt the hot tears well in her eyes and let them run unchecked down her cheeks.

There was so much water running down her face no one would be any the wiser and there was too much noise to hear her muted sobs. She would be all right in a minute. She just needed to release all her fear and anxiety and frustration. Then she could be brave again. She had to stay in control for Richard, so she could do whatever had to be done, but just for the moment she wanted to indulge her oestrogen and be a girl.

As the rain tailed off so did the incline and Holly sighed with relief as the strain on her aching muscles eased. They were walking along an almost flat area now that undulated gently from time to time. The track was wider and she didn't feel like one wrong footfall, one slip, could mean instant death.

The two rebels in front of her held their weapons high above their heads as they entered a puddle that lay across the track. Holly thought it rather strange until she realised that the puddle was deeper than it seemed. They were hip deep in it before she could blink.

Holly sighed and trudged in, too. She refused to think about the bacteria and parasites and the myriad creepy-crawlies that were probably swimming around her in the soup-like brown water.

She could tell her almost pathological fear of creepy-crawlies was going to get a real workout in the jungle. Not quite the way she'd hoped to confront it! Richard, who had been privy to her bug paranoia on more than one occasion, had enough to worry about without her squealing every time an insect landed on her!

The water became waist deep and her boots sank into the thick mud at the bottom grabbing at her feet each time she lifted one, making her progress twice as difficult. Every time something brushed her legs she had to suppress a scream. Did they have piranhas in this part of the world? Or water snakes?

She waded out the other side and turned and looked behind her at Richard, who was having to complete the chore with his hands tied behind his back. She wanted to wade back in and help him, despite having only just thought she never wanted to repeat the experience. She started to do just that but was prevented from doing so by a gun pushing into her ribs.

He smiled at her, a smile that said, I'm OK, it'll be OK and keep your chin up. The smile she gave him was kind of weary before she was prodded onwards again. She wanted to scream at them to leave her alone and let her rest but she remembered Richard had told her to keep her mouth shut so she set it in a grim line and plodded on.

Richard kept his eye on Holly's soaked form in front of him. He knew it was taking every inch of her courage to walk through the dirty water and not dissolve into hysterics. Holly didn't do insects or any kind of creepy-crawly. Yep, she'd be totally freaked by now.

How many spiders, cockroaches and other household insects had he'd killed at her insistence? Poor creatures innocently going about their business, unaware of the size-twelve boot descending upon them.

Holly lost track of the number of puddles and creeks they walked through. Each one seemed worse than the last, and she doubted if she'd ever been more drenched or more freaked out in her entire life.

Just when she thought she could go on no further, a clearing appeared ahead and she smelt the woodsmoke before she saw the fine wisps trailing heavenwards. As they approached, people came out to greet the soldiers and look curiously at the prizes they had brought with them.

Not that she felt like much of a prize. She was exhausted. Every muscle protested. She was soaked and her hair bedraggled. She longed to sit down and the sight of the fire burning in the background called to her on a primal level.

Pigs, chickens and the odd goat roamed freely around the central area. Young children eyed them with inquisitive stares, giggling and pointing and then running away to play. The camp was alive with noise—animal sounds, children's laughter, the crackling of the communal fire and adult chatter.

Somewhere in the background a woman screamed. Holly wondered for a moment if she was delirious because nobody seemed to be paying it any heed. The noise stopped, to be replaced by muted wailing and moaning. The unknown woman was obviously in pain. What was happening to her? Was somebody torturing her? Was that why no one seemed to give a damn?

'Why is that woman screaming?' demanded Richard. He had heard her pain and distress too, and his thoughts were running in a similar vein to Holly's.

'Relax, Sergeant,' said John, his voice full of derision. 'She is in labour.'

Holly almost sagged in relief, and she saw Richard's shoulders visibly relax. That certainly explained it. Holly had heard enough labouring women to be confident John was telling them the truth. She also knew that different cultures handled labour pain in their own ways. Still, her distress rang around the clearing and Holly hoped everything was OK.

'We will rest here for the night,' said John. 'We'll set out in the morning for the next camp.'

'Higher?' said Holly because the mere thought made her want to join the labouring woman and howl like a banshee.

'Higher,' he confirmed, and nodded to one of his colleagues who prodded them with his rifle butt, herding them into a rickety wooden shelter with a dry earthen floor. Some sort of woven fronds formed the roof and a fire burned in the middle of the floor surrounded by a ring of stones.

A door shut them in and through the wooden slats they could see two armed guards posted at the door.

'Are you OK?' Richard asked her.

Now was not the time to dissolve into tears but the concern in his voice was almost her undoing.

'Sore and tired,' she said quietly, 'but, still, I think I'm better than her,' she said, indicating the renewed screaming they could hear.

'Untie me,' he said, turning and presenting his imprisoned wrists.

'Oh, God, Richard, I'm sorry,' she said, attacking the ropes quickly. It took her for ever to undo them. The rain and Richard's attempt to loosen them had tightened them to the point of impossible.

'Richard, what a mess. Do they hurt?' she gasped as she pulled the last knot free. She lightly stroked the bloody rope burns encircling his wrists, pulling her fingers away as he winced at her touch.

'Like you wouldn't believe,' he said, assessing the damage himself. If he'd had his kit he could have dressed them properly, but he was just going to have to try to keep them clean and pray that they didn't get infected in the moist jungle environment teeming with bacteria.

There was a bucket of water sitting next to a pile of wood in one corner. It looked fresh and the bucket clean so he dipped the edge of his shirt into the water and squeezed it out over his wounds.

'Here, let me,' Holly offered, and knelt beside him.

She scooped small palmfuls of water and sluiced them over his wrists. It felt cooling and soothing and stung like hell all at the same time. She was gentle and he looked at her bowed head and his heart did a funny flutter thing that had no place in the predicament they were in.

'So, what happens now?' she asked, looking at him suddenly and catching him looking at her. She felt a constriction in her chest at the puzzled look she saw on his face.

'If we can't escape tonight, I guess we go higher.'

'I can't, Richard.'

'Sure you can.' He smiled at her. 'It's amazing what you can do with a gun poked into your back.'

'Do you think the outside world knows about us yet?' she asked, sitting on the floor, satisfied his wrists were as clean as she was going to get them.

'They might not have received the picture yet, but Kathleen and my CO are going to know we're missing. And Kathleen knows we were together. I suspect they're probably already searching for us.'

'And they're going to look for us here? In the mountains?'

'Once a ransom demand is made and it becomes clear the rebels are holding us, I'd say this will be the first place they'll look. Unfortunately there are quite a lot of mountains in this region and they cover an extensive tract of land.'

'So…we're screwed? We're going to die. It's over.'

'Absolutely not. Come on, where's that Pollyanna attitude? It ain't over till the fat lady sings.'

Another scream broke the humid air and Holly got the giggles. It wasn't exactly singing and it was only temporary fat but it was ironic nonetheless. Still, as omens went, it seemed kind of ridiculous so Holly didn't see the point in worrying. And when Richard's deep throaty laughter joined hers, the seriousness of the situation faded.

'Come on, then,' said Richard after their laughter had petered out. 'Socks and shoes off. Let's try and get our stuff dry before we have to get going in the morning.'

Holly followed suit, wringing the excess water out of her thick socks and laying them in front of the fire next to her waterlogged boots.

'It'll be dark soon. Once the camp settles for the night you can take your damp clothes off and dry them properly by the fire, but if you sit near enough you should be able to start the process.' Richard imparted this information very dispassionately. Whatever else he did, he must not think of a near-naked Holly or let her know the thought terrified him more than all the rebels in Abeil.

Richard was right. Darkness descended quite quickly and delicious smells from the communal campfire they could see through the slats of their prison made Holly's mouth water. Her stomach grumbled loudly and she realised she hadn't had anything to eat since breakfast.

Her hunger almost took her mind off their situation and then the woman having the baby would cry out again and it was all brought back into sharp focus. They were in the middle of the wilds, held hostage by a rebel army, and their future was uncertain at best.

At least having Richard by her side stemmed the hysteria that threatened every time she thought about their circumstances. Her arm rubbed against his as they sat with their backs to the fire and she yearned to snuggle into the circle of his arms and draw the quiet strength and confidence he exuded so effortlessly.

The door opened a little and a woman entered with two bowls full of plain rice. Holly devoured hers as if it was the grandest offering fit for a king. There was nothing in the bowl that resembled the aromas coming from outside but it was something to fill the stomach and beggars couldn't be choosers.

'I think we should get some sleep,' said Richard after they'd finished eating. 'How dry are you now?' he asked.

'My shirt and bra are dry but my cargos are still a little on the damp side.'

'Why don't you take them off and lay them in front of the fire for a while?' He tried not to let her see his concern at the thought of seeing her bare legs. 'I'll turn my back,' he offered hastily, and promptly did just that.

Holly stared at his back. She hadn't picked him as a prude. For goodness' sake, all he'd see was a bit of leg and now he was making her feel self-conscious. She quickly slipped her cargos off and spread them on the ground. 'What about you? Surely your fatigues are damp too?'

'I'll survive,' he said, his back still to her.

'Richard, I have seen naked men before.'

'I really don't want to discuss your sex life, Holly.'

She shook her head at his back and snorted. 'I meant I'm a nurse, Richard. But, hey, if you're having problems getting sex and me off your mind—'

'I do not have sex with you or anyone on my mind,' he snapped, turning to refute the point and immediately wishing he hadn't. Her legs were every bit as spectacular as he remembered. Petite and shapely. Standing before him in a black T-shirt and black, barely there knickers, it was suddenly easy to forget that two armed rebel soldiers were less than a metre away.

'Good, because I'm too tired and all that screaming is giving me a headache. I'm going to sleep,' she said, lying on the earthen floor a little way from the fire and turning her back to him.

Her hipster briefs rode up one cute butt cheek and Richard stared at the creamy flesh, mesmerised. Well, he couldn't take his trousers off now. There were things inside that were being more of a soldier than he was at the moment!

He followed her lead and turned his back to the fire, positioning himself close to the door so it couldn't be opened without him knowing. He tried to find a spot on the rock-hard ground that was the least uncomfortable. It certainly brought more meaning to the saying between a rock and a hard place!

Holly was exhausted. A deep exhaustion that seeped into her bones. She couldn't remember ever feeling so weary. Not even the regular screams that continued to come from somewhere behind them could stop her eyes from closing. Although somewhere she registered that they were more loud miserable moans now and that the woman seemed to be tiring. Too exhausted to find the energy to scream.

Well…she could certainly relate to that!

CHAPTER FIVE

RICHARD awoke to the door being opened onto his ribs. He sprang to his feet and took an immediate defensive position.

'Easy, Richard,' warned John, pointing the pistol at him, ever-present cigarette hanging from his mouth. 'We need your expertise.'

'What expertise?' he asked, hearing Holly stir behind him. 'Get dressed,' he said to her curtly, and turned back to John while still blocking the doorway.

'The labour isn't going well.'

'I'm no midwife, John. Don't you have someone here who usually handles that?'

'We used to but she didn't return to the camp after the typhoon. We assumed she was one of its many victims. Even the rebels lost people to the sea, Sergeant.'

'I'm a midwife,' said Holly, coming to stand by Richard. She swayed as she fought off the cloud of exhaustion that still hung heavily over her head. Her eyes felt gritty and sore.

'No,' said Richard, barring her movement.

'Yes,' she said. She took some comfort from the fact that he was obviously protecting her, but whoever the labouring woman was she needed help. 'It's OK, Richard. I want to help.'

'Good,' said John. 'You come,' he said to Holly, 'You stay,' he said to Richard. 'Don't think of doing anything funny. My guards will kill you without hesitation.'

'One moment,' she said, and quickly removed her contacts. Her eyes felt like they were on fire and something told her she'd need to concentrate. She flicked them into the fire, feeling a momentary pang. They hadn't been cheap but…there was no need to accessorise in the middle of nowhere.

Holly was led to a shelter similar to theirs further up the track. Every step was agony as her rested muscles protested their reuse.

'This is Mila and her mother Kia,' introduced John.

Holly smiled at the women confidently, trying not to betray her inner turmoil. She'd completed her midi last year but had been so disillusioned by obstetric intervention that she hadn't practised as a registered midwife.

'What's the problem?' Holly addressed Mila, who was lying on a low bed and looked completely and utterly exhausted. She looked so young, barely a teenager, her large belly dwarfing her.

'Kia says the baby is stuck,' said John.

'How long has she been in labour?' Holly looked at her watch. They'd already been here for about eight hours.

'Three days,' said John after consulting with Kia.

Holly had to stop herself from gasping. No wonder the poor girl looked so weary. Her mind raced. A prolonged labour, a small mother and a large baby. If the baby was truly stuck, in such primitive surroundings there would be little she could do. She needed to check its position first.

'I need Richard,' she said to John, 'and his medical kit.'

'No. Just you.'

'She needs rehydrating and if this baby arrives as flat as I think it will, it'll need some resuscitation. I need Richard and his bag. Now.'

John nodded sullenly and left. Richard was back in one minute.

'You got fluid in that bag?' she asked, barely acknowledging his presence.

'Saline, Haemaccel, Hartman's.'

'Get a cannula in her. Give her a litre of Hartman's. Any gloves?'

Holly was relieved to put the latex protection on. She knew from the briefings there was a high level of STDs among the locals and HIV was also prevalent. She hadn't wanted to come into contact with the girl's bodily fluids until she had protected herself.

She inserted a finger and could feel the baby's head right there. She was almost at the end. But what kind of shape would the baby be in? Was it still alive? This far down the birth canal a heartbeat was difficult to detect even if she'd had the right equipment.

An oil lamp gave reasonable light and Holly was glad for Richard's expertise as he easily slipped an IV in and hooked up some fluids.

'Let's run it in fully open,' said Holly. 'Once she's had it I want to get her up off her back. Get her squatting and see if we can get the baby moving with a position change.'

The fluid took fifteen minutes to run through during which time Mila had ten contractions and the baby remained stubbornly unmoved. Richard bunged the peripheral cannula and, with the help of John translating, they encouraged a slightly rallied Mila into a squatting position. Holly encouraged Kia to sit on the low bed behind her daughter and allow Mila to lean back against her between contractions.

Once Mila had adopted the best pelvic opening position, the head delivered quite quickly, despite Holly's best efforts to slow it down. The last thing she needed was for Mila's perineum to tear. How would she stitch it?

Luckily it didn't happen. How, Holly would never be able to say because the head was huge! Even badly moulded and looking rather cone shaped it was amazingly big. If this baby wasn't over four kilos she'd eat her hat.

As she lay down on the floor to get a closer look, Holly wondered if Mila had gestational diabetes. It would explain the huge baby and, particularly with no ante-natal care, the diabetes would have been largely uncontrolled.

Holly felt her heart rate settle, knowing they were over the hardest part. Only she was wrong. So wrong. It became quickly apparent that the shoulders were now stuck fast. Holly groaned inwardly. Shoulder dystocia? To think she had been worried about a perineum tear! This was much more dire. Much more fraught with complications.

She shouldn't have been that surprised, given the circumference of the head. The shoulders were obviously too broad to descend through the pelvis and the anterior shoulder was probably caught on one of the pelvic bones.

As far as obstetric emergencies went, this was up there. The cheeks of the baby puffed as a contraction tore through Mila but the baby, which should have just slid out, was stuck fast. Holly knew that the cord was being compressed as each second ticked by compromising the baby's oxygen supply.

She found herself yearning for the obstetric services that were on tap at a hospital. The very thing that had frustrated her as a student midwife was the one thing she needed now more than anything else. An obstetrician.

'What's wrong?' asked Richard. He had seen the play of emotions on her face and knew something wasn't good.

'Shoulder dystocia.'

'Oh.' He may have had limited obstetric experience but he knew enough to know it was a potentially life-threatening condition.

Luckily Holly had firsthand experience with dystocia. She'd been the only midwife in her student group who had witnessed a dystocia delivery.

He brought the oil lamp down closer to the action. 'You can do it, Holly,' said Richard quietly, and squeezed her arm.

She looked at him and looked at the faith on his face and she just knew that she'd walk over hot coals to prove him right. So, she wanted an obstetrician. Well, she didn't have one. She had herself and she had Richard—and she could do this. They could do this.

'Richard, when this baby comes out it's going to be flat as a tack. I'm going to need you to do the resus while I keep taking care of Mila. OK?'

'OK,' he said.

She hadn't expected such a confident reply and his conviction crystallised her thoughts. She straightened her shoulders. If he wasn't fazed then neither was she—they could do this.

Holly inserted a finger to see if she could loosen the shoulder off the shelf the pelvic bone had formed. She prodded and pushed and tried to rotate with no success, and as the seconds ticked by she knew the baby was getting closer to asphxia. She tried to gently rock the baby's head, hoping to dislodge it from its position. A bit like easing a cork out of a wine bottle. Still no success. Still the clock ticked.

An episiotomy was what she needed. A surgical incision into the perineum used to create more room by widening the birth canal.

'What are you thinking?' Richard asked, watching the concentration puckering her brow.

'That I wished I had the facilities to do an episiotomy.'

'I have suture material,' he offered.

Holly hesitated for a second and looked around her at the primitive conditions. 'It's too risky. If she haemorrhages from the site she'll die, and then there's infection.' She cast another look around her with the eyes of a nurse and saw potential bacteria sources everywhere.

She felt overwhelmed suddenly and cast Richard a helpless

look. Richard understood how she felt. Working in less than ideal conditions was almost second nature for him, but Holly was used to having a gamut of medical equipment and personnel on hand. He understood how alone it felt to be the one every one was looking to.

'Got a plan B?' he prompted.

His calm voice intruded on her helplessness. She looked at him and drew strength from his assuredness. She nodded. She had one more manoeuvre up her sleeve. She had to try and deliver the posterior arm to make room for the opposite shoulder. And if that didn't work she was going to have to perform the episiotomy and pray it didn't all go to hell in a hand basket.

He squeezed her arm encouragingly. She drew strength from his faith and turned back to her task. She took a deep steadying breath and inserted as much of her hand into the vagina as she could. She located the arm she needed, flexing it at the elbow and sweeping it up and across the baby's chest until it was delivered.

She didn't have time to congratulate herself. No time to rejoice. She had to hope she'd created enough room to rotate the body and apply downward pressure so the shoulder could finally be delivered.

And it worked. The shoulder cleared and she pulled the baby free of the birth canal. She lifted it up, looking at the not-so-little boy, momentarily triumphant before his pale face and silent mouth registered and she passed him hastily to Richard.

Richard's hand shook as he accepted the wet newborn. Holly had done her bit now it was his turn. OK. This was not his usual area of expertise but the ABCs still applied.

'Rub him vigorously with a clean cloth. Clear his mouth with your finger. Pinch his nose and sweep downward to remove all the mucus.'

Holly prattled off the orders as she continued to lie on her side on the floor, tending to Mila. Her eyes hadn't left her patient. Kia handed Richard a cloth and he did as he was instructed. Still the infant remained unresponsive. He could feel a slow carotid pulse.

'What's the heart rate?' she asked, looking at him momentarily, her ears tuned for a cry and becoming more alarmed at not hearing it.

'Forty.'

Their eyes locked for a second, sharing the seriousness of the situation. 'Don't let this baby die now, Richard,' she said.

Richard moved into action. Its heart needed to beat faster and he knew he was going to have to initiate some external cardiac massage and give the babe some breaths.

He lay the baby on the cloth on the ground and, using the tips of his index and middle fingers, rapidly pushed the centre of the baby's chest. His injured wrists protested the movement but he ignored them. He puffed some breaths into the baby's lungs by placing his mouth over the baby's mouth and nose. Once, twice, three times.

And then the baby coughed and then he spluttered and finally took a breath. The joyous noise of lusty cries filled the air and everyone in the shelter, everyone in the camp, breathed a collective sigh of relief. He watched as the baby pinked up rapidly, waving its arms around, apparently furious at its traumatic entry into the world.

He handed the baby boy to Mila, whose sobbing had turned to joy. She took him eagerly despite her exhaustion. Both Mila and her mother were crying, gabbling away at each other and talking to Richard and Holly with huge, broad grins.

'They are thanking you,' said John, cigarette drooping from his bottom lip.

She was relieved to see the baby waving his right arm around like nothing had ever happened. A high percentage of babies born with shoulder dystocia ended up with impaired or no movement in their affected arm. All the tugging and twisting and pulling required to get the baby out could stretch and irreparably damage the brachial nerve plexus situated in the baby's neck.

Thankfully there had been good outcome achieved tonight. Better than Holly had dared to hope for. But what if the baby had died? She glanced up at a very dispassionate John, his cold eyes watching her through a thin trail of smoke. Would it have been a death sentence for them if the baby had been stillborn?

Back in their own shelter again, Holly looked at her trembling hands and felt the muscles in her legs turn to jelly. She was shaking all over as she sat down and thrust her hands towards the warmth of the fire. The air was quite cool now and reaction to the events had chilled her even more.

'That was amazing, Holly,' said Richard, feeling on a real high, momentarily forgetting their situation.

Holly saw the gleam lighting his black eyes and recognised it instantly. It was the buzz that only witnessing the birth of a baby could give you. She knew that look intimately and it reminded her of the reasons she had become a midwife in the first place. Before the politics and power games of obstetrics had jaded her.

She only wished she could return it. At the moment she was feeling too...strung out. It had been a huge day. Being taken hostage had been bad enough, but the stress of holding a baby's life in her hands had been much worse. With the adrenaline rush over, all the what-ifs surfaced. She felt absurdly like crying again and the fire blurred before her eyes.

'You were amazing,' he said, and smiled at her.

She blinked rapidly. 'I was scared out of my mind.'

She shivered as a cool breeze caressed her bare arms. The pale skin puckered and she rubbed the flesh to warm it.

Her admission caused him to look at her, and he saw her blank expression and the weariness in every line of her body as she sat hunched by the fire. His old protective instincts stirred. 'You're cold,' he stated.

'A little. I'll just move closer to the fire,' she said dismissively because she was too emotionally raw at the moment to take his kindness. Suddenly all she wanted was for him to take her in his arms and kiss her and that made her feel even more wretched, because she didn't understand why she'd feel like this when there were so many more important things to think about. Like her life.

He shrugged off his long-sleeved fatigue shirt and draped it over her shoulders.

'I'm all right, Richard,' she restated in a firm voice. 'It's no problem. I'm not cold.'

The shirt was heavenly. It contained his body heat and his smell and she wanted to bury her face in it. Distant memories were being triggered. How many times had he comforted her when she'd needed it? Held her when she'd been upset. Kissed her better when she'd been hurt? He may have always kept a frustrating emotional distance but he'd never denied her physical closeness.

Accepting his gift would move her into dangerous waters. She was just managing to keep it together and as much as she was over him their situation was extraordinary and she needed a little human comfort now more than anything. The urge to feel his lips on hers was growing so powerful she could almost taste him.

'I said no, Richard,' she snapped, and shrugged the shirt off her shoulders so it lay in the dirt behind her.

'Hey. What's wrong?' he asked, gently grasping her chin and forcing him to look at her.

'Besides being kidnapped by rebels and dying for a cup of tea and being scared witless that baby was going to die and wanting my mother, you mean?'

'Is there more?' he asked, trying to make a joke, but he could tell by looking into her eyes that she was tired and fragile.

'Yes, actually, there is. I'm sitting next to a man who has no idea that just taking his shirt off for me makes me want to kiss him so badly I want to scream. But he doesn't want to kiss me, in fact, he dismisses me outright as just some young little piece of fluff. None of which should matter to me because we're stuck in the jungle with armed rebel soldiers at every turn, and it's highly likely I'll die from a rebel bullet long before sexual frustration claims me, but…there you go…that's how I feel.'

Oh, boy! She wasn't kidding when she said there was more. His gut lurched as her admission about kissing him twisted inside him. If only she new how tempted he was!

'I'm sorry for dismissing you as a young little piece of fluff because what you did tonight was incredible. And for what it's worth, I do want to kiss you, Holly. Very much. But nothing will change the fact that I'm fifteen years older than you and you want things I can't give you.'

'And what would you do if I just leant over and kissed you?'

At the moment he'd probably kiss her right back because she looked so small and fragile and feminine by the firelight, and that appealed to him on levels he hadn't even known existed. And she'd lain in the dirt tonight and refused to give up when a defenceless life had hung in the balance, and that appealed even more.

Richard swallowed. 'It would be a mistake, Holly.' He hoped he sounded more convincing than he felt.

The fire seemed to crackle louder between them, the insects outside grew noisier as the silence inside the shelter stretched. To hell with him, she thought, and moved her head, her lips, a little closer to his.

'Holly,' he warned quietly, when he could feel her breath mingle with his. 'Don't do this.'

'All you have to do is move away, Richard,' she whispered, staring at his lips.

She was right. All he had to do was get up and move away. Now. Right now. But…he couldn't. And he needed her to see it was wrong.

'Holly, please. It's not the time or place.'

He saw her shut her eyes, and he drew in a deep ragged breath as she moved her body back from his.

'Holly—'

'Don't, Richard,' she said quietly, turning her back to him and settling herself on the ground. 'I'm tired and tomorrow I'm going to be forced at gunpoint to climb another mountain.'

He touched her shoulder lightly. 'Holly.'

She shrugged it away. 'Don't touch me.'

Richard spent the rest of the night dozing, waking frequently, throwing another log on the fire and checking that Holly was OK. He told himself he was too alert, too wary to give in to the black abyss of sleep, but in his gut he knew he was scared. Too scared to sleep lest he should dream the dreams that haunted most of his nights.

He didn't want Holly to see his vulnerability. She had to believe he was strong. Invincible. That he could get them out of there. She thought he was a tough guy and that worked to his advantage. If she saw him at his worst, the strung-out mess his nightmares always reduced him to, she might lose faith in his ability to get them out of this alive. And that was to be avoided at all costs.

Richard was awake at the dawning of their second day of captivity and watched as the camp stirred to life. The first rays of sun poked through the canopy heating the moisture-laden air. Even this early, the jungle hissed and steamed around them.

He glanced at Holly, the early morning light filtering through the slats casting shadows against her skin. She'd rolled on her back and her shirt had ridden up, revealing her flat midriff and delicate waist.

He stared because he couldn't help himself. Her small high breasts, outlined in all their perfection by the T-shirt, rose and fell in unison with her respirations. Her mouth had relaxed and looked soft and very kissable.

He felt a stirring in his groin that by itself wasn't so unusual at this hour of the morning but had nothing to do with his diurnal rhythms. It was the memory of last night's kiss or near kiss. He could feel the anticipation, the longing as strongly this morning as he had last night. And even hours later, knowing he had done the right thing, it didn't lessen the impact.

Holly stirred and stretched slightly, recoiling instantly and becoming fully awake.

Her eyes came to rest on Richard sitting propped against the wall looking like hell, and she knew she wasn't just waking from a really bad dream. She was living it. Fortunately the intense pain in her legs overrode any lingering embarrassment from his rejection last night.

'I can't move, Richard,' she groaned. She really started to panic then. No way could she manage more mountain climbing today. Would they shoot her if she couldn't…wouldn't? Or would they let her crawl on her hands and knees?

Richard heard the agony in her voice. He knew how badly her muscles must be hurting today. Luckily for him, part of his job involved strenuous physical tests and pushing himself to the limits of endurance.

Today's journey was going to be a particularly horrific form of hell for her. Worse than yesterday. She needed to rest but that wasn't going to happen, and if they had a good opportunity to escape she would have to run. Run hard. There was nothing for it, she needed to warm her muscles up first.

'Stay where you are,' he ordered as he crawled to where she lay. He picked up her legs and plonked them across his lap.

'What are you doing?' she asked, half sitting, trying to remove her legs from contact with his body.

'I'm going to massage your calves and thighs. It's the only way you'll make it today.'

'Forget it. I'm never going to make it,' she protested again, trying to remove her legs and wincing as a sharp pain tore through her leg muscles.

He started to knead her calf muscles, knowing that they were too sore for her to move them away again. 'You can make it,' he said as his long fingers worked at the bunched fibres.

'I can't,' she whimpered as his fingers created agony and ecstasy in equal measure. Tears of pain stung her eyes and she swiped them away.

'You can and you will, and when I see a side path or an opportunity I'm going to yell at you to break. You're going to react instantly and run like the wind and we'll be free.'

His pep talk was more for his own benefit than hers. If he could treat her like one of his men, he could ignore that the flesh beneath his fingers was smooth and supple instead of bulky and hairy. That her ankle was delicate and her knee slim and the fact that her thighs led to an entirely different place to that of one of his men's.

Despite the torture, Holly had to remind herself that rebel soldiers were a mere metre away. Because if she didn't and she could actually physically get up without collapsing in screaming agony, she'd jump his bones, whether he liked it or not. His ministrations were so erotically painful she didn't know whether to scream or to purr.

Kia entered just as Holly thought she was about to drool in the dirt. She smiled at them shyly as Richard released Holly. She had brought them some breakfast and it smelt so delicious Holly knew she'd drag her aching body over an acre of broken glass to get to it.

Through their limited knowledge of each other's language Holly managed to ascertain that the baby was doing well and that Mila was recovering nicely. Holly could tell Kia had sympathy for their plight and she wondered if that could be useful.

When Kia came back to retrieve their bowls, Richard indicated he wanted to speak to John. Now they had gained some kudos with the delivery of Mila's baby, Richard felt it was time to exploit their deed for all it was worth. If he could find out where they were going and what the rebels had planned for them, it would have been a worthwhile exercise.

'You rang?' said John, standing at the doorway several minutes later, a sardonic smile in place.

Richard walked outside and away from Holly. 'We saved a child's life last night. How about you reciprocate and let us go?'

John laughed and it disturbed some birds nesting in the jungle canopy. 'Sergeant, you amuse me. Good try.'

'OK. Release Holly. You'll still have me. Consider it a gesture of good faith. Our government will look favourably upon it.'

John laughed again. 'Do you really think you were a random selection, Sergeant? We've been watching you and your mosquito foraging forays into Abeil for weeks. The red cross on your shoulder makes you very useful to us. Yes, we can get money for you. We can buy food and medicine and weapons, but as I've already said you are far more valuable to us.'

'Oh?' said Richard, intrigued despite himself.

'Fumradi is ill. He needs medical attention. We chose you.'

'Fumradi? The rebel leader?'

'Very good, Sergeant.' He smiled cynically. 'You are well informed.'

'Take him to a hospital.'

'No hospitals. He would be arrested as soon as he was admitted.'

'Take him to the army hospital. We treat anyone, regardless. It's part of our mandate.'

'No hospitals.' He dropped his cigarette and ground it into the forest floor. The steel in his voice would have done a sergeant-major proud.

'OK,' said Richard, holding up his hands. 'So let me get this straight. You abduct me at gunpoint, threaten my life, restrain me and keep me under lock and key, and expect me to treat one

of the people who perpetrated—worse, who no doubt ordered—this crime against me?'

'You are astute, Sergeant.'

'You could have just asked. This cross,' he said, pointing to
his sleeve, 'means, regardless of who you are or what you've
done, I'm honour bound to treat you. How far away is he?'

'We will get to top camp tomorrow,' said John.

'So, what's wrong with your leader?'

'He was wounded two days ago in battle. He is a very brave
man.'

Richard knew there were still skirmishes that occurred daily
in the disputed territories between government and rebel troops.
He also knew that the rebels had used the chaos and confusion
caused by the typhoon to reinvigorate the fight for independence.

'He has a fever now,' John finished.

Great, thought Richard. How the hell did they know that he
was even still alive? Fever meant infection and infections could
be deadly. 'Did someone remove the bullet?' he asked.

'I did,' John said.

'What if he's already dead when we get there? By the time
we reach him another four days will have already passed. If his
wound is infected it may be too late.'

'You'd better hope for your sake he's not, Sergeant. If you
are of no use to us then we'll have to revert to plan B and see
what your government is willing to pay.'

'They won't pay,' said Richard, his voice matter-of-fact.

'Then I guess you're in a spot of bother,' said John, and gave
a sickening chuckle.

'Two conditions,' said Richard. 'I won't be bound. I won't
be locked up. I give you my word I will not escape. I will treat
your leader but not as a prisoner, as an Australian soldier doing the job he came here to do.'

John considered it for a moment. 'Granted.'

'Release the woman.'

'No way, Sergeant. The woman is my insurance policy. She stays. That is not negotiable. When Fumradi is better we will release you both. I give you my word.'

'No deal.'

John laughed again and Richard was actually chilled by the harshness of it. 'You think I won't shoot her now, Sergeant? You want to test me on that one? Better still, I could leave her here alone with some of my soldiers that have a particular liking for white women.'

Richard felt the bile rise in his throat.

'You'll treat Fumradi whether she's alive or dead, because that's the kind of person you are. It's up to you what happens to your woman.'

Richard walked right up to John, closing the distance in an instant and grabbing the front of his shirt. He dwarfed the older man and took pleasure in the fleeting glimpse of fear he saw in the man's eyes. He heard the cocking of guns and the demands in a foreign tongue that he had no trouble translating, as nearby soldiers became nervous.

'You touch one hair on her head, she gets a scratch and everything that this cross stands for…goes out the window.'

John grabbed Richard's hand and forcibly removed it from near his throat. He took a step back. 'So we understand each other, Sergeant. You do your bit and I'll do mine.'

Richard turned away, not trusting himself to answer. Their situation had drastically improved. They would be kept alive while they were useful but the threat to Holly's safety, her life, burnt in his gut.

'If you can't save our leader, all bets are off,' said John to Richard's retreating frame.

Richard slowed and turned, the dank, sizzling heat of the jungle reflecting his seething mood. 'Oh, I can save him, John. And I will hold you to your promise. You can bet on that.'

CHAPTER SIX

EVERY step Holly took was agony. Even on level ground her calves and thighs screamed at her, but this steady incline was excruciating. To make matters worse, the humidity was oppressive. Sweat ran down her face and arms and trickled between her breasts.

They were largely protected from direct sunlight by the sparse canopy overhead, but the heat and the moisture made the march hard going. Holly felt as if she was constantly pushing against a wall of wet blankets.

The knowledge that they had been taken for a purpose didn't fill her with as much joy now as it had when Richard had first told her about it that morning.

'See,' she had said, 'not such bad people after all.' And he had given her a scowl.

But it didn't take her too long to figure out that Richard was the valuable one. Her capture had been purely incidental—she had been in the wrong place at the wrong time. So she wasn't needed. Putting it bluntly, she was expendable.

As he marched, Richard forced himself to concentrate on what he had in his pack that would be useful in treating his patient instead of how much he wanted to deck John. And how much he wanted to shake Holly.

Fluids and clean dressings. And antibiotics. But only a very limited stock of these lifesaving drugs, enough for one dose of each. If Fumradi's wound had gone septic it wouldn't be enough. It could buy them some time but getting a raging infection after his initial injury, one dose of antibiotics was like throwing a hand grenade at the Great Wall of China, hoping to reduce it to rubble. It just wasn't going to work.

Well, there was nothing he could do about it now. He had given his word that he would treat Fumradi and that's what he would do. For the moment at least, if nothing else, it gave them a potential reprieve.

Suddenly they heard helicopters overhead and John halted the party, ordering them all to get down low and stay still. Richard looked up and through the trees could make out the familiar shape of a Blackhawk.

'Is that one of ours?' Holly asked turning in her crouch position to Richard.

'Yep.' He smiled.

Holly smiled back at him and felt hope for the first time since this whole ordeal had begun. Even her muscles stopped aching for a magical moment. 'They're looking for us?'

'Absolutely,' he confirmed, and hoped he was convincing because he wasn't really sure. It wasn't unusual for Blackhawks and Iroquois to fly over this region. 'They know we're missing and they're searching for us, Holly.'

And the relief in her eyes and the smile she shone his way was worth it. If it gave her the impetus to keep going, if it gave her one small ray of hope that they would get out of here alive, he knew he would tell her whatever she needed to hear.

They heard the *wocca, wocca* of the rotors grow distant and John ordered them up again. Holly was amazed at how much lighter her step was. How the knowledge that there were people beyond this mountain who knew of their plight and were trying to help could spur her on and reinvigorate muscles that had previously been begging her to stop.

Richard noticed the spring in her step instantly. He'd been forced to watch the sway and wiggle of her bottom all morning, a different kind of torture, and definitely recognised a renewed perkiness.

They trudged on silently for another hour. Richard noticed Holly's steps becoming slower again. Had the jubilation caused by the chopper receded already? She tripped over a tree root and he heard pain in her muttered expletive. He needed to try to keep her spirits up.

'Tell me about your work at the orphanage.'

His voice startled her out of her misery. The only voices she'd heard for a while had spoken a foreign tongue and it felt good to hear English. And she was grateful for anything that took her mind off the burning in her legs. So she prattled on about her volunteer job for a while.

'Is it rewarding?' he asked when she had run out of things to say.

'Working with the kids, sure. I feel like I'm making a real difference, which is a nice change.'

Richard could relate to what she was saying. That was the part he liked most about his job. The fact that he made a difference to the lives of so many poor people caught up in such awful situations.

'But I don't think anything could have prepared me for the overwhelming sense of despair and hopelessness of these poor people. The scale of the destruction... I suppose I sound like some spoilt rich girl,' she sighed, sploshing through her millionth puddle in the track.

He laughed. 'You are.'

She laughed back. 'I guess you're right. I don't live in a disaster zone, and I have a wonderful family who are all alive and well so, compared to these poor people, I guess I'm pretty rich.'

In his book, that made her a millionaire. The gap that had always existed between them yawned ever wider. Just one of the reasons their relationship had been doomed from the beginning. They couldn't have had two more contrasting backgrounds if they'd tried. No wonder she looked at the world through Pollyanna eyes.

They trudged on, a companionable silence falling between them. 'Your turn,' said Holly.

'Oh, no.' Richard laughed.

'Come on, Richard, I've just spoken non-stop for half an hour. Talk to me about something.'

'Like what?' he asked.

'Tell me about your childhood.'

Great. Let's start with something easy, he thought. 'I don't think so.'

'Oh, come on, Richard,' she said, trudging around a rocky section of the track. 'I already know it wasn't the Waltons. We were an item for two years, I did manage to figure out some things. I hardly know anything about you. Indulge me. Did your parents divorce?'

Richard couldn't help the snort that escaped him. She seriously thought that divorce was the worst thing that could happen? She wanted to know? OK.

'My father was a wife-beater, my mother was a drunk. I raised myself. My father died in a bar brawl when I was twelve, and my mother drank herself to death a couple years later.'

Holly faltered. She'd had no idea. She'd occasionally seen past his tough-guy image and caught glimpses of hurt but this was so much worse than she'd ever imagined. When he had told her through tight lips that he'd come from a broken home she'd just assumed divorce. 'Any brothers or sisters?'

'No, thank God. That's about the only thing my parents did right. I think the fewer children that were exposed to my home life, the better.'

'So, you really have no family?' she asked incredulously. She hadn't believed him when he'd said so previously. She'd just thought he was estranged from them. How awful. How lonely.

'I told you already. The army is my family.' He heard the pity in her voice and couldn't keep the curtness out of his. He didn't need her sympathy.

Well, of course, the army felt like his family when they'd probably been the only true support system he'd ever had. They'd given him stability, safety and a shot at a career. And discipline and direction. More than that, knowing the man he had become, they had obviously also given him pride and self-esteem.

All the things that a family were supposed to give you but didn't if you were a kid from a dysfunctional home. She was finally starting to understand him.

But the facts of the matter didn't make his statement any less tragic. 'Oh, Richard,' she said, turning to face him, 'that sounds terrible. So…sad. Why did you never tell me?'

'I didn't need your pity then, Pollyanna, and I don't need it now. So don't waste your tears on me. I like my life just fine.'

'But there must be someone else. Anyone. Not just your job.'

'Nope.'

'What about your ex-fiancée? Surely she was your family?' Holly held her breath. He'd refused to talk about her when they'd been together. Holly hadn't even known until an army mate had let the cat out of the bag. 'What was her name?'

Richard sighed and gave in. If talking about his personal stuff kept her going then so be it. 'Tanya,' he said. 'She was very young.'

OK, so that's where his age hang-up came from. Holly mulled that over for a bit. He'd obviously been stung badly once before. Why had he never told her this stuff? Why had he waited until they were marching up a mountain with trigger happy rebels? Damn his he-man façade.

Richard felt a resurfacing of all his old angst and was surprised it still affected him a decade later. Yes, Tanya had been young but he had handled it badly. He should have stuck with his gut feeling all along and realised that a guy with his background made lousy marriage material. Kept his distance. Like he had with Holly.

But Tanya had been so pretty and she had been crazy about him and he had desperately needed someone to love him and someone to love in return. He'd just chosen the wrong girl and it had been a painful lesson to learn.

Holly's heart went out to him as she trudged along the track. How important would it have been to him to have made that relationship work? After the emotional void of his early years? She could sense his feelings of failure like a tangible aura.

'So, what happened?'

Richard sighed and rubbed his hands through his hair. He really didn't want to get into it. But one look at her straighter back and quick, easy strides and he knew that he'd bare his soul completely if it distracted her from her pain.

'She hated me being away with the army, which I was, quite a bit. I got posted to Darwin, which horrified her. I went up there to get settled and she was going to follow a little later. But I came home unexpectedly one day to surprise her, and found her in bed with another man.'

Holly gasped. Stupid girl! 'Oh, Richard,' Holly said, turning to face him, walking backwards. 'What did she say?'

'That it was my fault. That she was young and had needs and I was never around to fulfil them and no way was she ever going to move anywhere. And that it was over.'

Holly felt awful for him. 'I don't understand why you never told me any of this stuff when we were together.'

'Why would I?'

Holly turned back to the track. She felt her sympathy evaporating. She was getting ticked now. Had she meant so little to him? 'Because that is what people in relationships do, Richard. They share stuff like that.'

'Not me. I only told you now to keep your mind off your muscles and keep you putting one foot in front of the other.'

Holly felt like screaming. He was still treating her like a child. But as she trudged on, silently fuming, she had to admit their chatter had kept her mind of her aching body. Half an hour later, with her muscles starting to protest again and the road ahead disappearing ever upward, she broke her miffed silence. She was going to have to talk to him or throw herself off the mountain. Neither alternative appealed.

'So, how come you're still a sergeant?'

Richard stiffened and forced himself to keep going. 'I like being a sergeant.'

'I thought one of the reasons you were so keen to go to Africa was for the promotion opportunities. Isn't it every soldier's ambition to become a…brigadier or something?'

He smiled, easing the tension that had sprung into his muscles at the mention of Africa. 'I'm happy with my rank.'

'You always struck me as being more ambitious than that.'

'Sorry. I'm not.'

'Really?'

'Really.'

'It's just that you seem to have so much experience and expertise.'

'Look,' he said, becoming exasperated by her persistence, 'trust me on this one. I could be in the army till I'm one hundred and I'll still only be a sergeant.'

'How can you be so sure about that?' she said, wiping the sweat of her forehead with an even sweatier arm.

'Because…' He hesitated, wondering if he wanted to go into it, 'there was an incident in Africa…'

Aha! So she'd been right. Something had definitely happened while he'd been away. Something that had made him harder. More unreachable. Holly waited for further explanation. None seemed forthcoming. 'What sort of an incident?'

'I...broke some rules,' he said, trying to keep it as vague as possible. He really didn't want to think about it. He avoided thinking about it at all costs. It was bad enough that his dreams took him there most nights. He didn't want to talk about it in the daylight hours. 'Suffice to say promotion isn't ever going to be on the cards for me.'

'But—'

'Holly,' he interrupted, 'I don't want to—'

'Talk about it,' she finished.

'Bingo.'

Holly huffed out a frustrated sigh. Bloody men! Did he really think he was doing himself any favours by keeping things to himself? She stomped up the incline now. His tough-guy act wasn't fooling her. She remembered her shock at seeing him again. At how he seemed so much more distant. Machine-like even. Whatever it was, it must have been big.

'Well, I think they're mad.' She stopped abruptly and turned around and he almost careened into her. 'Surely the army is crying out for good leaders? People who are intelligent and dedicated and good at their jobs? I don't care what rules you broke. If you deserve a promotion, then it should be yours.'

Richard was surprised at the depth of her feeling. They were standing really close and her voice had husked over as she'd spoken. He couldn't believe she was showing him more forgiveness and loyalty than the army had.

John growled at them to keep moving and they turned back to the gruelling task of climbing higher. They stopped for a quick snack when the sun was directly above them and then hiked for another three hours in heavy rain.

Holly was relieved to finally reach another campsite and they were again herded into a structure similar to the one at the last camp. Holly didn't care. She was grateful to have stopped moving and sat on the hard earthen floor like it was the comfiest sofa in the world.

She pulled her socks and shoes off as Richard stoked the fire and wrung out the water from her socks. She lay back on the ground, her knees bent, revelling in the luxury of a horizontal position. Not even everything she had learned today could keep her from shutting her eyes.

'Oh, Holly, your feet!' exclaimed Richard.

She roused from the comforting layers of sleep that had quickly claimed her and half sat up. She had large, red, ugly blisters on her heels and over the bony prominence on the side of each big toe.

'Don't they hurt?' he asked, lifting each foot and inspecting the damage.

'Not as much as you yanking my sore legs around.' She winced. 'I didn't even know I had them until just now. I think the pain everywhere else is too intense to notice.'

Richard watched her fall back against the ground and shut her eyes again. She looked totally exhausted. 'I'm going to get my pack and dress those blisters,' he said, and wasn't surprised when she didn't respond.

Richard pushed open the door and the two guards placed restraining hands on his chest.

'I want my pack. I want to talk to John.'

The man appeared before him miraculously. 'Yes, Sergeant?'

'I need my pack. Holly has some bad blisters, I'd like to dress them.'

John spoke to one of the soldiers beside Richard and he left. He returned quickly with the requested pack. Richard picked it up and started to take it with him back to Holly.

'Oh, no, you don't. You take out what you need. We'll keep the pack.'

Richard felt his ire rise and gave John a mutinous stare. 'I gave you my word we wouldn't escape.'

'Take only what you need. The pack stays with me.' John's steely voice brooked no argument and Richard bunched his hands into fists by his side. He found the dressings, extracted them and then turned on his heel.

Holly stirred momentarily as he picked one foot up and then sighed in her sleep as he gently dressed her wounds. Blisters in such a moist, bacteria-rich environment could be a real problem, turning very nasty very quickly. The dressings he applied protected and cushioned them.

He replaced her feet back on the ground and watched as she turned on her side. Asleep she looked younger. Barely twenty. He shook his head and deliberately turned away so his back was to her and watched the camp activity through the wooden slats of their jail. He memorised every detail, knowing that he would be debriefed once they got back and any intelligence he could relay would be helpful. And he really needed to concentrate on something else!

He saw John approach an hour later and he rose to his feet and faced the door as it swung open, not wanting to wake Holly.

'We need you. One of our children has malaria, she's not doing very well,' said John.

Richard knew because malaria was his field that the young were hit hardest by this disease and that worldwide infant mortality from it was frighteningly high. Cerebral malaria, which was fatal, was too often a progression of the disease mostly seen in children.

He entered the darkened shelter and pushed through a small group of women who were huddled around a low bed. The baby, a girl, was lying naked and very still, and Richard noted her pallor despite the poor lighting.

He knelt beside the sick child and felt for a pulse. A commotion broke out around him. The elderly woman who had been holding the little girl's hand pushed at him and jabbered loudly, lifting the girl into her arms away from Richard's touch. She rocked the baby and her cries bordered on wailing. The other women joined in and Richard stood and looked enquiringly at John.

'What's wrong?' he asked. 'The girl is very sick, I need to examine her.' Richard tried to keep the alarm at the baby's condition out of his voice but even a cursory glance had told him she was severely dehydrated.

'Tuti's grandmother doesn't want a man. It is an old custom, not practised much any more. Girls are to be doctored to only by other women until they are married. I didn't think the old woman would be too fussy given the condition of the child.'

Having worked in many areas where local customs were sacrosanct, Richard appreciated the situation. But it was frustrating nonetheless. 'Where is the mother?' Richard asked.

'She was a victim of the typhoon. Mundi has cared for Tuti ever since.'

Richard's mind raced. They were wasting valuable time. He needed to rehydrate the baby and get her medical attention.

'Get Holly,' he said to Richard. She could be his eyes and his hands.

Holly was dragged out of a deep sleep by determined shaking. A rebel soldier, gun slung over his shoulder, was prodding her arm and jabbering insistently at her. She looked around for Richard, feeling frightened, but as he pulled at her arm it seemed he just wanted her to follow him.

She accompanied him, her heart banging in her rib cage. What had happened? What did he want? Where was Richard? The soldier hurried through the centre of the camp, startling chickens and children in his wake.

They entered a very noisy, crowded shelter and she almost sagged in relief when she saw Richard. There was a low, deep, anguished sound reverberating through the crowd of women and Holly got goose-bumps. It sounded mournful and her skin prickled with apprehension this time. Had somebody died?

'Holly, I need you,' he said curtly, grabbing her by the arms. 'We have a very sick baby on our hands. As a man, I'm not allowed to treat her. You're going to have to do it for me. Are you up for it? She's going to die if we don't get fluids into her.'

Holly didn't hesitate. 'Of course.' She was a nurse after all.

'John, I want all of these women out,' said Richard. 'Mundi can stay but I want everyone else to leave.'

John cleared the shelter. The women were reluctant but John's authority appeared absolute.

Holly knelt beside Mundi and assessed the baby. She spoke her findings out loud for Richard's benefit. She felt for the pulse and lost count it was so rapid. The baby was burning up, its eyes sunken, its lips dried and cracked. She felt the baby's fontanelle, noting how depressed it was. The baby was otherwise well nourished and Holly was thankful for small mercies. This little girl was going to need every ounce of her baby fat.

'How old is she?' Richard spoke to John.

'Ten months.'

'How long has she been sick?'

John spoke briefly with Mundi who was sponging her granddaughter's body. 'Her fever and chills started yesterday. She has also had vomiting and diarrhoea.'

'Has she bled from anywhere?' Richard asked.

More consulting with Mundi. 'No.'

'We have to get a line in, Holly. She's severely dehydrated. We'll give her twenty per kilo over an hour. I'll make up some ten per cent dextrose solution. Her blood-sugar level is probably dangerously low.'

Holly swallowed and tried not to laugh hysterically. Get a line in? Where? Big veins she could do. But little ones? Dehydrated ones at that? She quickly inspected the baby's arms and legs for signs of a vein. She was never going to succeed.

Richard got all the stuff ready for Holly while his brain ticked over. From the description of the symptoms it sounded like malaria. And as much as he despised John, at least he'd recognized an illness that was endemic among the people of Tanrami.

There was no way he could tell which of the four strains it was. All he could do was treat the physical symptoms and get her to Abeil, where she could have the proper treatment. He hoped he wasn't too late. He hoped Tuti wasn't in the stage of developing the life-threatening cerebral malaria and died before he could get her proper medical attention.

He watched Holly as he mixed some fifty per cent glucose with Hartman's solution to make the bag about a ten per cent dextrose mix. She was having difficulty finding a vein.

'Try the scalp,' he said, a needle cap between his teeth as he pushed the sugary solution into the bag of fluid.

His mind moved on. Weight.

'How much does she weigh, do you reckon?' he asked Holly. He figured as a midwife she'd be pretty good at guessing babies' weights.

Holly assessed the infant, trying to make an educated estimate. Not very much. 'About seven kilos…maybe?'

He nodded and filled the burette up with one hundred and forty mils of fluid. Holly could run it in over an hour once she got the drip in.

Holly inspected the scalp and mumbled thanks to Mundi, who drew a lantern nearer. Luckily the baby was bald so the veins were easier to identify. Or they would have been had there been any! There was nothing. Tuti was just too dehydrated.

'Forget it,' said Richard, handing her an intra-osseous needle. 'Use this. We don't have time.'

Holly looked at the rather brutal instrument. He was right. It was the quickest and easiest way for them to administer fluids, but she'd never placed one before, although she had seen it done and understood the theory.

The needle was basically a fancy screw that was twisted into the bone, accessing the bone marrow and using it to deliver fluid and medications.

She shut her eyes and sent a little plea out into the ether. 'Tibia?' she asked.

'Just below the knee, in the broadest, flattest part of the bone.' He nodded at her encouragingly.

Her hand shook as she grasped the large knob, positioned the needle so the tip pointed away from the joint space and pushed down firmly, twisting the knob in a screwing motion. She gritted her teeth as the sharp inner trocar ground through the bone. The baby didn't flinch, cry or move.

She felt a gentle give as the soft layer of bone marrow was breached and breathed a sigh of relief. The needle stood upright unsupported in the bone.

'Well done, Holly,' said Richard. It had been a tricky procedure, and she had managed it better than a lot of doctors he had seen. And Tuti couldn't have afforded her to fail.

Holy grinned at him, warmed by his compliment, and was surprised by his answering smile. It was a hundred-watt dazzler! He'd obviously been holding his breath too.

Richard passed her a dressing as she removed the central trocar. She secured the site and hooked up the IV line, adjusting the roller clamp to deliver the fluid in the burette over an hour.

'We need to evacuate her,' Richard said, turning to John, who was watching them dispassionately.

'No.'

'She needs hospitalisation. If it's malaria then it needs to be treated or she could die.'

'Many of our children die, Sergeant. What do you care?'

'I care about this child. I'm not going to stand by and watch her die from a totally curable illness.'

'She is a girl.' He shrugged.

Holly felt her ire rise and turned from her observation of the baby. She remembered Richard's warning to keep her mouth shut, but this was really too much! She wouldn't be silent in the face of such blatant discrimination.

'She is a human being. She has as much right to live and to medical care as the next child.' Holly's chest heaved as she swallowed her fear and confronted John.

'She can't fight and she's too young to work. She is just another mouth to feed,' John dismissed.

The coldness of his statement put a chill right up her spine. 'I didn't think the rebels were so primitive,' said Holly, rising to her feet, pulling herself up to her full five feet two and giving him a look of sheer disgust. 'Richard has been telling me you lot are dangerous and not to be trusted. I've been telling him he's wrong. Is he right, John? Are you just a band of barbaric savages or are you noble mountain people with a just cause?'

Holly's heart was hammering. She couldn't sit by and let him dismiss this child's life as worthless because of her sex.

Richard blinked at her outburst. She might be a woman but at the moment she was an angry one and she wasn't taking any prisoners. He stifled the caution that sprang to his lips. Maybe she could shame John into action.

Mundi let out a cry and Holly and Richard turned in time to see Tuti convulsing.

'Get her on her side,' Richard ordered.

'Yes, I do know that,' Holly snapped. She hadn't meant to sound so terse but her run-in with John had made her irritable.

Holly flipped Tuti on her side and waited for the jerking of her limbs to stop. Mundi sobbed and wailed and clutched at Holly's shirt. The old woman spoke to her with anguished eyes. Holly didn't know the words but the meaning was clear. Do something. Help her.

'Do you think it's related to her fever or a worsening of the malaria?' Holly asked Richard as the convulsions began to subside.

'It could be either,' he said, running his hands through his short hair. It was hot in the shelter and he felt a fine sheen of sweat lining his scalp. He couldn't be certain without vital tests. Tuti needed urgent hospitalisation.

'Well.' Holly turned and glared at John. 'Are you going to prove him wrong,' she pointed at Richard, 'and do the right thing?'

Richard held his breath. Holly's goading had hit the mark. John's face was puce with barely concealed rage. Richard hoped that Holly hadn't gone too far.

'She needs to go to Abeil,' Richard said, keeping up the pressure and trying to keep his frustration in check.

John nodded curtly and stalked out of the shelter. Tuti's limbs had stilled and Holly encouraged Mundi to sponge her grandaughter down. Richard followed John out.

John appeared to be organising an evacuation. Two soldiers scurried away and came back a few minutes later with a small stretcher.

'Let Holly go with them,' he said, interrupting the conversation between John and his men.

'I give the orders here,' John snapped, ignoring Richard's presence.

'Tuti needs a medical escort,' Richard persisted.

'Holly stays. You stay. Tuti and Mundi will go to Abeil as soon as you clear them to move.'

'It will take too long on foot. We could get a chopper from the field hospital—'

John pulled Richard's pistol out, cocked it and pointed it at Richard's head. 'They go by foot or not at all. Do not test my patience any further.'

Richard withdrew. He walked back into the shelter seething inwardly.

'How is she?' he asked Holly, and dredged up a reassuring smile.

'The same. Maybe a little less tachycardic. The bolus is almost finished. What's happening? Are they moving her?'

'Yep. Organising it now.' he nodded.

Holly smiled triumphantly, her spirits and hopes for little Tuti lifting dramatically. 'See, Richard, I told you. They're just misunderstood. It's going to be OK.'

Richard nodded again. She looked so happy, so righteous, he didn't have the heart to dash it all. She had had her first real glimpse of the disregard that John and his type had for human life and had managed to put a positive spin on it. He hoped she never got to see it as it really was.

Because it was ugly.

CHAPTER SEVEN

RICHARD slept. Two days of hard marching and only brief episodes of dozing the night before was a potent sleeping pill. The stress levels that had soared through his system, working on the dehydrated infant and their abduction and the subsequent worry about Holly's safety had left his tough-guy reserves seriously depleted.

He also knew that tomorrow was going to be his biggest challenge. Tomorrow he had to treat the rebel leader and earn their freedom. A million scenarios had circled through his head as he had reclined on the dirt floor of their prison and he had pushed them all aside to allow sleep to claim him instead. He was going to have to be alert. Their lives would depend on it.

Perversely, Holly couldn't sleep. She lay awake watching the steady rise and fall of Richard's chest as the firelight cast fingers of orange light across his body. She still quaked a little when she thought about her angry words with John but the result had been worth it. They had helped another person on their travels.

She shivered when she thought about how ill the little girl was. The fear she had see in Mundi's eyes and the desperation in her voice would stay with her for ever. So would the callousness of John. Had she been wrong about the rebels? No, when it mattered, John had done the decent thing. The honourable thing.

Richard mumbled in his sleep and her gaze rested on him

again. Her eyes caressed his features. His strong jawline was heavy with dark stubble, his short black hair peppered with grey and his lips slackened by slumber. In fact, the whole harshness of his face had disappeared, the severity of his features relaxed now.

It was great to be able to stare at him for a change. Two days of him following her had made her very conscious of her appearance despite their dire situation. When she had bought the cargos just prior to her departure from Australia she hadn't thought she'd be trekking through a jungle with an ex-lover behind her. If she had, she might have been more critical of how her butt looked in them.

Mind you, it probably didn't matter at this point. Every part of her must have looked like something the cat had dragged in. With no mirror to confirm her worst suspicions, she just had to guess. After two days without soap or toothpaste, she was more *au naturel* than she had ever wanted to be.

Still, she thought as sleep started to muddle her brain, at least she was clean—intermittent dousing with torrential rain saw to that. And didn't they say rainwater was good for your skin? Whatever. She'd kill for some soap and the opportunity to get naked and wash herself all over. Some shampoo and even a little moisturiser wouldn't go astray either.

And she only had four sticks of gum left in her pocket, which she had been sharing with Richard. Even if it didn't do much for oral hygiene, at least her mouth felt refreshed and her breath didn't smell like birdcage effluent. But, oh, if she ever got out of this alive, she was going to sit in a spa bath all day and pamper herself.

A couple of hours later she was dreaming about precisely that when a sudden shout woke her. She sat bolt upright, her muscles protesting the quick movement, disorientated at first. The fire had burned low, just a few coals glowing in the stone ring, and she heard the unmistakable sound of thunder and rain beating down outside.

Her heart rate settled as she realised the noise had come from outside and she glanced over at Richard to tell him it was just thunder. But he was asleep. Strange, very strange. Surely tough-guy, action-figure Richard would be instantly alert at a noise that had managed to drag her awake?

Nothing woke her. She was a shift worker. Her family called her log. As in sleeping-like-a. But Richard? Weren't professional soldiers supposed to sleep with one eye open or something? Weren't they supposed to be instantly alert if so much as a leaf crunched?

Then she noticed the sweat beading his brow and then he muttered in his sleep again and shook his head from side to side.

'No,' he shouted, and Holly nearly jumped out of her skin. That had been the noise that had woken her. It hadn't been thunder. It had been Richard. She watched as he muttered again and she saw the rapid movements of his eyes beneath his closed lids and guessed he was dreaming. Bad dreaming.

'No,' he shouted again, and she watched as his fingers curled into fists.

OK. What was she supposed to do now? The rain continued to thunder down outside so she doubted anyone in the camp had heard him. Did she just leave him and hope that he would wake of his own accord, or was she supposed to rouse him? The look on his face, twisted in agony, was too awful to bear. What was he dreaming about?

Her urge was to go to him and hold him. Whatever he was dreaming about, it was bad. He looked in so much pain, so alone. Maybe even if only his subconscious knew she was beside him, it might help him feel less alone.

She shuffled over and sat nearer. She reached for a log and threw it on the fire, poking at the coals with a stick to stir them up. She watched him a bit longer as he muttered to himself, still undecided.

And then he started to whimper. He sounded like a wounded

animal. It was such an anguished sound her heart squeezed painfully in her chest. She couldn't stand to listen to it any more. She lay on her side next to him, propped up on one elbow.

'Richard,' she whispered, and placed her hand on his firmly muscled chest. 'Richard.'

He either didn't hear her or couldn't wake from the bounds of his dream. She tried again, shaking him a little more firmly this time. Still nothing. And still a gut-wrenching whimpering that clawed at her soul.

Holly got down closer to his ear and whispered again. His head shook from side to side and she gently kissed the side of his face, close to his ear. 'Richard, it's OK. Wake up,' she said, and kissed him lightly again in the same spot.

She couldn't explain why she'd decided to kiss him. In fact, it hadn't even been a conscious decision. It had just happened on the spur of the moment. It hadn't even been sexual. Just one person trying to comfort another, a bit like a mother trying to soothe a frightened child. Because that's exactly what Richard looked like—a scared little boy.

'Richard,' she said again, kissing his sweaty brow. 'Richard.' This time she kissed a closed eyelid. 'Wake up, you're dreaming. It's OK, it's Holly. Wake up.'

She continued to whisper words of comfort and solace to him as she dropped gentle kisses all over his face. His fretting eased and she stroked her fingers through his hair and across his forehead. His face, contorted with a mix of emotions, relaxed and Holly snuggled her head against his chest and listened to the reassuring thud of his heart beating.

A few minutes later the head-shaking and muttering started again and Holly was quick to repeat her earlier ministrations.

'It's OK Richard. I'm with you. Holly's here. It's OK.'

Richard's eyes snapped open and the orange glow cast around the small area made them look even blacker. He looked at her, confusion evident in their dark depths. He didn't look fully awake to her so she kept whispering, telling him he was OK and that she was there for him. And it seemed like the most natural thing in the world to keep kissing him, dropping light kisses all over his face.

More importantly, he didn't even try to stop her. She stopped when he seemed more awake, his black eyes boring into hers, and laid her head back down on his chest for a while. His arm came up around her shoulders, scooping her closer, and she sighed and relaxed against him.

'You had a bad dream,' she said quietly. His heartbeat had steadied and the sound and feel of it beneath her ear seemed as natural as the rain beating down around them.

'Yes,' he said. 'I'm sorry. I didn't mean to wake you.'

Holly raised herself on her elbow. 'Don't be ridiculous, Richard. We can't control our subconscious.'

'I can,' he said, removing his arm from around her and putting it by his side between them.

Holly sighed. Now he was going to be a he-man about this? He seriously needed to open up a bit more. 'Tell me about it,' she said, lying back down on her side beside him, an arm propped beneath her head as a pillow, her body not quite touching his.

'It's not important,' he said.

'It is to me.'

'Why?'

'I want to be able to understand you. And because…you woke me.' She smiled. 'And it wouldn't be fair to do that and not explain.'

He gave her a half-smile back. 'Life, my dear Pollyanna, isn't fair.' And he promptly turned his back on her.

'Was it a premonition? Was it about us being killed?'

'No.'

'Being rescued?'

'Nope.'

'Your childhood?'

'Holly. Go to sleep.'

'Nope,' she mimicked.

Silence.

'Mosquitoes?'

Silence.

'Giant mosquitoes?'

More silence. She cast around for something else. She was getting kind of desperate now. 'Monsters?'

Richard flinched and squeezed his eyes shut. Now she was getting closer. He still felt the tempo of his heartbeat pounding through every cell in his body and the familiar nausea that the dream always caused rolled through his gut. He started counting to himself. Anything to divert his thoughts.

Twelve, thirteen, fourteen—

'Some other evil force that big tough guys are scared of?'

Why didn't she just shut the hell up? Fifteen, sixteen, seventeen—

'Please, Richard,' she said, unable to keep the pleading tone from her voice, 'talk to me.'

'Go to sleep, Holly,' he said gruffly.

'No. I'm going to guess all night. You may as well just tell me.'

Richard sighed. Unfortunately he believed her.

'Holly, enough,' he said, turning over to his other side so he was facing her.

'Please, Richard,' she whispered.

He shut his eyes. What the hell? If it meant that much to her and she'd actually be quiet, it'd have to be worth it.

'It was about the thing that I told you about today.'

'What? The Africa thing?'

'Yes.'

Holly held her breath. She felt like one false move, one wrong word would send him scuttling in retreat. 'What happened?'

'I killed someone.'

His bluntness pulled her up. His shuttered face was illuminated by the firelight and she could see the anguish etched there.

Think, dammit, think. 'You were a soldier in a war zone,' she said quietly, quelling the urge to stroke his face. 'I guess sometimes that happens? Right?'

'Wrong. I was part of a United Nations mission. Your weapon is to be used only if there is an immediate threat to your life.'

'And there wasn't?'

'Not to mine, no.' He grimaced as he remembered that day. 'I mean, how crazy is that? They can shoot someone, an innocent civilian, right in front of your eyes and you can't do a damn thing about it.'

'Is that what happened?' she asked softly. There was silence for a while and she watched as his eyes returned from a faraway place and came back to focus on her.

He nodded. 'I came across this rebel soldier on the outskirts of the camp who had rounded up a woman with two children. One was a baby and the other was probably no more than two. He was trying to prise the toddler away from her leg and she was screaming and crying and begging him to leave them alone.'

'Oh, Richard, how awful.'

'It became apparent he was making her decide. Forcing her to choose which child lived and which child died. He was so cocky. So…damn sure of himself. He knew I couldn't do a damn thing about it.'

'But you did.'

'Well, I wasn't just going to stand by and let him do that. So I intervened. I took out my rifle, pointed it at his head and…he laughed at me. He was only about nineteen or twenty but he was cold. Worse than cold. There was this maniacal, zealous glint in his eyes. He was so indoctrinated he couldn't see that an innocent woman and her children had no part in his stupid war. And he was getting such a sadistic kick out of terrorising her...' Richard shuddered as the chill that had swept through his bones that day revisited him.

Holly stayed silent. She could feel the tears welling in her eyes and goose-bumps prickle her skin at the eeriness of his tone. He had left her. She could tell he was back reliving that day.

'And then he grabbed the baby out of her arms and the mother was sobbing and wailing and begging him. She threw herself at his feet and clutched at his clothes and the toddler was screaming and he just laughed. This horrible, cold laugh. And even though I couldn't tell what she was saying, I could see she was offering herself instead. She kept pointing to her chest and trying to take the baby off him.'

Holly felt a tear leave her eyes and track its way down her cheek. 'So you shot him?'

Richard looked at her, her voice bringing him back to the present. He looked at her silently for a few seconds. 'No. Not then. I pressed the weapon to his head and demanded he give the baby back. And then...'

She watched the play of emotions on his face and gave him some breathing space. 'Then?'

'He sneered at me, took a step back, threw the baby in the air and while we all looked up he started to pepper the air with automatic gunfire...and I shot him. One bullet, straight through the heart. He dropped instantly.'

Holly bit back a sob as Richard's face blurred before her. She couldn't even begin to imagine the horror of what he'd just described. 'The baby?'

'The baby landed on the ground before any of us had a chance to catch it. He had taken a hit to his leg. I scooped him out of the dirt, picked the mother and the other child up and ran with them back to the casualty station. He was evacuated immediately. He survived.'

She saw the lines of strain around his mouth and eyes that retelling the story had caused. She touched his face with tentative fingers, stroking the deep furrows on his forehead. 'I'm so sorry, Richard,' she whispered. 'What an awful, awful thing to have been through.' She stroked his temples. 'What a terrible nightmare.'

Richard closed his eyes as her touch caressed his face. It was nice and he felt the tangible sense of dread recede. 'That's not the worst part of the dream,' he said, opening his eyes. What the hell? She may as well know it all.

'Oh?'

'It starts off with me witnessing an argument between my parents when I was a kid, about ten. My father starts to beat my mother and I'm crying and yelling for him to stop, and then suddenly the scene morphs into the baby incident, but I'm still ten and the soldier is ignoring me and I'm still helpless to stop it. Just as helpless as I always was at home.'

Holly heard the anguish in his voice. 'Hush,' she whispered, placing her fingers on his lips. 'You were a child, Richard. What could you do?'

'Something. Anything. I shouldn't have just let him beat her.'

His lips moved against her fingers and her heart filled with compassion. She tried to picture Richard as a frightened ten-year-old and failed. He seemed so capable. So sure of himself. But she could see the child in his eyes and she wanted to lend him some comfort.

Holly leaned forward and placed a gentle kiss against his passive lips. She pulled back slightly and saw the wariness creep into his black eyes. 'It's OK, Richard,' she said quietly, because he looked like he was going to bolt at any second. 'Just relax, it's OK.' She kissed the corner of his mouth this time. 'Tell me more about it. Were you scared…that day with the soldier?'

'Terrified,' he admitted, accepting another light kiss on his lips, feeling parts of his body stir to life. 'But I think I was angry…more than anything. Everywhere we looked there were such dreadful human rights violations and we were unable to do anything. There was this overwhelming feeling of impotence denting our morale. And when I saw him tormenting that mother…I think I just snapped. They reminded me so much of me. Alone and defenceless with no one to stick up for them. I was scared, yes, but primarily I was just pissed off.'

No wonder he was so screwed up, she thought as she listened to his story. She kissed him again on the lips and this time he kissed her back, their lips holding for a brief moment.

He felt her lips at his temple and then his ear. It was getting harder to remember that acute sense of impotence now. Holly's kisses were making him feel anything but.

'What I don't understand is why it destroyed your chance of promotion. The way I look at it, you were a hero that day.' And she kissed him full on the mouth to try and convey her belief. The world needed men like Richard. Noble men, ready to defend the weak and the downtrodden. She broke away, slightly out of breath to finish what she wanted to say before she forgot how to speak. 'They should have given you a medal for bravery.'

Her lips were moist from their kissing and mere millimetres from his. It was such a Pollyanna thing to say he kissed her again. It must be nice to live in her world, he thought as she moaned against his mouth, where everything was so simple, so clear-cut. Unfortunately UN conventions weren't so black and white. But to have someone so totally in his corner was a turn-on nonetheless.

'The justification doesn't matter. My life wasn't at risk,' his voice was husky against her mouth, 'I was reported and disciplined.'

'Do you regret it?' she asked.

'No,' he said, and gave her a brief hard kiss. 'I don't. If I had my time over again I'd probably do the same thing. You see, it was instinctive, pulling the trigger, there was nothing conscious about it. I had to stop him shooting at the baby. But killing another human being, no matter what the provocation, diminishes you, and realistically I didn't have to shoot to kill.'

She looked at the self-doubt in his eyes and for the second time in her life she fell in love with him. His heroic actions hadn't brought him any triumph. He'd saved a life but taken another in its place, and it had obviously taken a piece out of him.

She felt his conflict. How awful to have to make a decision in a split second when emotions were running high and a life was at stake. And to spend years with it on your conscience, trying to rationalise it and stop the nightmares. He was truly an honourable man.

He could have killed without conscience, without batting an eyelid, but it was the measure of the type of man he was that his actions had caused him much angst. Love surged through her, a stronger, more mature love than she had ever felt. Richard had changed and so had she. But one thing hadn't— Richard, her damaged hero, needed her love more than ever.

And there was nothing light or feathery about her kiss this time. She unleashed herself, pouring all her love and the pride she felt at his actions into the kiss. She moved closer so their bodies were touching, trying to imprint herself upon him, convey the depth of her feelings.

Richard reeled from the kiss, grabbing hold of her hip, almost drowning in the surge of need that swamped him. He held her face and joined in the mutual raging desire. His tongue plunged into her mouth and hers met his with equal power. He wanted her, there was still something between them that was useless to deny. He must have her.

Holly's heart sang. This. This thing between them had never gone away. She'd spent two years telling herself she didn't love him any more, but now she knew this passion and strength of feeling could never just be over. And he could deny it all he wanted but she could feel it emanating from every cell in his body, too.

She wanted him inside her so badly that kissing was exquisite torture. She didn't care that their circumstances were less
than the best. If she was going to die tomorrow or some time
in the next few days then she wanted to go knowing that for a
brief while he had loved her. She could feel his hardness pressing into her belly and gave in to the urge to touch it.

Richard almost jumped at the unexpected intimate pressure
on his erection as Holly fondled him. It brought him back to
earth with a thump. Whoa, there! This was getting a little out
of control. When had a spot of kissing become so serious?
They were in a jungle, for heaven's sake, with armed guards
outside their door!

He broke away from her mouth and she opened her eyes and
looked at him questioningly.

'Richard?' She frowned.

Her voice was husky and her lips were swollen from their
passion and her eyes had that glazed, drunk kind of look and
he very nearly kissed her again.

'We can't do this, Holly,' he said, drawing in deep ragged
breaths. He couldn't protect her properly if their relationship
became intimate. It would be too distracting and he couldn't
afford any lapse in concentration. It was important to stay aloof
from her and focused on his mission. Saving Fumradi and gaining their release.

He sat up, distancing himself from her stunned stare. He
could see her trying to get her head around what he was saying and not quite believing the words.

'Of course,' she said, shutting her eyes, already wishing she
had the last few moments back not to have made such a fool of
herself. But part of her wanted to cry out, Why not? If they were
going to die soon, why not go out on a sexual high?

'I'm sorry,' he said, his breathing now under control. 'I
shouldn't have let you kiss me.'

'No, I'm sorry. I was just trying to…comfort you. Your

nightmare…I wanted to help you forget.' It wasn't a total lie but she had to say it lest she told him the truth. A truth he wasn't ready to hear. Maybe never would be. That she wanted him and needed him and loved him in every way a woman could love a man.

Unfortunately their situation was complex to say the least. There were still too many of those barriers he'd put up in his mind for their relationship to blossom into something deeper. And particularly while they were still prisoners, she knew there was no way he was ever going to accept her feelings. That she knew for certain. He needed to be the big tough guy and focus, and he didn't want silly, girly admissions distracting him.

'Thanks,' he said, his back still to her. 'I don't need any help.'

'Yeah, I got that,' she said, and turned on her side away from him.

Holly slept badly for the remainder of the night. She relived the kissing in her mind over and over. It didn't help that he was so close. Her fingers itched to touch him as each wave of hot desire surged through her belly. She pressed a fist between her thighs and clamped her legs shut tight to stop the tingling sensation burning down there. She almost wished it was morning and she was marching up the mountain again.

Fortunately morning came soon enough and neither of them were in a talking mood as they ate their cold rice. Richard wanted to apologise again but felt it was probably better to just forget it had ever happened. She appeared to be giving him the silent treatment anyway. It didn't matter. Today was too important to their survival to worry about whether she liked him or not. It wasn't high school. This unfortunately was as real and harsh as life got.

'Come now,' said John as he opened their door. 'Today is the day you fulfil your purpose.'

Holly was pleasantly surprised to find that her muscle pain

had lessened. They were still sore but the excruciating agony of every step had eased considerably. She must be getting used to the punishing climb, she thought, and then grimaced at the sobering thought.

They moved out in their usual formation. Richard chose to zone out the sway of Holly's bottom by centering his mind on the challenges of the day. Fumradi had a bullet wound. It sounded infected. He'd need to probe the wound for any retained particles, clean it, administer some antibiotics and replace his fluid loss.

He knew he could do those things with his kit, easy. Should Fumradi require more intensive care, then they were probably toast. He'd know more when he laid eyes on his patient. For the moment all he had was an educated guess.

Holly put one foot in front of the other, mulling over the conundrum that was Richard to take her mind off the endless trek upwards. She'd learned another piece of the puzzle last night and shuddered as goose-bumps broke out on her skin despite the oppressively hot conditions. Richard had seen man's inhumanity to man up close and personal. That had to screw you up a little.

She hadn't really appreciated how complex he was until last night. She was no longer just dealing with his crappy childhood or his failed engagement to a younger woman but an incident of terrible human cruelty. It had hardened him and made him seem so much more unreachable than he had ever been before.

They walked for hours, the choppers of the day before nowhere in sight today. Holly's legs felt much better but two days of marching and not much sustenance was really testing her stamina. Exhaustion never seemed very far away.

Even the thought that they'd soon reach their destination wasn't enough to lift her mood. Yes, the endless walking would at last be over but she knew that their fate awaited them at the top and perversely she wished the mountain would stretch upwards for ever.

Holly smelt the woodsmoke long before the camp came into sight. As they neared, a young boy wandered down the track towards them and greeted the soldiers. He looked about five or six but given his state of malnutrition he could well have been older. His large protruding stomach stuck out from his ill-fitting ragged T-shirt and his skinny arms and legs didn't look strong enough to support even his feather-light weight.

He eyed them curiously but said nothing. He had large brown eyes, light brown skin and that solemn look she'd seen on so many children's faces since she'd been in Tanrami. His long dark hair looked unkempt, the fringe almost blinding him and the back brushing his shoulders.

The soldiers at the front of the procession unloaded their backpacks and gave them to the boy. She gasped as he uncomplainingly hitched them on his shoulders. His limbs looked like they'd snap under the extra weight and Holly swore she saw him sink a few centimetres shorter.

Her heart went out to him as she watched him struggle with his load. The men appeared to be finding his efforts funny. How could grown men burden such a small child with man-sized baggage?

She felt hot acid rise and burn in her chest. For the first time since their ordeal had begun, the total of all the despicable things she had seen hit her hard. She was beginning to feel real contempt for the rebels. Until now, despite everything, she'd still felt tremendous sympathy for their plight. But now there was just disdain.

Richard brushed past her and she wondered what he was doing. When he walked past the two soldiers ahead they tried to restrain him but he shrugged them off. He reached the young boy and placed a hand on one of the backpacks, stopping the boy in his tracks. He unloaded the child and shouldered the packs himself.

John brushed past her next and Holly kicked on some speed.

'Give the packs to the child. It is Tundol's job,' said John, barring Richard's ascent.

'You use a child to do a man's work?'

John's face hardened. 'He likes it. He is grateful to the freedom fighters.'

'What do you mean?' asked Holly from behind as she caught the conversation. She watched the child, who stood quietly regarding the adults' conversation solemnly.

'We found him in Abeil, scavenging for food. He was displaced during the typhoon. His family, his village are all dead.'

'He's an orphan?' she asked incredulously.

'Yes,' confirmed John. He flicked ash from the end of his cigarette in Tundol's direction.

'And you use him as a slave?' Richard's voice left no one in any doubt of his contempt.

'He earns his keep.' John bristled.

'As a packhorse? A mule?' demanded Richard.

'He is strong.' John shrugged dismissively.

'He's a boy,' Holly hissed. She felt hot tears scald her eyes at their callousness.

She looked at him and Richard saw her utter disbelief and disillusionment that people she had defended could do such a thing. She looked totally crushed and his heart went out to her. Shattered ideals were always hard to deal with.

John looked down at the sad-looking child with big, brown eyes and gave a curt order. He scampered up the track but not before Holly saw fear in the child's eyes. What had the poor boy been forced to do since the typhoon had separated him from his family?

'You want to carry Tundol's load, be my guest, Sergeant. But hurry. Fumradi waits for you.'

They fell back into line and arrived in the camp about ten minutes later. Holly was still too angry to fully appreciate the surroundings. Top camp was luxurious compared to the rudimentary dwellings of the lower camps. An impressive large abode dominated the area. It reminded Holly of the treehouse in the movie *Swiss Family Robinson,* which she had seen as a child.

It was made of timber and nestled in the thick canopy, high above the forest floor. The other living quarters weren't as big but were also elevated off the ground and a series of wooden bridges connected each to the other. It looked kind of surreal, like a magical forest kingdom.

Holly noticed Tundol as soon as they entered the camp. He was sitting alone near the sturdy animal pens, while a band of other children played happily together nearby. He looked so sad and alone and isolated.

The soldiers were greeted by a throng of locals, as they had been previously, and Holly took the opportunity to talk to Richard.

'I'm not leaving this camp without Tundol,' she whispered, placing her hand on his arm.

Richard looked at her and something inside him shifted. He recognised a kindred spirit and placed his hand over hers. She had seen an injustice perpetrated on an innocent child and had decided to make a stand. To look out for him, to defend him. And he, probably more than most people, understood how she felt.

Tundol's treatment had appalled him also, but he suspected that John probably wouldn't give the boy up easily. Maybe if they managed to cure the ailing rebel leader, they would have a good bargaining chip. If they didn't, and had to run?

A child would seriously hinder their progress. He glanced over at the boy and Tundol looked directly at him. Richard looked back at Holly and saw the purpose in her eyes.

'I don't want to leave him either, Holly, but it's too risky.'

'We can't leave him here with these, these…' She cast around for a suitable description. Something that would convey her utter disgust at their treatment of Tundol.

'Poor, misunderstood freedom fighters?'

She glared at him mutinously. How dared he throw that back in her face? So, she may have been wrong about these people. Did he have to rub it in? Her body was broken, her spirit was crushed. Wasn't she already defeated enough?

'Animals,' she hissed back at him, and couldn't even muster sorrow that her idealistic fantasy had been shattered in a million pieces.

'Come,' John interrupted, and signalled them to follow. 'There is work to be done.'

Richard felt his heart start to beat louder as they followed John up some steep wooden steps into the large home of the rebel leader. The house had looked big from the outside but the reality was even more impressive.

'Wait here,' said John at a doorway. He opened it and shut it behind him.

Holly felt…trepidation. What would they find behind the door? Could they help? And what if they couldn't? What did that mean for them and for that poor orphan child outside? She glanced at Richard and he smiled at her reassuringly, but she could see the same doubts assailed him.

John opened the door. 'Fumradi is worse. It looks like we're just in time.'

Great, thought Richard. Maybe John should have abducted a magician. John stood aside and Richard's worst fears were confirmed. The rebel leader was propped up in bed by several pillows and looked very unwell.

Richard met the rebel's leader blank gaze and knew with dreadful clarity he was looking into the eyes of a dead man.

CHAPTER EIGHT

THE first thing Holly noticed was the stench. It drifted over to them and she had to suppress the urge to wretch. She noticed a bloodied bandage on his right thigh and thought that if Fumradi wasn't septic she'd eat her hat. The smell of a purulent wound was something you never forgot and the rebel leader reeked of it. Great! We're dead, thought Holly.

A woman hovering around the bed, holding a cloth and wiping her leader's brow, caught her attention and Holly could see the worry etched on the woman's face. And quite rightly, too. Fumradi's skin had a distinctive yellow tinge, indicating jaundice and therefore probably liver failure. She hoped Richard had a magic wand in his pack.

And then as she advanced into the room with Richard she saw something even more alarming. Fumradi's skeletal chest vibrated with each boom of his bounding heart. She didn't even have to touch him to count his pulse, she could do it from the end of the bed. His heart was working at an alarming pace. He looked flushed and his forehead was beaded with sweat.

Richard knelt beside his patient and knew he couldn't save Fumradi. He doubted that even the high-tech medical care he'd get in a modern intensive care unit could have saved the rebel leader.

He was surprisingly young. Mid-twenties at most. 'Fumradi

is gravely ill,' he said, turning back to John. 'I cannot help him. He needs to be evacuated.'

'No evacuation.' John shook his head.

'He needs intensive care.'

'No hospital,' John reiterated.

'He's going to die,' said Richard, with barely concealed anger. 'Is that what you want? Are you going to tell those people out there that you let their leader die?'

'Best not let him die, then, Sergeant,' said John, his voice cold and hard.

Richard turned back, grinding his teeth together. He glanced at Holly on the other side of the bed and he could tell by the look on her face that her assessment of the situation was the same as his. Hopeless.

So, he thought. Fumradi would die. And that was going to be very bad for them. It was time to stop trying to change John's mind. He obviously wasn't going to budge. It was time to start thinking of ways to delay the man's death as long as possible and work out a way to escape.

'OK,' he said to Holly, quickly prioritising in his head the things they could offer him that could buy them some time. 'He needs fluids, antibiotics, his wound investigated and cleaned up. Let's get two IVs in and give him some colloid. We'll administer antibiotics and then we'll probe and clean his wound.'

Holly looked at him blankly. Surely he knew that Fumradi was still going to die, regardless of anything they did?

'I need my pack, John. Now.' Richard turned to see John disappearing out the door.

'Are you insane?' she hissed. 'He's at death's door and knocking really loudly. It doesn't matter what we do, he's still going to die.'

'Yes, I do realise that,' he replied quietly. 'I'm just trying to buy us some time.'

'For what?'

'To escape. You want to be here when they discover he's dead?'

'Of course not,' she said sarcastically. 'But how much time do you really think you can get us? If he's alive in an hour, I'll be amazed.'

Richard heard John's footsteps getting closer. 'He has to be, Holly. We need to get him through into the night. We're going to need the cover of darkness.'

Holly swallowed at the urgency of his tone. John handed the pack to Richard. It was three o'clock. Nightfall was sometime away yet. She glanced at Richard. He oozed confidence as he methodically pulled equipment from his pack. She couldn't help but compare him to the man she had kissed last night. He was gone. Only the machine remained.

He handed her an IV cannula. 'You get one in your side.' Maybe he could see the panic in her eyes because his hand lingered for a moment and he smiled at her encouragingly.

Holly's hand shook as she ripped open the packaging and assembled the tourniquet and other equipment she would need for when the needle slid into the vein.

Richard pierced his patient's skin, finding a vein immediately. Fumradi didn't flinch or protest at the sharp sting. 'John, can you ask her how long Fumradi has been unresponsive?' asked Richard, nodding to the woman who had been in the room when they had entered.

There was a brief exchange as Richard ran an IV line through. 'Since before lunch,' confirmed John.

Holly got a flashback and almost sagged in relief. Her hands were shaking so much she was sure she was going to stuff it up. 'When was the last time he passed urine?' Richard didn't look up from his task.

A further exchange. 'Yesterday.'

Holly glanced at Richard in alarm. Fumradi was in renal failure. His infected wound had obviously given him blood-borne septicaemia and had caused his kidneys to stop working. Untreated sepsis followed an ugly but predictable path, which usually led to multi-organ failure. His liver would be struggling too and his heart battling to keep it all together.

'OK,' said Richard, connecting the fluid to the cannula and jumping up from his squatting position. He opened the giving set up full bore. The two flasks of volume expander they were going to administer would help Fumradi's flagging circulation. And the triple antibiotics he was drawing up might temporarily knock the rapidly multiplying bacteria that were storming the man's system. He needed more than one dose but Richard didn't carry any more so it would have to do.

Holly hooked up her IV line and got it running. Richard handed her a syringe with an antibiotic in it, and she inserted the needle into the side port of the plastic line and pushed the drug into the drip. He did the same on the other side and as she watched the yellow fluid mix with the colloid solution, she crossed her fingers that it would buy them the time Richard was hoping for.

'Hold a mil back,' Richard said to her as he gave the last of the medication.

Holly didn't query him in front of an eagle-eyed John but she did look at him questioningly.

'I'll spray it into the wound,' he said. 'See if we can get a topical response.'

Holly blinked. OK, she'd never seen it done before with an intravenous preparation but Richard was the combat medicine expert. Or was he just clutching at straws?

'Shall we do the wound next?' Holly asked, changing her gloves.

'Yes,' he said, following suit.

Richard watched as Holly cut the dirty bandage away from their patient's thigh. He saw her nose wrinkle at the putrid smell and her shudder as the full extent of the infection was revealed. Pus oozed from the jagged wound that was about the size of an orange. Old clotted blood clung to the edges and the flesh looked dull and greyish. The stench intensified now the fabric barrier had been fully removed.

'Let's get it clean,' said Richard, straightening to remove himself from the potent aroma.

Holly sat back on her haunches, trying to mentally prepare herself. She was obviously going to have to work holding her breath. It was that or end up vomiting into the wound. Not that anything could make it any worse. The smell really was nauseating.

Richard pulled out a small sterile, single-use pack and opened it on the bed. There were two towels, several gauze squares, a small plastic bowl, a pair of long-necked forceps and a stitch holder. He filled the bowl with sterile saline and opened up some more gauze.

Holly turned her head and took a deep breath of relatively fresh air behind her, then moved reluctantly back towards the festering wound. She put the gauze into the bowl and watched as it soaked up the liquid. She picked up a square, squeezed out the excess saline and set about cleaning the wound.

The gauze glided across the rough surface of the deep wound, the tissue slippery beneath her fingers. As she discarded each piece of gauze she noted the greeny-yellow slime that coated them. Richard pushed around the edges of the wound, expressing pus that had become trapped in the jagged tissue.

Holly shifted away again, satisfied that the wound was as clean as she could get it, and sucked in some deep breaths of clean air. She watched Richard mix the remainder of the antibiotics together in one syringe and then add some saline to make the quantity up to ten mils.

Richard knew he was going to have to probe the wound. He didn't have the use of an X-ray machine to see if any shrapnel had been left behind. But he knew, given the amount of pus, that there had to be something still in there.

He put on another pair of gloves over the pair he was already wearing. Double gloving was essential for the procedure he was about to perform. It wasn't uncommon for foreign bodies such as shrapnel to cut through gloves. Two glove layers gave added protection in case the first glove was breeched.

He placed his latex-protected index finger into the wound, moving it around, pushing quite firmly, trying to locate any obvious retained fragments. Fumradi moaned slightly and Richard was surprised. Was the colloid having an effect already? The local woman tending the leader rushed to his side and mopped his brow again.

Richard thought he felt a large solid lump just below the surface in the centre of the wound. Ignoring the overpowering smell and his necessary proximity to it, Richard picked up the forceps. Not exactly the right tool for the job but they were all he had.

He inspected the wound closely and found a small opening in the bed of the wound. He pushed the forceps into it and probed around until the instrument hit the solid object. He closed his eyes as he manoeuvred the tips to grasp the foreign body. He wiggled it out slowly, encouraged by Fumradi's groans.

If he was responding to pain, their treatment was starting to have some effect. Richard knew it would only be a temporary rally, but it would give them some time and that was all he needed.

The offending object finally pulled free and Richard held it up to the light. A partial bullet fragment—no wonder the wound had been so full of pus, with this acting as a constant irritant. He dropped the metal object into the bowl with a dull thunk.

'Impossible,' said John. 'I told you, we got the bullet out.'

'Well, you left some behind,' said Richard, feeling a smugness he shouldn't have in the situation and a certain pleasure at John's loss of face.

'Let's dress it,' said Holly, jumping in as she felt the tension between the two men reaching a dangerous peak.

Richard broke his eye contact with John and got back to the task at hand. 'I'll just irrigate the wound with this,' he said to Holly as she prepared some soaked gauze. He squirted the antibiotic solution he had prepared earlier onto the surface of the wound and made sure he instilled it well into the area where the bullet fragment had lodged.

Holly grimaced as Fumradi protested the bite of the antibiotics on his raw, exposed flesh. She'd spilled enough antibiotics on paper cuts in her nursing career to know Richard's treatment would hurt like hell. When Richard had finished she placed a wad of wet gauze into the depression and Richard helped her bandage it in place.

He looked at her as she stuck tape to the bandage. She was holding up well under the pressure. He had no doubt that she knew the implications of failure. The fact they were going to fail was as immaterial as it was inevitable. They just had to do a convincing job.

Richard shuffled up closer to his patient's head. 'Fumradi,' he called in a firm voice. He shook the man's arm. 'Fumradi,' he repeated.

The man's eyes flicked the second time. Richard placed his thumbs beneath either eye and pulled down on the skin to expose the insides of the leader's bottom lids. He opened his mouth next and inspected the mucous membranes. He also picked up the leader's hands and inspected his nail beds.

Fumradi was desperately anaemic. Probably a combination of the blood Fumradi had lost through the initial wound to his leg and the septic process that chewed up red blood cells as quickly as they were made. The man needed a blood transfusion. Actually, he could do with several bags of blood but one could at least buy them some more time.

'He needs a transfusion,' said Richard.

Holly tried not to look at him like he'd grown a second head. A blood transfusion? Well, da, of course he did. She'd just go and check the blood fridge! 'Right? And we do that how?' she asked him quietly.

'I have the stuff in my kit but I'll need your help,' he said, and looked at her assessingly. She looked like she was only just managing to keep it together. But this was only the beginning. Later tonight he was going to ask so much more of her. If she baulked at this there was no way she'd be able to cope with being on the run. Being hunted. 'You up for it?'

Holly looked into his coal-black eyes and knew he wasn't just talking about the transfusion. Was she allowed to say no? That she was scared and she didn't want to die and that she loved him? But as she gazed into his eyes she saw his strength and his confidence and she knew that he needed her to have those things as well. That he'd get them out but she needed to put everything aside and concentrate on one thing only. Survival.

Holly felt her spine straighten. She'd do whatever was required of her to get the hell out of this godforsaken jungle and be able to tell Richard that she loved him. He wasn't going to accept it while they were still captive, so that was her goal. To get out, to survive, so she could start taking care of the man who stood before her. The tough-guy soldier with a bleeding heart and a damaged soul. Whether he knew it or not, he needed her and she'd be damned if she'd die in this jungle now.

'Ready when you are. Tell me what you need.'

Richard suppressed the 'good girl' compliment that sprang to his lips and pulled a fourteen-gauge needle from his pack and one of two sterile empty blood bags.

'Who are we going to bleed?' she asked.

'Me. I'm O neg.'

O negative—the universal donor. It didn't matter what blood type Fumradi was, it was safe to give him O-negative blood.

Richard also knew, as soldiers were screened before going away to places such as these, that he was clean.

He had no communicable or blood-borne diseases that could be passed onto another person. The army did it as a matter of course to ensure they had a known clean source of blood donations at their fingertips within their own forces.

Of course, he could have bled anyone here but not being able to check their blood type, plus the unknown factor of communicable disease, left Richard with little choice. Not that the disease angle was a huge issue for a dying man—Fumradi would be dead before he caught anything from a transfusion of questionable blood.

There was also another angle. If John could see that Richard was willing to give his own blood to save the rebel leader, that might win him some brownie points. Still, he had to weigh that against the fact that a sprint through the jungle would be better accomplished with all his current blood supply. Whatever way he looked at it, the fact remained—a transfusion would buy them valuable time.

The process of taking blood and starting the transfusion into their patient would take about half an hour. He handed Holly the tourniquet, sat on the edge of Fumradi's low bed and held his arm down at his side. She knelt before him on her haunches, and he gritted his teeth as her fingers stroked his skin, trying to find a vein.

She didn't really need to, she thought as a huge vein rose before her eyes from the constrictive pressure of the tourniquet. But contact with him made her feel more assured and…he had very nice arms.

'Just a scratch now,' she murmured, forcing herself to concentrate on the job. She didn't know why she'd said it. Habit?

She slid the large-bore needle into a bulging vein at the crook of his elbow. Richard clenched and unclenched his fist and they watched as his dark blood flowed down the tubing and into the empty bag that sat on the floor, using gravity to their best advantage.

'What are you doing?' asked John, watching them suspiciously.

'He is anaemic. He needs a blood transfusion. I'm giving him some of mine.'

John stared at them both for a while and Holly thought she could see admiration melt some of the ice in John's eyes. Then he laughed and they both looked at him.

'So you will be blood brothers?' And he laughed some more. 'An Australian army medic and his enemy, a rebel leader? Come, now, Sergeant, you must see the irony in that.' Further laughter escaped his thin lips.

'I told you already. I treat everyone who needs my medical expertise the same. Who you are or what you've done doesn't come into it.'

Twenty minutes later Holly was setting up the giving set and hooking the donation up to their patient—talk about fresh blood! She set it to run fairly quickly. The bag was as full as it could get so she figured there was probably five hundred mils in total. It should be complete in an hour which, given Fumradi's demand for fill, wouldn't be too fast.

'We've done all we can for now,' said Richard, turning to John.

'He looks better already,' said John.

Richard had to admit he did, too, but he also knew that the rally would only be temporary. Fumradi was too ill for such simple interventions to have an effect. It was just that after days of having no medical care at all Fumradi was bound to respond to basic fluid resuscitation measures. He had to feel a hell of a lot better.

'What happens now?' asked John.

'The blood transfusion should be finished within the hour. After that we wait. You should know it's not too late to get him to a hospital.'

'Tsk, tsk, tsk.' John smiled. 'You really need to have more faith in your abilities. You can stay with Fumradi,' he said to Richard. 'Holly, would you like to freshen up? I know how you women like to pamper yourselves.'

Holly looked at Richard.

'Where are you taking her?' demanded Richard.

'Relax, Sergeant. Just because we live in a jungle doesn't mean we are without class. Fumradi's house is very well appointed. I am showing Holly to the shower.'

Holly felt her spirits lift. What bliss. A shower? Really?

'She showers alone,' said Richard, a harsh edge to his voice.

Her spirits dropped like a stone. She hadn't even thought of the shower being anything other than her, a cake of soap and running water. She swallowed.

'But of course, Sergeant,' said John, his voice steely. 'I am insulted that you would think otherwise.'

Holly followed John, apprehensive now. She glanced at Richard and he smiled at her to ease her concern. She need not have worried. Aside from the vague creepy smile he gave her, John was as good as his word, showing her to the room next to Fumradi's and telling her this was where they would sleep. It was basic but had low beds and was a vast improvement on hard earth.

Then he took her to a room with a rudimentary shower. He showed her how to pull the lever and she watched as water sprayed out. He pointed to toiletries on a wooden shelf—soap, toothpaste and shampoo—and then left her.

Holly stood still for a moment, quite unable to believe the luxuries before her. And then she stripped. She had her clothes off so fast and was under the spray so quickly her teeth rattled. The water was cooling on her sweaty body and the soap and shampoo, although obviously not bought from an expensive boutique, felt wonderful against her skin and in her hair.

She was standing on an elevated slatted platform and the soapy water ran straight through the slats. Through them she could just see the forest floor beneath. She scrubbed her knickers under the shower. OK she was going to have to get back into them wet but it wouldn't be the first time this ordeal that they had been saturated. In fact, they had rarely been dry. At least they were clean and wet!

She wanted to stay longer, stay for ever, under the wonderful spray but the urge to return to Richard was stronger. She reluctantly pulled the lever and the stream cut off. She towelled herself quickly and got back into her clothes.

There was no toothbrush so she used her finger and no hairbrush so she used her fingers again to comb her short tresses into order. Then she noticed a smallish mirror and hesitantly inspected her face in it. Oh, God! She looked a wreck!

She threw the mirror down in disgust. There was absolutely nothing she could do about it now and if they ever got out of this alive and she managed to convince Richard to take a chance, he couldn't say he hadn't seen her at her worst.

Holly made her way to Fumradi's room. She passed a window that had no glass and noticed Tundol lugging heavy wood onto the pile near the fireplace. She was struck again by his solemnity. For her, he typified the typhoon crisis. It was about people. People such as little Tundol, who had been left alone to fend for himself.

He looked up and his solemn brown gaze met hers. They stared at each other for a few seconds, both captives in a strange environment, and then she smiled at him and waved. He stood by the fire, unmoving, and then she saw the barest smile touch his lips and he waggled his fingers at her ever so slightly.

Someone yelled for him and he broke contact, dropped the wood and scampered away. Her heart broke for him and she felt her earlier conviction return tenfold. She would not leave this camp without him. If they were going to escape then they had to offer him that chance as well. There could be people out there, looking for him.

She made her way to Fumradi's room and felt her heart pick up in tempo as each step drew her closer. What would she find? She pushed his door open with great trepidation. She stopped in her tracks when she saw him propped up in bed, talking to John.

She glanced at the almost empty blood bag. And then at Richard. He shrugged, plainly as amazed as she was. They had thought he would rally, but this much? True, beneath his illness he looked young and fit, but Holly would never have thought he'd improve this much.

John said something to the local woman who had been tending to Fumradi and she bowed and rushed out of the room, her eyes alight with joy and happiness.

'Our leader has returned to us,' he said to Richard and Holly. 'Tonight we celebrate with a huge feast. You may leave us now. Retire to your quarters. I will speak with you presently.'

Holly and Richard backed out of the room and she showed him where they would sleep next door.

'Did I really just see that?' Holly asked once they were behind closed doors.

'Uh-huh,' confirmed Richard. 'It's only temporary, Holly. It's not going to last. But at least we have a reprieve and some breathing space.' He was trying to be exuberant about it but she smelt fantastic and looked fresh and clean from the shower and he just wanted to crawl into a bed beside her and sleep for ever. The adrenaline surge that had buzzed through his system as he had ministered to Fumradi under John's eagle gaze had left him depleted and washed out.

'I know but…who would have thought he'd have rallied that well?'

'Well, he's got youth on his side. But he's still really weak, don't be fooled.'

A brief knock interrupted their conversation and the door opened.

'You have done well, Sergeant,' said John. 'Fumradi feels much better.'

Richard nodded. 'Good. Then I demand that you let us leave. You gave me your word you would release us when Fumradi was cured. I demand you keep it.'

'It is dark, Sergeant,' said Fumradi, smiling at his captive's audacity. 'If our brave leader continues to be well in the morning then I will keep my word. You will be freed.'

'I don't mind a midnight stroll,' said Richard.

'Be that as it may. Morning will be plenty soon enough. I ask that you remain in your room. I will be staying with him for the next couple of hours. I will let you know when I leave and ask you to check regularly on him after that. I wish to hear immediately if there is a change in his condition.'

John left without a backward glance. They stared at each other for a few seconds. Holly noted how tired Richard looked and guessed donating half a litre of blood hadn't helped.

'We don't have much time,' he said to her, leading her over to the two single beds and sitting on the edge of one. 'We need to talk about escape plans. I don't know how long Fumradi will last.' At least it would keep his mind off how fantastic she smelt.

She sat on the other bed and their knees almost touched across the small distance between them. He ran through everything he could think of about the plan. They would wait until everyone had settled for the night, providing Fumradi lasted that long and leave when the camp was quiet. That would hopefully buy them a few hours before they were discovered to be missing.

'What about Tundol?' she asked.

'If he comes quietly. But if he protests, we're going to have to leave him. We can't afford to have him alert the rest of the camp.'

Holly knew Richard was being sensible. But she also knew her conscience just wouldn't allow her to leave the boy behind.

'He'll come. I know he will,' she said vehemently.

They strategised for the next couple of hours while the noises from the camp outside indicated a celebration was going on. They could hear drums and a beautifully haunting instrument similar to wooden pipes echoing through the camp. Delicious aromas wafted up to meet them. Laughter and sounds of frivolity drifted their way.

She concentrated hard on what Richard was saying. He talked about their journey and the danger areas that the encampments posed and how to avoid them and the effort it would take to get out of this alive. He impressed on her his need for total trust and total obedience, and she swallowed her indignation and nodded her assent.

John came into their room and Holly started guiltily. Not Richard. His face remained impassive. Holly decided never to play poker with him. The man was good.

'Fumradi is tired. He wishes to sleep.'

Holly glanced at Richard. Obviously the rally was starting to wane.

'I trust you to check on him. I am joining the celebrations.'

'Sure,' said Richard. They couldn't make their move until after the celebrations had finished anyway. It would be important to know when Fumradi died. It could be the deciding factor in them leaving earlier.

'We'd better try and rest,' said Richard. 'There's no telling when we'll next get the chance.'

Holly felt her heart hammering in her chest as she reclined on the narrow bed. What they were about to do was dangerous. They could be shot and their chance over very quickly. But she knew she'd rather die running with Richard by her side than sit around and wait for Fumradi to die and be summarily shot.

A little while later a woman entered and brought them a huge pile of food in a couple of wooden bowls. They ate greedily aware that they would need plenty of energy for the night ahead.

Richard and Holly dozed on and off over the next few hours. It wasn't the hardest thing to do, considering their strenuous activity to get to the top camp. Even with a mind racing with what-ifs and the noise from outside, Holly managed to drift off, her tired body overruling her overactive brain.

Richard roused each hour and checked on the rebel leader. After a couple of hours it was fairly evident to him that Fumradi wasn't merely resting but had lapsed into unconsciousness again. He gave him a firm sternal rub and elicited no response. His pulse was weak and thready and his peripheral circulation was non-existent. They were running out of time.

He took some time to study the camp from the open window above Fumradi's bed and planned their escape route while the party continued to rage. The fire was burning brightly and as he scanned the area he noticed Tundol asleep on the ground under one of the treetop dwellings, despite the noise. He lay on an old sack and the only thing Richard could tell that was good about his sleeping spot was its proximity to the fire. Would the boy come with them?

He checked on Fumradi around midnight. The party was all but over. Richard could just see a few stragglers making their way home. They seemed to weave a bit and Richard was cheered by the thought that the whole camp may have indulged in a little too much of whatever alcoholic beverage rebels drank.

He left the window and stood looking down at the rebel leader. Was his chest moving? The door opened. It was John.

'How is he?' he asked.

Richard noticed John's unsteadiness. Dead, I think. 'He's sleeping peacefully,' said Richard, and hoped he sounded convincing.

John nodded. 'Well done, Sergeant. Get some sleep. Tomorrow you will be set free.' John turned and walked unsteadily out.

Richard waited until the door shut and quickly checked Fumradi's pulse. Nothing. He was dead.

He picked up his pack. They had to get out of here. Now.

CHAPTER NINE

HOLLY woke with a start when Richard shook her shoulder.

'What?' she whispered, disorientated.

'Fumradi is dead.'

The fuzziness cleared from Holly's mind immediately. 'Oh.'

'Yes,' he said. 'We have to leave. Are you ready?'

Holly jumped up, her heart starting to race as adrenaline surged through her system in preparation for their flight. She was as ready as she'd ever be.

Richard was fussing with their blankets and she wondered why he was wasting precious time. 'What are you doing?' she whispered.

'Trying to make body-shaped bundles in the beds in case someone checks on us.'

OK. That was smart. She helped him and stood back a couple of minutes later to admire their handiwork. It would do at a quick glance.

'What now?' she asked.

'Follow me. Step where I step. Stop when I tell you. Go when I say go and run when I say run. OK?'

She hesitated, suddenly feeling the enormity of what they were going to do. Would it be OK? He looked at her questioningly. She took a deep breath, nodded decisively and smiled at him. He was with her. Of course it would be OK.

They moved quietly through the silent house. Richard led her to a window he had passed earlier that backed onto the jungle. He indicated he was going out first and she was to follow him.

Being the back of the house, it was also closer to the ground so there wasn't much of a drop. Richard accomplished it easily. Holly threw his pack down to him and then took a deep steadying breath as she prepared to join him.

It wasn't quite as effortless as Richard had made it seem, but she managed to climb out and then let go, falling a short distance into the safety of Richard's arms. She slid down his body until her feet touched the crackly forest floor. She was breathing hard and felt her insides wobble at such intimate contact with him. He stared at her for a few seconds and then let her go.

Richard shook his head to clear the buzz that had fogged it when he had held Holly against him. He really didn't need this now. He needed to concentrate and be aware of everything around him, scanning for danger. They'd never get out of here alive if she was the only thing he was aware of.

He crept silently through the undergrowth and sensed rather than heard Holly following, which was not bad for a novice. He was trained in combat and stealth, techniques drilled into him until they were instinctive. She was obviously following his instructions to the letter.

They moved steadily behind the elevated shelters, sticking to the cover of the tree-line behind the camp. Richard could see the glow of the fire and used it to navigate his way around the camp. His gaze was alert, eyes darting back and forth, and his hearing was tuned in to the sounds of the night.

He heard a large crack and stilled instantly, melting into the night, indicating for Holly to do the same. His heart pounded in his ears. He heard the noise again and realised it was coming from the fireplace. He felt relief flood through him and he breathed again.

Holly tapped him on the shoulder and he turned to her. She

pointed past him and he looked back to what had held her interest, and realised she'd seen Tundol. He hesitated and she looked at him.

'What?' she mouthed.

Richard thought saving Tundol was the only humanitarian thing to do but it could also be a foolish move. What if the orphan didn't co-operate and woke everyone in the camp? What if he'd developed some strange sense of loyalty to the rebels who, even though they had enslaved him, had saved him from the streets? Could they afford to take the risk?

'What?' she mouthed again. Holly sensed Richard's reluctance but she would not leave without Tundol. If Richard thought she was going to turn her back on the defenceless child, he didn't know her at all.

He nodded at her and they continued their creep until they were directly behind the sleeping Tundol. Richard crouched low and indicated that Holly should stay where she was and he would go to the child.

She shook her head at him and pointed to herself. 'I'll do it,' she mouthed. She pointed to his chest and indicated that he should remain.

Richard shook his head firmly. She nodded hers back vigorously. Holly leaned forward until her mouth was pressed to his ear. She tried not to think about how she had kissed him there just last night. 'He'll come with me, Richard. Let me do it,' she whispered.

Her hot breath sent a wave of sensation to his groin. He ignored it and concentrated on the conviction in her voice instead. Even in the reduced light he could see she meant it. Every instinct he possessed told him no.

'Please, Richard, trust me.'

She was so sure about this. Maybe it was time for him to put a little of the faith in her that he had insisted she place in him? He nodded and then held his breath as he watched her creep forward.

Holly reached the sleeping child and shook him gently. Her eyes darted around the camp, alert for any trouble. Tundol opened his eyes and looked directly at her. She quickly pressed her index finger against her lips and placed a gentle hand against his mouth. He nodded at her and she let out the breath she had been holding then took her hand away from his mouth.

Holly pointed to herself and then turned and pointed at Richard. She crooked her finger at him and then held out her hand. And then she waited. She had no doubt by the keen intelligence she had seen in his eyes that he knew what she was asking. Would he come with them in their bid for freedom or would he refuse? And if he refused, would he turn them in?

Richard held another breath. Come on, Tundol. They didn't have all night. He was acutely aware that if the child yelled out, they were screwed. They might have to make a run for it earlier than he'd thought.

Holly's hand remained empty. She smiled at the child and continued to wait. Tundol smiled back and placed his hand hesitantly in hers. Holly gave him a huge grin and pulled gently on his arm. Tundol had the good sense to move quietly with her back to Richard.

So far so good, thought Richard. Stage one accomplished—get the boy. Now for stage two—escape the top camp without detection. Richard knew if they could do that then hopefully they'd almost be at the middle camp by dawn. He was counting on everyone in top camp being too hungover to notice they had gone or to realise their leader was dead.

They continued to skirt the outer perimeter of the camp until they'd almost reached the track that led down the mountain. Holly and Tundol were being impressively quiet. He spotted a sentry almost too late. They were about a metre from him when Richard realised.

It was quite dark. Overhead Richard could see a moon that looked almost full but only speckled light filtered through the canopy above. Luckily for them, although Richard was sure that John wouldn't see it quite the same way, the lookout was sound asleep, snoring softly, propped against a tree. A little too much party cheer?

He led his team a little deeper into the jungle to go around the sentry and then brought them back out onto the track a few hundred metres away from the camp. Richard couldn't help feeling relieved as stage two was completed. Hopefully the next bit would be easier. They simply had to make their way as fast as they could down the track before the sun rose or Fumradi was discovered.

Easy? Not really. If it were just him he'd be really confident of success, but not only did he have Holly in tow, there was also a child. The odds had narrowed considerably. Plus it was dark, which while advantageous on many levels made the trip on a mountain path that was often narrow and littered with swamps that much more treacherous. At least rainfall seemed to occur mainly during daylight hours. Dark he could handle. Slippery could be lethal.

He had a torch in his pack and pulled it out to light their way. He knew he was going to have to conserve the battery, so he switched it off whenever the moon lit their way in areas where the canopy was sparser.

Holly held on to Tundol's hand as they walked quickly down the mountain. She tried not to feel too jubilant. There was still a long way to go, she knew that. But the feeling of release she felt as her legs took her further away from John and the dead rebel leader helped her ignore the protests of her muscles at the cracking pace Richard was setting.

Little Tundol was practically running to keep up and she eased back a little. He didn't seem to be complaining but the last thing they needed was an exhausted child they were going to have to cajole to take every step or, worse, carry. His little hand was holding on to hers for dear life and she felt the enormity of his trust.

Walking through the darkened jungle was eerie. The muted moonlight threw weird shadows all around them and the animal noises that she'd only heard from the safety of their locked and guarded shelters seemed louder and closer. She felt a shudder ripple through her and swallowed. She'd never been overly afraid of the dark, but there was dark and there was this kind of dark.

The noise of the insects and the almost claustrophobic sense of teeming, seething jungle pressing in from all sides was kind of spooky. She held Tundol's hand a little tighter and reminded herself she was with Richard and he needed his escape partner to be mature. To be a woman. And she needed to prove to him that she wasn't a frightened little girl if he was ever going to accept her as an equal.

Still, it was especially unnerving, paddling through the puddles and swamps in the dark. It had been horrible enough in the daylight but the night made it tem times more creepy.

She wanted to call out to Richard to stay with her, but his long-legged stride was purposeful and he didn't need her fears slowing him down. She'd been tested many times during this ordeal and had not faltered. Had Richard noticed? She refused to undo her work when they were on the home stretch.

Having to help Tundol kept her mind off it to a certain degree. He seemed to be a good swimmer, which made the going a lot easier. If he was frightened about what the water held, he never let on. He just followed her uncomplainingly, and Holly thought that if a young kid could be brave then she sure as hell could.

They didn't speak. Richard turned and checked on them frequently but he rarely spoke to them. He had already explained to her that voices, particularly in the middle of nowhere and at night, could carry long distances. She knew that he was maintaining silence for a good reason but she was pretty spooked and could have done with some reassuring chatter. Even an argument would have done.

The first rays of daylight were filtering through the canopy when they heard a noise that put a chill right down her spine. It was a distant wailing noise, like an air-raid warning from an old black-and-white war movie. Except it was just one long loud note.

Richard stopped in his tracks and crouched low. Tundol flinched beside Holly and she felt his grasp tighten. The forest birds she hadn't even been able to see suddenly took flight in a loud mass flapping of wings and she jumped at their noisy departure.

And then the sound of gunfire. Distant gunfire but gunfire nonetheless. Sporadic bursts. Then nothing. Then some more. Had they found Fumradi dead? Or their captives escaped? Or both?

Richard hurried them off the path as more gunfire, closer this time and coming from the direction they were heading, started up. The game was up, their escape had been discovered. OK. Now it had started for real. From now on they really were running for their lives.

Richard guessed the gunfire and the booming noise had been a signal. The top camp was alerting those further down the incline that the prisoners had escaped. It meant they were going to be actively hunted now. People would be aware and on the lookout for them.

They were only about an hour's walk by his estimation to the middle camp. They had no choice now but to lie low, find a good hiding spot and get started again once night fell.

Richard left Holly and Tundol hiding behind a huge fallen log and scouted the area, trying to find them a good place to conceal themselves and avoid detection. He inspected both sides of the track.

To the left the mountain undulated away gradually, with thick forest and many potential places to lie low. To the right the drop was more pronounced, not ninety degrees exactly but definitely sharper and with less vegetation. It was also rockier. There were flatter areas but it looked less hospitable than the other side.

Richard thought carefully. The left side was the easier option. Finding a spot would be simpler and it would be safer terrain to be walking through once night fell and they had to leave their hiding spot and continue.

But it was also the obvious place to find them. Richard had to try to second-guess their hunters. He knew they'd be thinking the same as he was and would probably concentrate most of their search on the left side of the mountain.

So they had to go right. He clambered down the side, trying to hurry but be as surefooted as possible. If he fell, Holly and Tundol would have no one looking out for them. The thought made his search all the more desperate.

Richard found a rocky platform protected by an overhang in a heavily ferned area. The thick vegetation all but concealed it from the track above and, even walking straight past it, it wasn't easy to spot. He'd almost missed it.

Unfortunately, as he feared, he tripped over one of the many rocky obstacles and fell, putting his arm out to break his fall to prevent sliding further down the side of the mountain. A sharp pain ripped through his biceps and he had to bite down to prevent an expletive ricocheting around the jungle. He ripped off his fatigue shirt and noticed the nasty gash spilling out thick red blood.

Damn it! He didn't have time for this! He reached into his pack quickly and pulled out a bandage, quickly wrapping it in place. He would inspect his injury more when they were tucked away and hidden. For now he had to get back to Holly and Tundol.

He scrambled back to where he had left them, ignoring the pain in his arm. Holly looked scared when he lifted away the fern fronds he had cut to conceal their position. He noticed she was sheltering Tundol's body with her own and felt his heartstrings pull hard at her efforts to protect her charge.

'It's OK,' he whispered. 'It's just me.' He was glad when the fear left her face and she loosened her hold on Tundol. 'I've found a spot we can hide until tonight.'

Richard helped the two of them down the treacherous slope to the platform. It was a snug fit and they bunched together, putting the boy between them. Richard was satisfied they were as invisible as he could make them. And he crossed his fingers and hoped for rain.

And it did. Miraculously it rained all day. Torrential monsoon rain so typical of this time of year. Hard and steady, washing away any footprints that could be tracked and no doubt weakening the determination of the rebels. Driving rain made a manhunt hard going.

Not long after they had settled on the platform and just after the rain had started in earnest, Richard heard the distant drone of an engine. He glanced at his companions but they were both asleep. As it came closer, Richard recognised it as a trail bike.

He strained his ears to confirm it. Yes, it was definitely that. He didn't recall seeing one at the top camp but it was certainly coming from that direction. They must be desperate to locate them if they were bringing out a trail bike in such dangerous, slippery conditions.

Richard felt the throb of his injured arm and took the opportunity to inspect it a little closer. The bleeding had effectively stopped but as he pulled at the edges of the gaping wound he knew it should be sutured.

Holly stirred and opened her eyes and caught Richard inspecting his arm.

'Richard,' she gasped, looking at the jagged wound that looked about ten centimetres long. 'What happened?'

'Shh,' he whispered, placing his fingers against his lips. 'It's nothing,' he dismissed.

'Let me look,' she insisted in an angry whisper.

He acquiesced because he thought that at least it would shut her up. He tried not to grimace as her fingers probed the edges.

'It needs stitching,' she hissed.

'Yes, but it won't kill me. It'll wait.'

'Richard,' she whispered, trying not to let her exasperation at his he-man attitude show, 'it should be closed. It could become badly infected in this environment. Not to mention the scarring.'

Richard snorted quietly. Typical of a woman to think of the scar factor. He was a man, for heaven's sake, and a soldier to boot. A scar was nothing. 'Well, unless you're going to suture it there's nothing I can do.'

'What?' she whispered. 'Big tough guy can't suture his own wounds?'

'I have to draw the line somewhere.' He shrugged.

'I'll do it.' The thought of him surviving this terrible incident and then dying of infection a couple of days later was too much to bear. She loved him. She was going to do whatever it took to have all of them alive at the end of this ordeal.

He got the suture holder and the nylon out of his kit and handed it to her silently. What she'd said made sense. Wound closure in this environment was essential. An intact integumentary system was vital in a place teeming with bacteria.

'Local?' she asked.

He shook his head. 'None. We're going to have to do this the hard way.'

Was there any other way for him? 'Oh, Richard…no,' she gasped in a horrified whisper.

'Yes.' He nodded. 'It's OK. It won't hurt for long.'

Holly hesitated and Richard knew she was going to need a push. 'If you don't think you're up to it…'

Holly took the bait, looking at him mutinously. How much more did she have to prove to him? Her hand trembled as she grasped the sharp instrument with the suture holders. She glared at him and instead of cringing as she forced the razor-edged curved needle through his skin she felt almost sadistically satisfied.

He didn't even wince. She stared at him as she looped the nylon around the tips of the stitch holder and pulled it taut. Nothing. No grimacing, no clenching of fists. Not a flicker of pain or a hint of pallor.

The procedure became a match of wills. The rain and the presence of a slumbering Tundol faded from her consciousness. Each drive of the sharp through his skin became more forceful than the last. Damn the man! Did nothing touch him? Was he completely incapable of any emotions? Flinch, damn it!

She met his eye and wanted to scream as he stared calmly back at her. She plunged the needle through again. How could he stoically sit and have such pain inflicted on him and still look like he didn't need anybody? How was she ever going to reach him if she couldn't even get him to react to extreme provocation?

Richard's mouth flattened into a grim line and he gritted his teeth as the needle sliced through his skin. The throb had been bad—Holly's handiwork was worse, bordering on savage. But he knew there was more than a minor procedure happening between them. It was about more than simple suturing. It was about proving to her that he didn't need anything or anyone. That he was tough. That he didn't need to lean on her.

'All done,' she said, as she tied the last stitch in place, still waiting for some kind of reaction. A sigh of relief? The expulsion of a pent-up breath?

He wordlessly handed her a waterproof dressing and she almost missed his breath stuttering into the air between them as she opened the sterile packaging. She glanced at him and realised that it had taken all his self-control to endure her ministrations and was surprised to feel no satisfaction.

'I'm sorry,' she whispered, instantly contrite, as she stuck the bandage in place. Because she was. Did he realise inflicting pain on the man she loved had cost her emotionally? Sure, it'd felt good for a moment when she'd been trying to goad a reaction from him, but in the aftermath her actions had only appalled her.

The gentleness of her fingers made up for the brutality of her suture job, and he almost forgot the throb that pulsed through his biceps. 'It had to be done.' He shrugged.

She looked away. Maybe, but she could have been kinder. Holly turned to tell him as much but he was sitting with his head back against the rock, his eyes closed. His face looked pinched, emphasising the forbidding harshness of his features. Maybe he would sleep. Heaven knew, they both needed it.

He tried. He really did but the throb in his arm made sleep elusive and the intermittent passing of the trail bike kept his senses alert as it travelled back and forth, hunting its prey. On a couple of occasions he also heard voices from the track above him, which made sleep impossible. Luckily no one even came close to their position.

Tundol woke after he'd been asleep for several hours and Richard placed his fingers over his lips. The rain was belting down and he doubted if anyone could hear them, but silence was a good practice for them all to get into. He dug around in his pack and gave Tundol one of the hard biscuits from the rations he carried in his pack.

The boy devoured it and beamed at Richard when he had finished it. Richard had to smother a laugh. The boy had the most engaging smile and Richard could tell that before an environmental disaster had orphaned him, he'd been a happy carefree kid.

Holly woke too and accepted a biscuit after she'd pointed to Richard's arm and he had indicated it was fine. She looked at it dubiously and Tundol nodded at her encouragingly. The biscuit tasted like sawdust, she thought as she slowly gnawed around the edges. Half was about all she could stomach and she gave the rest to Tundol, who hadn't taken his eyes off it once. He did a good impression of the cookie monster without the noise and Holly looked at Richard and shook her head.

The dry biscuit had made her thirsty and she mimed bringing a glass to her mouth. He pulled from his gear a small bowl similar to the one from the sterile packs and after careful surveillance of the area outside their hidey-hole he pushed the bowl beyond the overhang.

He dragged it back in a minute later, overflowing with fresh rainwater. They drank greedily, all of them. At least water wasn't going to be a problem, thought Holly, even if the diet was basic.

The rain didn't let up, which was both good and bad as far as Richard was concerned. There'd be many more water pools and muddy quagmires to traverse, but it had hindered the rebels' search and given the fugitives cover. But it also reduced their visibility and if it continued into the night the going could be quite treacherous, particularly as they made their way toward the bottom camp.

He looked at Holly and watched her bent head as she ran her fingers through Tundol's hair and hummed quietly to him as she snuggled his little body close to hers and rocked gently. She was doing magnificently. They both were. He only hoped that continued.

Richard realised suddenly how much Holly had grown during this experience. She was no longer the carefree spirit she'd been when she'd come to Abeil. This experience had stomped on that very effectively. He took a moment to lament it.

It was the very reason he hadn't wanted her here in the first place. He had always admired her carefree young spirit and had known from experience that places like this tended to trample on people's souls. He had seen her face some harsh truths on this journey and unfortunately learn some stuff about humanity that no one should have to know.

Richard dozed lightly. His eyes were closed but his senses were acutely tuned into the outside world. A voice, a twig snapping, a leaf rustling and he was fully, instantly awake. Alert. Even the lightening of the rain or the dimming of the light roused him immediately.

Darkness descended and Holly was pleased to be moving off when Richard finally indicated he was going to check things out. It was difficult to sit in one spot, so close, and not be able to pass the time by chatting. Silence had never been a strong suit of Holly's and the enforced muteness was frustrating.

Richard came back and they shared a tin of cold spaghetti. The adults gave the lion's share to the boy, knowing that as long as they drank and had something in their bellies they could rely on their bodies to find the energy they would need. Tundol needed it more than they did.

Holly took the little boy's hand once again and squeezed it as they prepared to move off the platform, out of the safety of hiding and into the uncertainty of exposure. He squeezed it back and grinned at her, and Holly was once again cheered by his spirit.

They didn't go back on the track but walked parallel to it along the side of the mountain. Richard had to use his torch a lot and it was slow going, particularly as the rain didn't let up.

But he wanted to get around the middle camp before they tried the track again. In fact, he was pretty sure there would be sentries all along the path so he was going to need to be extra-vigilant. He decided to keep to the rougher side of the path as it would be the least patrolled by the rebels. Let's face it, he thought, you'd have to be crazy to attempt it, especially in the dark!

Richard halted them after they'd been walking for a few hours. His torch told him they had reached the end of the road in this direction. The mountainside dropped away before them.

They were going to have to go back up towards the track, cross over and try the other side.

Richard, Holly and Tundol lay on their stomachs beside the track, concealed by long grass. Richard waited and watched for fifteen minutes before he was satisfied that their was no rebel activity. Even so he crawled across the path on his stomach and made Holly and Tundol follow suit, only rising to his feet once they were back amongst the trees.

The going was much easier on this side, the slope much gentler, and there were more trees to conceal them. But he was having to use his torch more constantly as the rain meant visibility was very poor.

Holly tapped Richard on the shoulder a couple of hours later. Tundol was out on his feet. She had been practically dragging him behind her the last hour or so. They were standing on one of the many narrow tracks that led off the main one. It was a sticky, muddy quagmire.

'We need to rest for a bit,' she shouted over the pouring rain.

'Shh.' He frowned.

Oh, yeah, right. Like anyone could hear them over the racket of nature! Holly was sick of being silent!

'Tundol is exhausted,' she hissed.

'We can't afford to stop,' he hissed back.

'We have to! He can't go on any more. We're going to have to carry him.' The rain slapped into her face and water rivulets ran down her fringe and into her eyes.

'Then we carry him,' he snapped in a loud whisper, 'but we don't stop.'

She glared at him mutinously. The rain ran over his unshaven jaw and droplets of water hung off his long black eyelashes. Even mad as hell and in the pouring rain, there was something about him that just made her want to kiss him. Loving someone who didn't love you back was awful. Loving someone who seemed incapable of loving was hell!

'He's a child,' she hissed at him as she picked up the sleepy boy and cuddled him to her chest. Tundol laid his head against her breast and shut his eyes.

'We can't stop.'

They glared at each other for a few seconds, breathing hard. And then something so totally unexpected happened Holly didn't even have time to scream. The ground beneath her feet subsided, knocking her on her rear, and she was swept down the mountain with a very awake and terrified Tundol clinging to her.

Richard was also caught up in the mini-landslide. It was like a natural waterslide, the well-defined narrow track becoming a shute that barrelled them along at high speed, along with mud and rainwater.

Holly held on to the frightened child for dear life as her butt hit every stone, twig and tree root on the path. She didn't think about the possibility of the ride ending by them plunging over a precipice and falling to their deaths or ploughing at great speed into a tree. She just held on to Tundol and shut her eyes.

To think she had spent money at water parks to give her this exact thrill—never again. After a trip on mother nature's slide she'd be happy if she never saw another in her lifetime.

Her heart thundered and she could feel Tundol's beating a frantic rhythm as well as she held him tight. Leaves slapped at her face and arms, whipping her as she rushed past. Down, down, down they went. She refused to think that this could all end badly after all they'd been through so far. It just wouldn't be right. It wouldn't be fair.

And she'd never told him she loved him, she thought as her life flashed before her. That just wasn't right either. They might be words he didn't want to hear but Holly knew that she was going to tell him whether he liked it or not. She didn't want to take those words unspoken to her grave. She wanted them out so he knew. So he knew that someone in the world loved him.

Then, as suddenly as it started, the ride stopped and she felt herself lifting into the air and then falling, falling. She held Tundol tight and prepared to fall to her death. When she landed on her butt in a muddy swamp she couldn't quite believe her luck.

Richard splashed down beside her a few moments later.

They were all silent for a few moments, reflecting on the ride. The rain continued to sluice over them and they could hear the falling water behind them.

And then Tundol giggled. He sat up and rested back against her bent knees and laughed. They looked at him for a few seconds and then Richard joined him. His deep chuckle gave her goose-bumps and she stared at him in amazement. What happened to being silent?

Tundol chattered away excitedly at them in his own language, giggling intermittently and pointing at them. Now the ride was over and they were alive, he was obviously revelling in the adrenaline rush. Holly laughed too because suddenly she was alive and that was all that mattered. She had lived to tell Richard she loved him.

'Let's rest for a couple of hours,' Richard said, sobering slightly. He figured they were so off track the rebels wouldn't be looking for them here. At first light he'd try to figure out where the hell they were.

Richard located some reasonably dry shelter beneath a big old tree. They took cover under its huge branches, sitting with their backs to the trunk. Tundol lay down on the soft mattress of leaves and Holly and Richard reclined against the trunk so that their bodies were mostly lying flat on the ground but their heads were supported by the trunk.

Holly was too exhausted to say anything. The rush of adrenaline as they had slid down the mountain and the days of hard exertion had really taken their toll. She drifted off to sleep, only to be woken a few minutes later by a stinging sensation on her abdomen.

Half-asleep, she rubbed the spot and the pain intensified. She lifted her shirt up and her hand came into contact with some slimy sort of bug. It took all her willpower not to scream.

'Richard,' she whispered, trying not to sound as frantic as she felt.

'Hmm?'

'There's something crawling on my tummy,' she whispered frantically.

Richard flicked his torch on and shone it on her stomach. Three fat leeches were having a feed. He noticed her lying rigid with her eyes closed and smiled to himself. 'It's just a leech, it won't hurt you,' he murmured.

Holly opened her eyes and looked into his amused face. 'I don't care, Richard. Get it off,' she snarled.

'What is it with you and leeches, Pollyanna?' he teased. 'You seem to attract them somehow.'

Holly couldn't believe he was choosing now to show his sense of humour and his human side. Or that he had even made a reference to that meeting before he had left for Africa and had become a changed man. Not now, Richard, not when she was muddy and soaked through and had a leech feeding off her stomach!

'Richard! Get it off!'

'Them, actually,' he said, 'there's three.'

'Three? Three?' Oh, God! She was covered with leeches! 'Richard! Do something!' She tried to keep her voice low but the desperate note gave it a squeaky quality.

Richard chuckled and shuffled down so he was closer to her abdomen. How many times had he rescued her from creepy-crawlies? He set about removing them.

'Make sure you throw them far way,' she said through gritted teeth. 'I don't want them visiting me again.'

Richard chuckled again and threw the poor creatures a good distance away.

'Ow! I cant believe how much they hurt,' said Holly, inspecting the reddened areas where they had attached themselves to her skin.

'Oh, poor Holly,' he teased. 'Leech magnet.' His head was level with her stomach and he brought his face down and kissed each red area playfully. She had the flattest stomach. She was so petite. He placed a hand against her abdomen and was amazed to see that it nearly spanned her waist.

She placed her hand on his head as he ministered to her wounds to push him away but was mesmerised by the sight of his head against her belly. His salt-and-pepper hair against her white skin. Her hand stilled and his spiky military cut felt good beneath her touch.

Richard wasn't quite sure what possessed him but as he felt her hand in his hair he knew he shouldn't have started it. He glanced up at her and their gazes locked. He felt heat slam into him, white hot. She was so beautiful. If they weren't in this jungle, if she wasn't so young, if he didn't have a million reasons not to…

He pulled her shirt down abruptly and moved back until he was sitting totally upright against the trunk.

'Richard?' she asked quietly, her belly still burning from his gentle kisses.

'Go to sleep Holly.'

She sighed and turned on her side, cuddling into Tundol's body. Great advice, Richard. Now, tell me how.

CHAPTER TEN

RICHARD woke as a glint of sunlight pierced his shut lids. He looked at his watch. Six a.m. The rain had stopped for now. At least his uniform might have a chance to dry out. He looked down at the fabric that covered his body and regarded its muddy, tattered state.

This uniform had always made him proud, made him feel good about himself, that he was making a contribution. If he hadn't been so dog tired and strung out, he knew he'd be ashamed of its dishevelled state.

He glanced at his two companions. Holly was still sleeping on her side, her arm hugging Tundol close. He remembered how he'd kissed her stomach last night and felt the heat kick in again. What was it about this woman? No one had ever got under his skin this much. Not even his fiancée. He'd spent a lifetime protecting it with layers of armour. How had she managed to pierce them?

He shook his head. It didn't matter. Nothing was more important at the moment than getting them back to Abeil safe and sound. Time to stop daydreaming about milky-white, petal-soft skin and how much he had yearned to lay his head against her abdomen and shut his eyes. Reconnaissance. That's what he needed to be doing.

He pushed himself away from the tree and ignored the parts

of him that ached. In fact, he ached just about everywhere so it was an almost impossible task. But with over half of his mission accomplished, he could grin and bear it.

He walked a short distance away, his senses alert. He looked back up the mountain and saw the route they had travelled so unconventionally last night. It had definitely followed the course of a narrow track. He looked beyond the quagmire where they had landed and tracked the pathway further down as it disappeared into the trees.

Where did these side tracks lead to? Were they short cuts to the camps? If they followed this path, would it lead them to the bottom camp or just get them helplessly lost? One thing was for sure—they had to keep heading down if they wanted to get off this mountain.

Richard woke his fellow escapees. Holly regarded him warily, obviously still feeling a little awkward from last night. He wished he could erase what had happened. Go back to the precise moment he'd taken total leave of his senses and take another path. But he couldn't. If she wasn't adult enough to let it be, that was her problem. He was back in control of his body and last night didn't register a blip on his horizon.

'Let's eat and then move out.' He spoke in a low rumble.

Holly felt stiffness in all her joints and she winced as she sat up and leaned back against the tree. Between stiff muscles, a sore back, a bruised butt, leech bites and Richard's kisses, she hurt all over.

'Let me look,' Richard said, when he noticed her grimacing.

She flinched from him as he tried to pull her shirt up at the back and he ignored it. Large surface abrasions all over her back stood out against her pale skin. Some of the areas had obviously bled and dry blood had crusted in some areas. There were the beginnings of several small purplish-black bruises also.

'It's OK,' she said, shrugging him away.

'Your back bore the brunt of the slide,' he said.

'It's OK,' she repeated. Her back was sore but not more than anywhere else. 'Yours must be just as bad,' she commented, remembering he had taken the same trip as her. She went to lift his shirt but he pulled away.

'It's fine,' he said tersely.

Don't touch me. Yeah. He was coming across loud and clear and her heart broke a little. How was she ever going to reach him? How was she ever going to convince him to let her love him?

They ate another sparse breakfast in silence and moved out shortly after. Richard didn't like travelling by day. OK, the canopy muted the light, but they were still going to be more visible than if they had the cover of night. If they could find and then skirt the last camp, he'd pull them up for a rest and continue the rest of the journey in the dark that night.

They followed the track that had collapsed under their feet last night and swept them down the mountain in a torrent of mud and water. Richard crept from tree to tree, trying to keep the track in sight so he could assess their whereabouts. It meandered down through the forest and, as Richard had suspected, led them to the bottom camp.

They could smell the woodsmoke of the communal fire and Richard guessed they were quite near. He went deeper into the forest to avoid detection as they gave the inhabited area a wide berth. But just when they thought they'd passed the dangerous bit, they were proved wrong.

Richard and Holly looked up as they heard a shout behind them. They'd been spotted!

'Follow me. Run,' Richard snapped.

Holly felt adrenaline rush through her system and despite every ache and pain she surged forward, Tundol in tow, keeping Richard's back in sight, mimicking his actions as he ducked and weaved between the trees.

She realised he wasn't running as fast as he could, that he was trying to keep to a slower pace so he wouldn't lose her and she was grateful. She was about as scared now as she had been any time in the last five days, and she knew if anyone could get them out of this, Richard could.

A couple of gunshots reverberated around the forest and she heard bullets whizzing past her ears. OK. Scratch that. Now she was scared. More scared than any time in the period of their captivity.

Richard knew they had to create as much distance between them and their hunters as possible, so he ran hard and expected Holly and Tundol to keep up. He tried not to run blindly. They were going to need to know where they were should they manage to shake their pursuers.

Then he applied a bit of strategy. He could still hear the rebels chasing them but they had dropped back so he decided to slow and backtrack towards the camp and try to outfox them. After all, the rebels wouldn't be expecting that.

Holly and Tundol followed his movements. He could hear her harsh breathing and knew he was asking a lot of them. But this game wasn't over by a long shot, and he'd be damned if he'd just throw in the towel while he had breath left in his body.

Richard could see the shelters of the bottom camp now. He was getting closer. Maybe they should hide around here somewhere until the men pursuing them had run a good distance in the other direction.

Richard looked frantically around for somewhere good to hide, but couldn't find anywhere that would give them the protection they needed. He took a moment to gather his thoughts. His lungs heaved in his chest, dragging in oxygen, out of breath from their sprint through the humid, seething jungle.

And then it came to him. The camp! The perfect place to hide. Right under their enemies' noses! He whispered his idea to Holly and saw shock and doubt flit across her face.

'Trust me,' he whispered.

Holly followed him, with Tundol holding her hand tight. Trust him. But don't touch him. Don't love him. He asked too much of her—didn't he know that?

Richard chose the shelter that backed almost directly onto the jungle. It would be easiest to enter without being seen and would make their exit just as unnoticeable—hopefully. They just needed an hour. One hour to hide somewhere while the rebels searched the jungle. Then they could leave and head in another direction.

He looked in through the slats and it appeared to be empty. They entered quickly and he crossed his fingers that the occupants wouldn't return for a while. He stood by the door while Holly and Tundol sat on the low bed. She opened her mouth to speak to him but he shook his head vehemently and pressed two fingers to his lips. They had to observe total silence!

Holly didn't quite understand his reasoning for bringing them right into the heart of the enemy. She shook herself mentally. Listen to her! The enemy. She was thinking like a soldier now. Like Richard. Whatever had happened to her beliefs about the freedom fighters? Being abducted, that's what. And being confronted with their treatment of Tuti and Tundol.

Whatever Richard's reasoning, she trusted that he knew what he was doing. He was the big tough-guy soldier after all and he had kept them alive thus far. She had freaked at a few leeches. Out of the two of them, she'd have to say he was totally in his element.

And then it struck her. He was. This was what Richard did. This was what he was good at. Standing watch at the door in his less-than-perfect greens, he was every inch the soldier. She remembered his comments about the army being his family and she had to admit he looked right at home. Had he been right all along? Was their no room for her in his family?

She saw Richard freeze suddenly and then heard approaching chatter. She gathered Tundol to her side and pulled him up with her to stand beside Richard and behind the door.

The door opened and Holly shut her eyes. Was this it? The door shut and Holly opened her eyes again at the gasp that left their unwanted visitors' lips. Two sets of eyes stared at her, at them. Two familiar sets of eyes. It was Mila and Kia. The baby Holly had delivered was sleeping at Mila's breast.

Nobody moved for a few seconds. Holly felt sure they all must be able to hear her pounding heart. What was going to happen now? But then Kia smiled at them and Mila grinned and the two women turned to each other and spoke in their language. Holly let out a breath.

Richard let one out, too. The women they had helped a few short days ago were pleased to see them. They seemed safe for the moment but how long would it last? Had saving Mila's baby and probably Mila herself counteracted the loyalty these women felt for the rebel cause and for their menfolk? He doubted it.

Richard heard the trail bike again and they all froze as the bike drove into the central camp area. Mila and Kia talked together again and Mila gave the baby to her mother, who put him in a sling-style apparatus attached to her front and ran out the back into the jungle. Kia smiled at them and nodded.

Richard glanced through the slatted wood and noticed John getting off the bike. A small crowd gathered around him and soon the rebels that had chased them entered the camp, looking despondent and weary.

John yelled at them. He ranted and waved his arms around furiously. He addressed an older man in particular and Holly blinked when he slapped the grey-haired elder across the face. Kia's lips flattened into a slit and her forehead furrowed into a frown. She muttered under her breath.

As they watched the scene, Mila came running towards John and the other men from the jungle behind them. She was flapping her arms excitedly and jabbering away. Richard felt his heart rate slow right down and pound in his chest. His breathing slowed too and he shut his eyes, preparing himself for her betrayal. Had their ministrations meant that little to her? Or was blood truly thicker than water?

He opened his eyes again in time to see John and the other men turned in the opposite direction. Mila was pointing to the opposite side of the path, where they'd been the night before until they'd crossed over and ended up on the waterslide of a lifetime.

She jabbered some more, continuing to point down the other side of the mountain. John interrupted her and appeared to be giving orders. He snapped and pointed the same way Mila had then picked up a long stick and appeared to be drawing in the dirt with it. He was laying a trap.

Ten minutes later the rebel men ran off in the direction Mila had indicated. John got on his bike, turned around and followed his men. Richard breathed and smiled at a beaming Kia who had also been watching. Had Mila just lied to protect them?

Mila entered the shelter with a huge smile, nodding at her mother and at them. It appeared she had. Richard was eager to move out again. There was no telling how long the men would search in the wrong direction. They needed to get as much of a head start as they could.

He picked up his pack. Kia left them and Mila placed a hand on his arm. It appeared she wanted him to wait. Richard agreed but knew he couldn't wait too long.

Kia returned in a moment with a sack and gave it to Holly with a large grin. Holly opened it and the aroma of cooked food hit her square in the face. She thanked the women profusely. At least they could have a decent meal next time they stopped.

Kia indicated that they should follow her. Her grandson slept peacefully in his sling. She exited the shelter first, checked both ways for anyone who could be watching and then motioned them out. Mila waved them goodbye and Holly waved back as they followed the girl's mother back into the jungle.

Richard was humbled and amazed by the lengths to which Kia was going to help them. She'd sheltered them, hidden them, organised a diversion and was now guiding them to safety. Richard knew that the penalty to her would be high if she was caught collaborating with the escapees. And yet she was doing it anyway.

Maybe Holly had a point. Maybe you couldn't paint everyone with the same brush. Maybe they were just people who felt unjustly treated and were fighting for a little equality. Some chose armed rebellion. But not all. And not all approved of the methods of some of the others.

She led them to another side track. 'Abeil,' Kia said, and pointed down the track.

The old woman grabbed his hands and Richard felt humbled by her sincerity, feeling a tightness in his chest at the emotion clouding their goodbyes.

They had crossed each other's paths only briefly but each had had a profound effect on the other. Kia was a proud mountain woman who looked like she'd been around for the duration of the civil war. Yet still she had put politics and years of hate aside to help someone who had helped her.

Tundol and Richard set off down the track, leaving Holly to say her goodbyes.

'Thank you,' said Holly, clutching the older woman's hands and squeezing them tight. She felt all choked up by Kia's courage and generosity.

'Thank…you.' Kia nodded in return, gripping Holly's hands firmly, and Holly saw tears in the old woman's eyes. 'Thank you.'

Holly stroked the babe's head for a brief moment and felt honoured to have helped him into the world. For as long as she lived, she would have a connection with this baby. It seemed bizarre and fitting all at once.

Kia pointed down the track towards Richard's back. 'He good man. Make good father.'

Holy felt tears blur her eyes as she watched Tundol and Richard holding hands. She nodded at the old mountain woman, unable to speak.

'Three boys,' she said, grinning an almost toothless smile and holding up three fingers. 'You and him. Three boys.'

Holly stared at Kia as her words sank in and Kia cackled with laughter at the look on Holly's face. She looked so old and wise that Holly was tempted to believe her. She kissed Kia on the cheek and set off after Richard and Tundol, her mind boggling with Kia's prediction.

With the advantage of better light and the knowledge that their hunters were far away, Holly found their trip down the track less nerve-racking. The urgency hadn't dissipated but the heart-in-your-mouth-stuff had lessened.

Being shot at had been very frightening. Disturbingly it hadn't seemed to overly affect Tundol and she doubted whether Richard had even noticed. It sure as hell had scared her.

They stopped after a few solid hours of walking down the muddy track. Richard found them a secluded spot where they were relatively obscured and they tucked into beautifully smoked ham, unleavened bread and fresh sweet-tasting berries. It was like a banquet compared to the last few days and they ate until every morsel had gone.

Richard decided to not rush over their meal. They had done well to get this far and he knew he had been driving a young child and Holly, who at times didn't look much older than the boy, very hard. He knew how much his body hurt and he was trained and fit.

Holly had to be suffering ten times more than him. The nasty abrasions on her back would be pulling taut as part of the healing process and the salt from the sweat that must be running down her back would be stinging like mad.

Holly enjoyed the leisurely, sumptuous lunch and savoured

every moment. The events of last night, their death-defying slide down the mountainside and the bullets whizzing around her head were never far from her thoughts.

She tried to focus instead on how near they were, how in a few hours they'd be off this godforsaken mountain and she could have a bath and sleep in a proper bed. They were wonderful thoughts but still her mind flashed images of last night on her inward eye.

'What are you thinking about?' Richard asked, fascinated by the range of emotions that flitted across her face as she ate.

Holly jumped. She'd been so engrossed in her own thoughts she'd almost forgotten he was there. She smiled at him, pushing the unsettling images from her mind.

'About a bath. A long, hot, sudsy spa bath with divine smelling salts and aromatherapy oils,' she sighed as the vision floated before her.

He laughed and she joined him. It felt good to be able to talk and laugh and not have to worry that the sound of their voices would betray their position. They were so close to freedom it was such a heady liberating feeling.

Looking at the much more relaxed Richard, she made up her mind that it was now or never. She had decided last night as she had been swept down the mountain that she was going to confess her love whether he liked it or not. But then, with the leeches and plain exhaustion, she'd let it slide.

That morning, as bullets had rained around her, she had nearly met her maker again without having told him her feelings. She didn't want to wait another second. Waste another minute.

She took a deep breath. 'Richard.'

'Yes, Holly,' he said, his head bowed as he helped Tundol with something.

'I want to talk to you. I don't want you to say anything, just listen. OK?'

Richard stopped what he was doing and regarded her seriously. 'Holly—'

'I know you don't want to hear it, Richard—'

'Holly. Not now. OK?'

'Yes, Richard. Now. I've been nearly killed twice in the last twelve hours. I don't want to go another step without getting this off my chest.'

'We're not out of the woods yet,' he said, and then smiled at his own joke.

She ignored him. 'I love you, Richard. I've never stopped loving you. Yes, I know you think I'm too young and naïve and that you don't need me, or anyone for that matter, and that you're happy with your cosy military family of thousands and that I need more life experience and that I should sleep with more men—but you know what? I'm not Tanya. I would never sleep around. And when we were together before, I never understood your commitment to your job. But I do now. I know that the army isn't just what you do but who you are, and I would never ask you to give away something that is obviously dear to you. And it's OK. You're screwed up—I get it. But I can handle it, we can handle it together, Richard. You need someone who's going to love you despite the nightmares in your head and the sadness in your soul, and I'm that woman, Richard.'

Holly didn't stop to draw breath. She ploughed on, wanting, needing to say everything that was in her heart. 'I look at the torment within you and it makes me love you more, because you did something brave to save someone's life when you didn't have to, in fact, when you were forbidden to, and you've suffered emotionally and professionally because of it. But I know when I look at you that you would do it again in the blink of an eye because despite everything, despite your screwed-up childhood and the betrayal of one seriously stupid woman and all the horrible things you've seen as a soldier, you are a decent, kind, humane man. And I love you for it. Please Richard, let me love you.'

Richard stared at her while she unburdened her soul. Her eyes expressed her utter desperation.

'I'm sorry,' she sighed. 'That came out all jumbled and not very articulate. What I'm trying to say is that I understand it won't be easy but that's not a reason to not try.'

Richard stared a bit longer. No one had ever said those things to him. It was the most articulate, emotional speech he'd ever heard. She'd said it with such passion and such conviction he was convinced that she honestly believed what she'd been saying. But the young always thought they were bulletproof and in his experience very few could be persuaded differently. He didn't want to be there when she realised it. Realised that a man with a screwed-up past made terrible partner material.

'Holly…can we talk about this when we're back in Abeil?'

'No. I love you, Richard. Aren't you going to say anything?'

Richard checked his watch. This conversation had to end. They needed to go. 'I told you already, I don't need anyone in my life.'

'Yes, I know, the army is your family. Can't I be part of that? Let me be your family, too.'

Richard heard the note of desperation in her voice and let the fantasy of coming home to Holly each night take hold for a second. It was appealing on levels he didn't want to acknowledge, not least because right now they were as far away from the fantasy as they could be.

He turned away from her and pulled on his pack. 'Come on, Tundol,' said Richard to the boy, who was watching their conversation with interest. 'Time to go.'

Holly watched the boy and the man walk away from her. She saw Tundol squirm his hand into Richard's and she sighed when Richard opened up his hand to the skinny little orphan. He had walked away from her challenge but if he thought that would put her off, he was wrong.

He had just offered a little boy he barely knew a measure of comfort and reassurance and she wiped the tears that spilled from her eyes. Tears of frustration and love and pride. How could one man evoke so many emotions? She gave up trying to find an answer and followed the two males who had come to mean so much in her life.

They marched downwards for another couple of hours. Periodically they could see through the thick foliage of the trees to the flat lowland below and knew they were getting closer and closer to the bottom. Holly could almost taste freedom.

But, as Richard had said, they weren't out of the woods, and just to prove him right, just as her quads were rejoicing in flattish ground, John materialised from the long grass that grew around the bottom of the mountain.

The first Holly knew of it was the yelp of pain that Tundol gave and his hand being ripped from hers. She turned, reacting that split second too late, and John held Tundol firmly in his grasp. Richard's pistol was held at the little boy's temple.

'So…we meet again, Sergeant,' said John with a hostile smile.

'But how?' Holly was confused. How had he known? Everything had happened so fast. She looked at Tundol, brave little Tundol, and outrage filled her as she saw the tears tracking down his face. With all that they'd been through in the last two days, she had never seen him look more afraid.

'I returned to the bottom camp in time to see Kia coming back from further down the track. I had a hunch…'

Holly felt sick. What did that mean for Kia?

The how didn't matter to Richard. 'Let him go, John. He's just a boy. An orphan.'

Holly recognised both steel and contempt in Richard's voice. She couldn't believe this was happening. Not when they were so close to freedom.

'You didn't fulfil your promise, Sergeant. Fumradi is dead. But…you knew that already. And as the new rebel leader, I must hold you accountable.'

So, John had succeeded Fumradi. Interesting. 'I told you we couldn't cure him,' said Richard. Whatever he did, he had to keep John talking. He knew he could take the older man, he just had to get him to release Tundol. 'Besides, it's what you wanted isn't it?'

'What's that, Sergeant?'

Richard saw John's eyes cloud with questions as his irritatingly sure smile slipped a little. Oh, yes, maybe if he made John angry enough, he could get Tundol released. He refused to think about the similarities between the present and the horrific incident he had witnessed in Africa.

Flashes of that day assaulted his inward eye and he knew he had to suppress them and keep focused on the here and now. He had no intention of anyone getting hurt. Not even John— although the urge to wipe the smug smile off his face was strong. But Richard knew he could do that with words.

'Well, that was your plan all along, wasn't it? Once Fumradi was out of the way, you could assume the leadership. It's not fair, is it John, when these young upstarts assume positions of leadership that should belong to us? So, you left a little of the bullet behind...' Richard watched John intently for any sign of weakness, any flinching from his current position. He was poised and ready to pounce at any opening.

'You think I would put ambition before the life of our beloved leader? Really, that is not the way of a freedom fighter.'

Holly watched their dialogue getting more and more furious as it went on. John had to be joking. They were that close! That close to a hot, deep bath. If he thought she was going to let him end it for them now when they were so close, he had another think coming.

And to hold a child, an innocent child, hostage like that. Hadn't he already treated Tundol appallingly enough? To put a gun to his head and use him to manipulate them was unspeakable. She could feel the blood pounding through her head and thrumming through her veins. Her lungs demanded more air and she clenched her fists at her sides.

Never in her life had she wanted to see someone die so badly. She didn't even have time to be shocked by the thought. This despicable human being who had threatened their lives during this ordeal, had locked them up and manacled them, had just stepped over the line. More than that—he was threatening the man she loved and a defenceless child.

She looked at Richard, who was continuing to bargain with John and edge his way closer. Was this how he had felt on that awful day that still fuelled his nightmares? This white-hot impotent rage that was burning in her gut? This fury at how callous and disregarding people could be? As she watched helplessly, Tundol's muted sobs reached out to her, and she wanted John dead more than she wanted anything else in the world.

'Oh, come on, John. You could have had him evacuated to a hospital at any time, yet you didn't. Instead, you abduct us and we walk for three days before we even get to him.'

'Fumradi refused to leave his house. He ordered me to bring you there,' said John, his voice tinged with agitation.

'As you knew he would,' Richard goaded.

'Why, you…' John raised his gun and made to strike Richard across the face.

Yes! That was the right button, Richard thought, and knew he had John now. He caught John's arm easily as it arced downwards and blocked the lightning-quick punch that followed from the other fist. Tundol, free from John's hold, ran back to Holly and Richard began to try to shake the gun loose.

Tundol catapulted himself into Holly and she hugged him close. She could feel his frantic heartbeat against her abdomen and his sobs being muffled in her shirt. Her rage bubbled over as she watched the two men struggle and with Tundol safe in her arms she felt her restraint snap. How dared John hurt Richard? If he was going to mess with the man she loved, he'd better be prepared to take her on, too.

Richard squeezed the older man's wrist hard. He could hear bone crunching and John yelped and let the gun go. It fell to the ground. Now all he had to do was get it himself. He made a dive for it but John, who was no slouch in hand-to-hand combat, dragged Richard back by the feet.

Richard flipped himself over, preparing to launch himself up at John, but was surprised by the force of the man as he threw himself on top of Richard, straddling his chest and landing a punch on Richard's jaw.

His head swum momentarily. John took advantage of his disorientation, punching Richard in the face again. Richard could taste blood in his mouth. John placed his hands around Richard's throat, squeezing hard and pushing down on Richard's windpipe.

Holly watched as John tried to strangle the man she loved. She couldn't just sit by and let it happen. She prised Tundol off her and was about to launch herself at John's back when her eyes fell on Richard's discarded pistol. She didn't hesitate. She walked the short distance, picked it up off the ground, crept up behind John and pressed it to the back of his head.

'Get off him. Now!' Her voice was surprisingly firm. It didn't betray a fragment of her inward quaking. And inside she was seriously quaking. But her fury at John gave her an outward calm and after days of feeling frantic and helpless, the gun suddenly gave her power.

John's hands stilled instantly and he let go, raising his arms in a surrender motion. He rose slowly and Richard scrambled out from beneath him.

'Stay down,' Holly demanded in a voice that would have done a heroine from a horror movie proud.

'Well done, Holly,' said Richard, brushing himself off. 'Give me the gun.'

'No way,' she said through gritted teeth. 'I'm going to make him pay.' And she cocked the gun.

CHAPTER ELEVEN

RICHARD heard a note in Holly's voice that made him believe she was serious. He looked at her, her chest heaving, her eyes fixed on the back of John's head, her arms held out straight, both her hands gripping the pistol. He recognised the look on her face. Hatred and impotence and rage. She was mad as hell and wanted revenge. He knew how that felt. But he also knew how it felt in the hours and days and the months and the years after. And he didn't want her to go through that—ever.

'Holly.'

She didn't answer. She was so focused on the back of John's head he doubted whether she'd even heard him.

'Holly,' he repeated, louder this time, and she glanced at him briefly. 'Don't do this, Holly, you'll never forgive yourself.'

'He kidnapped us, he terrorised us, he enslaved Tundol. He has to pay, Richard. He has to.'

'He will, Holly. But not like this.'

'Why not? Why not like this?' She glanced at him quickly again, licking her dry lips. 'Jungle justice. He would have killed you or me without thinking twice.'

'You do this, and you're no better than him.'

'He just tried to choke you to death,' she said, her eyes beseeching him. 'He's a rebel soldier. You told me they were desperate and would stop at nothing, Richard. You told me that. Well, I believe you now.'

'No, Holly. All he is at the moment is an unarmed man,' he said, edging forward as he started to see the first signs of doubt creep into her eyes. 'If you do this, you're going to have to live with yourself for the rest of your life. Trust me, killing another person diminishes you as a human being, no matter what the justification. You want to end up like me? So screwed up I can't commit to anyone and a head full of nightmares I can't stop?'

'But if we let him go, he's going to continue to terrorise innocent people. You were right, Richard. A rebel is a rebel is a rebel.'

'Was I, Holly?' he asked, inching forward some more, still holding his hand out for the gun. 'What about Mila? Kia? If I was so right, they would never have helped us. But they did. I was wrong, Holly. You were right. We can't tar everyone with the same brush.'

'OK, maybe not, but we can him,' she said, poking John in the back of the head with the gun. Richard was making sense and her thoughts were confused now. She felt her anger dissipating. Didn't he have to pay for what he'd done to them?

'We can let the justice system deal with John,' Richard cajoled, sensing Holly was wavering. 'His kind of justice doesn't work among decent human beings.'

Holly's heart was still racing and her mouth was as dry as the desert. Was he right? She'd been stretched to the outer limit of what she'd thought she was capable of in the last few days, and she'd been surprised. She never would have thought herself capable of toying with a man's life. She'd never even fired a gun before. But here she was.

'And that's what you are, Holly. You're not this person looking for revenge. You're scared and you've been through a terrible ordeal, but this isn't you. Don't ruin your life. I'm telling you, you'll never get past it.'

Holly looked at Richard. The note of sincerity jarred her out of the hate and anger that had been clouding her vision. She saw the hurt and the pain in the depths of his black eyes that was always there. That he carried around with him every day. He believed what he was saying. She didn't want John's death on her hands. He was right, killing the rebel soldier just brought her to John's level.

She took a pace back and lowered the gun. Richard took two strides and caught her as she sagged, removing the gun from her unprotesting fingers. He pulled her close to his chest and he could feel her body trembling violently.

'I'm so sorry,' she sobbed into his chest. 'I don't know what came over me. I've just felt so powerless and suddenly…I wasn't.' And she sobbed some more.

Richard held her and told her it was OK and that it was over now. He understood about feeling powerless. He had been a powerless child and he had jumped in boots first defending a powerless woman. He understood the despair that powerlessness bred. He rocked her gently and Tundol joined them. He put his arms around Holly, too.

Richard noticed John inching away and he aimed the gun at the man who he despised at this moment more than the soldier he had shot through the heart. Despised him because he was responsible for turning Holly into a vengeful robot instead of the happy, zany, high-spirited person she was. He only hoped the old Holly wouldn't take too long to come back.

'Don't even think about it,' Richard ordered, and John froze.

They stayed there for a while, Richard comforting Holly until she felt better and then securing their prisoner.

'What now?' she asked.

'We're nearly at the bottom. When we get there we'll lie low til nightfall. We'll be easy targets for anyone from the mountain to take a pot shot at us if we go now.'

'What about him?' asked Holly, glancing at John sitting on

the ground a short distance away, his hands tied behind his back. She expected to still feel hatred but she only felt sorrow. Sadness that they lived in a world where the people within it couldn't get along.

'We'll take him with us and see he's brought to justice.' He smiled at her. 'We're nearly home.'

She smiled back and Tundol joined in also. They could see Abeil in the distance and Holly felt happy for the first time in days. Her heart filled with love for this man who had stopped her from doing something she would only have regretted. It seemed like the most natural thing in the world to open her mouth and tell him so, but she hesitated.

'You were right when you said that killing John wasn't me. Do you know how you know that about me?'

He looked at her warily. 'How?'

'Because we're the same, you and I, in lots of ways. You knew that about me because you recognise it in yourself. That beneath all the hurt and crap that's tainted your life you are basically a kind, decent man, Richard Hollingsworth. And that's why I love you.'

Every time she said it the words slammed into him like a sledgehammer to the gut. He refused to entertain such ideas out here. 'Really? You love me and think I'm a decent man, and yet I killed someone.'

'Yes, but you didn't have a choice. You did what you had to do to save an innocent family. I did have a choice. There were no lives in imminent danger, just a choice to make between right and wrong. Thank you for knowing how I was feeling and the words I needed to hear.'

He stared at her for a few seconds. 'Come on,' he said gently, 'let's get this show on the road.' He shrugged his pack on and pulled John to his feet with the ropes that bound his wrists.

It took them just under an hour to finally get off the mountain completely. They came out in a different spot to where they had first been driven, but it didn't matter. Abeil beckoned and in a few hours it would be dark and they could move out across the open plain and walk to their freedom.

Holly's heart soared and she danced a little jig with Tundol. The three of them looked like such a ragtag bunch of escapees. Their clothes were covered in mud and torn in places, and their skin was caked with days' worth of grime. But they were almost free.

Richard secured John to a tree. His mission was nearly complete. Holly joined him back at the treeline and they watched Tundol run around nearby like a crazy thing, like a child instead of a packhorse. He'd been so long up the mountain he was obviously enjoying his freedom.

Tundol saw a butterfly and chased it. He chased it and chased it until Richard called him back, concerned he had gone too far. He was worried there might be snipers on the mountain that could easily pick them off from their elevated vantage point. They had come too far to have tragedy befall them now.

The child obviously didn't hear him or was too engrossed in his game.

'I'll go,' she volunteered. Holly felt a bit like chasing butterflies herself.

She ran off after Tundol and Richard went and checked on John, testing the security of the bonds. John started to laugh and Richard looked at him questioningly. John nodded his head and Richard followed what he was looking at. There was a discarded sign laying on the ground nearby. Richard didn't understand the writing but he did understand the picture—landmines!

The next few moments happened in slow motion when Richard thought about them afterwards. He turned back to where Holly was chasing Tundol and yelled out, 'No-o-o-o.'

He was running out after them at the same time. He was careful to step where she had stepped, but it was too late. The

click as Tundol activated a mine sounded so loud to his ears
that it reverberated through his head. He saw the explosion in
slow motion, too. Tundol being thrown in the air and Holly, who
had been two paces behind him, dropping to the ground so suddenly it was as if she'd been cut in two.

He realised the explosion had been small and his mind was
already guessing that the device was probably old and malfunc-
tioning. He reached Tundol first. He was screaming in agony.
His right foot had been all but blown off. It clung to the rest of
his leg at the ankle by a macerated portion of skin. It was bleeding profusely and Richard knew he had to put a tourniquet on
it or Tundol would bleed out through his wound.

'Holly,' he yelled. 'Holly.' He whipped off his belt and pulled
it tight just below Tundol's knee. It wasn't great but it would
have to do until he got his kit.

'I'm fine, Richard,' she said. 'Just see to Tundol.'

He did a quick head-to-toe check-up on the boy but he
seemed to have escaped remarkably unscathed everywhere
else. He picked the orphan up and carried him over to Holly.
In the back of his mind was their exposure to eyes from above
and the location of further explosive devices. He had to do a
quick treatment and get back under cover.

'Holly,' he said, reaching her side, searching her from head
to toe. He noticed she was holding her stomach where a wound
was flowing freely with blood.

'I'm OK, I think I just copped a bit of shrapnel. How's
Tundol?'

Her voice was small and Richard was alarmed at the amount
of blood he could see. 'I think he'll lose his foot but I've put a
tourniquet on.' He ripped her shirt right up the middle with brute
force and his heart sank at what he saw. She must have copped
a flying chunk of metal to create a wound that size. 'I'll get
some fluids running when I get my kit.'

'Get it now, Richard,' she urged him. She could hear

Tundol's cries and they were thrusting daggers into her heart. 'And give him something for the pain.'

Richard couldn't remember ever feeling this scared. Not on the many dangerous missions he'd been on. Not confronting a masochistic rebel soldier. Not with his parents. Not in the last few days.

Holly had a critical injury. She needed surgery. There was very little he could do to stem the flow of blood out here when he couldn't even tell where it was coming from. Richard checked Tundol again as he took off his shirt and then his T-shirt beneath. The flow of blood from Tundol's wound had practically stopped.

He shoved his T-shirt on top of her wound and pressed hard. It was the cleanest option he had.

He shook his head. No. No. No. She would survive. He hadn't come this far to lose her now. That just wouldn't be right.

'Holly,' he said, 'I'm going to carry you back to the treeline. You and Tundol. We need to get out of plain view.'

'OK.' She yawned sleepily. 'Just look after Tundol.'

Richard picked up Tundol and plonked him on his back, piggyback style. He scooped Holly up into his arms as gently as he could and cradled her to his chest. She cried out in pain and Richard felt an ache in the centre of his chest like he had never felt before. And then he ran, bolting back to the cover of the trees.

Gunfire from further up the mountain chewed up the ground behind him and Richard ducked lower and weaved a little with his precious cargo, but still kept to the area of ground he knew to be safe. It didn't make him feel any better that his decision to move his patients had been vindicated.

He placed Holly gently on the ground and Tundol sat beside her. He made a snap decision. One or both of them could die without immediate surgical intervention. He felt fear crawl through his gut. He had to summon help.

He grabbed the flares from his pack and stood away from the treeline a little. He let off two red ones and then a green in quick succession. It was his company code for soldier in distress. He knew they'd be seen back at the army hospital and that help would be sent immediately.

Richard didn't have time to watch the display of the flares burning in the afternoon sky. He had to get back to Holly. Both her and Tundol needed fluids.

Richard tore open his pack and grabbed the gear for an IV line. Tundol's wound was still looking good but he knew that the tourniquet could only stay on for so long. He prioritised in his head. IV and fluids for Holly. Then for Tundol.

As he snapped the tourniquet around her arm, he realised he was chanting to himself. Don't die. Don't die. She was too young and had survived the horror of the last few days. It wouldn't be fair for her to die when she was so close to getting that bath.

'Holly, I'm putting in a drip,' he said, and was alarmed at her lack of response. 'Holly,' he yelled, and shook her.

Her eyes fluttered open. He slid the needle in and she protested slightly. He had fluids running into her as fast as possible within two minutes.

He reluctantly left her side to put an IV into Tundol. The boy watched with great interest as Richard slid the needle into him. His pain appeared to have subsided as the tourniquet slowly constricted not only the blood supply but the nerve supply to the foot and leg. It was no doubt quite numb by now. Richard wrapped it in a sterile towel and then bandaged the towel in place.

He smiled at the orphan they had both grown so fond of and the boy smiled back. Tundol pointed to Holly.

'I know, Tundol, she'll be OK. I promise,' he said, ruffling the lad's hair, trying to be positive when inside he was scared out of his mind.

'Holly? Holly,' he said, shaking her, and noticed the coolness of her skin. He checked her pulse. She was quite tachy-cardic. He heard the *wocca, wocca* of distant helicopter blades and felt a surge of relief. He wished he had a radio. He could alert them to his exact position and warn them of the landmines and the two casualties he had with him.

Holly felt wonderfully warm and she could see the most intensely beautiful white light. It was beckoning her and she wanted to go it. It was so inviting and she knew without anyone telling her that beyond the light was a wonderful world where everyone lived in peace and harmony.

She heard Richard's voice float down through the layers of fog. It was OK. She had told him she loved him. She had got it off her chest, so it didn't matter now that she was being called to a different place. She'd go to the light happily, knowing that she had reached out to him and told him the truth.

'Holly, Holly. Wake up. Help is nearly here,' he said, applying a wad of sterile dressings in place of his soaked T-shirt. 'Stay with me, Holly.'

His voice was so demanding, she thought absently as the light came closer. It was OK. She had tried to get him to love her. There was no shame in her failure. She had shared her love, that was the important thing.

Richard was going out of his mind with worry. 'Goddamn it, Holly.' He shook her pale, limp form and felt tears prick at his eyes. 'Don't you dare die on me. I love you, dammit, don't you dare die!'

Richard had suddenly never felt more certain about anything in his life. It was like he was seeing her for the first time, really seeing her. Seeing the woman, not the girl. The woman he loved. She couldn't die now, not when he had finally realised the truth.

She smiled at him then, a serene smile. Her eyes flicked open. The silly man was trying every trick in the book to keep her from the light. 'It's OK, Richard. You don't have to tell me now because I'm dying. It's beautiful here.'

Goddamm it, no! He had been so wrong about her. She had taken everything this ordeal had thrown her. And she hadn't whinged, complained, nagged, thrown a tantrum or broken an ankle. She'd done everything he'd asked of her and she'd done it without question or complaint.

He had rejected her advances because of their age difference and had dismissed her out of hand as a girl, a child. Well, she may be young but she was a woman, not a child. Hadn't she proved it? Hadn't she proved it plenty during this gruelling ordeal? Why had it taken something like this to make him realise?

'No. No.' He shook his head. The sound of the rotors was louder. He could see them now. 'I love you, Holly, with all my heart and soul. I think I always have but I just couldn't admit it to myself. You've got to believe me, my darling.' Richard felt himself choking up. 'Don't leave me. I need you, Holly. I want you to be my family.'

He gathered her up in his arms and held her close, trying to convey the depth of his emotion through his touch alone.

'It's OK, Richard,' she whispered. 'You don't have to pretend.'

'No.' He shook his head and pressed his face into her neck. What could he say to convince her? He knew she was at the brink but he'd read enough near-death stories to know that people could decide to go or to stay. And he wanted her to stay.

And then it came to him. He recited a string of numbers, his face pressed close to hers. He repeated the sequence again and again.

He knows my phone number, she thought absently as she reached her hands out to touch the light. How darling. How sweet. How... He knew her phone number? How come? He'd certainly never rung it. She pulled her hand back to her side and moved towards his voice.

'You know my phone number?' she asked.

'Oh, Holly, I couldn't get the damn thing out of my head,' he cried, seeing her coming back to him. 'I carry it in my wallet. Look.' He let her go and dug his wallet out of his back pocket. He took out the tatty napkin with her writing on it and she opened up her eyes and looked at it.

'You kept it?'

'I tried to throw it out,' he said, his voice husky with emotion.

'Why didn't you?' she asked.

Richard heard her voice getting stronger. 'Because I was in love with you. I just didn't realise it till now. I've always loved you, Holly.'

'Don't cry, Richard,' she whispered, weakly wiping a lone tear tracking down his face with her thumb. 'What's that noise?' She frowned.

Richard could see the markings on two helicopters now. They were almost here. 'The cavalry, darling. The cavalry.'

'Is Tundol OK?' she asked.

Richard sagged against her and kissed her cheek lightly. She was back. Now he had to get her to medical help, a.s.a.p.! He knew he was taking a risk but he had to get out from his safe position and alert the searching helicopters. He hoped the rebels were lousy shots. He ran out from the bushes to wave at the helicopters.

The downdraught from the choppers as they hovered above him almost knocked him over. He indicated for one chopper to send someone down, and within seconds a man was being lowered.

'Sergeant, we've been looking for you,' yelled the soldier over the rotor noise.

'Well, you've found me,' Richard yelled back. 'We're standing in the middle of an old minefield. This area is safe enough for the chopper to land and there seems to be a safe corridor that way.' Richard indicated the pathway back to their hideout. 'I have two casualties, one with a foot practically blown off, the other with major abdo trauma. And there are snipers shooting at us.'

The chopper medic nodded and tugged on the rope and he was winched back up. Richard ran back to his patients and was relieved to see Holly still conscious.

Gunfire burst out from somewhere in the jungle. The rebels were firing at the helicopters now. The Iroquois returned fire, peppering the direction of the sniper with a loud clatter of bullets. The Blackhawk landed soon after while the Iroquois kept up the covering fire from above.

Two soldiers jumped out once the chopper touched down and ran towards Richard. He met them halfway and reluctantly handed over Holly to one and Tundol to the other. They ran back, crouching low, and loaded their patients into the chopper, taking off as soon as everyone was inside.

Richard sat on the floor of the chopper, shaking as reaction finally set in. He noticed as they lifted off and peeled away back in the direction of Abeil that John was still tied to the tree. He had his head turned to protect his face from the force of the churning rotors as they took off. He would send a crew for the new rebel leader later. For the moment they were safe. His mission was complete.

EPILOGUE

HOLLY and Tundol were rushed to Theatre after their fifteen-minute trip back to the hospital. Richard was debriefed extensively over the following days and relieved of his duties and ordered home early. He sought and was granted permission to stay by Holly's side. She stayed in hospital for a week, the landmine projectile having nicked her mesenteric vein but luckily causing minimal damage to her bowel or other abdominal structures.

Richard was teased mercilessly by his men as he sat day and night beside her, holding her hand and telling her he loved her. He'd been through the scariest experience of his life—nearly losing the woman he loved—and he didn't want to waste any more time.

'I've got a surprise for you,' he said the morning of her discharge. She was to fly home to Australia the next day.

Holly looked into his black eyes and saw his love for her shinning in their depths. She couldn't believe it had taken her nearly dying for the stupid man to realise what she meant to him. She sat up in her bed and closed her eyes. 'Oh, goody! I love surprises.'

Richard grinned at the excitement on her face and was tempted to just kiss her instead. Damn this open bloody-plan design! He beckoned to Tundol, who was waiting outside, and when she opened her eyes, he was sitting on Richard's lap.

'Tundol! I've been asking for you!' she exclaimed, and opened her arms. The little boy threw himself into them and Richard felt more than a little emotional himself as he watched a tear track down her face.

Holly had been so happy when Richard had told her the orphanage had located Tundol's mother, who had been searching for him for three months. They sat and chatted for a while with Tundol, his hair cut short like Richard's, content to sit in Holly's arms and listen to them.

Holly watched Richard walk away with Tundol as he led the boy outside to his waiting mother. She looked at their joined hands and felt her heart contract. He was going to make such a fabulous father.

She smiled at him when he returned.

'You know, Kia told me we were going to have three children,' she said softly.

He looked at her dubiously. Children? What sort of father would he make?

'Three?' He swallowed hard.

Holly saw the doubt and panic in his eyes. She understood that with his background he'd be worried. But she wasn't. She'd seen him with Tundol. She'd seen him with Tuti and with Mila's baby. And the five kiddies form the orphanage who he had made glove balloons for. He was going to be great.

'Three little boys, all like their father,' she confirmed.

'I hadn't thought about kids,' he said.

'Richard, I'm going to treat you so good,' she whispered, 'that making babies with me will be all you can think of.'

He looked into her eyes and the promise that they held gave him an insight into a life he'd never had or even imagined he could have. A life he hadn't even known he wanted. Until now.

She gave him a long, deep, intimate kiss on the mouth to convince him that everything would be OK. The hospital staff and patients whistled and cheered.

'Get a room,' somebody called.

And Richard was just too happy to care that his reputation as a hard-ass soldier was totally shot.

Mistress: Hired for the Billionaire's Pleasure

INDIA GREY

Dear Reader,

I'm honoured to be included in this collection celebrating military men and supporting the work of Help for Heroes. This particular story has a very special place in my heart because I loved writing it so much, and fell in love with its hero before I'd got to the end of the first page.

Orlando Winterton is an RAF pilot, and I couldn't have written the book without the help of someone doing the job for real. He answered numerous e-mails (from various locations around the globe) containing some very odd questions, and the information he gave me inspired the story in all sorts of ways. He was even kind enough to read the book when it came out, and a tall, dark and handsome RAF fast-jet pilot with a Mills & Boon® romance in his hand is a sight you don't see every day!

I so loved Orlando that, as I write this, I've just submitted the second of a two-book series featuring another military hero (*Craving the Forbidden*). The courage, selflessness and dedication to duty that define these men also makes them obvious romantic-hero material, but I'm very aware that the life-altering situations in which I put my fictional characters are a difficult and far-from-romantic reality for many of our servicemen and women. Doing background research for the books gave me a small insight into some of the challenges they face; challenges which don't perhaps have a straightforward happy ending. Fortunately, Help for Heroes is there to provide both practical and emotional support, so thank you for contributing to their fundraising by buying this book.

My original book was dedicated to the heroes of the RAF, but this seems like a good opportunity to extend heartfelt appreciation to the people who serve in all capacities across all the forces, and the families who miss them when they're gone, and support them when they come home.

India

A self-confessed romance junkie, **India Grey** was just thirteen years old when she first sent off for the Mills & Boon® writers' guidelines. She can still recall the thrill of getting the large brown envelope with its distinctive logo through the letterbox, and subsequently whiled away many a dull school day staring out of the window and dreaming of the perfect hero. She kept those guidelines with her for the next ten years, tucking them carefully inside the cover of each new diary in January, and beginning every list of New Year's Resolutions with the words *Start Novel*. In the meantime she gained a degree in English Literature from Manchester University and, in a stroke of genius on the part of the gods of romance, met her gorgeous future husband on the very last night of their three years there. The last fifteen years have been spent blissfully buried in domesticity, and heaps of pink washing generated by three small daughters, but she has never really stopped daydreaming about romance. She's just profoundly grateful to have finally got an excuse to do it legitimately!

For all the heroes of the RAF...and for one in particular.
F.W.—with thanks.

PROLOGUE

'IT'S not good news, I'm afraid.'

Orlando Winterton didn't flinch. A thousand years of aristocratic breeding and a lifetime of ruthless self-control made his lean, dark face perfectly expressionless as the ophthalmic consultant looked down at the file on the mirror-shiny expanse of Victorian mahogany that separated them.

'The test results show that your field of vision is significantly impaired in the central section, indicating that the cells of the macula may be prematurely breaking down...'

'Spare me the science, Andrew.' Orlando's voice was harsh. 'Let's just cut straight to the bit where you tell me what you can do about it.'

There was a small pause. Orlando felt his hands tighten on the arms of the discreetly expensive leather chair as he tried to read the expression on Andrew Parkes's clever, careful face. But the blurring in the centre of his vision that had brought him here was already advanced enough to make this kind of sensitive judgement difficult. He waited, listening for clues in the other man's tone.

'Ah. Well, I'm afraid the answer to that is not very much.'

Orlando said nothing, but he felt his head jerk back slightly, as if he had been struck. There it was, that soft note of pity he had dreaded. A quiet death knell.

'I'm sorry, Orlando.'

'Don't be. Just tell me what's going to happen. Will I still be able to fly?'

Andrew Parkes sighed. It was never easy being the bearer of news like this, but in Orlando Winterton's case it was particularly cruel. Andrew had been a friend of Orlando's father, Lord Ashbroke, until his death four years ago, and understood that in joining the RAF both of Ashbroke's sons were following a long and distinguished family tradition. He also knew of the intense rivalry that burned between Orlando and his younger brother Felix. Both were exceptional pilots, both had risen through the ranks with astonishing speed to hold one of the most envied roles in the Royal Air Force—that of flight commander on the cutting-edge, controversial Typhoon Squadron. Orlando, the elder, had recently surpassed Felix by achieving the status of Officer Commanding Weapons Flight—the highest flying position.

To cut short such a glittering career was a terrible blow to have to deal. There was no pleasant way of doing it, so he was left only with the option of being honest.

'No. Given the information I have in front of me I have no choice but to sign you off with immediate effect. It'll take a while for a firm diagnosis to be made, but at the moment all the signs point to a condition called Stargardt's Macular Dystrophy.'

Still Orlando didn't move. Only the muscle flickering beneath the lean, tanned plane of his cheek hinted at the emotion that must be raging beneath his impassive exterior.

'I can still see. I can still fly. Surely this can remain confidential?'

The consultant shook his head. 'Not as far as the RAF are concerned. Who you choose to tell in your personal life is your decision. Your ability to live a completely normal life will be unaffected, for the moment at least, so no one will need to know until you feel able to tell them.'

'I see.' Orlando gave a short, bitter laugh which was edged with despair. 'My life will be normal "for the moment at least." I guess you're about to tell me all that's going to change?'

'I'm afraid it's a degenerative condition.'

Orlando stood up abruptly. 'Thanks for your time, Andrew.'

'Orlando, wait—please—there must be questions you need to ask…other things you want to know…?'

His voice trailed off as Orlando turned back to face him. His height and the powerful breadth of his shoulders made the desolation on his face all the more terrible.

'No. You've told me all I need to hear.'

'I have some literature for you to read when you're ready.' Andrew slid a leaflet across the desk and continued in a tone of forced optimism. 'A diagnosis like this can take some time to sink in, and it helps if you have someone to talk to. Are you still seeing that super girl? Quite a high-flyer—lawyer, wasn't she?'

Orlando paused, seeming to weigh up his answer. 'Arabella. She's a corporate financier. Yes, we're still…seeing each other.'

'Good.' Andrew gave a relieved smile, and added carefully, 'And Felix? He's home at the moment, isn't he?'

'Yes. We were both taking some time out at Easton before beginning another tour of duty next week.' He smiled bleakly. 'It looks like he'll be going alone.'

Emerging from the consulting room into the London street, Orlando blinked.

It was an overcast January day, but even the cold grey light filtering through the dark clouds hurt his eyes. He didn't let himself hesitate, refused to reach out for the reassurance of the handrail at the side of the stone steps.

He would do this without support of any kind. From anyone.

There was a hiss of air brakes and a bus moved away from the kerb in front of him, just as a shaft of thin sunlight broke through the cloud. Right ahead, high up on the building opposite, was an advertising hoarding, displaying a huge poster for some classical music CD. It showed a red-haired girl in a billowing ivy-green evening dress.

It was a picture he'd noticed countless times around London

since he'd been on leave, but he was suddenly struck by the realisation that until now he'd never really *seen* it. Like so much else. Letting out a deep, shuddering breath, he tipped his head back and gazed up at her. Her huge, luminous amber-coloured eyes seemed to be full of sadness as they locked with his, and though her pale pink lips were curved into the ghost of a smile they seemed to tremble with uncertainty.

At that moment it hit him.

Gazing up at her, he saw with brutal clarity everything he was losing. And he felt the darkness that would soon engulf his vision wrap itself around his heart.

CHAPTER ONE

One year later

IT WAS barely light as Rachel let herself out of the front door of
The Old Rectory and closed it silently behind her. The damp chill
of early morning curled itself around her, and her slow outdrawn
breath made misty plumes in the bitter February air.

Already the house was stirring, but only with the impersonal
band of cleaners and caterers who had come in early to obliter-
ate the traces of last night's party and prepare for today's celebrations. Even so, making her way carefully across the grass,
Rachel felt the back of her neck prickle with fear that she was
being watched. Swiftly she headed in the direction of the high
hedge that separated the old house from the churchyard, not
really knowing why—only that she had to escape from the house
and try to find somewhere where she could think.

And breathe. And step outside of the relentless march of
events towards the moment she couldn't even bear to contemplate.

In her hand she carried a half empty bottle of champagne that
she had picked up from the table in the hall on the way out. Last
night's pre-wedding party, for a handful of the most influential
of Carlos's music industry friends, had apparently gone on into
the small hours—although she herself had gone to bed around
midnight. No doubt he'd be furious with her for not staying and

'making an impression', or chatting up the right people, but her head had ached and her heart had been leaden with dread at the coming day. She'd pleaded tiredness, but had ended up lying awake until the last cars had left in a noisy series of slamming doors and shouted farewells at about three a.m., bearing Carlos off to the plush country house hotel where he was to spend the final night of his long years of bachelor freedom.

And in the darkness Rachel had wrapped her arms around herself and shivered with horror at the thought of what the following night would bring.

Ducking though a low archway cut into the beech hedge, she found herself in the churchyard. A thin mist hung low over the ground, giving the place an eerie air of melancholy which suited her mood perfectly. Tugging the sleeves of her thick cashmere sweater down over her hands, she hugged the bottle to her and walked slowly around to the other side of the church, out of sight of the house. Everything was grey, black, silver in the early morning light. She tipped her face up to the leaden sky, watching the rooks circling above the spire of the church, and felt nothing but despair.

A gust of icy wind whipped her hair over her face and made her shiver. Up ahead, in the shadow of an ancient yew tree, stood the largest grave of all, set slightly apart from the rest, topped by an imposing stone angel with its carved wings partly furled and its pale face downturned. Rachel found herself drawn towards it.

Beneath the canopy of the yew it was sheltered from the wind. The angel gazed down at her with blank eyes, and the expression on its sculpted face was one of infinite compassion and resignation.

He's seen it all before, she thought bleakly. Those pale, sightless eyes must have witnessed countless weddings and funerals, extremes of joy and tragedy. She wondered whether there had ever been another bride who would rather be going to her own funeral than her wedding.

Sinking down onto the dry earth beneath the angel's cold, pale feet, she took a swig of champagne, then leaned her cheek against the lichened stone. The sides of the tomb were carved with rows

of names and dates, some of which were worn away almost to il-
legibility and obscured by moss. But the name nearest to her was
still sharp and clear. Tracing her fingers over it, she read the words.

The Hon. Felix Alexander Winterton
of Easton Hall
Killed in active service to his country
HE GAVE HIS TODAY THAT WE MIGHT HAVE
OUR TOMORROW

She looked up at the angel with a watery smile and raised the
champagne bottle. 'Cheers, Felix,' she whispered. 'But in my
case that was a real wasted gesture.'

Orlando hardly noticed the cold as he got out of the car and
walked towards the churchyard. Cold seemed to be his natural
element these days. Cold, and gathering darkness, of course.

His last visit to Andrew Parkes had not brought any positive
news. His sight was deteriorating more rapidly than Parkes had
initially predicted, and he'd advised Orlando that it was now imperative he gave up driving.

He would. Today was the last time. The anniversary of Felix's
death. He'd come down to his grave early enough to avoid any
traffic, taking the private lanes through the estate. At high speed.

The nature of the condition was that his peripheral vision was
pretty much unaffected, while his central field of vision was
nothing more than a blur—like a dark fingerprint on a camera
lens. Getting around wasn't yet a problem, but it was the finer
details that were quickly slipping away from him. He could no
longer read faces, recognise people without them announcing
themselves, or carry out easily the million small things he had
once done without even thinking. Fastening the buttons on a
shirt. Making coffee. Reading his mail.

But he would die before he let other people see that. Which
was why he had come back to Easton, and solitude.

Pausing in the shelter of the lychgate, he looked up to where a group of rooks circled above the church, their ragged wings black against a grey sky. Everything was fading to the same monochrome, he thought bleakly, screwing up his eyes to scan the churchyard, where the headstones looked bone white against the dark fringe of bare trees and the shadowy bulk of the yew over the Winterton plot.

Something caught the corner of his eye. A flash of red in the gloom. He tilted his head, standing very still as he tried to work out what it was.

A fox? Slinking back to its earth after a night out hunting? And then he located it again,

A girl. A red-headed girl was sitting on Felix's grave.

'What the hell do you think you're doing?'

Rachel's head snapped upwards. A man stood in front of her, towering over her, his long dark coat and dishevelled black hair making him look both beautiful and menacing. His face was every bit as hard and cold as that of the stone angel, but without any trace of compassion.

'I—nothing! I was just…'

She struggled to stand up, but her legs were cramped from sitting on the ground, her feet numb with cold. Instantly she felt his hands close around her arms as he pulled her to her feet. For a moment she was crushed against him, and she felt the wonderful warmth and strength that radiated from his body before he thrust her away. Still keeping his vice-like grip on her upper arm with one hand, he removed the champagne bottle with the other, swilling the contents around as if gauging how much was left.

'I think that explains it.' His lip curled in distaste. 'Isn't it a little early? Or do you have something particularly pressing to celebrate?'

'No.' She gave a short laugh, and had to clap her hand to her mouth as it threatened to turn into a sob. 'I have absolutely nothing at all to celebrate. I was aiming more for Dutch courage.

Or oblivion.' She could feel embarrassing tears begin to slide down her cold cheeks and gave an apologetic smile, stroking a hand over the weathered stone. 'Peaceful oblivion. With lovely, heroic Felix here.'

The dark man didn't return the smile, letting go of her so abruptly that she stumbled backwards and had to lean on the gravestone for support.

'He'll be thrilled to know that a little thing like death hasn't made him lose his touch with women.'

The bitterness etched into the lean planes of his face made Rachel wince. She took in the dark shadows under his slanting eyes, the crease of anguish between his highly arched black brows. Horrified realisation dawned.

'Oh, God, I'm so sorry...you knew him?'

There was a pause. And then he held out his hand with a bleak smile that briefly illuminated the stark beauty of his face.

'Orlando Winterton. Felix's brother.'

She took his hand and, registering the warmth and steadiness of his grip, felt a sudden irrational urge to hold on for dear life. For a brief moment his fingers closed around hers, strong and steady, and she found herself wishing he would never let go.

He withdrew his hand, and she felt the colour surge into her cheeks.

'I'm Rachel. And I'm sorry...about your brother. Was he a soldier?'

'Pilot. RAF. Shot down in the Middle East,' Orlando said tersely.

'How terrible,' she said quietly, curling up her fingers. They tingled where his skin had warmed them.

He shrugged. 'It happens. It's all part of the job.'

'You're a pilot too?'

'Was.'

'It must take incredible courage. To know that every day when you go to work you're staring death in the face.'

He let out a harsh laugh. 'I think there are worse things to stare at than death.'

Rachel sighed, sinking down onto the dry earth at the foot of the tomb again. 'Tell me about it.'

Above her, Orlando Winterton and Felix's angel towered like twin protectors. She leaned her head back against the stone and lifted the bottle towards them before taking a long swig. 'To courage—the real kind. And to Dutch courage—which isn't nearly so honourable, but sometimes has to suffice.'

From the edge of his vision Orlando had an impression of dark eyes in a pale face, a generous trembling mouth, a glorious tumble of fiery hair that stirred a memory in the back of his mind and left him with a sudden fierce longing to see her properly. He could sense the despair rising from her like a scent, but whether this was due to the peculiar instinct that had developed as his sight deserted him or because the feeling was so bloody familiar he couldn't be sure.

She held out the bottle to him. He took it, but didn't drink, instead setting it down on top of the Winterton tomb. 'So, Rachel, what's so bad that you're reduced to sitting out here in the freezing cold drinking with the dead?'

She gave a mirthless laugh. 'You do *not* want to know.'

She was right. He didn't. His own suffering was enough to occupy him on a full-time basis. So why did he find himself saying, 'I usually decide for myself what I want and what I don't want.'

Rachel looked up at him. He was staring straight ahead, and there was something in the dark stillness of his face that made her want very much to confide in him.

'I'm getting married,' she said desolately. 'Today.'

She saw one dark brow shoot up before his face regained its habitual blankness. 'Is that all? Congratulations.'

'Uh-uh. It's not a "congratulations" situation. It's…'

Her voice trailed off as she tried to convey the awfulness of what lay ahead. This afternoon, standing in church before people she mostly neither knew nor cared about making vows she didn't mean… And worse, much worse, knowing that tonight she and Carlos would be man and wife, with all the expectations that carried.

Orlando Winterton shrugged his broad, dark shoulders, his gaze fixed straight ahead. He looked so distant, so controlled, so very, very strong that she felt her chest lurch. How could he understand? She couldn't imagine that this man had ever bowed to the will of anyone else in his life.

'Weddings don't generally happen by accident or without warning. Presumably you had some say in it?' He levered himself up from the gravestone and, thrusting his hands deep into the pockets of his coat, began to move away.

'No,' she said in a low voice.

There was something in the way that she said it that made Orlando stop, turn, and walk back towards her. His deep-set slanting eyes were the most extraordinary clear green, she noticed, and he had a strange, intense way of looking at her, his head tilted backwards slightly in an attitude of distant hauteur.

'You're being forced into this?'

Rachel sighed heavily. 'Well, there's no gun against my head… But, yes. Forced pretty much covers it.'

The last thing he wanted to do was get involved, but his sense of duty, dormant for a year beneath self-pity and bitterness, had seemingly chosen this moment to rouse itself. Wearily he rubbed a hand over his eyes. 'In what way?'

'There's no way out,' she said slowly. 'No Plan B. No choice. This wedding is the culmination of a lifetime of work by my mother.' She laughed. 'If I don't go through with it she'll probably kill me.'

But that was almost preferable to what Carlos would do to her if she stayed and married him. She knew, because he'd done it to her already.

'You can't get married to please your mother.'

The words were laced with scorn, and Rachel felt her head snap back as if she'd just had an ice cube dropped down her spine.

'You don't know my mother. She's…'

She hesitated, shaking her head, trying to find a word for Elizabeth Campion's single-minded obsession with her daughter's musical career; the combination of guile and icy manipulation that would have made Machiavelli green with envy, which had enabled her to bring about the ultimate coup in the form of Rachel's engagement to Carlos Vincente, one of the industry's most influential conductors.

'What? A convicted killer?' Orlando's voice was hard and mocking. 'A cold-blooded psychopath? Head of a crack team of hired assassins?'

His cruelty made her gasp. 'No, of course not. But—' It was impossible to keep the desperation out of her voice. She so badly wanted to make him see what she was up against, but the words darted around in her head, refusing to be pinned down, while all the time he held her in that cool, detached gaze. 'Oh, what's the point? Just forget it. I can't make you understand, so there's no point in trying. Please, just leave me alone!'

'To drink yourself into a stupor? If that's what you want…'

He turned away, and Rachel felt a surge of panic. She had to grip the stony folds of the angel's robes to stop herself from reaching out to hold him back. It was ridiculous, of course; he was nothing more than a passing stranger. But something about the intensity in his face, the bleak self-control in his voice, the immense strength in his shoulders, had made her believe for a moment that he could help her.

Rescue her.

'It's not what I want, but I have no choice!'

He stopped and slowly faced her again. He seemed to look right past her face and into her soul.

'Of course you do. You're young. You're *alive*,' he said with ironic emphasis, gesturing with one elegant hand towards his brother's grave. 'I'd say you have a choice. What you really lack, Rachel, is courage.'

Rachel felt her mouth open in shock and outrage as she watched him walk away. He moved slowly, almost wearily, in spite of his endlessly long legs and athletic build.

He knew nothing—*nothing* about her. How dared he say she lacked courage?

He was way off the mark. Wasn't he?

Courage. Mentally she examined the word. It wasn't a quality she'd ever been taught to value or develop. Obedience, yes. Discipline, perseverance, patience, selflessness—yes, yes, yes, yes...

Not courage. Courage had always seemed like just another word for selfishness.

Orlando Winterton disappeared from view through the gate to the road, and a moment later she heard the roar of a car engine starting up. Straining forwards, she saw a low dark sports car speed past in a shower of gravel and take the unmarked turning to the left of the churchyard. In the silence following its disappearance she was suddenly aware that she was gripping the carved robes of the angel so hard her short fingernails ached.

She felt bereft.

Closing her eyes, she allowed herself to remember the feeling of his hands on her arms, and the moment when she had been held against his chest. She felt again the roughness of his thick woollen sweater against her cheek, smelled the warm, faint tang of expensive aftershave that had clung to the collar of his long, exquisitely tailored black coat.

In that moment she'd felt as if she was safe. As if she'd come home. As if she'd finally found the shadowy figure she'd spent her childhood yearning for—the one man who would protect her from—

'Rachel!'

Her eyes flew open as she recognised her mother's voice, and without thinking she darted back into the cover of the yew tree, hiding behind the vast slab of stone beside her. For a moment all was silent as she crouched there, her heart pounding inside her chest, her cheek resting against the chilly stone where Felix Winterton's name was carved.

'Rachel!'

The voice was closer now, and Rachel knew only too well

its shrill note of exasperation. *I'm twenty-three years old and here I am, hiding from my mother like a naughty child.* She squeezed her eyes shut and suddenly the face of Orlando Winterton swam into focus in the darkness, with that hard, bleak smile of his.

What you really lack is courage.

She hesitated, then stood up slowly.

Dressed in a figure-hugging pink velour tracksuit and last night's high-heeled mules, Elizabeth Campion was making her way in Rachel's direction with unerring accuracy, and the expression on her well-maintained face was murderous.

'I'm here.'

For a wonderful moment Elizabeth was lost for words as she watched her daughter emerge from the shadow of the monument, then the full force of her fury was unleashed.

'What in heaven's name are you doing?'

Rachel steeled herself against Elizabeth's indignant screech, letting her mind return to the last person who had asked her that. Except that Orlando Winterton hadn't said 'heaven'. She pictured his dark, tormented expression, concentrated on reproducing in her mind the exact gritty rasp of his voice as he had said 'hell'.

'Well? I'm waiting!'

With huge effort Rachel dragged herself back to her mother. 'I went for a walk.'

'You *went for a walk*?' repeated Elizabeth, like an apoplectic parrot. 'Saints preserve us! *Why* do you have to be so selfish, Rachel? Today of all days? Haven't I got enough to do with all the wedding arrangements, without having to chase around after you as well because you're just too selfish and immature to get yourself organised? Hmm?'

Reaching the path, Rachel opened her mouth to reply, but her mother had only paused for breath and wasn't actually expecting an answer.

'Carlos phoned. I had to tell him you were in the bath. Lord only knows what he'd say if he knew that you'd *gone for a walk.*' She made it sound as if Rachel had been skateboarding down the motorway.

'I thought it was bad luck for the groom to speak to the bride before the wedding?' said Rachel sarcastically. 'I'd hate anything to spoil our chances of a wonderful happy-ever-after.'

Her mother threw her a venomous glance. 'Don't you dare start all that now, young lady,' she hissed. 'You'll do well to remember how lucky you are to be marrying Carlos.'

Rachel stopped and swung round to face her mother. 'Rubbish! He couldn't give a damn about me! He doesn't love—'

'Shut up! Just *shut up!*' Elizabeth's face was contorted with rage. 'You think you're so clever, don't you? Well, let me tell you something, Rachel. *Love* is nothing but a silly fantasy. It means nothing. *Nothing!* Your father told me he loved me, and where did that get me? I nearly died giving him a baby he didn't even stay around to watch grow up. *Love* doesn't bring you *security*.'

Rachel felt a jolt as the word lodged in her brain like a bullet hitting the bullseye. For a moment she felt dazed and disorientated as conflicting images and sensations raced through her head. Orlando's hands on her arms, holding her up. Carlos's fingers digging into her thighs, hard and insistent, on that awful night in Vienna when he—

She had survived by ruthlessly separating herself from the person who had endured all that. That was Rachel Campion, disciplined pianist, obedient fiancée, dutiful daughter. Not the real her. But the trouble was it was getting increasingly difficult to remember who the real Rachel was.

She'd caught a glimpse of her back there in the graveyard. She was someone who wanted to be courageous. And secure.

She went back into the house and closed the door very quietly behind her.

CHAPTER TWO

AS HE passed the gatehouse into the long straight drive up to Easton Hall, Orlando put his foot down and felt the world fall away in a dizzying rush. The frustration and fury that had needled him on the short drive home was temporarily anaesthetised in the blissful blur of speed.

This was the place where he and Felix had raced—first on their bikes as small boys, then later on horseback and motorbikes. It was here that, returning home for his twenty-first, Felix's brand-new Alpha Romeo had been written off as Orlando had overtaken him and forced him into the moat.

Their rivalry had been as strong as their love for each other.

Protected by birth and privilege, made arrogant by wealth and good looks, they had thought they were invincible. But all it had meant in the end was that they'd had further to fall. All the money in the world, an unblemished bloodline and the looks of an angel hadn't protected Felix from a rocket attack in his Typhoon, and the lottery of genes that had made up Orlando's perfect face was now destroying his sight.

There was a certain biblical morality to it.

All too soon Orlando reached the bridge across the old moat and had to slow down. The drive narrowed as it passed through the high gateposts to Easton Hall, and he drove more carefully round the house to the garages at the back. Bringing the car to a standstill in the brick-paved courtyard that had once housed grand carriages, he let his head fall forward to rest on the steering wheel. His hands still held it, as if he couldn't bear to let go, to take the keys out of the ignition for the last time.

He was giving up his independence.

He felt his mouth jerk into an ironic smile as he thought of the girl in the graveyard. He'd been harsh with her, but her helpless distress had been like acid in his own open wounds. *She* could take control of her situation. For him, control was inexorably slipping from him, with the inevitability of day sliding into night; there was nothing, *nothing* he could do. And this was the first measure of his failure. Slowly he opened the door and got stiffly out, blinking in the thin grey light.

'Will you be needing the car again today, sir?'

Orlando hadn't seen the man emerge from the doorway of one of the outbuildings, but he recognised his voice easily enough. George had worked for Lord Ashbroke since Orlando and Felix were children.

'No.' *Not today. Not ever*.

Soon, Orlando supposed, he would have to tell George. Ask him to take on the duties of a chauffeur.

'Shall I put her away for you?'

'Thanks.' Orlando took the keys from the ignition and let his fingers close around them tightly for a moment. Then he tossed them in George's direction and walked across the yard into the house.

'There. You look lovely, darling.' Elizabeth Campion's hands fluttered around Rachel's face like tiny birds, smoothing a wayward curl here, teasing a fold of frothy lace there. The church bells seemed horribly loud, pealing out their tumbling scales with a threatening leer, but at least it made conversation unnecessary.

Beneath the shroud of her veil Rachel stood impassive.

She was glad of the veil. It separated her from the rest of the world in a way that seemed particularly appropriate, filtering out the unwelcome ministrations of her mother, screening her own increasingly desperate thoughts and emotions from view. In the mirror her reflection was smooth and expressionless, with its pure, blanked-out face.

'Right, then. I'd better go over to church,' Elizabeth said brightly, as she checked her watch and gave Rachel's dress a last little tweak. Chosen by Carlos, it was cut in the Empire style of a regency heroine—which, Carlos had said, would charm the Americans when she sat at the piano later. Elizabeth handed her a bouquet of waxy white flowers. 'Here, don't forget these. Now, wait until the verger comes across to get you. And then it's your big moment! For God's sake see if you can manage a smile, darling, please…'

The shrouded figure in the mirror nodded almost imperceptibly. Elizabeth bustled around, adjusting her large peacock-blue hat, spritzing on another cloud of perfume, picking up a pair of black gloves and thrusting her hands into them like a surgeon preparing to cut, before finally reaching the door.

She stopped, and Rachel felt herself go very still, waiting for a sign or a word that would mean all this could be stopped. Elizabeth's face was thoughtful.

'Such a shame your father didn't have the decency to stay around for this. It's the one day of his life when he could have made himself useful. Oh, well, darling. The verger's a very nice man. He'll be about ten minutes, I should think.'

Then she was gone.

A gust of air from the door rippled Rachel's veil.

Beneath it, Rachel felt as if she was choking. Fury and despair swelled inside her, and without thinking what she was doing she found herself tearing off the veil as a series of shuddering sobs ripped through her.

She had to get away.

Glancing wildly around her, she picked up the keys to the car Carlos had bought her as an engagement present. She had always felt the gesture had been akin to putting a caged bird beside an open window, but suddenly it was as if the door to her cage had been left open and she had one fleeting chance to fly.

She ran down the stairs, her wedding shoes clattering on the polished wood, her breath coming in shaky gasps. Fumbling with the catch on the front door, she peered out for a second, before throwing it open and rushing across the gravel to the car.

Her hands were shaking so much she could hardly turn the key in the ignition, and then, when she did manage to start the engine, she shot forward with a sickeningly loud shower of gravel. She didn't dare look up at the house as she accelerated out of the drive and onto the road, wincing as she made the tyres squeal on the tarmac in her panic to get away. Whimpering quietly, she cast an anxious glance in the mirror, half expecting to see Carlos run out onto the drive of The Old Rectory, or her mother appear at the roadside, a bright flash of peacock-blue in the February gloom.

The main entrance to the church where all the guests had gathered was around the other side, but still the road seemed horribly exposed, and almost without thinking she found herself taking the narrow turning alongside the church, down which she'd watched Orlando Winterton drive that morning.

It was a single-track road, overhung with high hedges and spiked, naked branches of hawthorn that made it almost like driving through a tunnel. She leaned forward over the steering wheel, gripping it so hard that sharp arrows of pain vibrated along the taut tendons of her hands and down her wrists.

Behind her, the peal of bells echoed eerily through the leaden air, and the sound made her press her foot harder on the accelerator, trying to put as much distance between her and the church as quickly as possible. Ahead of her the lane twisted around blind bends, making it impossible to get any idea of where she was going.

She hadn't even thought of that. Where *was* she going?

In fact, where was she? Panic pumped through her in icy bursts. Looking around her wildly, she wondered whether anyone had realised she was gone yet. Would the verger have found her missing by now? Maybe it wasn't too late to go back. No one would have to know. All she had to do was find somewhere to turn round in this godforsaken lane. She could slip in as quietly as she'd left, replace the veil, and let the rest of her life continue as planned.

Carlos and her mother were right. She couldn't possibly cut it on her own. She couldn't even run away without getting lost.

It had started to rain, a thin mist of drops that beaded the windscreen and blurred the world beyond to a watery grey. Frantically trying to remember how to work the windscreen wipers, Rachel eventually located the right lever, only to discover that the blur was caused not by rain but by tears.

The road was bumpy and potholed, and there was nowhere to turn. She pressed her foot harder to the accelerator, trying to make the noise of the engine drown out the sound of the church bells in the distance. They were fainter now, drifting eerily over the dank, drab fields with a ghostly melancholy that was horribly funereal. The hairs rose on the back of her neck. Suddenly everything seemed sinister—loaded with menace. Her heart thudded madly as she glanced again and again in the rearview mirror, expecting to see the headlamps of Carlos's huge black car getting closer, dazzling, hypnotising, until they engulfed her.

Someone must have seen her go. Someone must have heard. He would have guessed that she had gone with that terrifying instinct he had for sensing her fear and exploiting it until she was helpless to do anything but submit to him...

She could almost feel his hot breath on her neck, and, letting out a whimper of terror, had to look quickly over her shoulder to reassure herself she was imagining it.

Twisting her head back again, she saw that the road in front had narrowed suddenly into a low-sided bridge. She swerved, but did so too sharply, cringing at the sickening sound of metal against stone as the nearside wing glanced off the wall. Numb with horror, she kept going, accelerating off the bridge with a screech of tyres and swinging out onto a straight stretch of road. She should stop, check the damage to the car, but darkness crouched menacingly in the hedges and fields beyond, harbour-

ing all manner of nameless horrors—all of which paled into in-
significance at the thought of Carlos gaining on her. She imagined
him pulling up alongside her as she stood in the deserted, darkling
lane, getting out of the car and coming towards her with that look
in his eyes that she would never be able to forget...

A sob tore through her, and she felt herself buckle, as if she'd
been punched in the stomach, as the memories bubbled up
through the thin crust that had sealed them in, like a mental scab.
Her lungs screamed for air. It was all she could do to keep her
hands on the wheel and not fall into the yawning chasm of panic
that had opened up beneath her.

What you lack, Rachel, is courage.

Orlando's voice cut through the fog—calm, steady, reassuringly blank. And then suddenly up ahead she saw the shape of a
large building, dark against the pewter sky, and twin gateposts
reared up on either side of the road. Weeping with relief, she sped
towards them as a dim memory of a story she'd read as a child
came back to her—where someone had had to race across a bridge
to safety before a headless horseman caught them and all was lost.

She screeched through the gates and slewed the car round on the
gravel in front of the huge, dark house, praying there was someone
home. Someone who could help her—hide her—in case Carlos was
making his way through the dark, dripping lanes towards her.

Turning off the ignition, she sank down in the driver's seat,
waiting for her heartbeat to stop reverberating through her entire
body and for enough strength to return to her trembling legs to
allow her to walk up to that imposing front door. What if there was
no answer? She pictured herself knocking, hammering with all her
strength as the sound echoed through vast, empty rooms, and all
the time the headlights in the distance were growing closer...

And then, as she watched, a soft light spilled out across the
gravel as the door opened and a figure appeared. Scrabbling at
the door handle with shaking, bloodless fingers, she threw herself
out and had to lean against the car for a moment as relief
cascaded through her.

A second later relief had turned to anguished recognition.

There in the doorway, like a dark negative image of the angel in the churchyard, stood Orlando Winterton.

Orlando flung open the door and frowned into the gathering darkness. He had heard the sound of tyres skidding on gravel but it took a few seconds for him to bring into focus the very expensive, very damaged silver sports car which looked as if it had been abandoned in front of the house.

Arabella.

She'd phoned last night and announced in that cold, efficient way of hers that she wanted to see him. He couldn't imagine why: everything in Arabella's life was glamorous and high-functioning. She had no room for weakness—a fact which she had made perfectly plain at the time of Orlando's diagnosis. Maybe she'd developed a conscience? he'd thought cynically as he'd slammed the phone down, having told her exactly what she could do.

But she always had liked to have the last word. Orlando's face was like stone as he stood in the doorway, waiting for her to get out of the car. He wondered what tack she would take this time—mockery or seductiveness? Either way, he was immune. That was one thing he could be grateful for: when you lived in hell already, no one could make it any worse.

The car door opened and a slender figure sprang out, ghostly white in the winter gloom. Orlando felt his head jerk upwards slightly as he desperately sought to bring her into his field of vision.

Not Arabella.

She stood against the car, and even with his failing sight, even in the gathering February dusk, he could see that she was trembling. She was wearing a thin white dress that blew against her long legs, and her bright hair was like a beacon in the blurred centre of his vision. It lit up the darkness. Red for danger.

Red for passion.

The girl from the graveyard.

Slowly he walked down the steps towards her. Frozen by the

icy wind that stung her bare arms and whipped her hair across her numb cheeks, Rachel watched him helplessly, suddenly finding that her brain was as frozen as the rest of her, but that something, somewhere deep inside of her just wanted to fling herself into this man's arms.

In the distance she could still hear the discordant peal of the church bells, and she gave her head a little shake, trying to regain a rational hold on the situation. The trouble was, she wasn't sure there was one.

'I'm sorry,' she said, in a voice that was little more than a hoarse croak. 'I didn't mean to come here. I didn't know... The road—I didn't know where it went—I was just...driving...'

He looked down on her from his great height. His massive shoulders were rigid with tension, but his face gave nothing away. 'Driving away from your wedding, I take it?'

'Yes. I couldn't...do it.' She spoke very carefully, breathing slowly and deliberately to keep herself together. 'I waited until the last possible minute to see if something would happen to stop it, but it didn't...and then...I knew I couldn't do it. I ran away... because you were right, I...'

She took another steadying breath, but at that moment the church bells stopped abruptly. Silence seemcd to fold around them like fog. Rachel felt her hands fly to her mouth, her eyes widening in horror as the implications of that silence sank in.

They knew. They'd found she was missing. And Carlos... Carlos would be...

Frantically she pushed her fingers through her hair, looking wildly about her as terror gripped her once again. Without knowing what she was doing, she wrenched open the car door.

Orlando was beside her in a flash, his arms closing around her waist, pinning her own arms to her sides and stopping her escape. She struggled against him, twisting her shoulders frantically, but his strength was enormous. Effortlessly he held her against him.

'Let me go! I have to go *now*! They'll come after me and—'

'No!' His voice was like sandpaper. He swung her round to

face him, his hands holding her upper arms again, as they had this morning in the churchyard. 'You're not going anywhere in this state. You're staying here.'

He felt the fight go out of her. She slumped into his hands, so that he was holding her up. Over her head his eyes were fixed on an unseen point in the distance as he gritted his teeth and fought to control the emotions that warred within him—impatience, hostility, exasperation, resentment.

And the prickle of arousal that had fuelled at least some of those.

He felt his mind shut like a steel trap against it. Those feelings had no place in his life now. But it was the scent of her hair that had done it, the weight and warmth of it as she thrashed in his arms that had made him feel momentarily as if he had been punched in the solar plexus.

She raised her head, so he could make out the milk-white curve of her cheek. 'I couldn't stay…' she said dully. 'It's too much to ask…I can't…'

He let her go and took a step away, slamming the car door with unnecessary force. 'Do you have anywhere else to go?'

'No.'

'Well, then,' he said with biting sarcasm, 'let's skip the part where you put up some token resistance, shall we? I think this is one instance where you really don't have a choice, and it's not as if I don't have room.'

Rachel looked up at the house, noticing it properly for the first time. Built of red brick, with a central grey stone porch, its blank windows stretched away from her on both sides, and she could make out a steeply pitched roofline and vast elaborate chimneys against the heavy sky. It was beautiful, but huge and dark and utterly forbidding. Just like its owner.

He had started back towards it, and now looked impatiently over his shoulder.

'What are you waiting for?'

The acid in his tone stung her raw emotions. 'I can't leave the car here…someone might see it… And my things…' she wailed, aware that she sounded like a hysterical child, but too distressed to care.

He stopped and came wearily back towards her, his hand outstretched. 'Give me the keys and I'll get someone to move the car.'

She handed them to him and watched numbly as he went round to the boot and took out her large designer case.

'You planned your escape well,' he said wryly.

'No...I didn't plan it at all. This was packed yesterday. For tonight...' Her voice trailed off and he gave her a wintry smile.

'Your wedding night. Of course.'

He had to consciously turn his thoughts away from imagining what was in there, selected in anticipation of a very different night from the one that now awaited her. Whatever it was, whatever expensive, seductive confections of silk and lace lay folded carefully inside, she'd have no need of them here. The wing where he intended to put her hadn't been used in a year at least. It was freezing.

It was also as far away from his room as possible.

Following him up a flight of steps and through a hugely high door, Rachel shivered. She felt like Beauty entering the castle of the Beast.

And then she caught sight of her dim reflection in an ornate gilt mirror in the hallway and let out a breath of ironic laughter at the thought.

Beauty? Who was she kidding? Her hair, brushed and tamed by dedicated professionals only a couple of hours ago, had since been swept by both wind and her own frantic fingers, and was now tumbling over her shoulders and around her face, giving her a slightly deranged appearance. Her eyes, expertly made up by a make-up artist, were huge and glittering with unfamiliar shadow in the ashen oval of her face. The dress only added to her appearance of a nineteenth-century waif on her way to the asylum.

Ahead of her, Orlando hesitated in a doorway at the end of the dark hallway, tall, effortlessly elegant, with broad, straight shoulders and that aristocratic upward tilt of his head. She felt a sharp twist somewhere inside her as she glanced up at him.

There was something about him that touched nerves in her that were too sensitive. Too sensual. And that terrified her.

Courage...

'This way.'

The imposing entrance hall opened onto a smaller hallway from which the stairs rose in a graceful sweep around two walls. He had started to ascend, keeping close to the wall and brushing his fingers against the painted panelling as he went. Mesmerised, she watched, feeling her flesh tingle almost as if it could feel that feathery touch. At the top of the stairs he turned to the right, along a dark corridor. Rachel glanced around her, noticing the silk-shaded wall-lights at intervals on the emerald-green walls, wondering why he didn't turn them on. At least the gloom inside allowed her to get a good view of what lay outside, and she paused to look out of one of the windows. It overlooked a courtyard whose walls were formed by the house, built in a square around it. The courtyard was divided into quarters by four dark, square flowerbeds in which nothing grew.

He'd gone ahead, and she had to hurry to catch up, guided only by the echo of his footsteps on the polished oak floorboards. Even in her frozen mental state she was stunned by her surroundings. The house was astonishing.

'In here,' he said curtly, opening a door. Rachel followed him into a large room dominated by a huge marble fireplace and containing little more than a vast canopied bed upon which he threw her case.

'You'd better get out of that dress.'

The dusky afternoon threw deep shadows into the edges of the room. Instantly alarmed and on her guard, she let her gaze fly to his face questioningly. His expression was glacial.

Seemingly oblivious to her distress he strode over to the windows and pulled the curtains shut, plunging the room into velvet blackness.

Inside her chest, her heart hammered a frenzied tattoo.

He couldn't mean...? Was her mother right? Did all men just want to...like Carlos?

She wrapped an arm around a thick wooden bedpost, half clinging to it, half shrinking behind it. Her mouth was dry, her stomach quivering with fear. She felt the air vibrate with his nearness as he passed her in the darkness, heard the soft rustle of his movements, and couldn't quite smother her small whimper.

Then the bedside light clicked on, bathing the room in a welcoming glow and illuminating for a second the hard angles of his face before he moved purposefully towards the door.

'I'll be downstairs.'

She blinked, inhaling sharply in surprise. 'No—Orlando! Wait!'

He stood still. His broad shoulders filled the doorframe as he waited for her to continue, but her throat seemed suddenly to be full of sand. She looked helplessly at him, feeling her mouth open soundlessly for a second before the words came out in a dry croak.

'I...I...need help. With the dress.'

She saw him hesitate, then put a hand up to his head. 'Jeez....' It was something between an exhalation and a curse. And then he was coming back towards her, his face terrifyingly bleak.

Shaking violently, she turned, offering her back to him and bending her head forward so he could reach the top of the zip. She waited, feeling the goosebumps rise on the back of her neck as she anticipated his touch.

It seemed to take an eternity, during which she felt the tension building inside her like water coming to the boil. At last his long fingers brushed the hair off the nape of her neck and skimmed over the sensitised skin of her shoulders, leaving a shivering trail of sensation in their wake. He found the zip, tugged it halfway down, then stepped away, leaving her clinging to the carved bedpost as he wordlessly left the room.

She closed her eyes, desperately wanting to feel some sense of relief, and had to bite her lip against the wave of desolation and longing that washed over her instead.

She'd thought she'd be afraid of his touch, but that was because she was so used to being frightened she almost expected it. But this was something quite different. Something she'd thought she was incapable of experiencing, which had been unfurling inside her since he'd first held her against him in the churchyard.

With a thud of shock and a rush of liquid heat she realised the sensation that was quickening her pulse and filling her limbs with honeyed warmth was not fear.

It was arousal.

CHAPTER THREE

ORLANDO slammed a couple of peppers down onto the marble slab in the kitchen, took a knife from the block, and then reached to switch on the powerful spotlights that were angled down onto the worktop.

The bright light made him flinch.

He frowned, a muscle flickering in his jaw as he balanced the knife in one hand and held a pepper in the other. For a second he hesitated, steadying himself, before he began slicing with swift, savage strokes.

He had made a deliberate decision to accustom himself to the darkness that was fast closing in on him while he still had some sight left. He used artificial light as little as possible, but the kitchen was one place where he could not yet afford to let his fingers take the place of his eyes. His determination to maintain his independence meant that it was vital for him to be able to do as much as possible for himself—without asking for help or admitting weakness. Cooking had been of no interest to him in his old life—Arabella had seen to all of that with flawless competence—but a lot had changed in a year.

Not having to cook was one thing. Not being able to was quite another.

It was easy, he thought brutally, to lock himself up here alone and kid himself that he was doing OK. Managing. So easy to believe he was the person he'd always been when there was no one here to fool.

The arrival of this girl had made him see how mistaken he was.

Upstairs earlier…when she had asked him to unfasten her dress. That was the moment he had been forced to admit that the Orlando Winterton of a year ago was as dead and gone as his brother.

The old Orlando Winterton had been a master in the art of undressing women. The smooth, effortless removal of every kind of feminine garment was something he had excelled at, like everything else. But upstairs just then he had been assailed by panic as his mind had conjured tormenting images of tiny buttons, delicate hooks, and he had opened his mouth to tell her he couldn't possibly do it. The words hadn't come. He'd been afraid to tell her. Unable to deal with sensing her recoil, as Arabella had.

He swore with quiet venom.

So, yes, he might be *managing*. He might be maintaining some semblance of a normal and independent life. But it wasn't of any kind normality *he* recognised.

'Hi.'

She spoke quietly, but, momentarily distracted, Orlando felt the knife slip slightly and cursed again under his breath.

'I didn't hear you come in.'

'I didn't want to disturb you.'

Orlando felt anger rising inside him like acrid smoke.

It's a bit late for that.

Hesitantly she came a little further into the room, and he could see that she had changed into something dark—the same sweater and jeans she had been wearing this morning, maybe? 'I couldn't find you. The kitchen was the last place I thought of looking.'

'Really. Why's that?'

'I just thought that with a house like this you must have millions of staff. A chauffeur and a butler and all that—at the very least a cook.'

'No.'

His voice was sharp, and as if realising this he took a deep breath and dragged a hand through his hair. When he spoke again his tone was slightly softer, but he still gave the impression of making a huge effort to be polite. 'I have a housekeeper who comes in daily, and is in charge of a team of people who look after the house, and I employ a lot of people on the estate. But other than that, no. I chose to live here precisely because I wanted to be alone.'

Rachel came to a standstill in the centre of the room. He seemed to have placed an invisible exclusion zone around himself. *Keep away.*

'In that case I'm sorry to intrude on you like this.' Her voice was quiet, the emotion rigidly controlled. 'It's all such a nightmare, and I can't quite get my head around what I've done, but I can see now how awkward it is for you too.'

'You need to let someone know that you're safe,' he said curtly.

Rachel felt a small glow of surprise at his thoughtfulness. 'I have. I phoned earlier and left a message.' No need to mention that it had been on her own answer service at her agent's office, and that after she'd done it she'd dropped her phone out of the window and heard it crash into the shrubbery below.

'Good. The last thing I want is an irate fiancé turning up and accusing me of abduction.'

The glow was abruptly extinguished. 'Don't worry,' she said stiffly. 'If I could just stay for tonight, first thing in the morning I'll...go.'

Orlando clenched his fingers around the knife, steeling himself against the reproachful whispers of his conscience.

'Fine. As I said before, there's plenty of room. Just don't be surprised if you're left to yourself—I've got a lot on at work at the moment.'

'Of course not. What kind of work?'

'I have a private defence consultancy business, advising the MoD on all aspects of air defence,' he said with an edge of sarcasm. 'I also run the Easton estate and all its subsidiary companies. Would you like to see my CV?'

Rachel felt the colour rush to her cheeks as she realised she'd strayed too far into forbidden territory. And been warned off.

'I'm sorry,' she muttered. 'I ask too many questions. It comes of spending far too long on my own. I'm insatiably curious about— Oh God, Orlando—you're bleeding.'

For only a second did he falter, suddenly aware of the stickiness on his fingers. It must have happened when she'd come in to the kitchen and distracted him.

'It's nothing.'

'It's not! There's blood everywhere!'

Orlando glanced down. It was easy to see the bright flowering of red against the pale marble slab. Without a word he crossed to the sink and held his fingers under the tap. Jaw tensed, he kept his eyes fixed straight ahead.

Hesitantly Rachel came to stand beside him. 'Please, let me see. There's so much blood—it must be a deep cut.'

'It's fine,' he said savagely, but even he could see that the water swirling into the sink was deep pink. Too pink. Gritting his teeth, he kept his hand beneath the freezing stream of water.

He felt her fingers brush against his wrist. Warm, whisper-soft and infinitely tender, they closed around it and slowly drew his hand away from the tap.

For a moment Rachel felt him stiffen, and she thought he was going to snatch his hand away from her. Head tilted back, his eyes burned into hers with that angry intensity that betrayed the heat beneath his glacial exterior. She felt her stomach contract with that same powerful kick of emotion she had experienced upstairs as, for a shivering second, their gazes locked.

Tearing her eyes, from his she looked down at his hand. On the tips of both his index and middle fingers the blood welled darkly, and as she watched it fell in glistening beads which shattered on the pale stone floor. She sucked in a breath and bent her head, ashamed of her sudden urge to press her lips to his upturned palm. Wincing, she ran her thumb over the clean slice in the skin on his first finger.

It was deep.

His face was like stone, betraying not the faintest hint of emotion as the blood ran into her hand, dripping between her fingers onto the floor.

'We need to stop the bleeding,' she said weakly.

She looked up at him. He seemed a long way away, towering over her, scowling darkly...

He swore abruptly, succinctly, and Rachel felt his hands on her shoulders, guiding her backwards and pushing her into a chair, pressing her head down onto her knees. Then, holding the blood-soaked hand aloft, he turned away and in one swift movement pulled his shirt over his head. Bunching the soft cotton in one hand, he attempted to twist it around his damaged fingers.

The roaring in her ears gradually subsided, and Rachel lifted her head. Instantly she felt dizzy again. He was standing a few feet away with his back to her.

His *bare* back.

Breathlessly, helplessly, she let her eyes wander over the broad expanse of silken skin gleaming in the harsh spotlights, the ripple of taut muscles beneath it. Suddenly she could see exactly where that aura of barely concealed strength and power came from.

He was like a jungle animal—raw, physical, finely honed. But here, in this dark house, this sterile kitchen, it was as if he was caged.

Wounded.

Damaged.

One question filled her head. *Why?*

Dazedly she watched him make for the door, and half-stood. 'Orlando—I'm sorry. Is there anything I can do to help?'

The look he cast her was one of icy disdain. 'Sure. Finish cooking dinner.'

Shakily she opened the door of the vast, state-of-the-art fridge and stood motionless for long moments, clinging to the cool steel as she waited for normality to reassert itself.

Nothing looked remotely familiar, she thought dimly, gathering up what looked like a forlorn bunch of bloomless flowers, some slim greenish wands, some lumpen, unpromising-looking root vegetables. It was as if she'd been transported from Planet Normal to some alternative universe where everything was different.

Where a glance could make you tremble—not from fear, but with longing.

Where a touch could make you shiver—not with revulsion, but ecstasy…

She was suddenly aware that she'd come to a standstill in the middle of the kitchen, her arms full of produce. This was totally ridiculous, she thought wildly, giving herself a hard mental shake. Her life was in turmoil, and all she could do was fantasise about a man she hardly knew.

A man she hardly knew who was expecting her to cook dinner for him.

As if waking from a trance, she looked down at the bizarre items in her arms and let out a small exhalation of outrage. What was she thinking of? What the hell was she supposed to do with all this stuff? She was a pianist, for God's sake—a highly trained professional whose hands were exceptionally precious instruments, insured for thousands of pounds. She didn't *cook*…

Tossing her hair back from her face, she marched defiantly across to the island unit, intending to deposit the stupid green stuff and hunt down a takeaway menu instead. But as she approached she felt herself falter. The precariously balanced armful of ingredients slipped and tumbled onto the worktop, rolling to the floor as she saw the crimson pool of Orlando's blood still on the marble slab.

She stopped dead. And then stepped closer, stretched out a hand, and trailed her finger slowly through the dark red. She looked at her finger, at the glossy bead of his blood shining on its tip, as dark and precious as a ruby. There was something agonisingly intimate about it.

His blood.

The essence of him.

A shudder rippled through her.

'Everything all right?'

Orlando's voice from the doorway startled her from her thoughts, sent her hand flying to her throat in terror and confusion and shame.

'Yes...yes, of course.'

He came forward, dressed in a faded checked shirt, two fingers of his left hand bound up with gauze. 'You don't seem to have got very far.'

'No.' Making a conscious effort to steady her breathing, she lifted her chin and met his eye. 'I'm still clearing up. And I'm afraid I have no idea where to start with this. I've never cooked anything in my life, I don't know how to—'

He cut her off with a sharp, scornful sound. 'Then it's high time you learned.'

Rachel swallowed hard. Reaching for a cloth, she briskly wiped up the blood from the chopping board and shook her head. 'No. I'm no good at things like that....practical things.'

He gave a curse of pure, undisguised exasperation. OK, so Arabella might have been something of an *über*-achiever, but this girl seemed to take the word *incompetent* to a whole new level.

'What on earth makes you say that?' he said scathingly.

'How about twenty-three years of experience?' she retorted hotly. 'Or should that be twenty-three years of *in*experience? I've never done anything remotely domesticated!'

He couldn't see her toss her head, but he could certainly imagine it from the indignant tone of her voice, and maybe a little from the rustle of her heavy hair. Turning his mind resolutely from the mental images that instantly flared into life, he smothered a sneer.

'So now's your chance.' He picked up the knife. 'Come here.'

'No!'

Orlando froze. There was no mistaking the genuine anguish in her voice. For a long moment neither of them moved. He suddenly felt very, very tired.

'What are you afraid of?' he asked heavily, and then he remembered he was still holding the knife. 'Jeez, Rachel, I'm not going to hurt you for God's sake…!'

'I didn't think you were,' she whispered. 'It's just…' How could she explain that it wasn't that kind of fear, the fear of harm, that was causing her to tremble so violently, but fear of losing control. How could she explain that when she could hardly understand it herself?

He sighed. 'Come and stand here…'

Tentatively she took a step towards him, stopping a few feet away so he had to take her hand and draw her forwards. Gently, firmly, he positioned her in front of the marble chopping board and replaced the pepper he'd started to slice. She wondered if he could feel the frantic beat of her heart throbbing through her body, vibrating in the tiny space that separated them.

'Now…take hold of the pepper,' he said tonelessly. He was standing right behind her, and his voice close to her ear made a shiver run through her. She picked up the pepper in one shaking hand, holding onto it as if it was her last connection with reality.

'Good. Now, in the other hand pick up the knife.' His tone was carefully blank, but she could sense the tightly controlled frustration behind his words. Biting her lip in shame, she picked up the knife, watching the blade quiver in her uncertain grip until Orlando's hand closed over hers.

She gasped.

His arms encircled her, safe, strong, and she had to muster every inch of self-control she had to prevent her from leaning back into his embrace and letting her head fall on to his chest.

'No, I *can't*!'

She dropped the knife with a clatter and clenched her fists. Instantly he stepped backwards, and she turned round in time to see his uninjured hand go to his head, his fingers raking through his hair in a gesture of wordless exasperation.

'I'm sorry…' she said lamely. 'It's just…it's my hands. I have to be careful. They're…precious…'

He suddenly went very still.

'Precious?'

For a moment she watched as he half-raised his own hands, gazing downwards at them, at the fingers of the left one held rigidly in place by the bloodstained gauze. And then he turned away.

Precious. God, her shallowness took his breath away. *Her* hands were precious. Jeez.

She was unreal. His hands… His hands weren't just precious, they were his lifeline. This spoiled little girl would never understand that.

Not that he had any intention of her finding out.

CHAPTER FOUR

RACHEL'S eyes snapped open, and for a moment she felt suffocating fear as she stared into black nothingness. Her hands were twisted in the soft duvet, her fingers cramped, and the darkness was filled with the sickening thud of her heart.

Whimpering quietly, she unravelled her hands from the bedcovers and held them out in front of her as her eyes gradually adjusted to the gloom. She had dreamed of Carlos—a bizarre, terrible dream, where he chased her down a labyrinth of narrow lanes in her wedding dress, a knife flashing in his hand. And she knew with the terrible certainty that came in sleep that he intended to damage her hands with it, in revenge for humiliating him.

And then suddenly Orlando was there, naked to the waist and standing between her and Carlos, shielding her, until the next thing she knew her wedding dress was scarlet with his blood. All she could do was hold his lacerated hands, knowing as the blood kept flowing that she had brought this on him.

Earlier on in the kitchen she had felt dizzy as his bare chest had been revealed…too shocked and too shy to take in what she was seeing. But while her conscious mind had been having a fit of the vapours it seemed her eyes had missed nothing—noting every muscle, every sinew, every inch of delicious flesh. And they had chosen the dead hours of the night to revisit them all in disturbing detail.

Her pulse raced, and her body twitched and throbbed with

strange, uncomfortable sensations. In the thick silence she could hear nothing but the thudding of her heart.

Until her stomach gave a deafening rumble.

The sound broke the spell and made her laugh out loud with relief. Of course—she'd eaten virtually nothing all day, which totally explained the bizarre feelings that buzzed through her nerve-endings.

She was hungry, that was all. So hungry.

She had no idea what time it was, but food suddenly seemed like an imperative. She longed for the normality of hot buttered toast or a cup of tea. God, a chocolate biscuit seemed like the most desirable thing in the entire world…

Apart from Orlando Winterton's chest. And his sinuous back. And his green, green eyes…

No! Resolutely she swung her legs out of bed and strode to the door.

It was bitterly, bitterly cold, but she kept going, too nervous and jumpy to want to take the time to retrace her steps and retrieve her clothes. Silver light flooded the corridor, and passing window after window she saw a full moon, swathed in diaphanous drifts of cloud trailing languidly across the star-spiked sky. Rachel slipped noiselessly down the stairs and stopped, suddenly disorientated and wishing she had paid more attention earlier, instead of concentrating on Orlando Winterton's bloody hands…

Bloody hands. The words made images she was trying to forget come flooding back, and again she experienced that painful fizz inside her, as if someone had just pressed an electrode to her heart.

Blindly she stumbled in what she thought was the right direction for the kitchen. But there were so many doors. She opened one door and hesitated on the threshold, trying to get her bearings. The room was huge—surely running the whole length of one side of the house—and in the silver-blue shadows nothing looked familiar. The walls were high and dark—possibly black—the furniture a mixture of beautiful antiques and startlingly modern pieces. But all of this faded into the background as her eye was drawn to a curved bay window in the middle.

In it, bathed in moonlight as if spotlit on a stage, stood a piano. A grand piano.

Without thinking she found herself crossing the room towards it on cold, silent feet, tentatively reaching out a finger and running it gently down the keys, so that a soft rattle was the only sound that resulted. They felt smooth, solid, expensive...everything that a good piano should be.

She let her finger come to rest on Middle C. And pressed.

The sound was rich and mellow, and it flowed right through her, reverberating against her tautly stretched nerves. Her stomach tightened, but her hunger was forgotten. Suddenly all that mattered was this instrument and the need to lose herself in its exquisite familiarity. Heedless of the biting cold, she sat down, placing her bare feet on the chill metal pedals, letting her fingers rest deliciously on the keys for a second and closing her eyes in relief.

After a day of confusion, this, at last, was something she could understand and control. This was her way of interpreting the world, expressing emotion—the only way she had ever been shown and the only way she knew.

The moonlight turned her hands a bloodless blue as they began very quietly, very tentatively, to play. Without thinking she found the piece that was flowing from her fingers was Chopin's *Nocturne in E Minor*, its haunting notes flooding the night and filling her head with memories.

Memories she hadn't allowed to surface before, but suddenly wouldn't be suppressed any longer.

Closing her eyes, she gave in to them. Gradually she became aware that the keys were slippery with wetness and she realised she was crying, her tears dripping down onto her hands. She played on, not feeling the cold.

Compared to the ice inside her, it was nothing.

* * *

Sitting at his desk in the library, Orlando rubbed a hand over his tired eyes and leaned back in his chair. Apart from the soft red glow of the dying fire, the computer screen in front of him was the only source of light in the massive room, and he had been looking at it for too long. His eyes stung.

Thankfully, much of his business was conducted internationally, so the long hours of the night when sleep would often evade him could be usefully spent working. His computer was state-of-the-art, fitted with the very latest in screen-reading software, which he had always refused to use, preferring instead to type by touch and magnify the words to a size that made it possible for him to read them.

Technically.

Tonight they seemed to slide across the edges of his vision and dissolve without penetrating his mind.

The Middle Eastern border situation he was dealing with was balanced on a knife-edge. Hired as a consultant on aerial tactics and weapons deployment by the government, he was monitoring the situation on an hour-by-hour basis, grimly holding out against sending planes into an area where they had about as much chance of surviving as a pheasant over the Easton beech woods in shooting season.

As he knew all too well. It had been on a similar raid that Felix had been shot down. Or that was the supposition: they'd never even recovered his plane.

Sighing, Orlando got up and went to stand at one of the long windows, feeling a gust of cold air as he pulled back the curtain and looked out. Around the relentless blackness in the centre of his vision he could see the courtyard was bathed in moonlight.

With something that felt almost like a physical blow he recalled Felix's kindness that last time when he'd come home on leave, at the time when Andrew Parkes had given Orlando his diagnosis. Felix had accepted it with resignation, and for the remainder of his leave had treated Orlando with a horrible gentleness bordering on respect. When he had said goodbye it had almost as if he knew it would be the last time.

He'd had no intention of their relationship carrying on as before, Orlando realised now. As far as Felix had been concerned, if Orlando wasn't the big brother he could compete with and look up to, he was no brother at all. Nothing.

Orlando leaned back against the wooden shutter, tipping his head back and banging it softly, rhythmically, against the paneling. The pain reminded him that he was still alive. Sometimes he felt that he was disappearing, that just as the world was fading before his eyes, so he was fading from the eyes of the world.

Somewhere in the distance he could hear music. Maybe he'd finally lost it? he thought with savage desolation, striding to the door and pulling it open.

But he hadn't imagined it. Music was rippling through the dark rooms of the sleeping house, filling the empty spaces with sweet, sad resonance. With emotion. With life.

In the doorway of the grand salon he stopped, his breath catching in his throat. The effect of the music in the moonlit stillness was profound—it vibrated through him, smashing down defences he had spent the last year building. The room was inkblack washed with silver, and he turned his head, so that at the edge of his vision he could see her.

She had her back to him, her head tilted up so that her glowing red hair cascaded down over the thin slip of pale silk she was wearing. He could see with startling clarity the gleam of her bare shoulder in the moonlight, the shadowed drape of silk at the narrow part of her waist, just before it swelled out into sumptuous fullness. Hungrily, helplessly, his eyes sought her, desperate for more; but, as always, the instant he looked directly at her she disappeared into the black vortex in the centre of his vision. He felt his hands ball into fists of frustration as the music tugged invisible chords inside him, reawakening the feelings and needs he strove so hard to annihilate.

He was hardly aware of crossing the room, was conscious

only of the thudding of blood in his veins beneath the soaring swell of music that was flowing with perfect fluency and exquisite grace from her fingertips.

Her *precious* fingertips.

He felt a moan of realisation escape him. Oh, God. He'd been so wrapped up in himself that he hadn't given her a chance to explain what she'd meant. He'd thought she was some silly, pampered princessy type, who didn't want to damage her false nails, but she was a *pianist*...

Remorse and self-loathing stole through him. His bandaged fingers throbbed and ached as he gripped the table beside him, waiting for this unwelcome, stinging insight into the man he had become to subside.

The music filled his head, each lovely, liquid note echoing inside the empty spaces of his heart. Until he noticed, above the piano, another sound.

An inhalation. A soft, swift gasp of indrawn breath.

He waited a few seconds. And heard another. The girl sitting a few feet away from him was creating that miraculous, moving music while crying her heart out very quietly.

He didn't want to go to her. He wanted to leave the room and go back to his study and his work. He wanted to wall himself up again, pack his heart in ice and put his needs, his desires, back in the past.

He wanted all of that, and still he found himself going towards her. It felt as if he was crawling over broken glass, but he couldn't stop.

Playing the last heartbreaking bars, Rachel closed her eyes and let her head drop backwards as the tears coursed down her cheeks.

Why had she played this piece?

It was the dream, perhaps, that had brought it all back. This was the piece she had played that horrible night at Carlos's apartment in Vienna, when he had forced himself on her for the first time. They had been engaged for about three weeks, and, coming back from dinner in a restaurant, her mother had pleaded a headache and gone straight to the hotel. There had been no question of arguing when Carlos had suggested she went with him to his beautiful penthouse for a nightcap, and she had done as she was told without demur. Just as she always had.

Until…

Until later. When she had felt his hands, damp and insistent, sliding up beneath her blouse as she'd played the Chopin. And then she had protested and fought with all her strength.

A sob escaped her.

Just at that moment she felt warm hands on her shoulders, sliding down her chilled arms to cradle her from behind. Letting out a cry, she stumbled to her feet, desperate to get away as her mind, made irrational by the terrible memories, made instant, impossible connections. Stepping away from the piano stool, she whirled round, adrenalin giving her movements an intense energy.

Orlando stepped back, holding up his hands. His face was entirely in shadow.

'It's you' she whispered, relief coursing through her. 'It's *you*.'

'Who did you think?'

She shook her head, looking away, feeling suddenly foolish and ashamed. Ashamed of the person Carlos had turned her into. 'I wasn't thinking properly…I was just…frightened. Of the dark. Does that sound stupid?'

He gave a low, mirthless laugh. 'No. Not at all.' He took a step towards her, into a square of moonlight falling through the huge windows, and it painted silver streaks in his black hair and shimmered on the hard planes of his lean face. 'You were crying.'

'Yes… It's ridiculous, but you were right. I totally lack courage in everything. I'm afraid all the time…'

She stopped as he reached out and lifted her right hand in his. Mesmerised, she watched as he looked down at it with his strange intense stare, turning it palm upwards and unfolding her fingers with a sweep of his thumb, as if he were spreading the petals of a flower. And then he placed his own damaged, bandaged hand over hers, and Rachel closed her eyes, unable to control the series of seismic shocks that juddered up her arm and into some locked-up, secret part of her. Her hands had always been her way of expressing herself, through the music that they created, but never had they brought her this kind of feeling. She felt as if she held a tornado.

'That's OK,' he said bleakly. 'It's OK to be afraid. It's how you deal with it that matters.'

Looking downwards, he could see the paleness of her skin against his. In the moonlight she was so white, like porcelain, and he found himself wondering whether, given the colour of her hair, she also had freckles that he couldn't see. He wanted to raise her hand to his lips, to feel the coolness of her flesh against his face and breathe in the clean, young scent of her. He let his bandaged hand fall to his side, but somehow his other hand remained pressed against hers, palm to palm. Her fingers were almost as long as his, though finer. But as they meshed with his he could feel their incredible strength.

She moved towards him until she could almost feel the electric current crackling in the small space that separated them.

'But I'm tired of being afraid. I want to be brave.'

She sounded both wistful and angry, and the words seemed to resonate in the charged air for a second. Then, her eyes never leaving his, she moved closer, closing the gap between their tense bodies, and stood on tiptoe to brush her lips against his in a gossamer-light kiss.

'Show me how to be brave,' she murmured.

His answer was a low curse as he captured her trembling mouth with a kiss of ferocious intensity. The miracle of his touch on Rachel's skin seared a path of purifying fire through the confusion and revulsion Carlos's touch had left in its wake. Suddenly, in the arms of this man, everything that had scared and confused her seemed so simple and so beautiful. One hand was still holding his, their fingers locked, but she lifted the other to his face, feeling the hard planes of his stubble-roughened cheek beneath her palm, feeling the leanness of his jaw as he kissed her with a passion and purpose that made the past irrelevant. His hand was in the small of her back, moving upwards and coming to rest between her shoulderblades, holding her against him with a touch so light it was almost as if he was afraid to crush her.

'Rachel…No.'

Orlando pulled away, his fingers still entwined with Rachel's, until he was holding her at arm's length. He knew he was a hair's breadth from surrendering control, but the lure of oblivion was incredibly powerful. To be, for a few blissful minutes, the man he used to be—powerful, capable, in command, omnipotent.

But he wouldn't use her for that.

'Please…'

She had her face tilted up to his, so that he could feel the warmth of her sweet breath fanning his cheek. She was shivering, and he could hear the yearning in her voice.

'You don't need this.'

With monumental self-control he turned, running a hand through his hair as his gut twisted with desire and agonising frustration. He felt as if he had been kicked repeatedly in the stomach.

'I do. Oh, God, Orlando, you don't know how much I need this. Please…' She was almost sobbing with longing.

He didn't turn, feeling his hands clench into fists, until the pain in his lacerated fingers provided a welcome distraction from his tortured conscience.

The last thing he wanted was a relationship, complications… companionship, for God's sake. He wanted to be left alone with his suffering and his pain.

But, sweet Lord above, he wanted her. Wanted to lose himself in her. Now. Right now.

Silently she had slipped through the shadows to stand in front of him, a pale, trembling moon goddess. He stared straight ahead, but in the moonlight he could see the silvery glisten of tears on her cheeks.

'I need you.'

Her whispered words broke down his last defence. With a moan of despair he gathered her into his arms and brought his mouth down onto her soft lips, feeling as well as hearing her answering moan of relieved surrender.

He could feel the frenzied pounding of her heart inside her shaking body. She seemed so scared, so vulnerable and needy, that his arms tightened around her, cradling her against the hard length of his body in an instinctive effort to warm and protect her. It felt so good. Her hands cupped his face, then slid to twine around his neck, her strong fingers massaging the base of his skull, pushing him downward, deepening the kiss, until his head was filled with nothing but the taste of her and the feel of her slender young body beneath the silky nightdress.

Reality melted away, and with it the demons and black dogs of despair. There was nothing now but darkness—a blissful darkness that only accentuated the powerful, miraculous sensations that were exploding inside him. Lifting his mouth from Rachel's, he buried his face in her fragrant hair.

'If we don't stop this now, I won't be able to.'

'Good.'

Her voice was low and fierce. *Carnal*, he thought, at the very moment when he felt her hands at his waist, slipping beneath his shirt and moving over the taut flesh of his stomach. All further thought became impossible.

Rachel felt his shuddering exhalation of breath in her hair as her trembling fingers fumbled with his belt. She was no longer shivering with cold, but with excitement. With heat.

At the beginning her overwhelming need had been to have the stain of Carlos's touch washed from her skin, but at that moment she couldn't have said who Carlos was. There was no thought in her head but Orlando, and she needed nothing but the feeling of his hands on her waist, his lips against her hair, her ear, her neck…

His thumbs swept upwards over the quivering skin of her midriff to run along the sharp ridges of her ribs. She was lost inside his kiss, but felt him gently pushing her backwards as her hands finally released the top button of his trousers and slid downwards. And then the silence was broken by a discordant clash of notes as her bottom came to rest on the piano keyboard. She was tearing at the buttons of his shirt now, her mouth never leaving his as her hands hungrily sought the warmth of his skin, pushing the fabric down over his massive shoulders, feeling them bunch and flex under her questing fingers.

He was so huge. So powerful. Dazedly, she tore her mouth from his.

'I want to see you,' she whispered.

He looked down at her, *into* her. His face was utterly unreadable. The moonlight bleached his skin to an unearthly white, so that he looked like the ghost of some heroic centurion. Only the rise and fall of his broad chest and the dark glitter of his eyes gave away the fact that he was real.

'You're so beautiful,' she murmured in wonder.

He didn't smile. With an expression of intense concentration he moved towards her again, and caught hold of the hem of her nightdress in his hands, drawing it slowly upwards over her head until she stood in front of him, spread against the piano, completely naked. His head jerked backwards as his hands slid upwards over the flat of her stomach, her arching ribs.

'So are you.'

The intensity of his voice sent a pulse of liquid need crashing through her, which was nothing to the deranging impulses that sizzled through her central nervous system as he cupped her breasts in his hands, shifting her weight backwards onto the piano. With another decadent, dissonant chord, she opened her legs and pulled him towards her.

It wasn't Chopin. It was a million times sweeter.

Their mouths found each other, and then he was lifting her, swinging her into his arms and carrying her across the room. For a second he lifted his mouth from hers, negotiating a path between the low mirrored table and the sofas, and then he lowered her gently to the floor.

She gasped as she felt soft, warm fur against her bare skin, twining her fingers luxuriously into it as she raised herself up and let her head fall backwards, arching her back as his lips traced a path of bliss down the column of her throat. She caught the back of his head, pulling him downwards, harder, until they were both lying in the thick fur, their mouths devouring each other, bruising, biting, tasting.

No moonlight penetrated their dark intimacy. The world was reduced to the sensations of the flesh. Abandoning his straitjacket of self-control, Orlando was lost in the feel of her hair in his hands, her lips on his neck. She smelled of roses, the warm smell of summer and purity and beauty, and as he entered her it was like regaining paradise.

She was exquisite. He heard her soft, throaty gasp and felt her clutch at his back, her strong fingers pressing into his skin, urging him deeper, demanding all of him, as she raised her legs and wrapped them around his waist, gripping him, cherishing him. And then her hands were cupping his face, imprisoning it millimetres from her own as her mouth captured his again, and he felt it open in a cry of high, primeval release.

She stiffened, and for a second was completely still, before he felt her shudder with ecstasy in his arms. It was too much. Helplessly he plunged headlong into blissful release, and as he did so the relentless, smothering blackness in his head was lit up with dazzling explosions of red and green and gold.

CHAPTER FIVE

'I CAN see angels.'

Rachel lay beside him, gazing upwards, and her voice was soft and drowsy and sated.

'Does that mean I've died and gone to heaven?'

Orlando stirred, rolling over to face her and propping himself up on one elbow. He could hear the smile in her words and wished he could look into her face. He wanted to kiss the corners of that smile and make it fade into something more intense and abstract as his lips moved further down her body. He wanted to see if that astonishing passion of hers lit up her eyes, made her skin glow...

But he couldn't.

'I doubt it, if I'm here too,' he said harshly. There was no peace and light in the place *he* inhabited.

'Don't say that,' she whispered softly. 'You saved me today. For that, if nothing else, you've earned your place in heaven.'

She pulled him down beside her again, sweeping her arm upwards in a wide arc, and then he understood. Remembered. He'd forgotten the carved plasterwork on the ceiling above them, and how at night the charcoal-grey-painted background seemed to recede into the darkness, making the angels depicted there come alive. He'd loved it as a child. But he'd stopped looking at it long before he'd stopped being able to see it.

'Look,' she murmured. 'They're so beautiful. I can't imagine that heaven could be any better than this, can you?'

Orlando sighed. Of course he saw nothing. The colours that had filled his head as he'd exploded inside her had faded, leaving a deeper darkness—like an empty winter sky after the fireworks were all finished.

'I can't imagine heaven exists at all,' he said with quiet brutality. There was no such thing as eternal bliss. All joy was fleeting, and came at a price. He had allowed himself this wonderful, unexpected release. But now it was over, and it was time to retreat to the safety of his walls of ice and steel.

In the velvet darkness he felt her hand against his face and tensed against the tenderness in her touch.

'Oh, Orlando, were you always so cynical?'

'No.'

'What happened? Was it Felix?'

He caught her hand, enclosing it in his, feeling the bones and sinews beneath the soft skin—feeling both her fragility and her incredible, surprising strength.

'Maybe.' The injustice that his brother's life—a useful, courageous life—had been extinguished while he was left to struggle on endlessly in a worthless one. That had made him cynical. 'There were other things too.'

'Tell me,' she breathed.

He dropped a kiss into her palm, curling her long fingers around it as if he were saying goodbye.

'No.' He got up in one lithe movement and reached for his clothes. 'There's nothing to tell. I lost something, that's all. Something I took for granted. And now I miss it. All the bloody time.'

Especially now. Especially right this moment, when I would give anything to be able to see you…

He turned away and, suddenly aware of how cold it was, reached up onto the high marble mantelpiece to feel for a box of matches. The kindling in the fireplace caught straight away and he straightened up, watching the small, brave flicker of flame take hold of the darkness.

Behind him, Rachel sat up slowly, tucking her knees up in front of her and resting her chin on them. 'You told me that it's OK to be afraid—that it's how you deal with it that counts.'

Orlando said nothing.

'I think the same could be said of loss. You can't change it. But you can deal with it.'

He gave a low, bitter laugh. 'You think so?'

His coldness took her by surprise. Suddenly she was aware that she was naked, and she felt foolish and exposed. It was as if the closeness that they had just shared had never existed. The barriers had gone back up.

'I'm sorry…I don't know anything about it. I'm a pianist, not a psychologist,' she muttered, getting up and looking around for her discarded nightdress.

He turned slowly round to face her, moonlight silvering his devastating, chilly face, firelight gilding his massive shoulders. Once again she was reminded of some gladiatorial warrior from mythology, and she wondered what had hurt him so badly. What—or whom.

'Why didn't you tell me you were a pianist before? I didn't understand about your hands—I thought you were being vain.'

He heard her soft exhalation. 'I don't know…maybe I thought you'd know. Some people do, you know—recognise me. Carlos's PR people did a huge poster campaign for my first CD.'

And in that instant, in a flash as bright, as dazzling as the glowing colours he'd seen earlier, he saw in his mind's eye the girl in the picture that day outside Andrew Parkes' office. Realisation hit him like the lash of a whip—sudden and shocking.

'I'm a philistine,' he said bluntly, turning back to the fire. 'I hardly ever leave this place—I'm far too wrapped up in work. The last time I attended a musical recital was in the officers' mess; it featured songs that I hope you've never heard, and it ended with the piano having petrol poured over it and being set alight.'

Rachel gasped. 'No! Why?'

'It's an RAF tradition. It happens every year.'

'But that's terrible! How could you bear to do it?'

He looked into the flames. 'It's just a piano,' he said simply, and the implications of his words seemed to drift and settle in the moonlit room.

'You're right. I forget. Sometimes I feel like it's my only friend.' She wrapped her arms tightly around herself and made an attempt at a laugh. 'In fact, let's face it, it is my only friend. I think it really hit me this afternoon, when I was all alone in that room, waiting to be taken to the church, that the only good relationship I've ever had in my life has been with the piano.'

Her loneliness was palpable. Orlando was struck by the irony: he had spent the last year brutally trying to shut out the outside world, while this girl was reaching out to it. He felt the ice around his frozen heart crack open a little.

'What brought you here? To a tiny place in the middle of nowhere like Easton?' He had to make an effort to keep the frustration out of his voice, but he needed to ask the question. Why had fate brought her here, to scrape the tender flesh off scars that were still healing, still hurting?

She sank back down onto the fur rug and pulled her knees up again, wrapping her arms protectively around them. 'Carlos's PR people found The Old Rectory, and thought it would be the perfect place for the wedding. Very English, very quietly grand— which all fitted in with the brand they created for me. They took out a six-month lease on it, but until the day before yesterday I'd never seen it. It could have been anywhere.'

The fire stretched long fingers of warmth into the room and painted her skin in peach and gold. Orlando had heard about the brain compensating for what the eye couldn't see, but until now he had never experienced it, or believed it was possible. But in that instant he could picture vividly the sadness in her amber eyes, the gentle swell of her upper lip, her delicate chin.

She got up slowly and walked towards him, her head bent so that the firelight made her hair glow like vintage cognac. Standing beside him, she pressed a hand against his chest, over his heart.

'I'm so glad it wasn't anywhere else,' she said with quiet ferocity. 'I'm so glad it was here.'

He took a deep breath and very gently moved her hand, turning away to spare her from reading the truth on his face; the selfish, hateful truth that he wished she'd never come into his life and smashed up the fragments he'd been painstakingly piecing together again. But then his attention was suddenly drawn away from her to a movement beyond, in the clear periphery of his vision. He walked towards the window, where the piano stood bathed in blue light.

Behind him Rachel stood, washed in fire-gold and spilling out warmth and softness. In front of him was a featureless waste-land of white.

He felt his lips twitch into a smile of irony as the symbolism hit him.

'It's snowing.'

'Oh…' She came to stand beside him, staring out in wonder at the enchanted garden. Snow already lay like icing on the clipped box spheres, making them look like fat cupcakes, and it had turned the bare branches of the trees into elaborate confections of spun sugar which sparkled in the moonlight. It was like a scene from *The Nutcracker* ballet. 'It's lovely…you're so lucky to live in such a gorgeous place…'

He smiled, and it was as cold and beautiful as the silvered winter garden in front of them. Goosebumps rose on her arms and a shiver rippled through her.

'Let's just say it's rather wasted on me.'

He stooped to pick up her nightdress from where it had been thrown, down by the piano, and untangled it, holding it out ready to slip over her head. Obedient as a child, she raised her arms, suddenly feeling very, very tired.

'What time is it?'

'After three.'

She stifled a yawn as it suddenly occurred to her that he had still been dressed when he'd found her. 'But you were still up…'

'Working. And checking over the arrangements for tomorrow.'

'What's happening tomorrow?

He took her hand, pulling her gently towards the door. 'The annual Easton Ball, to mark the end of the shooting season. It's an old tradition.'

'Oh, how lovely...' Rachel's drowsy mind was instantly filled with pictures of ladies in beautiful swirling dresses, men in black tie....Orlando in black tie...

Orlando gave a dry laugh. 'Lovely? No. I can assure you it'll be like the seventh circle of hell. The estate still makes a large part of its revenue from pheasant shooting, mainly by organising shooting parties for groups from big corporations and finance houses in London, and they all come down here solely to prove how macho they are. Tomorrow night the house'll be full of drunken City boys determined to down as much champagne as possible and impress everyone with their lord-of-the-manor credentials.'

'And you have to organise this thing?'

They were out in the darkened hallway now. The snow had changed everything, making the shadows blue and giving the air a muffled sense of suspended time. Rachel faltered, flinching as her feet touched the ice-cold marble tiles, and in an instant Orlando had scooped her up into his arms and was carrying her towards the stairs. Her eyes were on a level with his. They were narrow, slanting, impenetrable.

'Not really. I employ caterers and a party planner, and my extremely capable housekeeper does the rest.'

Above her, Winterton ancestors scowled down through the ages and through the darkness as they passed

'It must be horrible to have your house overrun with strangers.'

'It's the first time I'll have done it on my own.' For two years Arabella had taken over the job, with obsessive attention to detail, and she had organised lavish themed occasions that had looked marvelous on the pages of *Hello!* but had intimidated the Easton locals deeply. 'Last year it was cancelled because it was right after Felix's death.'

Safe in his arms, Rachel let her head fall against his shoulder. She could feel the steady, soothing beat of his heart against her ribs and looked up, seeing the strong lines of his jaw, the sinuous column of his throat. Emotion she was too tired to analyse solidified in her chest.

'It'll be hard without him,' she murmured.

'Yes.' Briefly he glanced down at her, and smiled. 'Though the year before he caused an awful lot of trouble by disappearing upstairs with the wife of a hedge fund manager. I had to give the guy a crate of vintage port to keep the peace. At least I won't have that to worry about this year.'

Rachel felt a small stab of surprise. 'Really? I imagined Felix would be like you, but you must have been very different.'

'No. We were as bad as each other. It's just that as the oldest I always had the most to lose.'

They were at the top of the stairs now. No moonlight penetrated the courtyard beneath the windows, and the corridor was in deep shadow. Rachel's head fell back onto Orlando's chest. He stared straight ahead, trying not to think about how good she felt in his arms, how right.

Because it wasn't right. It was impossible.

'Don't you ever turn the light on?'

'I don't need to. I've lived here all my life. I know my way around this house with my eyes closed.'

That, after all, was one of the reasons he'd come back.

In the bedroom he laid her on the bed and folded the covers over her, then stood back abruptly, his arms falling to his sides. Already they felt empty.

Turning to go, he had ruthlessly to suppress the masochistic part of his brain that was at that moment taunting him with thoughts of how it would feel to lie down beside her and hold her against him through the freezing hours of darkness, to wake up with his cheek against her hair and know that that red, vibrant, living blaze of colour would be the first thing he would see.

One night...just one night...

The agonising irony of the situation hit him like a punch in the ribs, momentarily winding him. He wanted her. He wanted her and the terrible thing was that having her just now had made him want her all the more.

How very optimistic of him to think that once would be enough.

But he'd had his chance to be open and he hadn't taken it, and his punishment was knowing that everything that had just happened between them was based on a lie. He'd deceived her into thinking he was something and someone he could never be. The person she'd just made such glorious, abandoned love to was the old Orlando Winterton. The one who had died a year ago.

He had almost reached the door when she spoke.

'Thank you.' Her voice soft and heavy with sleep.

'What for?'

'For having me.' He heard a breath of drowsy laughter which seemed to caress him in the dark. 'Not like *that*. I mean, having me to stay. Although…' There was a pause. 'Actually…like *that* too…' Her voice was slowing. She was almost asleep 'It was the first…time…'

He froze, adrenaline and guilt and remorse hitting him like a tidal wave. 'The first time?' He crossed the room again, back to the bedside, where she lay perfectly still.

He reached out a hand, finding the velvet-soft skin of her cheek. 'The first time, Rachel? You were a virgin?'

She stirred and exhaled—deeply, contentedly. 'No. But…it was the first time…. I've ever wanted it.'

CHAPTER SIX

RACHEL ran lightly down the wide staircase, running her fingers through her wildly sleep-tousled hair as she went. As she'd hurried along the corridor upstairs she'd seen that the courtyard at the centre of the house lay under a covering of white as thick and luxurious as the goosedown duvet which she had slept beneath last night.

And had, in the end, slept wonderfully well. It was as if Orlando had hushed the storm that had been raging inside her for as long as she could remember. She felt…liberated.

She had escaped from Carlos, and in the process she had discovered herself. Maybe she wasn't the incompetent idiot it had always suited him and her mother to make her out to be. After all, he'd said she was frigid, and he'd certainly been wrong about that…

This particularly enticing train of thought was interrupted by the sudden shrill ring of a telephone, echoing through the silent house. Looking round, Rachel traced it to a table in the entrance hall, and hesitated, not knowing what to do. There was no sign of Orlando—but then might he be in his study and would pick it up there? She walked on a few steps, but the ringing continued in a way that seemed to Rachel to be getting increasingly urgent.

She turned and looked back at the phone nervously. She'd never had to answer the phone for anyone else before. In fact she'd hardly had any need to answer the phone at all…

Courage.

For goodness' sake—it was a telephone, not an explosive device, she told herself disgustedly and seized the receiver.

'Hello, Easton Hall?' Pride suffused her at her new-found competence. 'Can I help you?'

'Ohh…?' It was a woman's voice, smoky, drawling, surprised. Rachel felt the confidence of a few moments ago evaporate. 'That's not Mrs Harper, is it?'

'N-no.' Rachel stammered. 'Can I take a message?'

'Well…' said the woman, and the short word seemed to crackle with indignation—as if Rachel was personally responsible for Mrs Harper's absence and had organised it on purpose. 'Could I speak to Orlando, please?'

'Oh…I'm sorry but I don't think he's here,' Rachel said faintly. 'I mean, I've only just got up and I haven't seen—'

'*Got up?*' repeated the voice, in a tone of utter disbelief. 'I see. In that case I do apologise.' The woman gave an incredulous laugh. 'I assumed you were one of Mrs Harper's helpers…'

She left the sentence hanging, making Rachel feel compelled to rush into an explanation. 'No—no, I'm just a friend…of…of Orlando's…'

Rachel winced at the blatant cliché.

'A *friend*?'

The woman's voice was suddenly sharp with animosity, and Rachel held her breath, wondering whether she should just put the phone down now, before she incriminated herself even further. There was a long pause, but then the woman at the other end started speaking again, her voice suddenly syrupy with concern.

'In that case, as you're a *friend* of Orlando, I wonder if you could maybe just…tell me how he is?'

Rachel swallowed, caught off-guard by this change of tack. 'He's…fine.'

There was a small sigh. 'I'm sorry. I know this must sound mad and you don't know me, but I don't know who else to ask. How is he *really*? I mean, as a *friend*? Does he seem miserable to you?'

Pieces of the jigsaw were flying into place with a speed that took Rachel's breath away. And her foolish, naïve happiness along with it. Her throat suddenly felt very dry. 'Yes,' she croaked. 'He seems miserable.'

'Oh, God…what a mess,' the woman said slowly. Her sexy, lightly accented voice was choked with emotion, and Rachel was ashamed of the strength of her hostility. She wanted to hurl the phone at the wall, as if that could somehow hurt the person at the other end. The person Orlando loved.

'But thank you,' continued the woman. 'It helps to know he's as unhappy as I am. It's mad that we're apart…you've told me all I've needed to hear to convince me to come back.'

'I'll tell him…' Rachel just managed to mutter through numb lips.

'No!' The response was instantaneous, and surprisingly sharp. 'No. Don't tell him. Don't say anything. I'd like to surprise him.' She gave a breathy, intimate laugh that contained no trace of any unhappiness at all. Only triumph.

Nauseous, Rachel was just replacing the receiver with a shaking hand when the front door was flung open. Orlando stood in the doorway, his broad shoulders blocking out the white glare behind him, snowflakes resting on his dark hair. He came towards her, a sharp line carved between his dark brows.

'Who was that?'

'She didn't give a name,' Rachel muttered, and jumped as the phone rang again. Orlando snatched it up instantly, his eyes blazing.

'Arabella?'

Rachel took a few stumbling steps backwards.

So that was it. She really should be grateful. It was far better to know before she made even more of a fool of herself than she had already.

Going into the kitchen, she tried to quell the biting sense of disappointment and hurt that burned in her chest. Last night had come with no promises, she had understood that perfectly, but she had at least wanted to be allowed to believe that for as long as it had lasted it had meant something.

The way he had looked at her—her throat constricted painfully as she remembered the intensity of his stare—the way he'd seemed to look beyond her face and into her soul. Now she understood why. *He hadn't seen her at all.*

He'd seen this Arabella. An image of a dark, exotic supermodel swathed in black satin sheets swam into Rachel's head as she mindlessly held the sleek designer kettle under the tap. She was just adding scarlet lipstick and a bottle of champagne to the image when she jumped back with a howl, as water sprayed copiously all over her.

Suddenly strong hands relieved her of the kettle and turned off the tap. Dripping and miserable, she looked up into Orlando's darkly scowling face and felt a further twist of pain.

'I was just going to have a cup of coffee, and then I'll go,' she muttered, not meeting his eye.

'Don't be ridiculous. Go where?'

He seemed distracted. Distracted and angry. And very cold. She felt her bruised heart shrivel a little.

'I don't know, exactly, but obviously I'll find a hotel or something. I have plenty of money...'

'No. You're not going anywhere.'

Orlando said the words as if it hurt him to speak them. It pretty much did. For the sake of his peace of mind he wanted her gone. For the sake of his conscience he needed her to stay. He wasn't quite sure what she'd meant by saying she'd never wanted sex before last night, but something about it troubled him deeply.

'But we agreed... It was just for last night.'

Abruptly Orlando moved away, going to stand at the other side of the kitchen with his back to her in a gesture which told her just as plainly as if he'd spoken the words out loud that as far as he was concerned *last night* was something he didn't wish to be reminded of.

'That was the housekeeper's son on the phone just now. He was ringing to say that Mrs Harper slipped on some ice on her way here this morning and is on her way to hospital now, with a suspected broken ankle and fractured collarbone.'

'Oh, poor her!'

'You're kinder than I am. My first reaction was far less self-less. Today of all bloody days.'

'The ball...of course.'

'Yes.' He didn't turn round.

He couldn't bear to look at her this morning, Rachel thought miserably.

'I want you to stay.'

The words cut through her thoughts, unexpected and shocking. 'What?'

He sighed, his huge shoulders rising and falling, his head drooping for a moment before he seemed to make a massive effort to conceal his exasperation and repeat the words.

'I said, I want you to stay.' He spoke through gritted teeth, with exaggerated patience, as if she were very stupid. 'I have to work. There's an incident brewing over border control in the Middle East, and I'm going to be in consultation with Whitehall and the Pentagon for most of the day. I need you...' He paused to suck in a breath. 'I need you to help tonight, and with getting everything ready.'

Rachel shook her head in bewilderment, trying to keep a grip on reality. For the briefest second she'd allowed herself to imagine that that pause after *I need you* meant something—that Orlando Winterton was asking her to stay because he wanted her, not because he was short-staffed.

'I can't—you know I can't! I'd be hopeless, Orlando. You know I'm completely impractical. I'd make a mess of it all, and spill red wine down someone's priceless designer dress or something...'

He spun round to face her, dragging a hand through his hair. His other hand, the bandaged fingers stained with blood, stayed limp at his side, and the sight of that small vulnerability made her heart skip a beat.

'Don't be ridiculous,' he snapped. 'There'll be caterers, for God's sake. I'm not asking you to be a *waitress*.'

The ice in his wintry eyes extinguished her flicker of compassion and left a smoulder of anger. 'Then what?' She raised her chin an inch, staring at him defiantly. 'If you don't want me to fill in as a waitress, what do you want, Orlando? A stand-in *mistress*?'

She stopped abruptly, heat and colour flooding into her cheeks as the absurdity of the word—of the accusation—sounded in her ears. *Mistress?* She sounded like a prim governess in a Victorian novel.

A smile spread across his face: slow, lazy, dangerously mesmerising.

'My *mistress*? No. I can assure you that there will be absolutely no need for you to take your duties that far, thank you. Though maybe it's just as well you mentioned it, so we can get things absolutely straight. I'm asking you to stay on for purely practical purposes, and whatever happened between us last night is completely irrelevant.'

Rachel bit back her gasp of hurt. 'And what if I don't want to stay?'

He shrugged, levering himself upright from where he had been lounging with deceptive indifference against the countertop, and took a couple of steps towards her.

'Then go. As soon as you've decided where. I'm asking for your help, not issuing a prison sentence.'

He was throwing her a lifeline. She knew that. Giving her time. So why was she hesitating?

She looked down at her hands. Subconsciously her fingers were stretching and flexing, getting ready for the two hours of practice she'd put in first thing in the morning in her old life. Her life with Carlos. The life she had run away from yesterday, with no thought of where she was going.

She shoved her hands into the pockets of her jeans and looked up at Orlando with a small, painful smile. Pride was a luxury she simply couldn't afford at the moment.

'Of course I'll stay,' she said in a subdued voice. 'Thank you. I'll make myself as useful as I can.'

He nodded curtly, his gaze brushing over her for a second, as cold and fleeting as snowflakes on her face. But then he turned and left the room, and it was like being abandoned in Siberia. Naked.

Orlando strode into the library and slammed the door.

The small act of violence made him feel slightly better for a second, before despair closed in on him again, cutting him off from the rest of the world. Like the snow, which was falling again outside in heavy, swirling flakes.

He ought to be proud of himself, he thought mockingly. For the first time in a year he'd done something selfless. Something altruistic. For the first time in the last twelve miserable, desperate, depressing months he had actually done something *heroic*.

And she'd reacted as if he'd asked her to embrace a boa constrictor.

Walking across to the desk, he felt his face contort into a grimace of self-disgust.

She couldn't wait to leave this morning. She had nowhere to go, but she was still planning to walk out of there. She could hardly boil a kettle, but she'd still decided she'd rather fend for herself than stay with him. Knives of pain shot through his damaged hand as it tightened convulsively into a fist.

Why?

Last night she had been different. He felt a moan of torment form in his throat as he remembered her softness, her compliance….her gratitude, for heaven's sake. And at the time he'd felt like the most callous bastard who'd ever walked, because he'd known he was going to have to let her down. This last minute role-reversal was unsettling and bewildering.

What had changed?

A thought crept in to the edge of his mind like a cockroach…unpleasant, and impossible to completely destroy.

Arabella.

Apart from his doctors, she was the only living person to know about his sight.

And she'd spoken to Rachel this morning.

Taking her coffee, Rachel wandered out into the hallway, feeling at a loss. In the distance she could hear the bangs and shouts of the teams of workers clearing the furniture in the long drawing room and setting up the tables in the dining room. The house felt so different today, when it was filled with noise and life. Last night—the moonlight, the silence, the snow—seemed to belong to a dream, unreachable and unreal.

She found herself standing in the doorway of the drawing room, although she couldn't remember consciously deciding to go there, and watched in a trance as two men with their shirt-sleeves rolled back lifted the last sofa and carried it out of the door at the far end.

The room was bare, except for the rug on the floor where Orlando had laid her, knelt over her as his hands had slipped over her body, trailing ecstasy as the angels above had looked down on them...

'Excuse me, you wouldn't happen to know where I could find Mrs Harper, would you?'

Rachel jumped. The voice at her elbow was incredibly well-bred, but decidedly frazzled. Turning round, she found herself looking into the face of a girl not much older than she was, but as different as it was possible to be. Sleek, elegant, sophisticated, she was the sort of girl you expected to see in the champagne bar of Harrods, surrounded by a group of matching friends called Henrietta and Lucinda.

She held out a beautifully manicured hand. 'Sorry, I'm Lucinda. From Ice and Fire? The party planners?'

'Oh—of course,' said Rachel, blushing. For a moment the name of Lucinda's business had thrown her. 'I'm Rachel. I'm terribly sorry, but Mrs Harper won't be coming today. She's slipped on the ice and broken her ankle.'

In sympathy with Mrs Harper, Lucinda's face fell. 'Oh, knickers,' she wailed. 'This sodding weather! I was *so* counting on having someone to help. Half of our office are in bed with hellish flu, which means I've come on my own. I had to set off at some perfectly indecent hour, and I've had the most nightmarish journey—'

She was interrupted by a loud blast of Handel's *Firework Music* from her huge designer handbag, and, glancing apologetically at Rachel, plucked out her mobile. As she turned away to speak into it Rachel had the chance to admire the exquisite cut of her black trouser suit, her shiny pale pink nails with their bright white tips. She looked capable and professional, Rachel thought enviously, pulling the sleeves of her beloved but decidedly distressed cashmere jumper down over her own plain hands.

With a vivid curse that was entirely at odds with the cut-glass tones in which it was spoken, Lucinda threw the phone back into her bag and turned to Rachel. 'That was the florist,' she said miserably. 'All the flights out of the Channel Islands have been grounded this morning, so the flowers won't be here.'

Rachel's heart went out to her. 'What you need is a good strong coffee,' she said sympathetically, taking Lucinda's arm. 'Come with me.'

In the kitchen, Rachel uttered a silent prayer of thanks that she'd watched Orlando fill the kettle earlier and knew how to do it.

'Thanks,' said Lucinda gratefully, taking the mug of coffee. 'You don't know how much I needed this. You're a lifesaver.'

Rachel smiled. 'My pleasure.' It was true. It was a pleasure to be doing something useful for once. 'Just tell me what else I can do to help.'

'Oh, don't say that or I might just take you up on it,' groaned Lucinda, reaching into the depths of her bag and pulling out some paracetamol. 'I feel rotten.'

'Oh, you poor thing.' Rachel regarded her sympathetically over the rim of her mug. 'Are you coming down with the flu, do you think?'

'Let's hope not. Or, if I am, let's hope I can keep it at bay until this party's in full swing.' Lucinda suddenly looked a lot less confident, and Rachel could see that much of the glossy sophistication was just a veneer. 'The thing is,' she went on miserably, 'the business is in a spot of bother, and this party could be make or break. I can't afford to mess this up—it's the perfect opportunity to get some new clients from amongst all these loaded financiers. That's why I was banking on the capable Mrs Harper.'

'I'm afraid I'm hardly capable, but I'll do whatever I can to help,' said Rachel apologetically.

Lucinda looked relieved. 'Would you? I don't suppose you could find a solution to the flower crisis, could you?'

Outside it had stopped snowing, but the temperature had dropped. Rachel's feet, in borrowed Wellingtons, hugely too big for her, crunched through a crisp crust of perfect snow as she trudged along an avenue flanked on both side by sculptural pleached limes.

There was something incredibly beautiful about their bare branches against the frozen sky, something poignant about the way their natural forms had been trained into rigidly controlled shape. They reminded her of Orlando, the way he'd appeared in the kitchen last night. Caged. Restrained.

Her arms were full of branches—some bare, some adorned with berries, some still covered in leaves the same coppery colour as her hair—her hands were scratched and torn, but she didn't care, and her cheeks were flushed with cautious triumph. Following the lime avenue to its end, she'd discovered a gate in the wall and, with difficulty, pushed it open, hoping to find neat borders of well-behaved shrubs. Instead she had found a tangled wilderness.

She'd almost turned back, but the thought of letting Lucinda down, of failing, had made her persevere. She was glad she had.

Ahead of her now, Easton Hall was a picture of English perfection, its ancient brick rosy against the stark, snow covered landscape. It was so beautiful, but there was something sad and empty about it—as if it knew that the best days, the happy times, were gone and there was only darkness ahead. Rachel wondered about all the previous generations of Wintertons who had lived and laughed and loved here; thought of family Christmases and summer afternoons with tea on the lawn, of parties like the one tonight in former years, when all the family would have been gathered…

Now there was just Orlando.

Her heart gave a painful twist inside her chest, as if it had been impaled on one of the thorny branches she carried. He seemed so isolated. She longed to draw him, and this magical house, back into warmth and light.

But of course, she thought sadly, dodging past the caterer's vans and pushing open the front door with her hip, if anyone was to warm Orlando's chilly heart or bring the smile back to his beautiful, hard face it wouldn't be her.

It would be this Arabella.

She paused, struggling to keep hold of all the damp, tangled branches as she kicked off the ridiculous boots. But, though they were far too big for her, they stubbornly refused to come off, so that she was reduced to hopping madly on one foot, desperately shaking her leg in the air while trying not to fall over.

At last the boot flew from her foot and skidded across the tiled floor, coming to rest at the feet of the person standing there. The person she hadn't noticed. The person who had just watched her stupid, ungainly embarrassing display and not stepped in to help.

Orlando.

'My God,' he said, in a cool, mocking voice. 'Burnham Wood comes to Dunsinane. The question is, *why*? We have plenty of kindling and firewood in the kitchen yard.'

Scarlet with exertion and embarrassment, Rachel eyed him mutinously through her armful of spiky branches.

'These are flowers for the tables,' she said haughtily.

Orlando's finely arched eyebrows shot up, eloquently communicating his scorn.

'Really?'

Rachel dropped her gaze. How could anyone manage to get so many syllables out of such a short word? Pig. No wonder he was alone. It was because he was insufferable.

She hesitated for a moment, horribly aware of her mad hair and unmade-up face. Her nose was probably bright red from the cold, and she desperately wanted to blow it. She sniffed, loudly.

'Yes, really. Now, if you'll excuse me…' She took a step forward, intending to sweep past him in an attitude of preoccupation and importance, but she'd forgotten she was still wearing one Wellington, which gave her a madly lopsided gait. She stopped, fury and humiliation warring within her as she had no alternative but to try to lever it off with her other foot.

Orlando took a step towards her, his face perfectly impassive.

'Can I help?'

It was too much. Desperate to end this humiliating encounter, and get as far away from him as possible, Rachel gave an almighty lunge to try and free her foot. Unfortunately as she did so she failed to step clear of the top of the boot and, unable to put her arms out, overbalanced.

He caught her effortlessly and set her back on her feet again. And then he stood back, snatching his hands away as if, instead of being chilled from the frozen garden, she'd been blistering hot.

'Thanks,' Rachel muttered stiffly, and, gathering the branches closer to her, resumed her progress across the hall, choking on the bitterness of the irony.

She had, after all, been the one to bring a smile back to Orlando Winterton's face. Such a damned shame, she reflected savagely, that it had been one of such complete and utter contempt.

The light was beginning to fade as Rachel finished the last of the arrangements and placed it on the table in the hallway.

Lucinda had brought heavy rectangular glass vases, tall

enough to support the height of the branches. They rose starkly out of the glass, and against the opulent grandeur of Easton Hall looked astonishingly sparse and elegant.

Rachel stood back and allowed herself a small moment of satisfaction.

She had tried something new, and she hadn't failed dismally. With a spring in her step, she went to find Lucinda.

She was in the dining room, talking to one of the hordes of caterers who had been traipsing in and out all day, carrying vast platters of salmon and lobster, endless dishes of salad, and every kind of spectacular pudding imaginable. But, going into the room, Rachel felt her attention drawn away from the array of food laid out on the long tables by the rising hysteria in Lucinda's voice.

'I quite specifically asked you to supply the candles. It's no good telling me now that you haven't got them!'

'I'm sorry.' The caterer's tone was firm. 'That wasn't the message we got. I double-checked myself this morning what we we'd been commissioned to supply, and candles weren't on the list.'

'So you're trying to tell me—?'

Rachel laid a hand on Lucinda's arm. She could feel her shivering violently.

'Don't worry. I'll go out and get some. The table arrangements are all done, so I've got nothing else to do.'

Lucinda turned to face her. She was deathly pale, but spots of bright colour burned high up on her cheeks.

'Would you?' Her eyes filled with tears. 'That would be fantastic.'

Rachel drew her away from the caterer, lowering her voice. 'Lucinda, you look dreadful.'

'I feel dreadful,' she said through chattering teeth. Two fat tears slid down her cheeks. 'I don't know what to do.'

'Go to bed,' said Rachel resolutely. 'You have to. You're obviously awfully unwell.'

'But I can't!' There's still so much to do!'

'Doesn't matter.' Rachel put her arm around her. Lucinda was burning hot and, crying in earnest now, virtually unrecognisable from the sleek, capable-looking girl who had so intimidated Rachel earlier. 'The caterers can sort out the drinks, and I'm going to buy candles right now. But you can't drive back to London like this.'

'No, I know…' She sighed, looking up at Rachel with puffy eyes. 'My godmother lives about ten miles from here, just beyond the next village. I'm sure she'd put me up.'

'Phone her,' ordered Rachel. 'I'll drop you off on my way into town.'

'Hadn't you better check with Lord Ashbroke?'

Rachel was about to say yes, but then she remembered the contemptuous look he had given her earlier, and his attitude of terrifying remoteness. 'I'm sure he's far too busy to be disturbed.'

'You're wonderful,' said Lucinda gratefully, giving her a weak hug.

Rachel smiled sadly.

That, unfortunately, was a matter of opinion.

CHAPTER SEVEN

THE snow had transformed the lanes along which she had hurtled so desperately only the day before. The black, glowering landscape was now hidden in a soft white blanket, which sparkled in the beam of her headlamps as if it had been sprinkled with glitter in preparation for tonight's party.

Driving carefully back to Easton, Rachel raised her hand, tentatively brushing it up the back of her neck.

She felt strange; oddly light-headed, and the sensation of the close-cropped hair at her nape brought an involuntary smile to her face in the warm fug of the car. She had gone into the hairdresser's completely on impulse as she'd hurried by on her search for candles, and had found herself seated in front of the mirror before she'd had time to think about what she was doing.

The face that had looked back at her had been pale and childlike. Her eyes had always been her best feature—large, as clear and warm as amber, and inherited from her father, her mother had once told her in disgust—but they gave her face a frightened look.

And as she'd sat there the words she had said to Orlando last night came back to her. *I'm tired of being afraid. I want to be brave...*

She'd taken a deep breath and heard herself saying 'Take it all off, please.'

Now, she glanced into the driving mirror, angling her head for a better view of herself. The hairdresser, horrified at the sacrilege of butchering such luxuriant hair, had flatly refused to give her a short crop, persuading her instead into the idea of a choppy, layered bob, cut closely into the curve of her skull at the back and angling sharply downwards, following the line of her jaw to finish in longer, spiky layers at the front.

It felt glorious. She slid her hand into the front, pushing it backwards, loving the way it stayed put now the weight of it had gone.

Only now did she appreciate what a weight it had been. Described by the PR people as being 'integral to the brand', her heavy hair had been entangled with the weight of expectation and responsibility. It had oppressed her and, while defining her image, it had stopped her from being herself.

She was free of all that now—in every way. It was as if Orlando Winterton had broken all the chains that had anchored her to her past with the same casual ruthlessness with which he and his fellow pilots torched pianos.

It was only natural that she should feel drawn to him, she thought sadly. It was inevitable, stemming from the same psychological imperative that made newly hatched ducklings bond with the first creature they saw when they emerged from the egg. He was the first person who had listened to her, the first person she felt had ever really *seen* her—seen through the image and past her porcelain-pretty face.

It was just such a damned shame he was in love with someone else. Suddenly she gave a gasp as the road ahead narrowed. She slammed her foot on the brakes, but too late, too sharply, and she felt the car glide across the icy road, completely out of her control. For a moment everything was suspended as in slow motion she watched the low wall ahead getting closer, brighter in the beam of the headlights…

And then there was a crunch, a jolt, a shattering of glass, and semi-darkness as the headlight on one side went out.

In the sudden thick silence Rachel let out a shaky laugh.

That bloody bridge again.

Which just went to show that knowing where the dangers lay didn't stop you falling right into them.

The house was completely quiet as she pushed open the front door and stood for a moment in the hallway with her bags of shopping. Cold, intimidating, dark—just as it had been when she'd stood here for the first time yesterday, almost deranged with terror.

The team of caterers must have finished here and be getting themselves organised in the kitchen. Apart from a glimpse of long, white-clothed tables through the open door of the dining room beyond the hallway, there was no evidence at all that in a little under two hours this would be the scene of a party.

For a moment Rachel felt an icy fist of doubt bunch inside her stomach. *She* had been the one who had insisted Lucinda went home, so the responsibility for making things happen now rested firmly on her shoulders.

How had Lucinda put it?

Oh, knickers.

She set the supermarket bags down and looked inside them. Having her hair cut had taken up more time than she'd thought, and by the time she'd left the hairdressers all the small shops on the high street had been shut. Suppressing her panic, she'd remembered passing a huge supermarket on the way in, and there she had found boxes of thick ivory-coloured church candles and filled her basket with as many as she could carry.

Hurrying to the checkout, she had spotted, on a shelf of reduced post-Christmas stock, some fairy lights. Shaped like snowflakes, they'd reminded her of watching the snow fall last night, standing naked at the window of the firelit drawing room, with Orlando at her side…

For a second she had seen, more vividly than the boxes on the shelves in front of her, his deep-set, slanting eyes. Pale green, ringed with darkness. Tropical waters overlaid with ice.

It had come as a surprise to discover, as she'd paid for her shopping at the checkout, that as well as the candles she also seemed to have bought five boxes of the snowflake-shaped fairy lights.

Now, with trembling hands, she set to work.

Orlando stood in front of the mirror.

If he looked straight ahead, straight to where his face should be, technically he should just about be able to bring into the lower edge of his vision the buttonholes down the front of his dress shirt. But for the thousandth time the tiny mother-of-pearl shirt stud slipped from his fingers and fell to the floor.

He swore expressively, and was just about to get down and try to locate the stud with his hands when there was a soft knock on the door.

'Yes?'

God, he sounded like an ogre. He felt like a bloody ogre. He was losing his humanity along with his sight. Wrestling with self-loathing, he deliberately didn't turn his head as he heard the door open.

'Orlando?'

That voice. Soft. Like the cashmere she wore. But with a slight edge…a texture too…like…

'What?'

'I'm so sorry to disturb you.' She was crossing the room. In the mirror he caught a glimpse of movement behind him, a glimmer of her brilliant hair. 'I can't fasten this dress. I wondered if you could possibly do it?'

That again. He turned round slowly to face her. 'How does it fasten?' he said dully, holding up his bandaged fingers. 'Because I'm struggling too.'

'Zip. You should manage with one hand. And then I'll help you.'

He felt the usual, automatic kick of bone-deep, visceral resentment at the word, but gritted his teeth and said, 'Fine. Turn round.'

Did he imagine the small, sad sigh as she presented her back to him?

Instinctively he reached up with his injured hand to sweep the hair from her neck, but found nothing there. Of course—she must have fastened it up. Imagined visions of her bare nape rose tormentingly in his mind, but determinedly he kept his head lowered, his gaze fixed straight ahead, deliberately not trying to get it within his field of vision. His fingers sought the base of the zip.

It began low down, in the small of her back. His fingers skimmed across the luxuriously soft fabric to where it met the satin warmth of her skin and he almost snatched his hand away.

'Can you manage?'

That was what her voice reminded him of, he thought, brushing his thumb downwards, smoothing her dress. Velvet. Dark, luxurious, sexy velvet.

'Of course,' he snapped, tugging the zip upwards. 'Done.'

'Thank you.' She turned to face him again. 'Now you.'

Downstairs, the house was finally ready, and she hoped it was almost up to Lucinda's standard. But the time had sped by, and she had left barely half an hour to wreak the same magic on herself as she had on the vast, chilly rooms. Rushing upstairs, she had showered in record time and, with shaking hands, had brushed the lightest smudge of charcoal-grey glittering shadow over her eyelids, adding a slick of shimmering gloss to lips that already felt swollen and red. Finally she had slipped into the dress she was to have worn at her big recital in Paris, at the end of her honeymoon. A narrow, figure hugging column of dark green crushed velvet, it had come to no harm from being squashed into her suitcase for two days.

For five long minutes she'd struggled with the zip, before giving in and coming to find him. But from the moment she'd walked in here and seen him, his shirt open to the waist, the long cuffs hanging down over his beautiful hands, she had felt sick with desire. And now this was almost more than she could bear.

It was like some sophisticated form of torture. Picking up one of the antique shirt studs, Rachel tried to slot it into the lowest buttonhole, just above the place where his stomach swept down in a muscular arc beneath his ribs. Only centimetres from his bare skin, her hand trembled violently with the need to touch it. She gripped the stud between her fingers, focusing intently on the gold-hinged stem and waiting for the dizzying wave of longing to pass before she could fit it through the hole.

It was so stupid, so very, very stupid, to feel like this when he belonged to someone else. There was no point going back over what had happened last night—that had been before she'd known about Arabella, and had come with no promises, only pure, heat-of-the moment passion…

She shuddered, biting back a moan as the stud slipped through her fingers.

'Sorry—I don't know what's wrong with me.'

She dropped to her knees and swept a hand over the rough sisal floor covering, groping for the stud. Suddenly the symbolism of her position struck her—she was literally on the floor at his feet. She had to get a grip of herself. Standing up, she took a deep breath.

'Sorry. Try again.'

He had promised her nothing. She slid the stud into place and reached for another. *He had given her no reason to think he had any feelings for her whatsoever.* Another stud. *He hadn't even seemed to notice her hair.* What had she expected? That he'd take one look at her and decide Arabella wasn't the one for him after all? God, how ridiculous. Angrily, she picked up another stud.

And made the mistake of glancing up at him.

He was staring straight past her, over her head, his clear green eyes empty and bleak, his jaw tense, as if he was enduring some terrible private torment. She looked quickly away, sliding the stud into the buttonhole in the middle of his chest. Over his heart.

Arabella. He was wishing she was Arabella.

Misery fought with compassion. In that brief moment when she'd looked at him she had seen on his face an expression that exactly mirrored her own feelings. The difference was that she had the ability to ease his suffering a little. Arabella had told her not to say anything, but would it be so wrong to comfort him with the news that she was coming back?

He lifted his chin so she could put the last stud into the collar of his shirt, revealing the strong column of his throat. For a second she couldn't move, mesmerised by the pulse that jumped faintly beneath the smooth skin. In an instant all thoughts of Arabella fled her mind—along with everything else but the desperate urge to press her lips against it. Aware that her own heart was beating in perfect time, she almost bit through her lip in anguish as she snapped the stud into place and immediately backed away.

'Thanks.' His tone was utterly offhand.

She swallowed. If he had noticed her lack of composure, he was doing a very good job of not showing it. Probably because it embarrassed the hell out of him.

Or maybe he just didn't notice her at all.

'No problem. If that's all, I'll go…'

Gathering up a handful of floor-skimming green crushed velvet, she almost ran to the door, choking back the ridiculous urge to cry. The dress, the haircut, the eyeshadow and lipgloss had been wasted. He hadn't even glanced twice at her.

She couldn't get away fast enough, Orlando thought bitterly. He had sensed her awkwardness, and from it could deduce only one thing.

His suspicions were correct.

Arabella had told her.

Blackness flooded his heart as he turned to her with an icy smile. Let her squirm with embarrassment at his helplessness. Let her see exactly how big a mistake she'd made last night.

'Sorry,' he drawled, in a voice of molten steel. 'I'm afraid you'll have to do the cufflinks too.'

She hesitated, then came slowly back towards him. He could see that her hair half covered her face, giving him the agonising impression that she'd just stumbled out of bed—sleepy and tousled. As she bent her head over his outstretched hands he felt one silken strand brush the inside of his wrist.

Fire licked through him, searing his scarred emotions with fresh agony.

Her long, strong fingers worked quickly at the stiff cuffs of his shirt, folding them back, slipping the flat disc of century-old gold with its worn Ashbroke crest through the holes. He could hear her breathing, fast and shallow, smell the scent of crushed rose petals, with its whispers of summer and happiness, its memories of last night.

All things that he had lost for ever.

She straightened up and rubbed the palms of her hands down the narrow column of her fitted dress. Against the dark velvet the skin of her bare shoulders gleamed like mother-of-pearl.

'I can manage the rest,' he snarled, turning away.

'You're sure? Your tie?'

'I've done it often enough.'

'With one hand?' There was a break in her voice that sounded like anguish. Or pity.

He swung round and felt his fists clench, the throbbing in his fingers reminding him afresh of the ostensible reason for needing her help. Picking up the silk bow tie, he hesitated for a moment as his mind filled with dense, dark fog. Then, trying to keep the hostility from his face, he turned back to her and tossed the tie at her.

'No.'

She caught it, and for a second just stood—not daring to look at him, unable to bear his obvious distaste at having her so close. She threaded the band of silk through her fingers, twisting and pleating the expensive material, numbly watching as a tear fell onto it and slowly melted into the darkness.

'Do I have to beg?'

The ice in his tone made her gasp. Her head jerked up, and she gazed at him through a haze of humiliated tears. He gazed back, his green eyes glittering with cruelty.

'I'm sorry.'

Even in high heels, she had to stand on tiptoe to slip the tie around his neck. The proximity was almost unbearable. Staring fixedly at his lean jaw, she made a clumsy attempt to tie a neat, flat bow, but the pounding blood in her ears and the echoing drumbeat in her wrists, her heart, the top of her thighs, made her fingers flutter ineffectually at the heavy silk. She could feel the whisper of his breath fanning her brow and heard her own whimper of anguish.

'I can't—'

He swore abruptly as his hands closed over hers. His face was like granite. She was aware of nothing beyond his skin on hers as he wrenched her hands from him. 'Leave it. I'll do it.'

'How can you?' she cried, disgusted at her own inadequacy, her own emotional stupidity. 'I can do it—please, just let me try again…'

And then his hands were on her face, holding it, his thumbs brushing her cheeks as the tears soaked into the bandage on his fingers before he pulled away sharply and thrust his hands through his dark, dishevelled hair. He half turned from her, but she heard his exasperated sigh and felt herself die inside a little more. 'You're crying. Why?'

'Nothing. I'm being stupid. Take no notice…' She gave a sudden, bitter laugh. 'Not that you would anyway…'

He whipped back to face her. His eyes blazed with sudden searing, unidentifiable passion, but his voice was terrifyingly calm.

'What did Arabella say, exactly?'

Rachel felt her hands fly to her mouth. 'She…she told me not to tell you.'

Orlando went very still. Standing there with his head thrown back, the silk tie hanging loosely around his neck, he looked like a tortured Adonis, and she felt the breath being squeezed from her lungs by the sheer charisma of his presence as she waited for him to speak.

'I can guess.' He gave her a heart breaking twisted smile, and his tone softened so that the steel edge to it was almost imperceptible. Which only made it more dangerous. 'Discretion was never really Arabella's strong point.'

Rachel was like a rabbit caught in the headlights of a fast-approaching car. His face was completely expressionless, utterly remote, but the emotion that flared in his luminous eyes was terrifying.

'I think it's best that I…know…' She was backing away from him, unable to bear his nearness and his immeasurable distance a moment longer. 'I was in danger…in very great danger—' her voice broke into a dry sob '—of falling in love with you, you see.'

She stumbled slightly on the hem of her trailing dress, and then, yanking it up over her knees, turned and fled from the room.

CHAPTER EIGHT

STANDING in the hallway beneath the portrait of his great grandfather, Orlando drained one glass of champagne and picked up another.

The house was filling up. The level of noise rose as more parties of people arrived, greeting each other loudly, their confident voices ringing through Easton's vast rooms and all but drowning out the sound of Lucinda's string quartet. The ball showed every sign of being a huge success, and the weather, far from deterring people from coming, seemed to have forged a sort of Dunkirk spirit amongst the guests. In their midst, Orlando felt more isolated than ever.

It wasn't his damaged sight that set him apart from everyone else, though. It was his relentless, churning rage.

At Arabella. She'd probably told half of London that Orlando the heroic was now Orlando the pitiful. But he'd been a fool to expect anything else; she'd always been as hard as diamonds. It was what had first attracted him to her.

No. It was Rachel who had hurt him the most.

'I think it's best that I know—I was in danger of falling in love with you...'

Was.

Not now. Not now she'd found out the truth about him.

There was a blast of arctic air as another group came in, pausing to hand over tickets and coats to the door staff, cheerfully exchanging anecdotes about their difficult journeys as they helped themselves to champagne from the tray. Orlando knew that he should be there, playing the host, but even thinking about the effort required made him feel weary. Turning on his heel, he walked in the other direction—towards the inner hall, away from the throng of people.

The house looked stunning. Even through the acrid fog of his anger and the curse of his reduced sight, he could feel that Easton been brought to life. He had been so used to its shadows and darkness that he had quite simply forgotten that it could be so lovely. He ought to find Lucinda and thank her...

He felt his mouth quirk into a twisted smile.

But he'd have to recognise her first. He'd known her for years, but still his chances of being able to pick her out from all the other pedigree blondes at the party were utterly negligible.

Despairingly he shouldered his way through the groups of people who were clustered, talking in loud, braying voices, in the hallway at the foot of the stairs. He had just reached the door to the dining room when he stopped, his fingers tightening dangerously around his glass as he overheard two men behind him.

'Check that out. Coming down the stairs...'

The second man let out a low whistle. 'Hel-lo. Don't usually go for redheads, but for her I'd make an exception. Look at the t—'

Orlando stopped dead, adrenaline coursing through him. Technically, he was the host of this party. Did that make knocking one of the guests unconscious more acceptable, or less?

'I say, isn't it that girl from the posters? The pianist one? Hair's different, but I'd recognise her anywhere. Huge picture of her at Bank tube station last year. Used to make my journey to work quite uncomfortable, I can *tell* you...'

As they burst into guffaws of crude laughter, Orlando wrenched open the door into the courtyard and stepped out into the biting cold, feeling a small flicker of satisfaction as he heard one of them say, 'Bloody hell, it's freezing!'

He was shaking, so fired up with bitterness and adrenaline that it took him a moment to take in his surroundings.

The high-walled courtyard, where light hardly penetrated for most of the year, was bathed in the gentle glow of scores of candles. They lined the snowy paths, were clustered in flickering groups on the steps opposite and in each corner of the courtyard, and reflected a hundredfold in the rows of windows that looked out onto it.

His footsteps slowed as he reached the point in the centre where the paths converged and turned slowly round, exhaling heavily in a plume of frozen air.

Lucinda had done a great job, he realised with a small frisson of surprise. In truth, he'd only hired her because he'd known her vaguely from the old days and had heard her business was in trouble. But she was good. Amazingly good. The effect she'd created out here and in the house with firelight and candles was magical. Timeless, somehow, as if somehow the years had been peeled back and the house was in its heyday again.

He took one of the paths that crossed the courtyard and stood in the shadows against the wall, eyes closed, waiting for the unexpected tightening in his throat to ease.

The volume of voices and laughter suddenly grew louder for a moment, and then died down again, but the faint strains of the string quartet drifted through the frozen air, like warm, caressing fingers.

'Orlando?'

Rachel laid a hand on his arm and felt him stiffen instantly. His eyes flew open and, gazing up, she could see the candlelight reflected in their cold, glittering depths.

'I came to find you. I wanted to apologise…'

He cut her off ruthlessly with a swift, crushing sneer. 'There's nothing to *apologise* for. At least you were honest.'

'But I shouldn't have been. It was wrong of me to say that about…about falling in love with you when—'

'Save it,' he spat. He made to move past her, but she grabbed his arm, her strong pianist's fingers gripping him. He froze, holding up his arm where she held him, too bound by ingrained chivalry to shake her off, almost afraid of what might happen if he unleashed the fury that surged through him at that moment. Around him, the candles still flickered serenely, mocking him, taunting him with the memory of his momentary glimpse of a peace that would forever elude him.

'Let go of me, Rachel.'

'No! Please, Orlando, I want to explain—about Arabella. I didn't have a chance to finish before, to tell you that she—'

'I don't want to hear it!' he roared. His fingers closed around her wrist like handcuffs and brutally he wrenched her hand off him. But somehow his grip remained locked fast on her wrist and they struggled, her other hand coming up to his chest, pushing him away, beating against him, until neither of them was sure who was struggling against whom. With a desperate cry Rachel tried to break away, only to find he was still holding her, pulling her back towards him, into his body, and she fell against him, so that he had to grasp her waist to stop her falling.

And then suddenly his hands were on her back, and her lips were parting as his mouth came down on hers, and her fingers were entangled in his hair, pulling, pressing his head down harder, wanting more, wanting all of him. There was no tenderness in the kiss, just an urgency born of despair and frustration and pain and longing. She could feel the wall behind her, cold and damp, but she was glad of its solidity as she leaned back against it, unable to trust her legs to hold her up. Orlando's hands were on her shoulders now, pressing them back against the brick—or was she doing that herself?—her body helplessly arching towards him in an attitude of transparent need. She could feel her legs part, her hips rising upwards as his hand slipped downwards. His grip was hard, insistent, and it sent her to the brink of oblivion.

So what if he loved Arabella? *So what?* He was here, with her; this was real—the only reality she could think of. The world beyond this tiny space of shared breath, shared warmth, shared fire, was crushed out of her consciousness by his presence and his nearness and her own self-destructive will.

She needed him.

Now.

She needed him now, and if she didn't have him she thought she would die.

She heard him groan, his lips pressed against her neck, as his hand slid upwards into her hair, feeling the spiky shortness at her nape. She felt the sudden rush of chill air on her heated skin as he drew his head back and, opening her eyes, saw him gazing down at her with a despairing intensity that sent a wave of annihilating desire crashing through her, drenching her from the inside.

'Your hair…'

She didn't let him get any further. Taking his face in both her hands, she pulled him roughly down again. For a moment she let her quivering lips hover tormentingly over his, until she heard his tiny indrawn breath and knew he was as lost as she was. The moment stretched, deepened, as she slowly slid her tongue along the taut line of his top lip…

'Good Lord….' A woman's voice cut through the raw air, almost as cold and sharp as the icicles hanging from the eaves above them. 'I thought it was a country ball, not an orgy.'

Rachel felt Orlando stiffen and jerk upright, heard his low, savage curse.

She recognised the voice from the phone call that morning, but now it was stripped of its veneer of concern, revealing the viciousness beneath. Her eyes flew to the doorway. Silhouetted against the bright hallway beyond, her face illuminated by the candles into a grotesque mask of malice, stood a woman with long blonde hair.

'Arabella.'

With lightning speed Orlando moved so that he was standing between them, shielding Rachel with his body from the basilisk stare of the blonde.

'I told you I was coming,' she drawled. 'You should know me well enough to know that when I say something I mean it. I suppose I should consider myself lucky to have arrived in the middle of a party, when there was someone to show me in, since you're obviously far too preoccupied.' She tossed her blonde mane disdainfully. 'I left my things in the study and helped myself to a drink—you don't mind, do you?'

'Yes. I told you to stay away.'

'You did, didn't you?'

Slumped, shivering, against the wall, Rachel could hear the spiteful relish in her tone. She's enjoying this, she thought dully. Her moment of victory as she returns to lay claim to her man. She could picture the triumph on that tight, hard face, but could see nothing but the broad spread of Orlando's shoulders. She pressed her hands against the bricks to stop herself from reaching out and sliding her arms around him, desperate for the warmth and strength of him, but suddenly realised why he had positioned himself like that. Not to protect her from Arabella, but to hide her.

He was ashamed.

'But,' Arabella continued, 'unfortunately, darling, you Wintertons aren't the gods you once thought you were. You don't command the universe any more, and things happen whether you like it or not.'

He had taken a step forward as she spoke. Behind him, Rachel could sense his tension in the set of his shoulders, the proud tilt of his head. She closed her eyes, wishing she didn't have to endure the torture of seeing him go to her.

'What do you want, Arabella?'

'I have something to show you,' Arabella said matter-of-factly. 'Oh, dear—maybe that's not a very tactful way of putting it. Sorry, darling. But you'll forgive me when you find out what it is. It's in the library…' And with that she disappeared back into the noise and warmth of the party.

For a moment Orlando didn't move. Standing there, in the centre of the candlelit courtyard, he suddenly reminded Rachel of some early martyr, alone and palpably suffering. Slowly he turned his head. The candles cast deep shadows in the hollows of his face, making him look gaunt and haunted.

'Go,' Rachel croaked. 'Go. This is what she told me on the phone. What she asked me not to tell you. This is what I was trying to explain…'

He shook his head, frowning.

'What? *What*?'

'She told me that she was coming down here…coming to see you. She wants you back, Orlando. She told me not to tell you.'

'God, Rachel…I got it wrong. I thought…' His head dipped and he thrust his hands into his hair, then took a couple of steps towards her. She held up her hands.

'Doesn't matter. Please. I'm fine. Just go to her.'

She said the words. But she couldn't bear to watch him as he walked away.

'Sorry to drag you away from your guests,' drawled Arabella bitchily as she stood at Orlando's desk in the library. 'Not that you were doing much in the way of socialising. I must say I'm stunned to find you haven't lost that Winterton magic, Orlando darling. I'm delighted to see you're as attractive and commanding as ever.'

'Are you? I see no reason at all why you should care, as there's absolutely nothing between us any more.'

Arabella gave a dry, humourless laugh. 'Oh, darling, you don't know how devastatingly ironic that remark is.'

She paused, and he saw her walk around to the other side of the desk and bend to pick something up. He tilted his head back, trying to see what it was. Something large and cumbersome. He heard the heavy thud as she placed it on the desk, but couldn't make sense of the awkward shape.

'There. *There*, darling, is the reason why I care. Do you see it now?'

Her tone was spiteful. Orlando felt hatred harden into chips of ice in his heart.

'No, Arabella, I don't see,' he said in a low, savage tone. 'As you very well know.'

'I don't *know*, actually. I know what the doctors said, of course, and I thought by now you'd be helpless—an invalid.' She sounded aggrieved, as if she were almost disappointed to be proved wrong. 'But you seem completely normal—as that little nobody out there would obviously agree. I take it she doesn't know?'

'That's none of your business.'

'It's rather obvious from the way that she looked at you that she doesn't—like you're Prince Charming and Sir Lancelot all rolled into one. I'd keep it that way, if I were you—telling her that her hero is flawed would be like telling a child that Father Christmas doesn't exist.'

Orlando spun round, feeling for the door handle, knowing that if he stayed in the same room as her no amount of chivalry, training or good breeding would prevent him from giving vent to the violent impulses that fizzed and burned like overloaded electrical circuits through his nerve-endings. He wanted to get back to Rachel, but he paused for a moment and said, with quiet venom, 'I don't know why you came back, Arabella, but you needn't have bothered. There's nothing you can say that would—'

Orlando stopped dead as a thin, quavering cry rang out into the tense air from the direction of the desk. His hand froze on the door handle as his blood froze in his veins.

'Nothing?' challenged Arabella in the silence that followed. Her voice vibrated with unconcealed triumph. 'How about *come and meet your son*?'

Back in the hallway, the light and noise of the party were like an assault after the tranquil courtyard. Rachel looked around in bewilderment. Her lips were swollen with Orlando's kisses, her hair mussed from his questing, hungry fingers, and a combination of surging hormones and desperate longing made her feel edgy and wild. Thrusting her way through the crowd, she ignored the comments and whistles of the financiers and hedge fund boys in her wake, and made her way resolutely to the library.

She had to find out what was going on.

Her heels tapped on the marble tiles of the hallway as she approached the half-open door. She could see Orlando standing there, his hand on the handle, but then she felt her confident footsteps falter as she heard Arabella's voice…

'*Come and meet your son…*'

Rachel stopped dead. Through a crack in the door she saw Arabella's face. She bore the look of a chess grandmaster who had just uttered the word *checkmate*.

On the desk, from the depths of a bulky infant carrier seat, Rachel caught a fleeting glimpse of a tiny flailing hand before Orlando slammed the door shut, leaving her shivering on the outside.

'Is it mine?'

Arabella made a sharp, scornful exclamation. 'If you could see him you wouldn't be asking. He's Winterton through and through—from the top of his very dark head to the tips of his long, elegant fingers,' she sneered. 'If he wasn't I wouldn't be in the mess I am now.'

Orlando walked slowly over to the window, trying to keep as much distance between himself and Arabella. And this child. His head felt as if it was full of sand, and he rubbed his forehead with his undamaged hand, trying to clear it. Trying to rub away the images of Rachel that wouldn't seem to leave him.

'What mess?'

'Jamie's kicked me out,' she said dully. 'I thought the baby was his, but, given that Jamie is deliciously Scandinavian and blond, it's painfully bloody obvious that it isn't.'

'You must have known that from the dates?' Orlando ground out from between gritted teeth. Arabella left nothing to chance. Her body ran to the same strictly controlled timetable as the rest of her life.

He heard her sigh. 'It must have happened that last couple of weeks. When you were…told. Diagnosed. Whatever. Felix was home…' For a moment her voice faltered, and then hardened, almost defensively. 'It was a horrible time for me. I was so confused. I didn't have anyone to talk to…'

Orlando's face was a mask of contempt, and it dripped from every sneering word. 'Poor you.'

'It was hell! You never talked to me. You just pushed me away!'

'Funny,' said Orlando acidly. 'That isn't how I remember it. As I recall, you ran out of the room when I told you what Parkes had said, and went back to London that afternoon for some party.' He swore softly. 'Oh, God. What a coincidence. Jamie van Hartesvelt's party…'

'I was shocked…devastated—surely you can understand that! I needed space to think—to adjust,' Arabella protested. 'Suddenly you weren't the same person any more, the man I'd fallen in love with. And then, when I came back the next day, you hardly acknowledged my existence. If it hadn't been for Felix I don't know how I would have coped…' She was silent for a moment, and then added, almost in an undertone, 'Felix was good to me.'

'Of course he was,' said Orlando bitterly. 'Because he'd won. Everything we ever did was in competition with each other, and suddenly it was over. I was out. Defeated. He was the winner, so he could afford to be bloody *good* to you.'

'It wasn't like that! He was devastated too. He looked up to you so much, Orlando, and the thought of you being…weakened, being *reduced*, was almost more than he could bear! I wasn't surprised when I heard that he was dead. He shouldn't have been flying. He was still too upset.'

'Oh, for God's sake, spare me the guilt trip! I'm supposed to believe now that Felix's death is due to my selfish, embarrassing *weakness*? Jeez, Arabella—does it not enter your stupid, self-absorbed head that it's bad enough knowing that I'm here, sentenced to this bloody awful half-life, while Felix has been robbed of a useful, long, full one? Don't you think that's bad enough without you telling me it's actually *my fault*? Don't you think I'd change places with him without a second's hesitation? The only thing that makes it bearable is the knowledge that wherever he is now, he's laughing because he won. From here to eternity he's a *hero*, for God's sake!'

She raised her head, and it was lucky that Orlando couldn't see the look of cruel triumph on her face. 'Oh, yes,' she said quietly. 'That destroys you, doesn't it, Orlando? Felix died a hero, while you're living the life of a hermit.'

Above the drumming of blood in his ears, Orlando heard the sound of Arabella unbuckling the straps of the baby seat, and the soft sigh and whimper of the child as she picked him up. 'It's a bit of a come-down, isn't it, darling, after the accolades and the adulation? Just as well Felix did his bit to uphold the family name. Just as well he's a good role model for your son. That's why I called him after his brave uncle. Meet Felix.'

Orlando felt the blood drain from his face. The room was very still, very quiet. The sounds of the party were coming to them as if from a parallel universe, not merely from the other side of a closed door. Eventually Orlando spoke. His voice was hollow.

'Why? Why did you do that?'

'Because I did everything to make you love me,' Arabella hissed venomously. 'I was *perfect*. You have no idea how much effort it took to be perfect all the time, and it still wasn't enough. You didn't love me. You didn't need me. You had everything and I was just an accessory. But in all that time we were together I came to understand you, and I knew the one person who could really touch your impenetrable heart was Felix. You loved him, but you hated him, too.'

He had to hand it to her. Her aim had been to inflict the maximum amount of pain and she had succeeded. She was right, and he'd underestimated her. She'd made sure in the most subtle, agonising way possible that he would never be allowed to forget Felix's victory. Felix's heroism. His own fallibility.

'Well done,' he said bleakly. 'It seems you've won too. What now?'

'I haven't bloody well won. I'm the loser in all this, Orlando. It's destroyed my life, my career, my relationship, my *body*, for God's sake.' She was pacing briskly back and forth across the room, bouncing the inert bundle in her arms with alarming ferocity. 'It's harder than it looks, this parenting thing. No sleep. No going out. No time do have a bath or talk on the phone or go shopping. It's suffocating. Everybody's always on at me not to drink and smoke—as if I hadn't already given up enough.'

Orlando felt the sweat break out on the back of his neck as this insight into the early weeks of his child's life was starkly revealed. He stepped forward, his hands in his pockets so she couldn't see his clenched fists, but she was too wrapped up in herself to notice anything else.

Her voice had taken on a slightly hysterical edge. 'I can't do it any more, Orlando. I need a break. I'm going to Paris, and I'm leaving the baby with you.'

With huge effort Rachel forced a smile for the merchant banker whose hand was creeping rather too low down her back as he whisked her round the drawing room in a clumsy waltz. It was as if Arabella possessed some kind of supernatural power to slow down time, and was making the seconds drag by like hours as Rachel waited for Orlando to emerge from the library.

Not that there was anything to wait for, she thought despairingly. Orlando had only been using her to fill the gap left by Arabella's absence. She'd known that already. If she was any kind of a decent person she'd be happy for him that he'd got his great love back. And, not only that, that he'd got a baby...

She closed her eyes against the sudden rush of tears, but felt them ooze out from under her lids as she pictured Orlando's big, strong hands holding the baby, the lips that had so recently brought her to the brink of ecstasy dropping the tenderest of kisses on that tiny, downy head. And his eyes....his astonishing, glacier-green eyes…looking down into the face of his own child and being softened with helpless love.

As a child she had never known her father, and his absence had caused her to construct an elaborate image of the kind of person she would have chosen to fill his role. A perfect hero: strong, fearless, handsome, honourable. Like Orlando.

She buried her face in the shoulder of the merchant banker while she tried to puncture the misery that was ballooning inside her, but was unable to contain her moan of hopelessness. Unfortunately the merchant banker mistook the sound for pleasure, and instantly tightened his grip, dropping his head to breathe hot, whisky-scented fumes into her ear.

Her eyes flew open in panic and she tried to pull away, but his palm was damp and heavy on her bare back, pushing her body harder against his, so she could feel the pressure of his arousal. It was just like Carlos all over again—and for a second she felt the room tilt and swim as panic swamped her.

'My turn now, I think,' said a cold voice.

Instantly the merchant banker released her from his insistent embrace and melted away. Rachel stood in the centre of the floor, looking dazedly up at Orlando.

His face was ashen, utterly drained of colour and emotion, and his eyes were dark and haunted. For a moment they gazed at each other in wordless agony, before he very slowly placed his bandaged hand on her back and drew her into his arms.

He had rescued her again.

She felt so good. So sweet and uncomplicated after Arabella's savage guile.

The enormity of Arabella's allegation was like a boulder on his chest. It crushed him, so that he wanted nothing more than to thrust it away with all his strength. He didn't trust her.

'Boy or girl?' Rachel whispered.

He held his head very upright, for fear that if he felt her hair brush against him he would be lost.

'Boy.'

'How old?'

'Ten weeks.'

The music of the string quartet was soft and innocuous. Rachel moved with absent-minded fluidity in his arms, so that he could feel her spine flexing beneath his hand. Holding her so close was almost unendurable. Her voice was soft and distant.

'What's his name?'

Orlando's hand tightened convulsively on hers. He closed his eyes briefly.

'Felix.'

He felt her move her head, tilting it backwards so she could look into his face.

'Your brother would be pleased about that, wouldn't he?'

He laughed bitterly. 'Oh, yes. Extremely pleased.'

'Congratulations.'

He shook his head. 'No. Don't say that.' He gave a crooked, humourless smile and echoed her words from yesterday. 'It's not a "congratulations" situation.'

'How can it not be? You have a child...'

'I only have Arabella's word that he's mine.'

He'd always been careful. In those days he'd never been without a wallet full of condoms. Had always used one. Always.

In those days. But not last night. He hadn't used one then.

He swore softly.

Rachel stopped, standing still in the centre of the other dancing couples, in roughly the same bit of floor where he had lain her down less than twenty-four hours ago and lost himself in the miraculous softness of her skin, the evocative rose scent of her hair, the caress of her brilliant hands. Then she had been so uncertain, so vulnerable, but now he could sense her strength.

'She wouldn't lie about something like this, Orlando. Not in these days of...of DNA tests and everything. You're shocked just now—who wouldn't be?—but you have to believe her. You mustn't deny your child a good father. He deserves better than that.'

Neither of them moved. Orlando's face was like granite as he stared straight ahead. His narrowed eyes had darkened to the colour of winter seas, and were opaque with fathomless emotion.

'You're right.' he said slowly, letting his hand fall away from her back. His other hand still held hers, and for a moment he smoothed his thumb across her palm, sending sparks of desire shooting up her arm.

'Thanks for the advice.'

And then he very carefully let her hand go. Without looking back, focusing all his energy on making it to the door, he walked away, taking her words with him as certainly as if she had just carved them on his heart with a rusty nail.

She was right. So right. Little Felix deserved a great father. Which was why Orlando was going to have as little to do with him as possible.

CHAPTER NINE

THE party was coming to an end.

As Orlando walked through the dining room the caterers were clearing tables, and it dimly occurred to him that he hadn't seen Lucinda all night to thank her. He'd had more urgent matters on his mind.

Like his son.

Arabella was in no fit state to look after a goldfish, never mind a baby. The ball-breaking alpha-female whose chilling competence had always terrified the designer pants off the men she worked with had simply collapsed, leaving Orlando no choice but to pick up the slack. Baby Felix would have to stay at Easton while she got herself straight again, and, knowing Arabella, it wouldn't be long before she was with another man...

He stopped beside a table, leaning against it for a moment. He hoped to God it would be someone decent...someone who would stick around. Someone reliable and kind, who would kick a football around with Felix, teach him card games and read him stories. Someone who would be the sort of father Orlando could never be.

He would do everything he could for the child, of course— see that Felix was generously provided for, both in the short term and in his will, ensure that he received the best care and education. But he would do it at a distance. Felix would never have the burden of knowing his blind father.

On the table was a Chinese vase of his mother's, which had

stood in the same place for as long as he could remember. Now it held a dramatic arrangement of tall branches entwined with tiny, twinkling lights. Absent mindedly he reached out and touched one of the branches, thinking it must be something artificial Lucinda had brought from London.

It was rough and brittle. Real. Suddenly he remembered Rachel struggling through the door that afternoon, her arms full of cumbersome branches...

Had *she* done this? He'd sneered at her at the time, but maybe he'd underestimated her.

Briefly he cupped one of the tiny snowflake-shaped lights in the palm of his hand, feeling its warmth, able to see the glow it cast on his skin. It was only small, but the light was surprisingly powerful, and it transformed the stark branches into something beautiful. Something useful.

He closed his hand tightly around it, and the light went out.

For a moment he held it like that. And then he let it go and walked on to say goodbye to his guests.

By the time she finally climbed into bed Rachel ached in every bone of her body, and her face hurt from smiling.

Switching out the light, she lay in the darkness, willing sleep to come but feeling her eyes sting with the effort of keeping them closed. Her breathing seemed too loud, her heartbeat too fast, and her brain couldn't seem to stop endlessly repeating the same tortuous loop of thought, like a faulty recording. She longed for the release of oblivion.

She didn't know how long she lay there before she heard the unmistakable sound of the door clicking open, and watched as a thin sliver of faint light fell across the floor.

'Rachel?'

It was Orlando's voice, and as she replied she knew her own was suffused with a terrible, obvious hope.

Slowly his face swam into focus, a long way above her, ghostly and remote. 'I need your help.'

The hope died instantly. 'Of course…' She got out of bed, noticing that he had carefully stepped backwards to allow her to pass. She swallowed her humiliation and misery. 'What… what's happened?'

As they went out into the corridor she became aware of the distant crying of a baby, which got louder and more insistent as he hurried her through the darkness. As they turned into the front-facing landing it sounded unbearably distressing, and Orlando's fingers, trailing along the wall, fell back to his side and stiffened slightly as he approached a door halfway along the length of the corridor.

He hesitated, as if steeling himself for what lay beyond it, then pushed it open.

Inside, the light was on, and the sudden brightness after the shadowed corridor made Rachel blink. The room was in chaos, and as she stepped over the clothes dropped on the floor she recognised them as Arabella's—the tight black trousers and thin chiffon top she had been wearing earlier. One stiletto-heeled boot lay at an angle beside the bed, as if it had been thrown there hastily as she'd fallen into the bed.

Or been pulled?

With massive effort Rachel averted her mind from the image, and her eyes from mass of dark blonde hair fanning out across the white pillowcase, focusing instead on the scarlet, screwed-up face of the baby beside Arabella. The cries had reached fever-pitch, but she slept on, oblivious.

Rachel stood there helplessly, momentarily unable to think clearly. The noise was all-consuming and urgent, like a police siren, and she cast a panicky glance at Orlando.

He was leaning against the door, his head tipped back, his face utterly expressionless. It was as if he had been turned to stone. Her mouth opened to speak, but she was too shocked to find the words, too distracted by her desperate compulsion to stop the crying. Without thinking she went over to the bed and picked up the baby, holding him awkwardly at arm's length for a moment, before folding him into her body, cradling his head, rocking him, crooning.

'There…there…shhh…shhhhhh…'

Gradually, miraculously, the tiny red face relaxed and the ferocious cries subsided into gulping bleats. Still rocking, still whispering soothing nonsense, Rachel watched the baby's dark eyes fix on her, following the movement of her mouth, watching her intently as fat tears wobbled on his spiky dark lashes.

He was beautiful. She'd never seen a small baby at such close quarters before, and was taken aback by his perfection. Wonderingly she let her gaze travel over his ruff of soft black hair, the slanting, watchful eyes and the lovely mouth that were so heartbreakingly similar to…

'Thank God for that,' said Orlando coldly from the door.

Rachel was unaware that she'd been smiling until she felt that smile die on her face as she looked up at him.

'Oh, my God…' she breathed. 'You bastard. You were so keen to pick up where you left off with *her*—' she tossed a contemptuous look at the inert figure of Arabella in the bed '—that you forgot you had a child to consider. How could you? How *could you*?'

Orlando took a step forward into the room. His face felt like a mask—a hard, brittle mask, behind which he was slowly disappearing. Rachel had totally misunderstood the situation, but there was little point in enlightening her.

'Not easily,' he said coldly, 'when he makes a noise like that.'

'He just needed to be picked up!' Rachel hissed furiously. Orlando saw her lift one hand, shielding the baby's head as if she could protect him from the tension that spat and crackled in the room. 'He probably needs to be fed, for God's sake. Did that not occur to you? Or *her*?' She made a dismissive gesture at the champagne bottle that Arabella must have brought up with her while he was downstairs, dancing with Rachel in his arms. 'Or are *those* the only bottles she's interested in?'

'I'm afraid so,' he said tonelessly, picking up a large black leather bag. 'Milk and bottles are in here, I think. As well as nappies and whatever. Could you do it? I have something important to see to.'

'Important?' she repeated quietly, taking the bag from him. '*Important?* Bloody hell, Orlando, you amaze me. I thought you were...' Awkwardly she hoisted the bag onto her shoulder, trying not to disturb the baby. 'Well, it doesn't matter what I thought. I can see how wrong I was. You're not worthy of being a father. Your heart is made of stone.'

She stormed past him, and when she'd gone he shut the door quietly behind him and went to stand at one of the windows on the landing, looking down into the courtyard below. The candles had all burned out, leaving nothing but shadow. Panic and despair rose inside him, swift and choking, taking him by surprise so that he had to gasp for air.

She was right about one thing. He wasn't worthy of being a father. How could he be when he couldn't see to make up a bottle, couldn't trust himself to carry his tiny son downstairs? But she was wrong about the other. His heart was not made of stone. How much easier everything would be, he thought with savage desolation, if only it was.

A rose-pink dawn was creeping over the snow-covered lawns and stretching tentative fingers into the shadowy kitchen. Sitting uncomfortably in the big Windsor chair, Rachel struggled to keep her eyes open.

In her arms Felix slept peacefully, his pinched face now softened and replete. For long hours she had gazed at it, watching his eyelids flicker, his exquisite mouth twitch into a miraculous tiny replica of Orlando's ironic, crooked smile. His skin was pale, transparent, warmed now by the soft light of the new day, but it was his hands that captivated her most. She watched them flex and curl, as expressive and eloquent as those of his father.

Hovering halfway between sleeping and waking, she found herself unable to think of anything other than Orlando's hands.

She let her head fall against the high back of the chair and felt delicious warmth wash through her as she remembered him undressing her in the moonlight, his fingers moving over her quivering skin, brushing her face, closing over hers as she struggled with his tie...

Her eyes closed, and she was suddenly struck by a vivid image of him walking ahead of her through the gloom, his long fingers brushing the wall, almost as if...

Her head jerked upright, her eyes flying open.

Coming into the kitchen, Orlando walked straight over to the kettle, snatching his hand away as he touched its hot surface. He whirled round.

Rachel was curled up in the big Windsor chair at the head of the long kitchen table. He could see that her knees were tucked up, her head awkwardly resting to one side. He couldn't tell if she was asleep or not, nor see any sign of the baby.

Swiftly he crossed the room, coming to stand over her. As he did so she raised her head, and although he couldn't see her eyes, he could feel them burning into him.

'You should be in bed,' he said gruffly.

There was a small silence, in which he heard her soft, indrawn breath. 'Yes,' she said eventually, with barely controlled anger. 'Yes, I should be in bed. I'd love to be in bed. But that particular luxury was reserved for you and Arabella.'

Orlando turned away and went back to the kettle. He hadn't been to bed, but he didn't tell her that. He'd been up all night, thinking, planning, and had waited until a decent hour this morning to phone an old friend from his RAF days, whose wife was a doctor in a general practice. She had confirmed that it sounded very much as if Arabella was suffering from post-natal depression, and that it would be best for everyone if he supported her decision to have a complete break from the baby.

But she, like everyone else, didn't know of his own medical problems.

'Where is he?' he asked casually, as he switched on the kettle and reached for a mug.

'Here,' she said sardonically, as if she were stating the blindingly obvious.

Fair point, he thought grimly.

Out of the corner of his eye he watched her unfurl her long legs. The baby was nestled against her, and he understood now how she had curled herself around him, cradling him with her body as he slept. Her feet were bare, and she was wearing nothing but the ivory silk nightdress he had peeled off her so hungrily two nights ago.

He felt his heart thud uncomfortably in his chest as guilt, gratitude and a handful of other, far less noble emotions and impulses clashed inside him.

She was standing up now, and he could see the baby's dark head against her creamy shoulder. She must be freezing.

'Why didn't you go back to bed? He's asleep, isn't he?'

She gave an incredulous gasp. 'And do *what*, exactly, with *your son*? Where was I supposed to put him down? You asked me to look after him and I said I would—although believe me I wouldn't have been so accommodating if I'd known it was going to be for half the bloody night! Stupidly, I thought you meant just until one of his parents could tear themselves away from their joyful reunion to come and take over!'

Her furious words exploded and died in the quiet kitchen.

Orlando gave her a cool smile.

'Sorry. It was unreasonable to leave you with him for so long.'

'Too right it was unreasonable! I know nothing about babies. I've never even picked one up before. I didn't know what to do...'

'He doesn't seem to have any complaints.' Orlando nodded curtly at Felix, whose small, starfish hand had come up and grasped a lock of Rachel's hair. He turned away and busied himself with the coffee, to try and distract himself from the sudden surge of acid envy and resentment that rose in the back of his throat. History was repeating itself, he thought with sardonic self-mockery. Felix would be delighted to see his namesake cradled so tenderly in the slender arms of the girl Orlando craved. It seemed the old rivalry was set to run and run.

'He's lovely,' said Rachel softly. 'Which just makes your behaviour all the more despicable. And as for Arabella…'

'She's not well,' Orlando said shortly.

'Wh-what do you mean?'

'Post-natal depression. She's completely unfit to look after a child.' Some sense of loyalty and protectiveness to the baby prevented him from adding that even if she hadn't been ill Arabella felt the same way about babies as most people did about plague-carrying rats.

'She's in a bad way,' he continued blandly. 'The guy she was living with in London dumped her because he suspects the baby isn't his.'

'For crying out loud, he'd be mad not to,' Rachel snapped. 'Look at him, Orlando. Just look at him!' Deftly she moved the baby from her shoulder to the crook of her arm, and crossed the kitchen towards him. 'He's *yours*—can't you *see* that?'

Her voice was raw with contempt, and her words seemed to reach inside him and wrap around his heart, squeezing all the good, honourable, civilised feelings out of him.

'No,' he said very quietly. 'No, I bloody can't.'

There was a long silence. Neither of them moved. He could feel the blood thrumming through him, filling his head with a primitive, insistent pounding. *What had he just said? What the hell had he just said?*

He'd all but told her.

Great. Excellent idea. Tell her. Shock her into leaving or shame her into staying out of pity and guilt. Perfect.

He glanced dismissively down in the direction of the baby. 'I don't see the likeness at all, actually—I'm much taller than he is, for a start—but at the moment that's hardly the point. The fact is, Arabella needs a break. She wants to go to Paris for a while—

she's booked herself into some private spa or something. Which means I'm left holding the baby.'

'Huh!' said Rachel scathingly. 'Don't you mean *I* am...?'

He looked down at her, fixing his eyes on where he thought hers would be, staring into the blackness in the centre of his vision and picturing the luminous amber eyes that had haunted him for weeks after he'd seen that poster. It took all his self-control to keep every trace of emotion out of his voice as he smiled grimly.

'Funnily enough, I was just coming to that.'

CHAPTER TEN

THERE was no more snow in the week following the party. The garden, which had been so suddenly transformed into an enchanted wonderland on the night of Rachel's arrival at Easton, slowly thawed back into damp, grey reality. Like her hopes.

It had been a terrible week, during which she must have asked herself a million times what the hell had made her agree to Orlando's request that she stay on to look after Felix. After all, there were countless compelling reasons for saying no. The fact that she knew nothing about babies might have been a good one to start with.

Straightening up, and tossing another tangle of branches on the pile she had already hacked down, Rachel felt the ache in her shoulders. On the amount of sleep she'd had in the last five days it was perhaps stupid to be out here in the biting cold, making futile attempts to tame the walled garden, but it felt good to be doing something, and the growing mountain of cuttings combined with the ten metres or so of pathway she had cleared gave her a sense of achievement. It also beat staying inside the house, where the atmosphere was several degrees colder than out here in the freezing air.

She paused to survey what she had done so far. With the worst of the brambles and overgrown weeds stripped back, the bones of the formally laid out garden were beginning to emerge. Yesterday she had had the very great excitement of discovering an old stone seat in what had obviously once been some kind of rose arbour. Felix's pram stood there now, and she wandered over and sank down gratefully beside it, looking in at him as she did so.

He was still asleep, thank goodness, his long black lashes sweeping over his flushed cheeks, no doubt exhausted by yet another wakeful night.

He wasn't the only one, she thought ruefully.

After five broken, sleep-deprived nights she was light-headed and spacy with fatigue, aching in every bone and muscle, and more ill-equipped than ever to deal with the constant demands of looking after a small baby. She felt as if she'd been abandoned in the middle of the Amazonian rainforest without a map or a compass. The fact that she wouldn't have known how to read a map or use a compass was almost irrelevant; it was the abandonment that hurt.

Since Arabella's departure, Orlando's withdrawal from both her and the baby had been total.

Looking down into Felix's sleeping face, Rachel felt a stab of anguish. In spite of everything—the torturous nights, the endless challenge of making up bottles and changing nappies—he was utterly adorable. Orlando's relentless refusal to even acknowledge him was as incomprehensible as it was devastating.

She had been so utterly sure that he was better than that. In him she had thought she'd found a man who proved that Carlos's shallowness and her father's fecklessness weren't common to all men. That heroes still existed.

Wrong.

Sadly she tucked the pashmina she had wrapped Felix in more snugly around him, wishing she could keep out the hurt of being unwanted as easily as she could keep out the cold. Impulsively she trailed a caressing finger down his plump rosy cheek, and instantly felt a thud of alarm.

It felt hot. She thought straight away of Lucinda, and the speed with which she'd succumbed to that awful virus. Flu could kill babies, couldn't it? Did Felix have flu?

She took a step backwards, breathing out slowly and trying to quell her mounting panic. Of course he didn't have flu, she rationalised. Lucinda had gone by the time Arabella had arrived; he hadn't even been in contact with her. He felt hot to her because her hands were so cold.

Nevertheless she found herself turning the pram and beginning to hurry back towards the house. He'd slept for longer than usual that morning, but she'd put that down to the two hours he'd been awake in the early hours. She'd fallen into a weary routine at night, bringing him downstairs when he refused to be settled by a bottle, and propping him in his car seat while she played the piano. So far it had never failed to soothe him, and, equally importantly, she found it soothed her too, by giving her something familiar to hold onto. A reminder that she was actually good at something.

Last night she'd played for longer than usual; surely that was why he was sleepy this morning? He couldn't be ill. He couldn't be…

Reaching the back of the house, she hefted the pram over the scullery step and bent down over the sleeping baby. Apart from the hectic flush on his cheeks he seemed fine—his breathing was normal and he was deeply asleep. He'd be crying if he was ill, wouldn't he?

Determinedly she kicked off her boots and walked into the kitchen. She was overreacting, she told herself sternly as she took a pizza out of the fridge and, pulling off its cellophane wrapping, slid it into the vast stainless steel oven for lunch. She was too tired to think straight, never mind make anything more sophisticated. After all, what was the point? Orlando hadn't shown any interest in the things she had taken trouble over. She'd spent all afternoon making laboriously spaghetti Bolognese the other day, and he hadn't even come out from his office to try it.

Wearily she shrugged off the old wax jacket she had pinched from the boot room and went to hang it back up, looking into the pram as she passed. Felix's cheeks were positively glowing now.

Rachel felt an icy jet of adrenaline pulse through her as she pressed the backs of her fingers against his skin.

Her hands were tingling as the warmth seeped back into them, and against them he felt burning hot. She gave him a gentle shake, hoping to see his eyelids flutter open, but they stayed firmly, ominously closed.

'Oh, God,' she whimpered, seizing him and picking him up, still swathed in the pashmina. Clutching him to her chest, she rushed back into the kitchen.

Please, Felix, please…

'Orlando! *Orlando!*'

Startled out of sleep, Felix instantly began to scream, his face turning wine-dark with outrage. Rachel laid him on the table and with shaking hands began to undo the fiddly buttons on his pale blue coat. She needed to get him out of it so she could see him properly, but his back was arched, his small body rigid with fury as he cried.

'Orlando!'

God, he really was hot, she thought in panic: his face was burning to the touch now, and as she pulled down the neck of his vest she could see an angry red tide spreading down his chest. Dear God…what was the matter with him?

'Orlando…' she croaked, picking up Felix and holding him against her shoulder, automatically rocking him as blind panic choked her.

'What's wrong?'

He was there in the doorway, and she let out a cry of relief. As he came towards her his face was completely impassive, and in that moment she felt again his strength, the sheer unshakable capability of this man.

'I don't know… It's Felix. I don't know what's wrong with him. I think he's ill. He's so hot, and he won't stop crying, and—' She could hear the hysteria in her voice as she raised it over the noise of Felix's screams, but was powerless to control it.

In one swift movement Orlando's big hands had closed around the angry, bellowing form of his son and taken him from her. For a moment he held him upright, at arm's length, as the baby yelled in rage, and then, cupping one hand under Felix's head, with the other supporting his back, he began to rock him firmly.

Felix blinked, let out a half-hearted hiccupping gulp, and stopped crying, his dark eyes fixed on the face of his father.

The world beyond the steamed-up windows of the warm kitchen faded into a monochrome blur and time hung suspended. The only sound was the low, comforting hum of the fridge; the only movement was the rhythmic rocking motion of the small baby in Orlando's strong, able hands. The angry flush had faded from his cheeks now, and his eyes were bright. Rachel felt she was intruding on a very intimate encounter, but was powerless to tear her eyes away from Felix as his dark, curious gaze met and locked with Orlando's.

And then, with an sudden look of astonished joy and recognition, Felix's face broke into a wobbly smile.

Rachel's hands flew to her mouth. In that instant all the fatigue and frustration, all the confusion and insecurity evaporated, and she found herself torn between laughter and tears.

'He smiled,' she whispered incredulously. 'Orlando, he actually smiled…'

She glanced up and felt the fragile bubble of happiness pop. Orlando's face was as cold and hard as granite.

'Which just goes to show that he's fine,' he said curtly, thrusting Felix unceremoniously into her arms again. 'Now, if the immediate crisis is over, maybe I could get back to work?'

He was halfway across the kitchen before Rachel found her voice again. Unfortunately sensible words were a little harder to locate.

'God…you…you…. How *could* you? He *smiled*! Don't you understand? That was his *first smile*!'

Orlando didn't flinch. Not a flicker of emotion passed across his perfect face.

'I'm not surprised. He hasn't exactly had much to smile about, has he?'

Rachel gasped as if she'd just been winded. 'You bastard. You absolute, irredeemable *bastard*! It means *nothing* to you, does it? You are so bloody wrapped up in yourself that you can't see what's going on right in front of you!'

Orlando's mouth quirked into a humourless smile at that. 'Interesting. Please, do go on,' he said, very softly.

Rachel tilted her chin and looked at him. 'You're letting him down, Orlando. With every day that passes you are letting your child down more and more spectacularly. And I can't just stand by and watch you do it. He needs you!'

'In that case maybe you'd like to go and talk to the American Chief of Defence about international security issues while I change nappies?' Orlando's voice was quiet, and terrifyingly polite, but there was a lethal edge to it that should have set alarm bells ringing in Rachel's head. But she was too tired, her emotions too raw, to pick up on the atmosphere of dangerous calm that had suddenly fallen.

'International security?' The words flew from her mouth in a rush of scorn. 'Oh, *please*! Forget saving the world for a few days, can't you? What about the security of your *son*? He doesn't need a goddamned superhero; he just needs a father!'

'I see. Is that all?'

His eyes were narrowed to dark, glittering slits, but his face was expressionless. Suddenly his absolute indifference was too much. It was as if a dam had burst inside her and all the frustration and anxiety and anger and longing of the past week had been unleashed in one crashing tidal wave.

'No,' she said through bloodless lips. 'Seeing as you asked, that is not *all*! You told me I lacked courage, and I listened to you—I learned from you—and, boy, have I got braver. Which is why I'm going to say this. *You* lack courage, Orlando. You might have been some hot-shot fighter pilot, you might have risked your life on a daily basis for the service of your country, but only because it made you look good, *heroic*, so that girls like Arabella would throw themselves at your feet and into your bed. Well, good for you. But it's time to grow up now. This is where the real business of being a hero starts—and, you know, it's hard and it's thankless, and it means you have to stay up all night and you don't even get laid. But you have to give your son someone to look up to.'

Orlando stared at her, his head tilted backwards in his habitual attitude of utter disdain.

'That was quite a speech,' he drawled mockingly. 'You've obviously spent plenty of time carefully identifying my numerous shortcomings. Am I to assume that your thorough character analysis includes no redeeming features whatsoever?'

She glared at him as her eyes filled with tears. 'If you'd asked me that a week ago I would have had a very different answer. I thought you were the most astonishingly brave and strong person I'd ever met. But now I can see that I mistook bravery and strength for callousness and coldness.'

He nodded slowly. 'In that case it's just as well I've been looking into making more permanent arrangements for Felix. You'll be delighted to know I've spoken to an agency, and they can have someone here by Monday.'

Rachel stepped backwards, as if she'd been slapped. She could feel the blood draining from her face and her eyes widening in shock.

'No!'

'It'll be better for all of us.'

He turned on his heel, making for the door, but she caught up with him, placing herself and Felix in front of him. 'Orlando, no—you can't! He's had too much change in his life already. He's just got used to me…and—and I've just got used to him!' She was aware that she sounded as if she was pleading, but she was too shattered to care. All she knew was that the thought of leaving Felix was unbearable, and she found herself impulsively reaching out and touching Orlando's arm.

It was a very, very bad move indeed. As her fingertips brushed his skin she almost passed out with longing.

Leaving Felix? If only it was that simple.

'He managed without you before; he'll manage without you again.'

Rachel tried again, feeling as if she was arguing for her life. 'I'm doing OK now, honestly. I can look after Felix just as well as anyone—it's been a tough week, but the worst is over now, and I've learned so much. Especially when you think of how clueless I was when I first arrived—'

She broke off, looking round in alarm, suddenly aware of a horrible smell of burning plastic coming from the direction of the oven. Orlando beat her to it, swearing viciously as he opened the door to release thick clouds of noxious black smoke.

'The pizza!' Rachel wailed. 'But it's not even supposed to be ready yet!'

Swiping ineffectually at the smoke, she grabbed a towel and pulled out the shelf. Melted plastic dripped down between the bars from the polystyrene disc on the base of the pizza, which Rachel had forgotten to remove. Holding it at arm's length, she crossed the room and deposited it in the bin.

When she turned back she saw a flash of grim triumph on Orlando's face.

'You were saying?'

It would be better when she was gone, he thought bleakly as he crossed the hallway. Felix would get used to someone else…someone who didn't cook pizza with the plastic still on, and make damning accusations when she was in possession of only half the facts. Someone who didn't put the radio on and dance with him in the kitchen, or wrap him in her soft, rose-scented scarves, or soothe him when he was fretful in the night by playing Chopin to him in the moonlight.

Orlando's first heroic act had been to let her stay at Easton. His second would be to let her go. Felix would forget. It was just his father who was sentenced to a lifetime of remembering.

CHAPTER ELEVEN

'HUSH Felix…please, darling… It's all right, it's all right…'

Rachel gritted her teeth and tried to make the straps of the car seat meet across Felix's furiously squirming body as his howls intensified, inches away from her ear. With her car out of action, she had borrowed Orlando's to come into the village for supplies, but it was so ridiculously low that she had to virtually bend double to fasten the seat in place. As hostile to babies as its owner, she thought viciously, bashing her head against the top of the car as she stood up.

'Bloody, *bloody* hell!' Rubbing the back of her head with one hand, she picked up a bag of shopping with the other and threw it into the car. It hit the catch of the glove compartment, which fell open, disgorging its contents into the shopping bag. Felix screamed even louder.

Rachel slammed the door, closing her eyes briefly as the noise was abruptly, blissfully, reduced. Since her encounter with Orlando at lunchtime she had felt as she had just before her wedding—filled with helpless dread at what lay ahead. The difference was that then he had been the one to show her a way out. This time he was the cause of her anguish.

But she had come a long way in the last week. It was amazing, she thought miserably, considering Orlando hadn't been talking to her for most of that time, exactly how much he had taught her. The meaning of the word orgasm was one. That she could influence the course of events if she felt strongly enough was another.

And, boy, did she feel strongly about this. She had no intention of just walking away from Felix now. She knew too well what being rejected by your father and growing up in a loveless home felt like.

Making a visible effort to collect herself, she walked round to the driver's side and got in, starting the engine and turning on the radio in an attempt to comfort Felix.

But he was tired and hungry and refused to be soothed. Rachel drove quickly, one hand stroking his cheek, frantically trying to quieten him. But then, as Chopin's *Nocturne in E Minor* came on, filling the small space of the car with memories and longing, she gave up, and they both cried all the way back to Easton.

Rachel longed for an hour-long soak in scented water to calm her frazzled nerves and soothe the ever-present ache in her neck and shoulders, but there wasn't time to bath both Felix and herself before making a start on dinner. She'd discovered that the village boasted an award-winning butcher on the high street, and had thrown herself on his mercy, telling him she needed to cook something foolproof but fantastic. He'd recommended duck, fresh in that lunchtime, and told her exactly what she had to do. She wanted to get Felix settled for the night before making a start.

At the last minute she decided to get into the bath with him, shivering as she stepped into water which, to her, felt only lukewarm. As a tiny concession to vanity she added a dash of her rose-scented bath oil, and, lying back in the chin-deep claw-footed bath, with Felix beached on her chest like a baby seal, she was overwhelmed with anguish and love.

Where would she go if she had to leave here?

Her old life now seemed as remote and unimaginable as snow on a summer's afternoon. Musingly she calculated the date, working out that the concert she had been scheduled to give at the end of her honeymoon was due to take place in just two days.

Idly trickling water on Felix's back, she thought of Carlos. He'd always appeared to her like some evil puppet-master, controlling the world around him as effortlessly as he controlled his orchestra, but surely this situation was beyond even *his* influence? He would have had to cancel the entire tour. The thought gave her a shameful moment of pleasure.

Felix was almost asleep now. Tenderly she gathered him up and stepped out of the bath, wrapping him in a towel and laying him gently on the floor while she slipped back under the water to wash her hair for the first time since the party.

It was hardly the most luxurious beauty regime, but it would have to do. Tonight wasn't about seduction. Tonight was about sense. She wanted to impress Orlando with her maturity and competence—show him she was indispensable, not irresistible. After all, she'd tried that before and it hadn't got her anywhere. He'd managed all too easily to resist her from the moment Arabella had reappeared.

Rinsing the last of the shampoo out of her hair, she sighed and stood up. Even if she'd had all the time in the world there was no point in going to any more trouble anyway. Orlando always looked straight through her.

Downstairs in the kitchen, she set Felix down in his little bouncing chair while she boiled water for his bottle and unpacked the shopping. There was no sign of Orlando, but that was hardly unusual, she thought sourly. Felix was at his most adorable, his hair standing up in a soft dark halo from the bath, his tiny feet in the white sleepsuit kicking excitedly. As she passed she couldn't stop herself from taking them in her hands and raining kisses on him, revelling in the scent of him and in his tiny gasps and gurgles of pleasure.

'You're gorgeous.' She smiled, putting her finger into the palm of his hand and letting him curl his own small fingers around it in a surprisingly strong grasp. 'You're gorgeous and strong and handsome, no matter what your miserable excuse for a father says…. Yes, you are,' she cooed. 'And it's his problem if he can't see it…'

There was a cough from the doorway.

'Sorry to intrude on what's obviously a *private* conversation,' said Orlando acidly, 'but I came to get a drink. Don't let me disturb you.'

Standing up quickly, and disentangling her finger from Felix's octopus grip, Rachel felt a hot rush of colour flood her cheeks. Not that Orlando noticed, of course. He went straight to the fridge and took out a bottle of Sancerre. There was a careful deliberateness about his movements. He looked terribly, terribly tired, she thought, with a sudden flash of compassion which she quickly squashed.

It served him right. He should spend more time with his son and not work such stupidly long hours.

She managed a stiff smile. 'I'm cooking tonight. I hope you can stop work.'

He took down a glass and turned away while he sloshed some wine into it. 'I doubt it,' he said tersely.

It was suddenly very still in the brightly lit kitchen, and Rachel's soft exhalation of frustration and disgust was very audible.

'Fine. Doesn't matter.'

Orlando turned round and leaned against the marble worktop, his eyes boring into her over the rim of his glass. They were as pale as the wine, she noticed with a thud of irritation, feeling a horrible, unwelcome warmth begin to unfurl in the pit of her stomach and spread outwards into her limbs, like wreaths of smoke. His hair was untidy, where he'd been pushing his fingers through it, and there were lines of fatigue around his eyes.

'It's work.'

She busied herself spooning powdered milk into Felix's bottle. 'No problem. I just thought we could…talk. About Felix. But,' she said nonchalantly, 'if you're too busy that's fine by me. I'll eat alone.'

Her body was saying something completely different. His

presence changed the atmosphere in the room, charging it, instantly making the vast kitchen seem too small, too full of his broad shoulders, his penetrating gaze. Oblivious to the currents of hostility swirling around him, Felix gurgled away happily. Rachel was furious to find she'd lost count of how many spoonfuls of milk she'd put in the bottle.

'OK—look, I'll try.' He sighed heavily, making his way to the door, and Rachel felt her chest constrict with annoyance. 'I'll try. Just so long as you promise you're not cooking pizza.'

It was all she could do not to turn round and hurl the tin of powder at him as he left the room, and she allowed herself a small moment of self-congratulation at her admirable restraint.

He hadn't even noticed Felix. Hadn't so much as glanced at him.

Leaving the bottles to cool, she turned and scooped him up, nuzzling her cheek against his soft fuzz of hair. 'Oh, sweetheart, how could he fail to adore you? You're so lovely.' Frowning, she cradled his warmth against her and rocked him absent-mindedly as she finished emptying the shopping bag.

Right at the bottom was a leaflet. She took it out, glancing at it as she went to the bin to throw it away. It must have fallen out of the glove compartment when it had come open.

For a second everything seemed to stop. The clock on the wall, her footsteps across the stone-flagged floor. Her heart. And then it all came rushing back again, with a rushing of blood in her ears. Felix squirmed and whimpered in her arms, and she realised she was crushing him against her as a succession of emotions rampaged through her and understanding dawned.

Her hand shook as she held the leaflet and re-read the title. *Living with Sight Loss. A Patient's Guide.*

At ten past eight Orlando took a deep breath and opened the door of the library. It had been an incredibly exhausting week, with the Middle Eastern border crisis growing more tense and volatile by the minute. His ambitious tactical strategy had, at one point, seemed to be taking fourteen airmen directly to their own funerals, which had tested his reserves of inner strength to their absolute limit.

He'd just heard that the last plane was safely home.

He felt light-headed with relief. Now he wanted nothing more than to go to bed and sleep, deeply, for about a year. Or at least until Monday, when Rachel would be out of the way and he could slide quietly back into his uncomplicated life. His empty, isolated life, free from inconvenient feelings and painful emotions.

Out in the hallway it was quiet, but a surprisingly delicious smell of cooking was drifting through from the kitchen, and he realised with a small jolt of surprise how ravenously hungry he was. Distracted by work, he'd hardly given a thought to food all week, surviving on coffee and snatched slices of toast. He approached the dining room, thinking to walk through it to the kitchen to find Rachel, and came to a standstill in the doorway.

The room was lit with the glow of candles, placed in the old silver candelabra right in the middle of the table and in rows along the mantelpiece, where they were reflected in the mirror. The curtains had been left open, so in the blackness of the windows the candles shone like stars. The light they gave off was surprisingly bright. Soft, gentle, beautiful...but amazingly strong.

Just like the courtyard at the ball.

Which reminded him of several things—most of them in the territory marked *Dangerous*, but one of which was that he'd meant to try ringing Lucinda again. He'd telephoned her office yesterday, only to be told that she was still off sick, but that she'd asked for her sincere apologies to be passed on to him, along with assurances that he wouldn't be invoiced for the party organisation. At the time, he'd thought there had been some mix-up, and had quickly dismissed it. Now, seeing the candlelit room, he wasn't so sure.

Rachel had created those eccentric, stylish arrangements of branches at the ball. What else had she done?

He'd been very quick to dismiss her as being fey and primadonna-ish, just because she was so very different from Arabella...

Thank God.

Arabella was right. He'd never really loved her, but he'd admired her sharp mind, her well-maintained body and her aggressive high-achieving personality. Looking back on it now, he could see that he'd chosen her in exactly the same way he'd chosen his cars. Quite simply, he always had the best, the fastest, the sleekest model available. It would never have occurred to him to look at anything less, but the fact was that when the terrain had got rough, fast and sleek had been no use to him at all.

And, standing there in the familiar room that suddenly felt so different, he wondered whether if he hadn't been faced with losing his sight he'd ever have seen that. If it hadn't been for the curse of this damned disease everything would be as it was before: he'd still be flying, still with Arabella, and, if she was to be believed, Felix would still be alive. Would he go back?

'I hope this isn't keeping you from anything important?'

Rachel's voice from the opposite doorway was soft and hesitant. He turned his head in her direction, locating her in the dim, flickering light by the coppery gleam of her hair. He felt suddenly absolutely wiped out by the longing to feel it under his hands again.

He shook his head, walking towards her. 'No. It's been a bloody awful week. But the crisis appears to be over.'

'Crisis?'

'Border defence,' he said briefly, following her into the brightly lit kitchen. Going over to the fridge, he pulled out a bottle of champagne. 'We're celebrating.'

'What are we celebrating?'

'Survival.'

Rachel moved to the cupboard to get down glasses as he tore off the foil and effortlessly eased out the cork with his thumbs. His fingers had healed enough for him to have taken the bandages off now, but she could still see the livid dark red scars. Evidence of a more hidden suffering.

She felt unbearably shy, totally unable to look at him and yet paralysingly aware of his nearness. Since she'd read the leaflet things kept coming back to her…slotting inexorably into place— filling in the gaps to make a picture she'd almost known was there all along, from the moment she'd watched him trailing his fingers along the wall as she followed him upstairs. She'd judged him so harshly.

'Here.' Briskly, she took the bottle from him. 'I'll pour this if you could open some red. I should have done it earlier, but I couldn't find the corkscrew.'

He didn't want her to know. She respected that, and she would make it easy for him. God alone knew she'd made it difficult enough already, by repeatedly taunting him for not making enough fuss of Felix. For not being heroic.

She stopped, setting the bottle down for a moment, waiting for the bubbles in the glass to subside again, along with the fizz of remorse and longing that rose up inside her. God, but he was more heroic than she could ever have imagined. To have lost what he'd lost and bear it alone…

She suddenly remembered what he'd said that night when they'd made love. It seemed like a lifetime ago now, like something that had happened to someone else, but his words came back to her just as vividly as if he'd just spoken them. *'I lost something… Something I took for granted. And now I miss it. All the bloody time…'*

Picking up the two glasses, she held one out to him, making sure she put it into his hand.

'To survival.'

'And the end of the crisis?' she suggested quietly, silently cursing the transparent need in her voice.

Orlando took a long mouthful of champagne. 'For the time being,' he said resignedly. 'For tonight, at least, it seems peaceful enough. Tomorrow we can all start thinking of new ways to tear each other apart.'

'Is that how it seems?'

He was looking straight ahead, his eyes glassy with tiredness, a muscle flickering in his cheek. 'Sometimes. It's necessary and inevitable, but, yes. Sometimes I just get tired of planning for the next attack. Always being on the defensive.'

There was a long pause. Rachel averted her eyes from his ravaged, beautiful face and picked up the bottle. She had to have something to do with her hands, otherwise she wouldn't be able to stop herself from reaching up and taking his face between them and smoothing away the lines of exhaustion.

'Shall we go through?'

Orlando set down his glass and dropped his head into his hands while Rachel went back to the kitchen to get the food. He was relieved she'd turned down his offer of help; he was suddenly so overwhelmed with exhaustion he could hardly move.

Which made the effort of getting through dinner without giving himself away extremely unappealing, he thought despairingly. He let his head fall back and closed his eyes.

He heard her come back in. He heard the muffled clink as she put dishes down on the table. But above all that he heard the rustle of her clothes as she walked, the tiny sigh of her breath. And he realised that, despite being so tired he could barely think straight, every nerve was wide awake and taut with awareness of her presence. Her closeness.

He opened his eyes.

'You look shattered,' she said softly. He could hear the smile in her voice, but also the quiet note of anguish, and had to steady himself against it. He could feel his defences slipping, and he couldn't afford to leave himself exposed.

'I'm fine.'

She was leaning over the table, her skin gleaming in the candlelight. She was wearing some sort of dark top, low cut at the front, and he could make out all too easily the dark shadow of her cleavage. He felt his aching body instantly stir into life, and allowed himself a wry smile in the soft gloom. Just as well he couldn't see more. He'd be beyond control if he could.

The smile faded as lust kicked him in the ribs. His sight might be wrecked, but there was nothing wrong with his imagination. Or his memory.

'I hope you're hungry?'

'Ravenous,' he said dryly.

'It's duck. The lovely man in the butcher's shop told me how to cook it and everything, so hopefully I won't poison you, *but*—' She broke off, pausing to suck juice from her thumb before leaning over to take his plate. 'Obviously advising about the meat was as far as his expertise went.' She sounded breathless and apologetic. Orlando found he was smiling.

'Go on…'

'Well…I didn't know what else to cook. Or rather, I did, but I sort of forgot that I'd have to think about other things—I mean, there's a lot of things to think about cooking, and I didn't know how to cook anything else, *so*…' She put another dish in the centre of the table. 'It's chips, I'm afraid.'

Orlando let out a shout of laughter.

'I know, I know, I'm a disaster. And there I was, hoping to impress you with my supreme capability and domestic excellence, and I've blown it. Anyway, I thought if I shredded the duck we could just, you know, help ourselves. I didn't think we'd need knives and forks. Sorry.'

'Don't be.' Orlando lifted his glass to his lips and looked over at her as she sat down. The smile on his face felt unfamiliar. And good. And she'd just saved him from the tedious business of concentrating on cutlery and all the other complicated paraphernalia that waited to catch him out on every formally laid dining table. Which left him free to concentrate on her. 'Duck and chips is my absolute favourite,' he said gravely, leaning over and taking some of the velvety shreds of meat.

'Stop it. I'm trying.'

The light of the candles cast an incandescent aura around her, so he could see the outline of her cheek, the slope and swell of her throat and chest. He felt his throat constrict with sudden, crushing desire.

'I know you are. I'm grateful. And I owe you an apology.'

It was Rachel's turn to mock. 'Yes, you do. Probably more than one. Where would you like to start?'

'Careful,' he said lightly. 'I struggle with the concept of admitting weakness of any kind. It would be a good idea not to push it.'

He heard her soft breath of laughter. 'I see. And what if I tell you it's not weakness? What if I tell you that admitting to being less than perfect is a definite strength?'

He frowned as her words sank in. His voice seemed to have deserted him. Picking up a chip, he ran it slowly around the edge of his plate, soaking up juices from the perfectly cooked meat as he played for time.

No. Don't…

'Well…for a start I underestimated you….assumed the worst.'

'Oh, yes? I don't like the sound of this.'

'I never thought…' he began slowly, then stopped to take a mouthful of wine. Setting down his glass carefully, he gave her an ironic smile and continued. 'I never thought that duck and chips would work so well together.'

'*Orlando Winterton!* If you think that *that* is going to do for an apology, then—'

She broke off abruptly.

'Then what?' he asked quietly. He knew he was straying into dangerous territory, that tiredness was making his defences slip, but it also made it difficult for him to care.

'Then I will be extremely disappointed in you,' she said primly.

Orlando smiled painfully. 'I'd hate to disappoint. OK, I did underestimate you, and as a result I think I owe you a thank you as well as an apology. Would I be right in thinking that last week's ball was orchestrated largely by you rather than Lucinda?'

'No, not at all. She worked amazingly hard. I did hardly anything…'

'I see. Not the flower arrangements?

'Well, yes. But…'

'Not the candles in all the rooms, and in the courtyard?'

'Yes, I did that, but it was n—'

'It was *great*,' he said with quiet emphasis. 'It was perfect. This house hasn't looked like that for years. It brought it alive again, and I can't tell you how good that felt. It's been empty and dark for a long time.'

'It doesn't have to be.'

Her voice was very low, and he could sense her fear, her hesitancy, and behind it her naked longing. It made him want to get up and drag her across the narrow width of table between them and kiss the living daylights out of her.

For long, long moments neither of them moved. He heard the soft sound of her lips parting, and in the swirling, pulsing darkness in front of his eyes he pictured her tongue moving across them, moistening them…

And then, from the baby listening alarm in the kitchen, Felix's wail cut through the silence.

CHAPTER TWELVE

BURYING her burning face in Felix's milk-scented neck, Rachel gave herself a stern telling-off.

What was she thinking of? She'd set out to prove to Orlando how dependable she was, how capable and sensible. She wanted him to realise she was the best person to look after Felix, and behaving like some rampant nymphomaniac was hardly the right way to go about it.

'I am hopeless, Felix,' she whispered into his soft hair, before placing him back into the creaking depths of the antique Winterton crib. Instantly his mouth opened in a wail of protest.

'Oh, baby,' Rachel said in anguish, 'you mustn't cry. I have to go downstairs. I have to tell your gorgeous daddy that he mustn't get anyone else to look after you.' Felix screwed up his face and cried harder. 'Hush-a-bye, sweetheart. Hush-a-bye...'

It was no good. Sighing, Rachel scooped Felix up and held him against her shoulder, rocking and soothing with quiet desperation. 'I've already messed up with the food... Please little one, *please*...I need to talk to him. It might be the only chance I get... It's for your sake, you know. I can't bear the thought of leaving you...' She paused, pressing a kiss onto the top of Felix's head, and, dropping her voice to a whisper, added, 'Or him. I can't bear the thought of leaving him either...'

Standing at the window, she drew back the curtain an inch and gazed out into the darkness. There was no moon tonight, and the garden was shrouded in blackness. A hundred shades of black. She thought of the path she had discovered, the stone seat that had been hidden by tangled undergrowth and years of neglect. There was so much here that she wanted to do, so much that she had already grown attached to.

And at the centre of it all, dark and compelling, was Orlando.

On her shoulder Felix snuffled and hiccupped. Rachel felt his head lift questingly, and realised with a sinking heart that he wasn't going to go back to sleep without a bottle.

She sighed. 'Oh, sweetheart... You're as stubborn as your father. I give in.'

'You shouldn't,' said a low voice from behind her. 'You're far too nice for your own good. You should stand up to both of us.'

Cupping Felix's head, she whirled round.

She could see nothing but Orlando's silhouette against the light from the doorway behind him, his broad shoulders filling the space.

'Ah.' She sighed, turning back to face the dark garden again, swaying gently and rubbing the baby's small, curved back. 'I tried that earlier, remember? You asked me to leave.'

He waited for a heartbeat before answering. 'Not as a punishment.'

She could feel him behind her. A little way away, not close. But close enough for her skin to tingle with awareness and her stomach to tighten. She spun slowly round to face him. 'That's how it feels,' she said bleakly as her eyes filled with tears. 'That's exactly how it feels. And I know it's unreasonable, and it's my own stupid, stupid fault, but I've fallen in love with this boy...'

With a stifled sob she shifted Felix gently from her shoulder to settle him in the crook of her arm. He gazed up at her, his eyes dark and gleaming.

'I know I had no right, because he's not mine—he belongs to Arabella, and to you, but he's so lovely I couldn't help it. I didn't want it to happen. I wish it hadn't—'

'Don't say that.'

'But it makes it all so much more painful. I was supposed to be persuading you tonight to let me stay—proving to you that I was capable and efficient and the ideal person to care for Felix. But I've messed it up by forgetting to cook vegetables and crying *again*. No wonder you've found someone else to look after him, since most of the time I've spent in your company I seem to have been in floods of ridiculous tears.'

'Not ridiculous. It's been a pretty intense week. And anyway, that's not the reason I found someone else.'

'Then why?'

'I'm trying to break the habit of a lifetime and think of what's best for someone else for a change.'

His voice was as harsh and bleak as a Siberian dawn. Rachel bit her lip as a fresh tide of tears filled her eyes. She should be pleased that he was thinking of Felix, that he wanted what was best for him. It was awful of her to be so selfish.

She swallowed. She had to respect his right to make decisions for his son. Hell, there had been enough times over the last week when she had been desperate for him to show that even he'd noticed him. Maybe if she knew that he was going to be more involved she wouldn't mind leaving so much. If she just knew that Felix was going to be loved...

'Just promise me...' she said in a shaky voice. 'Promise that whoever looks after him will love him. I know he needs someone who'll know all about weaning and getting him into a proper sleep routine...'

She was momentarily distracted by Orlando's soft exhalation of amusement.

'You mean someone who'll know how to get him back to sleep without a personal Chopin recital every night?'

'Exactly—someone efficient and organised. But someone who'll love him too.'

'Arabella's efficient and organised. I'm not sure the ability to be loving and patient exists alongside those qualities.'

At some point, she couldn't say how or when, they had come

closer together, so that now they were standing with Felix almost cradled between them. Their heads were bent downwards over him. With a wrenching sensation inside Rachel remembered that Orlando couldn't see the way Felix's dark eyes shone in the dim light, the contours of his beautiful mouth. She took a deep, shaky breath.

'He's so like you, Orlando,' she said with quiet deliberation. 'His eyes might be blue, not green, but they darken like yours when he's cross or upset... And it's there in the shape of his mouth, with its perfect cupid's bow upper lip, and in his dark, arched eyebrows, and even in his hairline...'

It was a risk, she knew that, and the stakes were high. Orlando Winterton was the proudest, most remote person she had ever met; the barriers he had placed around himself were high and unbreachable. Slowly, hesitantly, she groped for his hand in the darkness and, taking it in her trembling one, brought it up to Felix's head.

She looked up at him. He was standing with his head tipped back in that way that she had always taken to be indicative of disdain, but which she now understood was to enable him to make the most of his limited field of vision. In the half-light his face was shadowed and impossible to read.

Anxiety twisted inside her. If she got this wrong she could lose everything, but since she was going to end up doing that anyway it hardly mattered. If her instinct proved right, Felix might just end up with a father.

'Even his hands are like yours. He's got your long, tapering fingers, and your beautifully shaped fingernails.'

Orlando hadn't moved his hand. It still rested against Felix's cheek, and Rachel watched, mesmerised, as his thumb very lightly caressed the whisper-soft hair at his temple. When she lifted her gaze she saw that the expression on Orlando's face was one of exquisite agony.

'I'll make a promise to you,' she whispered hoarsely. 'I promise that I'll go quietly—no more arguing or pleading—if you'll just show me that the person who will look after Felix and love him will be you.'

Orlando's head whipped sideways, as if she'd slapped him. He spoke through gritted teeth.

'I can't.'

'You can.' She kept her tone low, determined. 'You have to work, so of course you need the person from the agency to do all the day-to-day stuff, but you can be the one who *loves* him, the one he loves back and looks up to…'

He gave a low gasp of exasperation and pain and shook his head. 'Not going to happen…'

Rachel took a deep breath. 'Well, if you won't, I'm not leaving.' Then, heart pounding, she handed Felix to him.

'Think about it while I get his milk.'

Orlando took his son, his gaze fixed glassily ahead as Rachel silently left the room.

He didn't look down. He didn't have to.

Rachel had described him so lovingly that even without trying to fix his ruined gaze on something above Felix's face in order to bring it into the edge of his sight he could picture him. Maybe it wasn't accurate, maybe it owed a lot to countless dusty albums full of remembered pictures of himself and his brother as dark-eyed, dark-haired babies, but it had made his child real.

As if to emphasise this fact, Felix uttered a soft, clear sound that reached right into Orlando's heart and wrapped itself around it. He dipped his head, closing his eyes as his mouth brushed the top of the baby's downy head and breathed in. He smelt of baby powder and roses, and Orlando felt a knife turn in his ribs.

In the past nightmarish week his careful defences had been battered by a succession of powerful emotions. But he was used to keeping emotion at bay. He was a defence expert, for God's sake. He knew all the tricks.

Keep information on a need-to-know basis. To the point. Impersonal.

But she'd really got him now, hadn't she? Somehow, without him even noticing she had simply dissolved all his barriers until his heart lay exposed—as defenceless as the child in his arms.

God, for the first time in a year he felt almost human. Downstairs, sharing a meal in the candlelight he had forgotten, actually forgotten, that he wasn't *the person he used to be*, as Arabella had put it. Suddenly that person had ceased to matter. He was himself now, and Rachel had made him that.

But with humanity came pain. He could feel it now, crouching in the velvet darkness around him, waiting. He could open his heart to Felix, and take on the anguish of knowing he would never be a proper father, or he could keep him at arm's length, and as a punishment have to endure the torture of having Rachel close but impossibly forbidden.

Orlando Winterton was no stranger to suffering. But losing his sight was like a paper cut compared to the agonising prospect of losing his heart.

Rachel stood in the doorway, frozen with indecision, the bottle in her hand.

Orlando stood over the crib, Felix in his arms, his astonishing, heroic face lined with anguish. She longed to go to him, was almost bent double with the rush of longing that swept through her as she let her gaze travel over his massive shoulders, with their sense of restrained power, and down his strong arms to where Felix's small head nestled in his elbow.

She longed to go to him but she didn't want to intrude. This was what she'd hoped for. She couldn't break the moment now.

So she stayed where she was, watching in silent hope and fear and longing as Orlando lifted Felix higher in his arms and dropped a kiss onto the top of his head.

Maybe she did make a sound, because the next thing she knew he was looking towards her. Had she not known, she would never have picked up the almost imperceptible note of uncertainty in his low voice.

'Rachel?'

She went forward into the room. 'Here's his milk.'

'You do it.'

'Uh-uh. You have a magic touch—he's almost asleep already. If I take him he'll wake up again.' She put the bottle in his hand. 'Look—you just hold it for him like that, and he's clever enough to take it for himself…' Felix's little questing mouth found the teat of the bottle and sucked powerfully. Rachel watched surprise flicker over Orlando's shadowed face as he felt the tug, and then she quickly turned away, walking over to the bedside table and turning on her iPod, unleashing the first shimmering notes of Chopin's *Nocturne in E Minor* into the room.

Orlando's mouth twitched into a smile. 'I thought he preferred a live performance?' he murmured, so quietly that she had to go and stand beside him to catch what he was saying.

'I guess I'd be lying if I pretended I only played for his benefit,' she whispered apologetically.

He frowned. 'You miss it?'

'Of course. It's been my life for as long as I can remember. It's like losing a part of myself.' Suddenly she realised what she was saying, and stopped just in time. 'Oh…' she breathed in relief. 'He's asleep…' Gently she took the bottle from Orlando. 'You put him down. I'll be outside.'

She left quickly, before he could argue. Waiting on the landing, she listened intently, praying that Felix wouldn't choose this moment to do one of his amazing instant wake-ups.

He didn't. A few moments later Orlando came out and pulled the door half shut. As he turned round Rachel saw with a shiver that the barriers were back in place. His face was perfectly blank. She stepped forward.

'You see? You did it. You did it brilliantly. You fulfilled your side of the promise, and so now I have to fulfil mine.' She was trying hard, so very, very hard, to keep the break from her voice. 'You've shown me that you'll love him and look after him, so now I have to do as I promised and go quietly.'

'No. *No.*'

He took a step towards her, pulling her into his arms with something like desperation. He heard her cry out in sorrow and longing in the instant before his mouth found hers, and he felt her need as forcefully as he felt his own. It was agonising, impossible to endure, when the prospect of release was so within reach—like withholding drugs from an addict; he knew it was for his own good, but, God, he didn't care any more. At some point this evening he had gone way, way beyond caring about what might happen to him in the future, or about anything that he had been or felt in the past.

Everything was simple. He wanted Rachel. He wanted the firelight and the candleglow and the warmth and her vibrant, blazing hair. He was tired of endless darkness and cold.

'Orlando—' She tore her mouth from his, and he felt her hands push his face from hers, holding him at arm's length. 'I can't—'

She had been going to say that she couldn't settle for just one night, but the words died on her swollen lips as she looked into the indescribable green of his eyes and knew that she could. Whatever he was offering, she would take it. If she had to leave him tomorrow it would be better to have something to hold on to, to remember, than nothing.

'Rachel?' His voice was sharp, his eyes blazing into hers searchingly, and she had to remind herself that he couldn't see her, couldn't read the blatant longing in her face.

'I can't help wanting you,' she said in a hoarse whisper, dropping her gaze from his tortured face and pressing her mouth to the hollow at the base of his throat.

'I know.' It was a moan of despair. 'I've tried, but I'm lost…'

'Then we're lost together,' she sobbed, reaching up to pull his mouth back to hers, breathing in the scent of him, feeling the hardness of his stubble-roughened jaw against her palms. They stumbled backwards, and then she felt him grasp her hands, and he was pulling her along the corridor, quickly, urgently, until they both broke into a run.

They turned a corner into the front landing, where there were no lights on, and the inky shadows enveloped them. Rachel's footsteps slowed uncertainly and Orlando turned, taking both her hands in his strong, sure ones, drawing her forward.

'You're afraid of the dark?'

She stopped, her hold on his hands tightening, so he couldn't help but be pulled back to her. 'Not when I'm with you,' she said throatily, standing on tiptoe to reach his ear.

The low note of desire in her voice seemed magnified in the blackness. A second later Orlando was scooping her into his arms and striding down the remainder of the corridor to his room. Kicking open the door, he hesitated just inside the threshold to find her mouth with his, and her hand went up to hold his head, sliding across the hard plane of his cheek until her fingers were entwined in his hair, pressing him deeper into her.

He let her slither from his arms, setting her back on her feet so his hands were free to explore and reveal. The room was velvet black, and they were both sightless; he could feel her hands clumsily seeking the buttons to his shirt, fumbling to work them free. Her own shirt was soft, clinging perfectly to her narrow body, and without hesitation he swept it over her head.

He groaned as his hands found the rose-petal perfection of her skin, dropping his head hungrily to the silken dome of her shoulder, scraping his teeth against it, feeling the powerful shudder of desire that shook her as he trailed his fingers around her ribs to the fastening of her bra. Helplessly she grabbed his shirt in her fist, twisting it, pulling…

'I can't… Orlando—take it off.'

He pulled it over his head and she heard the soft sound it made as it landed on the floor at their feet. She took in a shivering gasp. For a moment they stood inches apart, unable to see each other but exquisitely aware. Then Rachel took a small step towards him, so that her nipples skimmed his bare chest. It was all she could do not to cry out in devastating ecstasy as she heard his indrawn breath and felt his head tip backwards.

It was the point of no return. Grasping her shoulders in both hands, he crushed his mouth down on hers, and she felt herself dissolving, disappearing into the chasm of yearning that she'd been tiptoeing around all week. She didn't know how they made it onto the bed, how the rest of their clothes disappeared, was only aware of the feel of him under her damp thighs, the hardness of his jutting hip bones, the concave sweep of his stomach, ridged with muscle, and beneath that the smooth, hard length of his erection. She was kneeling up, over him, and his hands came up to hold her steady, spanning her ribs, measuring, discovering, moving reverently over her breasts, her collarbone...

He was *seeing* her, she thought hazily. And that was her last coherent thought as she gripped him with her knees, rising up to take him inside her, and abandoned herself to blissful sensation.

CHAPTER THIRTEEN

IN DREAMS Orlando could always see perfectly again.

Falling into a deep, grateful sleep for the first time in days, with Rachel's head on his chest, he saw her properly. She was wearing her wedding dress, as she had had when she'd arrived at Easton and got out of the car with her vivid hair blowing around her like a pennant, and as she walked towards him her amber eyes were incandescent with love.

The picture was shattered as the telephone on the bedside table began to ring.

Rachel felt Orlando move beneath her, the sonorous beat of his heart fading from her head as a shriller sound took its place.

The phone.

She felt a dart of alarm. Telephones ringing in the middle of the night were only ever bad news weren't they? But every inch of her was still blissed out and glowing from Orlando's touch, and the outside world still seemed a long, long way off. With Orlando she felt safe.

In the darkness she could dimly make out the sweeping arc of his arm, moving over her to pick up the telephone, could feel the flex of his muscular chest beneath her cheek. She found she was smiling as she listened to his husky sleep-drenched voice.

'Orlando Winterton.'

And then she felt the smile dissolve from her face as he sat up. Moving sideways onto the cold pillow, she heard him swear viciously. She could just make out the muscles moving beneath the skin of his broad back as he thrust a hand into his hair. When he spoke his voice was steely.

'*Hell*. How is she?'

Rachel's heart had begun to thud uncomfortably, and the heavy contentment in her limbs had been replaced with icy pinpricks of dread. She could hear the voice on the other end of the phone, but not make out what it was saying. It sounded ridiculously tiny and innocuous; how bizarre that it could shatter her brief moment of happiness.

'What do you mean, you can't tell me?' Orlando got up angrily. For a moment she caught a brief glimpse of his magnificent body before it melted, ghost-like, into the blackness of the huge room and she was left with nothing to do but listen.

'I know I'm not her next of kin…but I'm the *father* of her *child*, for God's sake!'

So. There was no mistaking to whom he was referring. Or the anxiety in his voice.

Quietly Rachel slipped out of bed and found her way back to her own room. Without Orlando the darkness of the old house frightened her—but not nearly as much as the emptiness inside herself.

'She's in hospital. They won't tell me any more, other than that she's asking for me. I have to go.'

Rachel nodded wordlessly and, balancing Felix on one arm, collected up the breakfast cups and plates with the other. In the grey light of early morning, Orlando looked utterly shattered, his narrow, slanting eyes shadowed, his face gaunt and pale. How pathetic of her foolish heart to want so desperately to fold him into her arms when all that anguish was for someone else.

Bloody Arabella.

'I've made phone calls. All the Paris flights are booked up until this evening, so I've called in some favours with the RAF. We leave from Northolt at eleven.'

Rachel's head snapped round. 'We?'

Orlando sighed and pushed a hand through his hair. 'Sorry. I should have asked. She'll want to see Felix, so I'd like you to come with me.'

It was a measure, thought Rachel desolately, of her utter en-slavement to him that she only could feel relief. How astonish-ingly humiliating. She was actually *glad* to be accompanying him to the bedside of the woman he loved, because being left behind without him was too terrible to contemplate.

'OK.' She gave a wan smile. 'I'll go and get some things together.'

Orlando got up from the table and pushed his chair in with a violent scraping sound that set his teeth on edge. What was one more lie to add to the sprawling web of deception that his life had somehow become? he thought viciously. Arabella hadn't asked to see her son; she wouldn't be so selfless. No. Orlando wanted Rachel to come for far less noble reasons.

Because he couldn't face the journey on his own.

And because he was terrified that if he left her she wouldn't be there when he got back.

George drove them to the airport in Lord Ashbroke's old Daimler. Orlando sat in the front, with Rachel in the back, beside Felix in his car seat. As they drove through the high gateposts she turned round and gazed at Easton through the rear window, wondering when she would see it again.

If she would.

And, if so, under what circumstances.

For one difficult, painful, wonderful week she had felt as if it was her house, and she had allowed herself to care for it just as she cared for Felix. She had invested something of herself there as she had pottered about in that bright kitchen and torn her hands on brambles in the old walled garden.

The thought of Arabella returning as mistress of Easton was unbearable.

The only thing that was worse was the thought of her returning as mistress of Orlando.

There was what seemed to Rachel to be an entire uniformed squadron waiting to greet them on the tarmac as they pulled up alongside the small but luxurious plane. Orlando Winterton was certainly *somebody*, she realised, watching him from under lowered eyelashes as crewman after crewman saluted him. Not a flicker of emotion crossed his face. However, as the engines started and the plane began to gather speed along the runway, she noticed that his knuckles showed bone-white through his skin as his hands gripped the armrests of the cream leather seat.

'Last night...' She was looking straight ahead, and so missed the fleeting pained expression that crossed Orlando's face. 'Last night when you asked me whether I missed the piano... You knew the answer already, didn't you? Because that's how you feel about giving up flying?'

'Yes.'

It was impossible to explain that feeling. He missed it viscerally. It had been so much a part of who he was, and defined the part of him that had died that day in Andrew Parkes's office—the heroic, risk-taking, thrill-seeking part.

He closed his eyes briefly, tensing himself for the question that would inevitably follow. *Why did you give it up?*

But she said simply, softly, 'I can understand why. It must be an incredible feeling.'

Relief washed through him, but it was tinged with despair. Last night, when he'd kissed her in the corridor outside Felix's room, he'd crossed a line. That was the moment when he'd accepted that he wanted her...not just at that moment, but for longer. For ever. But he hadn't even told her the truth about himself yet.

He had to, of course. Soon. But...

God. How ironic. He was *afraid*. He, who had berated her from the moment they met for her own lack of courage, was frightened. And she had shown, time after time, that she was brave in ways he was only just discovering.

'It is. There's nothing like it,' he said gravely.

But that wasn't true either. Last night—with her hands in his hair, her mouth on his mouth, her legs around his waist—*that* had felt like flying, with the light coming up over the horizon and the dew forming rainbow diamonds on his wingtips. Holding her as she'd shuddered and cried out in his arms…*that* had felt like flying home into a clear pink and gold dawn.

The car that awaited them was long, black and impossibly shiny. It reminded Rachel very much of a hearse—which, given her mounting sense of dread, seemed horribly appropriate.

It was as if for the past week she and Felix and Orlando had lived in a sort of Eden, cut off from the rest of the world at Easton Hall. It had hardly been idyllic…most of the time she had felt lonely, confused and isolated…but it was only now that she realised how much strength and comfort she had gained simply from knowing Orlando was nearby. Looking back, she suddenly saw the days that had passed there as peaceful and sheltered, and the nights when she had played the piano into the listening darkness as magical.

As they inched their way through the Paris traffic she felt totally unprepared to return to reality. The world beyond the tinted glass of the car window seemed loud and aggressive, full of busy, indifferent people and glaring, garish sights and sounds. She sank back into the leather upholstery, closing her eyes and mentally searching for something to counter the assault of unfamiliarity and hostility. It was a trick she had been taught by one of her piano teachers, to calm herself down before a performance. All she had to do was pick an image and concentrate on it very hard, carefully filling in all the sensory details…

Standing holding Felix in the semi-darkness with Orlando. Close to him…looking down at Felix. Reaching out, feeling for Orlando's hand, her skin brushing his—feeling its warmth, the reassuring heaviness and solidity of his hand, hearing the whisper of skin against skin. Breathing in…slowly, steadily…the smell of warm, babymilk softness...and beneath it, like a haunting, bass note, Orlando's dry, masculine scent. Lifting his hand, bringing it up to Felix's head, raising her gaze to Orlando's face...

He breathing quickened, and she felt her heart-rate double as her mind, too far advanced down that particular track, refused to be called to heel. But then she was aware of other things—of the car slowing, making a sweeping turn, coming to a standstill.

She didn't want to open her eyes. She didn't want to let reality back in.

'This is the hospital.'

The tableau of the couple with the baby in the darkened room faded, and she slowly opened her eyes.

Orlando was reaching for the door handle. She watched his long, elegant fingers deftly move along the walnut inlay of the door to locate it and, once they'd done so, hesitate. He turned his head back towards her.

'I don't know how long I'll be. It's best that you go on ahead. I'll send a message to the hotel if she's up to seeing Felix.'

His eyes seemed very dark, opaque with emotions Rachel didn't want to think about. Feelings that had nothing to do with her and everything to do with the woman he was just about to see. There was a moment...a long, shimmering moment of unspoken possibility...when she wanted to find something to say that would sum up a fraction of what she was feeling. She didn't blame him for going to Arabella. She knew out of the two of them the other woman had the greater claim, she had never been led to believe anything else. It was just that she would have liked, in this last few seconds before he opened the door and was swallowed up by the outside world again, to tell him how much it had meant to her, this enchanted time. How very, very much.

He turned his head, so she could see him in profile. She caught the movement of his throat as he swallowed. She bit her lip hard, knowing that if she were to speak the only words that would come out would be *I love you.*

And then it was too late. He threw open the door and the world came rushing in, with a blast of sleet-edged air and a cacophony of city noise. Rachel watched him get out of the car in one lithe movement, his broad shoulders shielding her from the worst of the damp and cold for a second before he stood aside.

Her mouth opened in horror.

It was like an explosion inside her, spreading quickly outwards as the information was relayed to different parts of her body. There was a split second when it was just her eyes that registered the large poster on the building behind Orlando, advertising a concert that was taking place tomorrow night, and then the rest of her body caught up, going into full shock response as she stared at her own smiling face.

Orlando leaned back into the car—coming between her and Rachel Campion, concert pianist.

'We need to talk,' he said gruffly.

Rachel didn't answer. Her mind was in uproar. Craning her head to look past him, she looked again to see if, in her shock, she had initially missed the part that said the concert was cancelled. Surely Carlos and her agent and the PR people should have publicised the fact that it wasn't going ahead by now?

'Rachel, please…' Orlando's voice was infinitely weary and seemed to come from a long way away. 'I'm sorry to bring you all this way and abandon you like this… Look, I promise we'll talk later.'

'What? Oh. OK…'

Orlando's face darkened. She sounded utterly distant, utterly preoccupied. He'd spent the entire journey feeling absolutely eaten up with remorse for his emotional cowardice, steeling himself for this moment. He'd tried to bridge the chasm that he'd created around himself—only to find that she wasn't remotely interested in crossing it.

He straightened up and slammed the door, then waited until the car had pulled slowly away before he turned and went slowly up the steps to the hospital.

His head ached. Away from the familiarity of Easton, his reduced sight made every small thing a grinding challenge, so that just finding his way down the labyrinth of corridors towards the ward he was directed to triggered the same adrenaline surge he'd used to get during dangerous night-time search patterns over the North Sea.

He came to the end of a corridor, where it opened out into another high, elegant hallway. At the end was a desk. The nurse greeted him by name as he approached.

'Ah…Monsieur Winterton? It's good that you're here. Mademoiselle de Ferrers has been asking for you.'

'How is she?'

'Well, physically she is improving, there is no reason why we shouldn't discharge her in the next day or so, though mentally we are…concerned.' Orlando detected a distinct edge of frosty disapproval in her tone. 'She is finding it very difficult to come to terms with the fact that she will be scarred.'

Orlando felt as though an icy hand had closed around his throat. 'Was it a car accident? Was she driving?'

The nurse had picked up a clipboard and was examining it. 'No, *monsieur*. She had cosmetic surgery,' she said tonelessly. 'A breast-lift at an unregistered clinic in Switzerland. The surgeon was not aware that she had so recently had a child. It was too soon to do any kind of procedure, and unsurprisingly she suffered severe infection. She checked in here two days ago, and our doctors have done their best, but the scars may never disappear.'

The icy sensation dissolved, and was replaced by the much more familiar one of slow, burning anger. He managed a stiff smile.

'Thank you for your help. Now—may I see her?'

CHAPTER FOURTEEN

THE car door was opened and Rachel got out stiffly. The hotel in front of her looked a lot like Buckingham Palace, she thought dimly. Or how Buckingham Palace would look if it had been made over by Parisian designers: authentically period, but at the same time outrageously cutting-edge and chic.

Perhaps to ensure she didn't create a bad impression in the highly polished reception hall, in her faded jeans and ancient cashmere sweater, she was ushered straight to a room by a porter who looked as if he'd just stepped out of an advert for Armani suits in French *Vogue*. He carried the car seat as if it were an unexploded bomb, while in it Felix grizzled, and Rachel followed wordlessly, her mind so taken up with questions and suspicions that she hardly noticed the splendour of the halls and corridors they passed through.

What was Carlos up to?

Having delivered her to a suite the size of the average family home, the Armani porter dissolved away again. Rachel picked up Felix and looked slowly around her. The room in which she was standing was straight from a film set. Four tall sets of French windows opened out onto a wrought-iron balcony, each set framed by excessive amounts of sumptuous swagged silk. The walls were painted pale gold and inlaid with silk-damask panels, and the furniture was upholstered in the same shades of gold and ivory. The overall effect was swanky interior design magazine meets Madame Pompadour. Rachel wasn't sure if she ought to be wearing a crinoline and a powdered wig, or designer hotpants and a feather boa.

The air was heavy with the scent of the hot-house flowers which were placed in fleshy arrangements on every polished surface. Opening a door at the far end of the room, she found herself facing an enormous bed, over which a cascade of grey and gold striped silk spilled down from an antique corona of twisted gilt leaves.

Miserably she surveyed it. It was almost indecently romantic—a bed for making joyous, decadent love in, she thought dully, for spending lazy, lust-drenched afternoons in and drinking vintage champagne…preferably from each other's navels.

She turned away sharply as her mind veered straight back to last night, and her body obligingly provided an instant sensory replay. Darts of remembered bliss fizzed along her nerve endings as she recalled how he'd held her, running his brilliant, beautiful hands over her body, unleashing a storm of desire in her that had been almost violent in its intensity.

And the worst bit was, she couldn't be sorry. Even knowing what she knew now, even being here, on her own in the most romantic city in the world, while he went to the bedside of the woman he loved, she couldn't regret what they'd done.

Jiggling Felix absent-mindedly, she found herself standing in front of another closed door. She pushed it open, expecting perhaps a bathroom, and felt tears of self-pity spring to her eyes as she took in what it was.

Another bedroom, small and narrow this time, with a single bed covered in sensible blue and white check.

He'd booked a two-room suite. This must be her room.

The short, grey day was already giving way to night. Rachel had carefully measured out the afternoon by playing with Felix and giving him an early and much drawn out bath in the exquisite temple-like atmosphere of the *en-suite* bathroom, grateful for the sound of his squeals and gurgles in the oppressive atmosphere of such luxury. All the time her confused brain had ricocheted between tormenting thoughts of Orlando, sitting at Arabella's bedside holding her hand, and needling thoughts of Carlos.

Eventually, driven to distraction by the incessant questions hurtling around her brain like leaves caught in a whirlwind, she seized the telephone and dialled Reception, nervously stammering out an enquiry about the concert that was being advertised and the possibility of obtaining tickets. There was a pause, during which she could only just hear the concierge tapping details into a computer over the hectic hammering of her heart, before he came back to say he was very sorry, but the concert was all sold out.

'It is still going ahead, then?' she confirmed weakly.

The voice at the other end sounded surprised. *'Oui, mademoiselle.'*

Rachel had only just replaced the receiver when the phone rang again. Thinking it was the concierge, telling her he'd enquired further and had discovered he was mistaken, she grabbed it eagerly. But this time he was telling her that a car was waiting for her downstairs.

The first thing she saw, before she'd even set foot in Arabella's room in the hospital, was Orlando. He was asleep, stretched out on a square and uncomfortable-looking sofa opposite the doorway, with one arm falling to the floor like in the pre-Raphaelite painting of *The Death of Chatterton*.

Rachel stopped on the threshold as her heart jolted painfully against her ribs. Seeing him there gave her an extraordinary, powerful feeling of homesickness as well as longing. After the lonely hours in the gilded splendour of the hotel, the unfriendly city streets, in the strangeness of the hospital he looked achingly familiar. His head was thrown back, his dark hair falling away from a forehead that, in sleep, was smoothed of all its anger and its anguish. His beautiful lips were slightly parted, and one hand rested on his chest, his palm upturned, his fingers slightly curled.

Without thinking she crossed the room and, setting down Felix in his car seat, let her gaze travel over Orlando. There was a bone-deep ache inside her as she watched the slow rise and fall of his chest, the languid, almost imperceptible pulse in his neck. On the hand which lay across his chest she could see the still-raw scars on his fingers, and she was instantly transported back to the kitchen, to the breathless moment when she'd held him and his blood had run into her own hands and she'd felt his pain. She couldn't stop herself from reaching out to touch him...

The next moment she almost jumped out of her skin as an amused, mocking voice came from the direction of the bed.

'Darling, forgive me for intruding on this private act of worship, but I don't believe we've met properly.'

Rachel whirled round. 'Oh! Sorry! I was just...I mean, I didn't...' She was blushing furiously, aware that whatever she said was just going to make the situation worse. 'Sorry. I'm Rachel.'

Arabella was sitting up against a mountain of snowy pillows, wearing a silk wrap beneath which Rachel could just see bandages covering her chest. Aside from that, she didn't look ill at all. The eyes that were regarding Rachel so shrewdly were subtly made up with mascara and shadow. Through the fog of her humiliation Rachel noticed that they didn't even flicker in Felix's direction.

Arabella's immaculately glossed mouth spread into a slow, incredulous smile. It was as if she had suddenly come across a winning lottery ticket in an old handbag. *'Rachel,'* she said wonderingly. 'Yes, of *course*. How *amazing*.'

'Amazing? I'm sorry...I don't know what you mean?'

Arabella gave a soft laugh, but her narrowed eyes never left Rachel's face. 'You're too modest, Rachel. Far too modest. Here was I, thinking you were some sweet local girl Orlando had unearthed at Easton, but you're not, are you? Far from it—you're *Rachel Campion*, concert pianist and, according to those in the know, the Next Big Thing.'

Rachel shook her head emphatically, unaware that she was edging towards the door. 'No,' she protested. 'Uh-uh. Not any more.'

'What do you mean? You're the toast of Paris, darling. Your face is on every street corner in the city advertising this spectacular concert. Soon, isn't it?'

'No. I mean, yes, the concert's tomorrow. But...' Rachel shook her head, struggling to maintain her grip on this conversation. 'I'm not doing it. I...left my management. The concert should have been cancelled—I'm sure it has been, in fact... They just haven't taken down the posters...'

Arabella cut through her stuttering resistance. 'I don't think so, angel. Some friends of mine have tickets. And surely you're under contractual obligation to go through with it, anyway?' Her pretty, pointed face still wore an expression of avid fascination which Rachel found sinister. She wanted to cover her ears with her hands and close her eyes to block out what Arabella was saying. Contractual obligation? she thought wildly. What did that mean?

'Darling, do sit down so we can talk properly.' Arabella patted the bed beside her and gave a throaty laugh. 'I'd hate to wake Sleeping Beauty over there—and, Lord, what a beauty he is. Of course that's part of the problem, isn't it? That's why you've turned your back on your fabulous but no doubt very demanding career? You've fallen in love with him, haven't you? Don't bother denying it, sweetie, because it's absolutely pointless, I'm afraid. It's written all over you.'

Rachel turned her head away. Her eyes were drawn back to Orlando's lean, elegant form on the sofa. She was suddenly too tired and too confused to think or argue any more, and she felt the denial that had sprung to her lips wither and die there.

'I'm so sorry...' she whispered hoarsely.

'Oh, darling, don't be silly!' Arabella's voice was full of concern. 'It's I who should be saying that to you. Love's never easy at the best of times, and loving Orlando Winterton... Well, let's just say you're not the first to get your fingers burned in that particular fire.' She paused, then added abruptly, 'I suppose you've slept with him?'

Looking down into her lap, Rachel nodded miserably, so missed the glint of malice in Arabella's eyes.

'Oh, dear. And that must have given you hope that your feelings were reciprocated?' Arabella reached out a hand and tucked a strand of hair behind Rachel's ear. 'Well, there's no easy way to say this, angel—but I hate to see such a lovely and talented girl throw her life away on a lost cause, so I'm going to be utterly straight with you. I want Orlando and I to give things another go. For Felix's sake.'

Rachel closed her eyes and felt her whole body tense as Arabella's words penetrated the fog of confusion in her head.

'Now, don't get me wrong,' she continued. 'I really don't believe in couples staying together just for the sake of the children—especially if one of them is in love with someone else. But the thing is, Rachel darling...I don't think that's the case here. Has Orlando *told* you that he loves you?

Rachel shook her head dumbly as hot, stinging tears gathered in her eyes and began to overspill.

'No.' Arabella held her hands up apologetically. 'Stupid question. You've hardly known each other any time, and Orlando's hardly the type to use the word freely. I think it took him a good year to finally say it to me.' She eyed Rachel thoughtfully, an expression of extreme solicitousness on her face. 'There's one thing, of course, with Orlando. One thing that's absolutely key to understanding him. He's intensely proud, as you may have guessed, and intensely private. But he will take down those barriers for people that he cares about. People he *really* cares about.'

This whole encounter had taken on a nightmarish dimension. Rachel half expected Carlos to appear in a puff of smoke, like a pantomime villain. Only the persistent throbbing in her head and the dull ache in her chest told her that this was real. That she couldn't just open her eyes and make the sound of Arabella's husky, insistent voice fade back into the shadows.

'There's something you should know about him, Rachel—something I think that, if he had any plans at all to include you in his future, he would have told you…' She paused dramatically, fixing her piercing blue eyes on Rachel, watching her intently. 'He's going blind.'

'I know.' Rachel lifted her gaze to Arabella's and for a moment saw a flash of surprise there. 'I found out by accident. I borrowed his car…there was a leaflet in the glove compartment about it and it all fell into place…'

'Ah. So he hasn't told you himself?'

'No,' Rachel whispered.

'Well, maybe he hasn't had the chance?'

Rachel thoughts flew back, for the millionth time, to last night. He could have told her then. All the time they were having dinner, or upstairs in Felix's room, he could have told her. She shook her head slowly. Arabella's hand came out and covered hers.

'Of course, it doesn't necessarily mean he doesn't love you,' she said carefully. 'It's just that it *is* a fairly major thing to keep from someone if you intend to be around them for any length of time, isn't it? It's so awful for him—we've had a *long* talk about it this evening… He says it's got worse lately. It's a degenerative condition—maybe you know that from the leaflet? It affects only the central part of the eye, which is why he can still maintain such a damned good impression of normality, but he can't see anything in the middle of his vision.' She gave a little regretful pout. 'Which means, my darling, that he's never seen your pretty face. I'm sure if he had he would have fallen in love with you on the spot.'

Sorrow and hurt were bunching up inside Rachel, making it difficult to breathe. She wanted desperately to snatch her hand away from its imprisonment in Arabella's cool grip, but felt oddly powerless. Events just kept coming at her, like a succession of waves battering an exhausted swimmer who wasn't sure she had the will to stay afloat any more.

'It wouldn't have made any difference,' she said through dry lips. 'It's you he loves, Arabella. I've known it all along.'

Arabella's mouth quirked into a smile of satisfaction as she leaned back on her bank of pillows. 'I don't know about that,' she said girlishly, twisting a lock of her streaky blonde hair round a finger. 'But, yes, in his own way I think he does. Anyway, I think we can make it work. For Felix. It's so important for him to grow up in a family environment, I think—which is why, if Orlando hadn't come back, I would have taken Felix to Brazil.'

'Brazil?' Rachel echoed faintly, her heart thudding.

'Yes. My family all live there, and he would be surrounded by cousins and aunts and uncles...which of course are no substitute for a father. '

Her blue eyes bored into Rachel's with meaningful intensity, and with a shiver of disgust Rachel recognised the veiled threat behind the words. If Orlando didn't go back to Arabella, she would take his son to the other side of the world.

Pulling her hand away, Rachel stood up. She found herself instinctively drawn back to Orlando. She couldn't help it. Right from the moment she'd first seen him she'd felt somehow that he represented home for her. Without him she felt utterly directionless.

Right on cue, Arabella spoke. 'So, what about you, darling? What will you do now? I think, in a way, all of this has worked out rather well. Your concert—your big break—is tomorrow. There's still time to go back, sweetie, isn't there?'

'But I can't. I still have Felix to look after—'

'Oh, don't be silly! You don't think I'd be cruel enough to make you stay on as nanny *now*, darling? Of course not—Orlando and I will manage. Together.'

'Oh.' Humiliatingly, Rachel felt her face crumple as sobs shook her body. 'In that case...I don't know. I can't think...'

'Well,' said Arabella firmly, 'I think you should go to the hotel now and get a good night's sleep. And then in the morning you can come back here and we'll talk about it. All right?'

Mute with misery, Rachel nodded.

Deliberately, wanting to imprint the moment on her memory for ever, she reached out a hand and touched Orlando's face. In sleep, the torment had left it, and he looked simply remote and heroic—one of King Arthur's knights, awaiting the call to greatness again. Raising her fingers to her lips, she kissed them, and gently brushed her fingertips across his exquisite mouth.

Behind her, she heard Arabella give a little hiss of disapproval. When she spoke her voice was sharp. 'Don't wake him, sweetie. There's a good girl. He's obviously exhausted, and I just want him to have a chance to rest. I think that's reasonable, don't you, darling?'

A spark of anger glowed in the darkness of Rachel's heart. Suddenly she wanted to turn round and shout at Arabella that it *was* her fault Orlando was tired, *her* fault for bringing him all this way when there wasn't even anything much wrong with her. For a dizzying moment she closed her eyes and imagined the terrible relief of standing there and unleashing all her rage and resentment and bitterness and grief onto the smug figure in the bed, but then it passed, and she was left feeling just unbearably sad.

'I won't wake him,' she said flatly. 'I just want to say goodbye. To them both.'

Crouching down beside the car seat, she dipped her head to nuzzle Felix's hair, breathing in his wonderful scent as she dropped a kiss onto his warm head. And then she stood up, looking down on Orlando while the tears streamed down her cheeks. An odd, disjointed memory of a story book she'd had as a child came back to her, where the princess's tears had fallen on the blinded eyes of her handsome prince and his sight had been magically restored. It suddenly struck her as being a horrible distortion of a happy-ever-after. She would love Orlando whether he could see or not.

'No need to make a big thing of it,' Arabella said sharply. 'You'll see him in the morning.'

It didn't make any difference. Rachel knew that this was still goodbye.

As a woman in the male-dominated world of corporate finance, Arabella de Ferrers had learned to make the most of her advantages. Her success, therefore, was due not only to her incisive business mind and excellent head for figures, but to her great cleavage, her long legs, and her instinctive understanding of how to use them.

She'd been a major player, but fate had dealt her a series of bad hands. She wasn't just fighting for a position at the top any more, she was fighting to stay in the game. And she wasn't overly troubled with a conscience when it came to sticking to the rules of fair play.

She might have lost a few of her marketable assets, she reflected thoughtfully, but she was still a formidable adversary. And she still had plenty of contacts. It had taken has a little under ten minutes to discover the name of Rachel Campion's agent and inform him where Rachel was staying.

Now all she had to do was keep Orlando here until the morning, when Rachel would be safely back in the clutches of her very grateful agent, and maintain a suitably compassionate expression when she broke the news to Orlando of Rachel's defection. Switching out the light, Arabella allowed herself an exultant smile.

That might be the hardest part of all.

There was a knock at the door.

Rachel heard it as if from a great distance. The sound meant nothing to her, so she simply ignored it. Anyway, she felt too tired, too stiff and cold, to get up and cross the room to open it.

She was sitting on a chair by the window, and had been for a long time. At the beginning—hours or days or a lifetime ago?— she had been looking out at the street below, in case a car pulled up and Orlando got out.

There had been lots of cars. Whoever would have thought that so many people would come and go in the secret hours of the night? She couldn't say at exactly what point her hopes had died. Only that as the meagre light of the new day had gradually leaked into the room it had become apparent that they were as cold and stiff as she was.

There was another knock, louder this time. Slowly she raised her head, frowning.

Maybe she'd missed him getting out of the car down on the street below? Maybe he'd come straight up to her, without stopping at the desk to ask for the key…?

With a tearing, wrenching gasp she stumbled to her feet. Her legs were shaking as hope and adrenaline surged through her, and she threw herself across the room, her arms outstretched, blindly groping for the lock on the door, wrestling with it for agonising seconds before flinging it wide open.

'Orlando—'

She stopped, her chest rising and falling with desperate, racking sobs as she tried to make sense of what her eyes were telling her.

There, standing in the doorway with a look of compassionate concern on his face, stood Carlos.

CHAPTER FIFTEEN

ORLANDO stormed into the reception hall of the hotel. At this hour of the morning it was already busy, with people settling bills and checking out, or waiting in little groups before setting out on whatever excursion they had planned for the day. Bypassing them all, Orlando went straight to the desk. Seeing the murderous expression on the face of this intimidatingly tall, compellingly handsome man, the couple who had been querying their bar tariff stepped aside.

'Miss Campion in the Orangerie suite?' Orlando snarled. 'Has she checked out?'

'*Pardon, monsieur…* There are other people waiting.' The small and officious concierge didn't look up from his computer screen. This was a mistake. If he had, he would have been better prepared for the moment when Orlando reached across the desk and grabbed him by the lapels of his well-tailored uniform.

'I'm sorry,' Orlando said with devastating politeness, 'but this is urgent. Just tell me…*has she checked out*?' He let go.

Throwing a look of blatant dislike in Orlando's direction, the man began tapping details into the computer. At length he looked up.

'*Non, monsieur.*'

He didn't meet Orlando's eye, looking instead at a point just over his right shoulder, where the lifts were situated. He gave a brittle smile.

'Can I have the key, please?' Orlando said harshly.

'Hold on please, sir,' the concierge said silkily. He took an eternity to come back with it, by which time the red-haired girl he had just seen emerging from the lift with her distinguished-looking companion had crossed the lobby and been ushered out into the street.

Backing away from the desk, Orlando totally missed the small, superior smile on the concierge's face. His heart was hammering a panicky tattoo against his ribs as hope churned with icy fear inside him. *She hadn't checked out. That meant she must still be upstairs. Didn't it?*

He hammered on the lift call button, and was relieved when the doors slid open straight away. But, stepping inside, he nearly blacked out with annihilating longing as he breathed in the faint scent of roses. Desperately he looked around. The lift doors were closing, shutting out the clear part of his vision, and the dark vortex at its centre obscured his view of the lobby through the narrowing gap. He opened his mouth to call Rachel's name, but the doors slid inexorably shut, leaving him shouting into the insulated silence of the lift.

Slamming his fist against the door, he felt the structure shake beneath his feet. He spun round, searching frantically for the control panel, and then gave a violent curse of rage and self-disgust as he realised he couldn't even see which number to press. Slowly, laboriously, he felt his way along them, counting.

When he finally reached the suite he threw open the door.

'Rachel!'

His voice was so raw with emotion that he hardly recognised it as his own. He strode through the horribly quiet room, knocking over a vase of flowers, flinging doors open, feeling his hopes being relentlessly slashed as each one revealed an empty room. Eventually he was back where he started, with no choice but to face the facts.

Arabella had been telling the truth for once. Rachel was gone, leaving nothing behind but a lingering scent of rose petals and his whole life in ruins.

Arabella's voice seemed to hang in the heavy, oppressively heated air. *'She's a world-class pianist with a glittering international career, Orlando. Even you couldn't be selfish enough to want her to give all that up for a life of complete isolation with a blind recluse.'*

How bloody arrogant he'd been.

He had booked this ridiculous hotel suite with such definite plans. Here, he had thought, away from the crushing familiarity of Easton, he would be able to open up to Rachel and finally hack through all the secrets and misapprehensions that lay between them like a forest of thorns. She was brave and strong and loving—if anyone would accept him as he was, flawed and damaged, she would. He'd even been hopeful enough to ask for a two bedroom suite—what he'd had in mind for her afterwards definitely wasn't suitable for Felix to witness.

But such was his own selfishness he hadn't considered Rachel herself. Her life. Had he ever really thought of her as Rachel Campion, world class pianist? Sickeningly he recalled that first night in the kitchen, her horror at his lacerated fingers, her reluctance to pick up the knife. He remembered his unconcealed disdain. Even when he'd found out about her profession he hadn't given it much thought.

What had Arabella called her? The Next Big Thing?

Rachel had tried to tell him herself, hadn't she? She had said that not playing the piano had been like losing a part of herself. And he knew exactly how that felt. Why was he surprised that she'd gone back? Arabella was right. Going after her would be nothing short of cruel.

'Querida...are you feeling better?'

Carlos looked at Rachel with infinite concern as he came into her dressing room at the concert hall. Struggling with the zip on her dress, she felt herself stiffen at his approach, and clutched the green velvet protectively against herself.

'You still look very tired. I wish you had let us take you back to the hotel for some rest before tonight.'

'I'm fine,' said Rachel coldly. 'I needed to practise.'

'You are as brilliant as ever.' Carlos's voice was like oiled silk as he trailed a hand over her rigid shoulders. 'I am so glad to have my little star back where she belongs. You have no idea how worried we have been.'

'But I left a message. I told you I was safe.'

Carlos's small eyes glittered in the harsh overhead light. 'I know, and I tried to understand that you needed some time to think. I am a fair man, *querida*. I do not blame you. Deep in my heart I knew you would come back.'

Rachel fought a tide of nausea and felt her own nails digging into her arms. How she hated herself for proving him right. How she despised her weakness for giving in and going with him. But the point at which he had appeared at the door of that stiflingly lavish hotel suite had been the lowest of her life. Her resistance, her pride, her ability to think clearly had all completely deserted her, and she'd felt so profoundly alone that she would probably have willingly gone with an axe-wielding serial killer if he'd shown her a glimmer of kindness. It hadn't even crossed her mind to ask how Carlos had found her; it had just seemed like a masterstroke of fate that he had.

'So I gathered, from the fact you didn't cancel the concert. What would you have done if I hadn't come back?'

Carlos threw back his head theatrically and waved an arm. 'I make contingency plans,' he said airily, and then quite suddenly his expression changed. 'You humiliate me enough when you leave me at the church, Rachel,' he said with quiet malevolence. 'It took a lot of money and careful PR work to contain the damage. I do not want to have to deal with that again.'

'What were you going to do?' she asked, torn between not wanting to know and needing to find out the worst.

He walked slowly around her. He was so much shorter and squatter than Orlando, she thought with a shiver of distaste. She was no longer frightened of him. Just repelled. She would work alongside him for the remainder of this tour, and then...

The thought was like plunging head-first off a cliff into darkness. Then what? Without the piano, without Orlando or Felix, *then what*?

She was so gripped by horror that she almost didn't notice Carlos's touch on her back, his fingers crawling like insects across her skin and playing idly with the zip of her dress. 'You are not the only young, slender red-headed pianist, *querida*,' he whispered, his breath hot against her neck. 'How many times do I tell you? Rachel Campion is not just a person, she is a *brand*. If you are unavailable for the concert, we get an understudy for the role of Rachel. The public do not know. The hall is big. Everyone sees red hair and they think of you.' He laughed nastily, and shivers of loathing rippled down her spine. '*That*, my little one, is the power of marketing. Brand association. Brand identity.'

Rachel stared straight ahead, transfixed. 'What about the music?' she said tonelessly. 'You might find someone who looks like me, but what about someone who plays like me?'

'Ah. Ever the artiste. Well, not all pianists have your talent, it is true. The critics, no doubt they would be disappointed. They would comment on a lack of finesse, a heaviness of interpreta-tion...Rachel Campion does not live up to her early promise, they say, burned out so young—what a pity.'

As the implication of his words struck her there was a com-motion in the corridor outside. She heard her mother's shrill voice, and then a deeper one cutting through it. The next minute the door burst open, and Rachel felt a thousand-volt surge of relief and hope as she found herself staring straight into Orlando's face.

It was blisteringly angry.

'What do you think you're doing?' said Carlos imperiously, but without stepping out from behind Rachel.

'I need to talk to Rachel.' Orlando's voice was like a rusty blade. 'Alone.'

'Impossible,' said Carlos haughtily. 'Before a performance she must not be—'

His words were choked off as Orlando reached over Rachel's shoulder and seized him by the arm, dragging him forward and twisting it up behind his back.

'You must be the bastard who forced her to sleep with you.'

Carlos made a strangled noise, which was turned into a high-pitched cry as Orlando jerked his arm further up his back.

'And then you tried to force her to marry you. You're a conductor, no?'

Carlos gave a whimper of assent. 'I imagine,' Orlando went on icily, 'that conducting with a broken shoulder wouldn't be easy. So let's just say that if you ever touch her again your career will be over.'

He thrust him towards the door. Muttering darkly and straightening his clothes, Carlos attempted to make a dignified exit.

Orlando and Rachel stood facing each other. Rachel found she was shaking uncontrollably, though he was utterly still. He was staring straight at her, his eyes dark pools of anger, rimmed by the thinnest band of pale green ice. For a long moment neither of them spoke. Then, seeming to make an effort to rein in his fury, Orlando put his hands in his pockets and came slowly towards her.

'So,' he said with quiet venom, 'you ran away again. It's getting to be quite a habit.'

She took a couple of steps backwards, stung beyond belief at the hostility in his tone. Slumping against the wall, she bent her head.

'Is that what you came here for? To tell me again that I lack courage? Because if you did you're wasting your time and your breath. I already know.'

'No.' There was an edge of darkness in his voice that sliced through her heart like a guillotine. 'I came to see if you were all right. I came to see for myself that you'd left of your own free will. That you'd made a *choice*.' He shook his head in bewilderment. 'I couldn't just let you go without trying to understand why.'

Rachel took a deep breath in, trying to steady herself, trying to steel herself against the heartbreaking necessity of lying. She was doing it for Felix. For Felix and Orlando, and their future together as father and son. It was a love worth sacrificing her own small, ravaged heart for.

'I was surplus to requirement,' she said with admirable calm. 'Felix has both his parents now. He doesn't need me.'

'*What about me?*' Orlando lashed out, then stopped and turned sharply away. She saw him raise his hand to his face, his long fingers massaging his forehead as he paced restlessly across the floor. Reaching the door, which Carlos had left open, Orlando kicked it viciously shut and turned back to face her. 'You don't think that I deserved some sort of an explanation? A goodbye at least?'

He leaned back against the door, looking dangerously calm and almost languorous. Only the terrifying darkness in his eyes and the tense set of his jaw betrayed his fury.

'If I'd said goodbye I was afraid you'd—say something to make me stay.'

He slammed his fist against the wall. 'Jeez, Rachel. What do you take me for? Some kind of tyrant? Is your opinion of me so very, very low that that you think I'd blackmail you to stay when you wanted to leave?'

Leaning against the wall opposite him, Rachel let her head fall back as her body was racked with anguish. Every second, with every painful beat of her heart and every deep shuddering breath, she wanted to throw herself into his arms. All her noble intentions to do what was right for Felix were suddenly engulfed by the tidal wave of need that crashed through her as she registered the strength of his emotion.

'I didn't want to leave,' she moaned. 'I didn't want to. I *had* to. For my own sanity.'

'*Why?*'

'Because I fell in love with you!' she shouted. 'And because you were unavailable—in every sense of the word. Sex—that was all that was on offer. The rest of you was out of bounds. I can't live like that. It'll destroy me in the end, loving someone who can't love me back. You've spent the whole time I've been with you keeping me at arm's length, and I know it's my fault for wanting too much, but I need more than that!'

His face was absolutely ashen. 'You're right,' he said through tight, bloodless lips. 'I did keep you at arm's length. But I had good reason to. I had a bloody good reason.'

'Did you?' she yelled. 'Did you really? Well, I'm glad. I'm glad all this misery isn't for nothing. But, just out of interest, maybe I could hear that very good reason now? It's far too late to make a difference, but I'd kind of like to hear it anyway.'

With a lithe movement of his shoulders Orlando levered himself from the door and stood before her, wearing a look of raw agony.

There was a sudden sharp knock on the door. 'Five minutes, *mademoiselle*!'

'*Oh, God…*' Rachel jumped, the green dress slipping from her shoulders as her hands flew to her face in panic. And then Orlando was there, holding her steady, his green eyes seeing right into the fear and insecurity inside her, calming it. 'It's OK. You're fine. Your dress…let me do it.'

Wordlessly she turned round, and the world stilled again as his fingers traced their now familiar path along her spine to the base of her dress. She let out a breath of hopeless laughter.

'What will I do without you to dress me?'

His hands closed around her shoulders and he turned her back to face him. Tilting his head back, he stared down into her face and spoke through gritted teeth.

'It's not too late.'

Rachel looked up into the face she loved for its uncompromising strength as much as for its undeniable beauty. For a moment she found herself wondering whether Felix would inherit his father's unshakable determination as well as his aristocratic features. She would never find out. But though she would never see him grow and change and become himself she still had a responsibility to make that journey as smooth as she could for him. That was why she had to do this.

'It is,' she whispered brokenly, and his grip tightened convulsively on her shoulders, as if she'd hurt him and he was tensing himself against the pain. 'I'm sorry, Orlando, but it *is* too late.'

There was another urgent knock at the door, and the voice called 'They're ready Miss Campion.'

Orlando let her go, holding his hands up as if in surrender for a second, before letting them fall helplessly to his sides. 'In that case I won't hold you back any more.'

He stood aside. Rachel was ghostly pale, trembling with the effort of holding herself together. The thought of playing in front of almost two thousand people in just a few short minutes was nothing compared with the emptiness that would come afterwards, when she came back in here and Orlando would be gone. These last few seconds seemed infinitely precious, loaded with a lifetime of meaning and feeling.

She hesitated by the door and looked at him with huge, troubled eyes.

'I just wish…' she said, in a voice that was low and filled with pain. 'I just wish you could have told me *why* you wouldn't let me near you, that's all. Because I want to know it wasn't something stupid, like the fact that you're losing your sight. You have to know that that wouldn't have made the slightest bit of difference to how I felt about you.'

Very slowly he turned his head towards her. He wore an expression of intense desolation.

'Arabella told you?'

'She did. But I found out for myself before that. At Easton.' Rachel opened the door. 'And it doesn't make you any less of a hero or any less of a father or any less of a bastard for breaking my heart. So get over it and stop hiding behind it.'

For a moment after she left he stood as if turned to stone, and then he rushed out into the corridor in her wake.

Too late. She was gone.

A few moments later a gust of air seemed to ripple through the building as it was shaken by a storm of tumultuous applause. But to Rachel, taking her place at the piano in the centre of the starkly lit platform, the applause and adulation of two thousand people was immaterial. She played for herself, and for Orlando and Felix, to express a grief that words could not adequately convey.

It was, quite simply, the performance of a lifetime.

CHAPTER SIXTEEN

London. Four months later.

'SO THIS is the heir of Easton?'

Andrew Parkes leaned over his desk and peered benignly at Felix. 'Gorgeous little chap, Orlando. Very like you—and his namesake, of course. Very like Felix too.'

Orlando gave a wry smile. There was perhaps good reason for that—as Arabella had maliciously revealed in one of their final arguments, before she'd left for her new home in Dubai with her oil executive fiancé. Orlando was indifferent; all that mattered was that Felix was staying with *him*. The oil executive didn't like children, apparently.

'So…' Reluctantly, Andrew stopped blowing raspberries at Felix and cleared his throat self-consciously. At six months, Felix was distractingly sweet. 'How are you?'

Orlando shrugged. 'No change. My sight hasn't deteriorated any further. I can still get around fine. I can change the odd nappy, if I have to, though don't tell the nanny that.'

Andrew Parkes nodded. 'Excellent.' Though that didn't explain why Orlando Winterton still had the look of a man who had just been released from the torturer's cell. 'And how are you finding the…er…adjustment, mentally.'

Orlando sighed impatiently. 'I'm doing all right, Andrew. People know now. I don't hide it any more.'

Or hide behind it.

'That's a huge step forward.'

Orlando stood up, deftly holding Felix against his body with one hand, and the little boy regarded Andrew with clear Winterton eyes while Orlando stared fixedly ahead. 'It's one thing coming to terms with it for myself, but I need to know what the chances are that Felix will have inherited this too.'

Andrew looked thoughtful. 'Slim, I'd say. It's a very rare disease, and for a child to get it both parents need to be carriers of a recessive gene. We can't test for the gene yet, but obviously Felix will be very closely monitored.'

Orlando's face was dark. 'Would it make any difference if I wasn't his father but my brother was? Would that make it less likely?'

'Probably not...' Andrew replied carefully. 'I assume you ask that for a reason?'

Orlando gave a wintry smile. 'My brother was apparently devastated by my diagnosis, and Arabella very generously offered him solace,' he said sardonically. 'Naturally it's all my fault. As is Felix's death. According to Arabella, he was too upset by the prospective bleakness of my life to be able to fly safely.'

'Ah...' Frowning, Andrew rested his elbows on the desk and steepled his fingers. 'I think, Orlando, I should mention something at this point that might ease your conscience a little. I can't say too much, but Felix had also been referred to me, as you were, following a routine sight test. His appointment was the week following yours. He telephoned my secretary to cancel it. He didn't book an alternative date.'

Blood drummed in Orlando's ears as the implications of what Andrew was saying hit him. 'You're saying that maybe Felix...?'

Andrew held up a hand to stop him. 'I'm saying nothing, because that would be in direct contravention of the Hippocratic Oath. No, I am merely letting you know of your brother's change of plans. From that,' he said emphatically, 'you may draw your own conclusions, and if they lead you to the realisation that you are in no way to blame for what happened to him that's only fair. As for this little chap—Felix the second—he's no more and no less likely to inherit the condition whichever of the two of you were responsible for his arrival in the world.'

'Thank you, Andrew.'

As Orlando carried Felix carefully down the steps to the street, he thought about what Andrew had just told him. He'd discovered a lot about himself in the last four months. Mostly things that Rachel had seemed to know right from the start. Like the fact that courage wasn't only measured by medals and military honours, and heroism wasn't about wearing a uniform and dying in a far-flung place.

What Andrew Parkes had just said only served to reinforce that.

He'd been so quick to assume that Felix was the brave one, that while he had been falling apart at home his brother had been out there protecting his country, upholding the family name. But maybe, just maybe, Felix had been the cowardly one. Faced with the same challenge, Felix had opted for the easy way out. Orlando had chosen to fight.

Though at times it was a bleak and bitter struggle.

Outside, the polluted city air was warm, and the afternoon sun slanted down between the buildings onto the acid-green leaves of the trees outside Andrew's consulting rooms. Automatically Orlando's imperfect gaze sought out the place where he'd first seen Rachel's picture over a year ago, on that dark, hopeless day of his first diagnosis.

At first he thought it was his mind and his sight playing tricks on him—another instance of the brain supplying the image that it wanted to see. He blinked and rubbed a hand across his face, hardly daring to look at it again.

But it was there again. Another picture. Blurred. Only visible to him in tantalisingly small pieces. But the date on the poster was today's.

* * *

Slumped in front of her dressing room mirror, Rachel squirted the dregs from a bottle of eye-drops into eyes reddened by not enough sleep and too many tears, before making a start on repairing the ravages four months of grief had wrought on the rest of her face.

It was a warm evening in June, but she was wearing her beloved old cashmere sweater to keep at bay the chill which seemed to pervade her bones all the time these days. The tour had been a massive success; every date had been followed by rapturous reviews from critics, who claimed that she 'imbued the music with hitherto unplumbed emotional depth', and that she was a 'courageous performer'.

The latter statement was the only thing that had brought a faint smile to her lips in months. She had paid a high price for that courage. It was a legacy of her time with Orlando.

Another was that Carlos had kept a hostile but merciful distance since the night Orlando had threatened him. Her mother, who had a much less rosy opinion of Carlos since he had tried to replace Rachel with a stand-in, was now much more of an ally, and while Rachel would never forgive Elizabeth for all the years when discipline had replaced love, at least she understood better now. Love was so very, very sore.

Glancing up at the clock, Rachel steeled herself for the knock at the door. Tonight was the last date of the tour, and though she was tired, she was also dreading life beyond the final encore. She was afraid that without this nightly exorcism, the demons inside her would slowly smother her.

The door opened and Elizabeth put her head round it. 'All set, darling?' she enquired brightly. Rachel nodded. 'Take off that dreadful old sweater, then, sweetie, and I'll see you afterwards.' Blowing a kiss, she disappeared.

Reluctantly Rachel got to her feet and peeled the sweater over her head, then stood for a moment looking at her reflection in the mirror. She was wearing another dress in her signature dark ivy-green, made of satin this time. Its neckline plunged down to a narrow band of beading beneath the bust, from where the fabric fell with bias-cut fluidity, artfully skimming the new roundness of her belly.

The other lasting reminder of her time with Orlando.

It was a glorious evening.

The sky, which had been an unbroken dome of Wedgwood blue all day, was now dotted with feathery fine tufts of cloud, stained blush-pink by the setting sun so they looked like the marabou trim on a bride's negligée. After two weeks of torrential rain the unexpected arrival of summer had created an expansive mood amongst the concert crowd on the balcony of the Bankside Hall. They lingered over their cocktails and champagne until the last possible moment, before making their way unhurriedly inside for what promised to be a fine programme of music.

Following the rave reviews, tickets to the concert had sold out with lightning speed, but tonight there were a few unclaimed seats as, swayed by the sudden spell of good weather, people had taken off to the country or to Ascot. Therefore it hadn't been difficult for Orlando to arrange a last-minute seat at the back of the hall.

What had been more problematic was persuading the girl on the door to let him take Felix in.

In the end she had been powerless to resist the old magic formula of devastatingly good-looking man with small baby and, muttering anxiously about losing her job, had let him slip through the doors when the lights were dimmed. She'd been rewarded with a kiss on the cheek, which more than made up for the worry of being found out.

With Felix fast asleep in his arms, Orlando slumped into his seat and steeled himself, as an eruption of applause told him that Rachel had just walked onto the platform. Tipping his head back against the seat, he could just make out her vivid hair, shining beneath the bright spotlights like flame.

For a second there was silence as the audience settled, and

then the opening bars of a Debussy prelude floated through the warm evening air.

An audible breath of collective contentment rose from the audience. Until that moment Orlando hadn't given a thought to the music, but as the sound filled the rafters and ran in rippling currents over his tautly stretched nerves he was transfixed. It reminded him so poignantly of when Rachel had been at Easton, and all the nights he'd sat at his desk, wrestling with life and death issues on the other side of the world, and she'd reached out to him through the cold blackness and reminded him of his own humanity. The irony was so perfect: he'd been handling a defence crisis, and all the time his own defences had been being stealthily undermined. And he hadn't even realised until it was too late.

Far too late.

Could there be any words more poignant than those?

Time ceased to exist as he sat there, hovering in a state of blissful painlessness, suspended between having her and not having her. He had grown so used to waking up alone, as yet another dazzling dream of Rachel faded, leaving him with his monochrome and lonely reality, that just breathing the same air as her for a couple of hours was, he realised desolately, better than being without her altogether. And, after so many months of firmly steering his thoughts away from Rachel, it was the greatest relief to just give in.

At length he was aware of the piece coming to an end, and for a moment there was absolute silence in the cavernous hall as everyone sat, still spellbound. Then there was an explosion of clapping.

In his arms Felix gave a start, raising his head and whimpering slightly before settling again. Orlando held his breath. Then below, on the rostrum, Carlos cued the orchestra into a Scarlatti sonata, and Felix, roused a second time, gave a loud, indignant wail.

Carlos made a vicious slashing motion with his baton and

whirled imperiously around. Instantly the orchestra ground to a ragged halt.

'A *baby*?' said Carlos in outrage. 'What is the meaning of this?'

Orlando got abruptly to his feet. Felix was crying in earnest now, the sound drifting up into the roofspace, thin and plaintive. In the audience curious muttering broke out as heads turned and feet shuffled, and then there was a collective gasp as the pianist herself got up and peered out into the crowd.

The murmuring was hushed again as everyone held their breath and waited for her reaction. Straining forward in their comfortable cherry-red seats, they eagerly anticipated a display of diva rage to complement the glowering indignation on Carlos Vincente's face. But instead they saw a look of naked hope and longing as Rachel Campion shielded her eyes against the bright lights that were directed on her, straining past them to look into the darkness beyond.

'Felix?'

It was no more than a whisper, but the microphone above the piano picked it up and amplified it so that above the crying of the baby everyone heard the low note of yearning in her voice.

'*Orlando?*'

As if operated by a central remote control, every head turned to the back of the hall. The man who stood in the central aisle, holding a crying baby in his arms, was tall, romantically dark and breathtakingly handsome. He also looked as if he had been struck by lightning.

The atmosphere in the hall was suddenly charged with electrifying tension. No one moved, and the only sound was the heart-wrenching cries of the baby.

Rachel sat down at the piano again. Softly, and with infinite tenderness, she began to play.

Chopin's *Nocturne in E Minor* rippled from her fingers in a magical, shimmering rainbow of sound, every note vibrating with love and longing. Even though the conductor had now left the rostrum, one by one the members of the orchestra joined in, until the hall was filled with the purest sound.

It was as if angels hovered in the rafters.

In the spotlights Rachel's tears glistened like falling diamonds. Her face was that of a suffering Madonna—full of pain and adoration and tortured bliss.

The Bankside Hall held one thousand three hundred people. By the time the music melted back into a shivering silence Felix was amongst the few who weren't crying. For a moment there was an absolute absence of sound. And then the muffled thud of a door shutting at the back of the hall.

When everyone turned to look, the man with the baby had gone.

And when they turned back so had the pianist.

The network of passages behind the stage at the Bankside was labyrinthine. Rachel's breath came in desperate gulps as she hurtled along them, alternating between hope and terror as she desperately tried to find her way to him.

He was probably here with Arabella, her head very firmly said. Or else she'd gone somewhere else for the evening and left him at a loose end with Felix...

But he had come, and that was something, her heart cried wildly. He had come, and she couldn't let him leave without asking to see him again. She knew how much he loved Felix—he had a right to know about his other child. Her baby.

The sound of her heels on the tiled floor echoed madly in the stark corridors as she ran, so she paused to slip them off and carried on, not caring what she looked like to the few straggling musicians and backstage staff she passed. Rounding a corner, she found herself on the mezzanine balcony that rose up from the Bankside's famous Art Deco entrance hall.

She rushed to the railing and looked down.

With the concert still technically not ended, the place was deserted—except for one man crossing the austere white space towards the door. There was no mistaking those massive shoulders, the narrow hips and long legs, the slow, deliberate walk. Or the infant, now quiet, in the car seat.

'Orlando... *Please*... Wait!'

His hand was on the door.

'You can't just leave like that!' she said wildly, the pain in her voice echoing around the stark walls.

As if in slow motion she watched his arm fall back to his side. Seeming to tense himself, as if in anticipation of some terrible blow, he turned round. His expression was rigidly controlled, his narrow eyes dark and hollow.

'I have to.'

She gazed down at him. Her chest was heaving with the exertion of running, and also with painful locked-in emotions. The air seemed to have been squeezed from her lungs and replaced with razorblades, and her eyes searched his face for answers to the questions she hardly dared to ask.

'Arabella? Is she waiting for you?'

For a second he looked almost bewildered, shaking his head as he said irritably, 'Arabella? She's gone. We were never together.'

Rachel could feel the metal railing biting into her aching fingers. 'But Felix...' she said desperately. 'She said if you weren't together she would take Felix...'

Bitter understanding suddenly flooded Orlando's face. With deliberate care he set Felix down on the floor at his feet. 'Another of Arabella's sophisticated tactics,' he said acidly.

A tiny spark of tentative hope glowed somewhere in the darkness of Rachel's barred and shuttered heart. 'Why are you here?' she asked, trying to keep the pleading note out of her voice. 'Why did you come?'

Below her, Orlando was standing perfectly still, perfectly straight, his face an emotionless mask.

'To see you.' He gave a sudden ironic laugh. 'To hear you. Whatever. It was worth it. You were astonishing.'

'But you're a philistine,' she protested, unable to stop the hope that was now spreading like wildfire through her whole body. Holding onto the balcony railing for support, she started to move along it towards the stairs, never taking her eyes off his pale, tense face. 'You said so yourself.... You don't even like music. You burn pianos.'

He gave a deep, shuddering sigh. 'You wouldn't believe how much I've changed.'

She had reached the stairs now, and she began to run down them on bare, silent feet towards him. Tears were streaming down her face as she came to a standstill in front of him on the second step from the bottom. Adrenaline and love and the same gut-wrenching desire she had always felt whenever she looked into his ocean-coloured eyes fizzed through her, making her brave.

'I don't want you to change...' she whispered fiercely. 'I love you just the way you are.'

Very slowly he lifted his hand and held it out towards her. The smile he gave her was one of unbearable sadness as he tilted his head back slightly, as if preparing himself for the firing squad.

'Oh, Rachel...' he said resignedly, 'I love you too. Far, far too much to ruin your life. You're too bright, too beautiful, too talented to throw yourself away on me. This is where you belong—and if I had any doubts about that before, tonight has put them all to rest once and for all. If we were to...' He faltered, and an expression of fathomless suffering flickered across his face. 'I'd only stand in your way, and I can't do that. I won't.'

For a moment Rachel couldn't speak, couldn't take in what he was saying. The words were like silvery, shimmering snowflakes, and for a second all she could do was watch them in wonder, terrified that if she tried to catch them they'd melt away. Hesitantly, she brought her hand up to his, and with infinite tenderness her fingertips brushed his outstretched palm.

'Again...' she breathed, her face streaked with tears. 'Say that again.'

Their fingers tightened, twisting together, locking fast, so that they were holding onto each other as if from either side of a deep and unbridgeable ravine.

'I love you,' he said harshly. 'I love you, but I won't hold you back. I won't take you away from everything you've worked for. You were right. Your hands are far too brilliant, far too precious for everyday life at Easton. I can't do it to you.'

'You don't have to.' Joy sang out of her voice, falling onto his bowed head like sunlight breaking through cloud. 'I'm doing it to myself. As of tonight, I'm retiring.'

'No—'

'Yes,' she said tenderly, emphatically, lifting her chin and gazing at him in a blaze of defiance and love. '*Yes*. This time, Orlando Winterton, you have *no choice*. As of tonight I'm starting my maternity leave, and there's nothing at all you can do about it.'

His head whipped violently upwards. His face was ashen, but his eyes burned with terrifying emotion.

'*What?*'

Gently she pulled the hand that was still entwined with hers downwards, and placed it on the slippery satin over her small bump.

'See?' she whispered.

And then suddenly he was pulling her into his arms, bringing his mouth crashing down on hers, and they were devouring each other with all the desperate longing of the past four months, all the hope of the next lifetime. When he finally pulled away Orlando couldn't tell whether the wetness on his cheeks was from her tears or his own.

As his hands moved wonderingly over her rounded stomach, moved upwards over the cold, slippery satin to the new fullness of her breasts, her eyes never left his face. The fierce, dazed longing there told her everything she needed to know.

'There's an expression...' she said slowly. 'An old proverb that says "Love is blind, but marriage restores its sight"...'

Orlando took her face in both his hands, gazing down at her with his intense, mesmerising stare. 'I don't want to have my sight restored,' he said gravely. 'I don't need to, because when I'm with you I see things more clearly than I ever did before. God,

Rachel, I do want to marry you. I want that more than anything.' He paused, frowning. 'But can you really live with this illness?'

She smiled into the clear pools of his eyes. 'I can't live without it. Because it's part of you, and I can't live without you. Your life is my life. Your problems, your joys, your triumphs, your children…all mine. Because you see things in me that I didn't know were there. You give me courage.'

He laughed, though his dark lashes were wet with tears. 'You're going to need it if this baby's a boy. Believe me, Winterton brothers are a nightmare.' Still holding her face between his hands, he pressed a kiss to her quivering lips, feeling them part beneath his, welcoming him into the darkness of their private heaven. He felt drunk with longing, drunk with love.

Behind them there was an embarrassed cough. 'Miss Campion… Excuse me…'

'Mmm?' Rachel murmured against Orlando's mouth.

'The audience are wondering if there will be an encore… They want more.'

Orlando groaned. 'They're not the only ones,' he said with a rueful grin, taking a step backwards and giving her a little push in the direction of the hall. 'Go.'

'I don't have to…'

'You do. Over a thousand people are waiting for you.'

'You and Felix are the only ones who matter.'

'We'll wait as long as it takes.'

She was halfway across the hall, but then she ran back to him and stood on tiptoe to brush her mouth across his ear, her fingers lightly caressing his neck as she breathed very softly, 'Five minutes. And then I'm yours—exclusively, for ever.'

Closing his eyes, he smiled languidly into her fragrant hair as her touch and the whisper of her breath against his ear sent shockwaves of ecstasy through his entire body.

Five minutes suddenly seemed a hell of a long time…

EPILOGUE

THE rose-petal-pink sun drifted gently down behind the garden's old brick walls and violet shadows gathered, darkening to deepest indigo beneath the sheltering limes. Felix ran ahead, the sound of his clear, pure laughter floating through the honeyed evening air as he reached the fountain which bubbled up through the stones at the secret heart of the garden.

Rachel's design for the old rose garden had been faithful to the original in spirit rather than in actual detail. Old-fashioned blooms still spilled abundantly over arches and pathways, but these had been re-laid to her exact specifications, using specially chosen materials. In the gentle days of the previous autumn, as her bulk had swelled, she had paced and sketched and directed a team of gardeners who had been under strictest instructions from Orlando not to let her do anything remotely strenuous. The completion of the garden had coincided with the arrival of a delicately beautiful baby girl, whom it had seemed only right should be called Rose.

Pausing now, in the golden summer twilight, a cool, moisture-beaded bottle of champagne clasped in one hand, Rachel looked back. The garden was at its most intoxicatingly perfect—ripe with blossom, heavy with perfume—but her joy in the achievement was nothing compared to the familiar surge of deep-down, wrenching love she felt as she watched Orlando walk towards her with his sexy, long-limbed stride, their daughter in his arms.

Although she was the first Winterton girl for three generations, seven-month-old Rose had the dark hair and thrill-seeking energy of all her male forebears, and she kicked and wriggled delightedly in her daddy's easy grasp.

The neck of Orlando's white wedding shirt was open, his tie long since discarded. A couple of hours ago, in a private ceremony in Easton's church, he had reverently added a plain band of old gold to the finger of Rachel's left hand that already bore the Winterton rubies. Afterwards, coming out of the church into the drowsy late-summer afternoon, the new Lady Ashbroke had taken her bouquet of apricot roses, gathered that morning from the garden, and laid them at the feet of Felix's angel.

They had returned to Easton, where all the estate employees and Rachel's new friends from the mother-and-baby group in the village had mingled happily on the lawn and drunk champagne beneath a soft, forget-me-not blue sky. It had been perfect. And yet Orlando had found himself longing for this moment, when he could have Rachel to himself again.

Beneath his bare feet the slate pathway felt like warm silk as he followed the ribbon of smooth stones set into it. This began at the doorway at the end of the lime walk and got gradually wider as the path wound its way to the centre of the garden, meaning he could instantly orientate himself. Rachel's idea, and just one of the many millions of ways she made his life better.

She made *him* better.

He followed her to where the stone seat stood, in its arbour of frothing white roses, and stooped to set his daughter down on the circle of flat cobbles around it. Instantly Rose hitched herself up onto her plump pink knees and, cooing with satisfaction, scuttled off in her precocious crab-like crawl to find her beloved Felix and the water. Orlando sat down beside Rachel, taking the glass of champagne she put into his hand. Her wedding dress was a simple knee-length shift of palest coffee-coloured silk, and he dropped a kiss onto her bare creamy shoulder.

'Are you sorry we're not jetting off somewhere exotic for a

honeymoon?' he murmured. Her skin was like the velvet of sun-warmed peaches.

'No.' She smiled, bending her head to expose the curving sweep of her rose-scented neck to his lips and sighing with pleasure. 'I'm glad. I love it here too much. At home.'

The shadows stretched and deepened, and the first tiny diamond stars flickered in the lilac sky above them. The children's laughter and muted shrieks of joy rose like soft moths in the hazy, fragrant evening. Sipping champagne, Rachel let her head fall back as Orlando's beautiful fingers moved languidly down her arm, trailing rapture. Through half-closed eyes she gazed at him, feeling the familiar unfurling hunger inside, watching as his mouth spread into a slow smile of recognition.

'Lady Ashbroke, would I be right in thinking that you're giving me *that* look?'

She breathed a low, wicked laugh and slipped her hand between the buttons of his shirt, feeling the muscles of his taut stomach tighten beneath her palm. 'How did you guess?'

'I can *feel* it.'

'How does it feel?' she whispered huskily.

'Exquisite.' He drained his glass of champagne and stood up, pulling her to her feet. 'But, unless you do something about it soon, extremely uncomfortable. Come on—time for bed.'

Rachel quirked an eyebrow. 'Us or the children?'

'Both.'

Laughing, Rachel gathered up a protesting Rose, raining kisses down onto her face and her fat little hands, while Orlando lifted Felix high, setting him on his shoulders. Together they made their way back up the path to the house through the blue evening haze.

A vast disc of gold hung over the rooftops of Easton as they approached.

'Moon,' said Felix sleepily, pointing. 'Big yellow moon.'

'Honeymoon,' said Rachel quietly, as Orlando's fingers closed around hers, his thumb caressing her palm. 'A perfect honeymoon.'

And, in every way possible, it was.

The World of Mills & Boon®

There's a Mills & Boon® series that's perfect for you. We publish ten series and with new titles every month, you never have to wait long for your favourite to come along.

Blaze®
Scorching hot, sexy reads

By Request
Relive the romance with the best of the best

Cherish™
Romance to melt the heart every time

Desire™
Passionate and dramatic love stories

Have Your Say

You've just finished your book.
So what did you think?

We'd love to hear your thoughts on our 'Have your say' online panel
www.millsandboon.co.uk/haveyoursay

- Easy to use
- Short questionnaire
- Chance to win Mills & Boon® goodies

Visit us Online

Tell us what you thought of this book now at
www.millsandboon.co.uk/haveyoursay

YOUR_SAY